The Scent of Rain
and Lightning

Nancy Pickard

The Scent of Rain and Lightning

A NOVEL

BALLANTINE BOOKS  NEW YORK

Published in the United States by Ballantine Books,
an imprint of The Random House Publishing Group,
a division of Random House, Inc., New York.

BALLANTINE and colophon are registered
trademarks of Random House, Inc.

LIBRARY OF CONGRESS CATALOGING-IN-PUBLICATION DATA
Pickard, Nancy.
The scent of rain and lightning : a novel / Nancy Pickard.
p. cm.
ISBN 978-0-345-47101-7 (hardcover : alk. paper)
1. Murder victims' families—Fiction.   2. Family secrets—Fiction.
3. Ex-convicts—Fiction.   4. City and town life—
Kansas—Fiction.   I. Title.
PS3566.I274S34 2010
813'.54—dc22   2010002092

Printed in the United States of America on acid-free paper

www.ballantinebooks.com

2 4 6 8 9 7 5 3 1

FIRST EDITION

Book design by Laurie Jewell

With love and appreciation for
libraries large and small

Acknowledgments

A novel's worth of words cannot sufficiently express my gratitude to my editor and hero, Linda Marrow. Heartfelt thanks to four people who inspired important epiphanies about this novel: Dana Isaacson, Sally Goldenbaum, Donald Maass, and Randy Russell. Love and thanks to my son, Nick Pickard, who knows about barbed wire and writer moms, and to my mother, Mary Wolfe, who knows when to offer a writer a cup of hot soup without asking how the book is going. Soup makes books go better. Thanks to my patient and supportive agent, Meredith Bernstein, and to my friends online and in the real world. Special thanks to the wonderful librarians at "my" library, the Central Resource Library of Johnson County, Kansas. Thanks to the residents of Gove County, who let me "steal" their famous Monument Rocks, reconfigure and rename them, and then plunk them down in a fictional county in the very real state of Kansas.

The Scent of Rain
and Lightning

June 9, 2009

UNTIL SHE WAS twenty-six, Jody Linder felt suspicious of happiness.

She hated that about herself, because it tended to sour some otherwise pretty damn fine moments, but this was Rose, Kansas, after all. Only the year before, a pencil tornado had dropped down and killed three people only a few miles from her hometown. A tornado, when the sun was shining! In the winter, there were ice storms. In the summer, there were grass fires. At all times, people she knew went bankrupt, lost their homes, their ranches, their jobs. Or, they died just when you least expected them to. A person could, for instance, belong to a nice family living an ordinary life in a small town in the middle of nowhere, and on some innocent Saturday night, violent men could drop in like those tornadoes and turn those nice people into the dead stars of a Truman Capote book. Such things happened. That wasn't paranoia. It was a terrible *fact* that Jody knew better than anybody—or at least better than anybody whose father had not been murdered when she was three years old and whose mother had not disappeared the same night.

Such things happened, and she was proof of it.

Therefore—the past having proved to her the unreliability of the present—happiness made Jody Linder anxious. Feelings of safety and security got her checking around corners, lifting lids off bins, and parting shower curtains for fear of what might be hiding there, because you just never knew. A killer could hide in the corner, bugs lurked in bins, spiders jumped out of bathtubs.

Happiness was fragile, precious, and suspect.

"No peak not followed by a fall," she believed, which explained her flutter of worry as she lay naked on top of her bed with Red Bosch in the middle of a suspiciously beautiful Kansas afternoon. The air smelled too good for such a hot day, the light penetrating her eyelet curtains looked too delicate for noon. Most foreboding of all, the sex with this man she didn't love had been too damned good to be trusted beyond the (admittedly fine) moments of her satisfaction and his. She'd kept her eyes open during the finale, which meant she'd caught Red smirking down at her, looking pleased with himself.

Don't flatter yourself, she'd nearly blurted, but then she thought, first of all, that wasn't kind and he didn't deserve it, and second of all, why *shouldn't* he flatter himself? Red was good at riding horses, rounding up cattle, baling hay, and this. She could hardly think of better talents in a man.

"Pretty girl," Red murmured, tracing a lazy finger down her sternum.

"Sweaty girl," Jody said, lifting his hand off and laying it back on his own damp belly.

He laughed, a self-satisfied growl, deep in his chest.

A hot, pollen-scented breeze blew through the open windows.

She smelled honeysuckle, which wasn't blooming yet, and lilac, which had already bloomed and gone. These things were impossible, they were all in her imagination, she knew, and they were just the sort of deceptions that the smallest feeling of contentment might spring on her.

She and Red lay sprawled on their backs like sated puppies who'd just had their bellies scratched for half an hour. Lying a few inches away from him, so their limbs couldn't touch and stick, Jody let out an irrepressible sigh of pleasure. Immediately, she wanted to take it back, suck the breath right back into her lungs, because God knew she couldn't let the universe be hearing any of *that*.

No peak not followed by a fall . . .

The sound of a vehicle turning onto her street made her turn her face toward the windows, alert to the possibility of unpleasant surprise.

"Did you hear that, Red?"

"What?"

"Shh!"

The sound of the single vehicle turned into the sound of a second truck and then another, which multiplied her alertness exponentially. Jody pressed her elbows into the bottom sheet and raised her head and shoulders to get a better listen. Traffic might not have been worth noticing in a place like Kansas City, 350 miles to the east, or in Denver, 250 miles to the west. But this was one of the quietest streets in a town so small she could hear people she knew start their cars in their garages on the other side of Main Street and know if they were late to work.

"Somebody just pulled up outside."

"Who?"

She threw him a look.

Sometimes she wondered if Red was one post short of a fence.

"What?" he repeated, half laughing.

He was thirteen years older than she, but sometimes Jody felt as if she were the more mature one. Abandoning him as he lay naked and limp on her bed, she peeled herself off her new white sheets. She slid down off the high old walnut bed with its new pillows and mattress cover and its new mattress and box springs. Once her bare feet landed on the equally bare walnut floorboards that she had polished and buffed until they glowed in the sunshine, she bounded to the windows—much taller than her own five feet four inches, their panes shining and cleaned, their borders rimmed in polished walnut—to check what was up. A road crew? Unlikely, given that Rose barely had the budget to keep its half-dozen traffic lights changing colors.

Jody peeked outside and got a shock that panicked her.

"Ohmygod. Red! Get up! Get dressed! You've got to leave now!"

What she saw from two stories up was the unnerving sight of her three uncles parking their pickup trucks in front of her parents' house, when she hadn't even known that two of the uncles were in town. She still called it her parents' house even though Hugh-Jay and Laurie Jo Linder had been gone almost all of her life. It was still their home to their only child—the descendant of a famous, violent night twenty-three years earlier—and it was still their home to everybody else in Henderson County, which was named for Jody's great-great-grandfather on her father's mother's side of the family.

"What is this fearsome thing I see?" she whispered at the high windows, mimicking Shakespeare. Her master's degree in English literature was a happy achievement, which, upon attainment, she had automatically shaded with doubts that she could ever find a job for teaching it.

"Who is it, your other boyfriend?"

Red's tone was joking, with an insecure edge to it.

"I don't have another one. I don't even have one."

That was blunt enough to be mean, and she immediately regretted it.

"What am I?" Red asked quietly.

Convenient was the adjective that popped into Jody's head but which she didn't say aloud. He was that, along with being the only available male for miles around who wasn't a child or a grandfather. Or a relative. She glanced back at her current lover-not-boyfriend, at his wiry cowboy self sprawled across her sheets. Her fingers knew that his long frame was checkered and slashed with scars, bruises, odd bumps where bones had healed awkwardly, and fresh little wounds. Red wasn't the most careful of cowboys. He tended to get bucked, bounced, and "rode over" more than your average rodeo rider, and he wasn't even one of those anymore, he was just an ordinary ranch hand. Maybe that's why she liked him, she sometimes thought, because that's all and everything Red was—just a cowboy, with no pretense of anything else, or more. It was also true that other men's bodies—the bodies of accountants, for instance, or lawyers, not that she'd ever been with such and really knew—were boring to her compared to the interesting terrain of cowboy skin.

"Well?" he challenged her.

She gave him an exasperated look—because the question irritated her and she couldn't think of any answer that was true without also being hurtful. She turned her bare back on him, returning her attention to the disturbing view from her window, hiding her naked self behind the new white eyelet curtains. The hot breeze coming through the open window blew dangerously around her, threatening to expose her nakedness to the street and to any uncle who happened to look up.

Jody sucked in her upper lip and held it between her teeth.

Red had sucked on a breath mint after lunch at the Rose Café, right before slipping into her house, her bedroom, and her. She could still taste peppermint in her own mouth, along with a tangy hint of hot sauce and an even tangier taste of him. She could still feel his callused touch on her skin, too, a feeling so real she would have sworn his rough hands had followed her to the window. They were not sensations she wanted to have with her uncles arriving.

They were also not activities the local high school had looked for on her résumé when they hired her to be their new English teacher in two and a half months. She had whooped with joy upon landing that job, but immediately tamped down her exuberance, because who knew how long she could stay employed in such an iffy economy? And what if she wasn't a good teacher, or the kids hated her, or their parents objected to *Catcher in the Rye*? There were so many things that could go wrong after something went right.

Tense as fresh-strung barbed wire, she watched from the second floor.

Three truck doors slammed, *bang, bang, bang,* with the solid thud of well-built vehicles. Now her uncles were walking toward each other. *What were they doing here, and why didn't she know anything about it?* Uncle Chase was supposed to be in Colorado, running the family's ranch on the high plains east of the Rockies; Uncle Bobby was supposed to be in Nebraska, where he ran a third ranch the family owned, in the Sand Hills. Uncle Meryl was supposed to be at his law office in Henderson City, the county seat, twenty-five miles away.

"Hey," Red said, in the tone of a man feeling ignored.

"Shh!"

From her hidden vantage point, she watched with growing alarm.

Now her uncles were meeting in a tall, wide-shouldered trio on the sidewalk in front of her porch, and now her uncle Chase was grinding out a cigarette on the cement, and now he picked it up and put it in his shirt pocket—not because he was so thoughtful, but because every rancher and farmer was wary of fire. And now her uncles were coming toward her front door together—big men dressed in cowboy boots, pressed pants, cotton shirts, and wearing their best straw cowboy hats for summer. The hats, alone, were a disturbing sign. The uncles usually wore their best hats only to weddings, funerals, and cattlemen conventions, preferring brimmed caps for everyday. Meryl even wore a bolo tie and one of the hideous plaid suit coats that her aunt Belle had never been able to excise from his wardrobe. He had matched it with a reddish-brown pair of polyester trousers that made Jody, even two stories up, wrinkle her nose. She knew what Meryl would say if she mocked his wardrobe: he'd say it fooled out-of-town lawyers into mistaking him for a bumpkin—to their sorrow and his clients' gain.

Their trucks also looked suspiciously clean, as for making formal calls.

They wouldn't have done all this for just any casual visit.

When her uncles went formal-visiting, they showered first and changed into clean clothes. Jody's grandmother, who was the mother of two of these men and a near-mother to the third one, wouldn't stand for any less. If a male in Jody's family stepped into somebody's house, he would, by God, smell of soap. Her uncle Bobby might be forty-one years old, her uncle Chase might be forty-four, and Uncle Meryl might be forty-six and have married into the family instead of being born into it, but they lived by the laws that all Linders lived by, the commandments that Jody's grandparents, Hugh Senior and Annabelle Linder, set down. You didn't show up in church dirty and smelling of horse. You didn't take your cow-shitty work boots into other people's nice living rooms. Most important of all, you didn't show up at somebody's house without calling ahead first, even if that somebody was only your niece.

They hadn't called first. She hadn't known they were coming.

And then they really scared her, because they rang her doorbell.

Only after that unprecedented announcement of their arrival did she hear her front door open, and a moment later her uncle Chase called out in his smoky baritone, "Josephus?"

It wasn't her name, which was Laurie Jo, after her mother.

Joe-*see*-fuss was her three uncles' nickname for her.

She clutched a fist to her naked breasts: had something happened at the ranch?

Was it her grandfather Hugh Senior, was it her grandmother Annabelle?

She didn't know what she would do without either of them; they had been the rocks of her life since her parents had gone.

"Jody?" Chase called, louder this time. "Honey? You home?"

He sounded tense, which wasn't like her coolest uncle.

In a flash Jody thought of their various wives and ex-wives, their assorted children and stepchildren who were her cousins and sort-of cousins. There were so many disasters that could happen on a cattle outfit. So many ways to get hurt, so many ways to end up in hospitals or funeral homes, so many ways to break hearts and families. She couldn't think of any minor calamities that would prompt her uncles to pay a special visit like this to her. They wouldn't do this unless there was something serious, something they couldn't just make a phone call to tell her, and worse—something that made them decide they had to tell her en masse.

"Jesus," she whispered, a half prayer, hurrying to pick up clothes to cover her naked body. She felt shocked, albeit without being surprised at all, since she believed that bad events followed good as inevitably as death followed life, and as frequently. The secret, she had decided when she was younger, was to try to anticipate it, so as to mitigate the blow. The problem with that philosophy was that it never worked; she was always surprised; no matter how far ahead she tried to look, bad news still hurt, shock still left her shaken. With a start, she realized she hadn't answered, so she yelled in a high voice, "I'm home, Uncle Chase! I'm upstairs, I'll be right there!"

"You want us to come up?" he yelled back.

"No!" she screamed. *God, no.*

On the bed, Red had bolted up to a sitting position at the first sound of that voice, which was the voice of one of the members of his extended family of employers. He also heard the terrifying offer to climb the stairs, and now he was trying to scurry out of bed and get dressed fast and silently.

"Go down the back stairs!" she whispered to him, unnecessarily.

"What the hell's Chase doing here?"

She glanced at her lover's face, tanned up to his hat line and furrowed now with anxiety, and it hit her at that inconvenient instant that she was going to have to do something about Red Bosch. When they first tumbled into bed, she'd assumed they were both just a couple of horny-toads hungry for sex in a county where romantic partners were as scarce as yaks. That, plus the fact that at least he wasn't married, and she did have *some* standards. But lately Red projected a possessive, boyfriend kind of air that worried her.

"I don't know! It's Bobby and Meryl, too! Go!"

Red fumbled as he picked up his jeans, dropping them. The huge metal buckle on his belt hit the wood floor with a clattering thump. They both froze for a second, staring at each other, and then continued hurrying into their clothes.

"They'll string me up in the barn if they catch me here," Red whispered.

"Are you kidding? You'll be lucky to get to the rafters!"

He half laughed, half shuddered at her serious joke.

Physical harm wasn't the real threat. It wasn't as if the uncles were going to thrash him for bedding their niece. Getting him fired at a time when ranches were foreclosing, not hiring—that was the risk.

Jody rushed into jeans, a bra, a T-shirt, and pulled on socks and cowboy boots, while Red dressed down to his own socks, picked up his boots to carry in his fingers, and then disappeared down the back stairs that led to the kitchen and the back door. She hoped that he'd had the sense to park his truck someplace nonincriminating. She took the time to run a brush through her hair, managing to flatten some of the dark curls that Red's long fingers had tangled. Even facing the possibility of an emergency, she couldn't show up in front of her uncles half groomed, not in the middle of the day when all decent Linders were supposed to be at work—as were their hired hands. Nothing much got by the uncles, not a bull trying to get to cows in another pasture, or a niece trying to hide her affairs. Besides, her grandmother would eventually hear all about this, including what her granddaughter was wearing, if it was anything out of the ordinary by her uncles' reckoning.

"I'm coming!" she yelled.

Finally, she hurried downstairs, hanging onto the banister, skipping steps in her loud, clomping rush to the bottom.

"What's going on?" she demanded of them breathlessly.

Three polished straw, immaculate summer cowboy hats hung on pegs on her wall, identical except for their bands: the sterling silver one was Meryl's, the twined black leather one marked Chase's hat, and Bobby's was plain with no band at all.

There they were, the avuncular blessings and banes of her life: Chase, who got more handsome every year, as if the cool restraint with which he held himself somehow firmed his jaw, widened his shoulders, slimmed his torso, dissolved the age lines on his handsome face, and brightened the blue of his eyes; Bobby, muscular and taciturn, with a broad face that was as inexpressively flat as the plains that surrounded them; Meryl, with his kind, canny eyes and a girth that came from Belle's fried chicken and a lawyerly life spent behind a desk. Two of them were the younger brothers of her late father; Meryl had been like a brother to him.

Her uncle Meryl's eyes frightened her at that moment, because they filled with wet sympathy when she looked into his flushed, beefy face. Meryl Tapper had been her father's best friend long before marrying her aunt Belle. His own large family hadn't valued ambition and education, so he'd gravitated toward the Linders, who valued those things and him.

Her uncle Chase's eyes were hidden behind sunglasses, which she thought suspicious in and of itself since he was standing in a dim hall-way. With his fashionable shades, monogrammed white shirt, tailored trousers, engraved belt buckle, and black boots, Chase looked like Hollywood's idea of a cowboy, except that he really was one, and an exceptionally good one at that. Jody had always heard that he'd been a fun and teasing charmer when he was young, but after her father died, Chase's lighthearted nature died, too. She knew him as a disciplinarian, tough-minded, sarcastic, protective, and bossy. Her uncle Bobby, looking as massive as the bull rider he once was, and as vigilant as the soldier he had also been, stood at the screen door, facing sideways to the street. She couldn't see his face, but she could see his left side, where the shirtsleeve hung empty, its cuff tucked into his belt. He'd left the arm in Iraq during the first Gulf War, a battle he hadn't known was ahead of him when he enlisted in the Army right after his brother's murder. Standing at her front door, Bobby looked as if he were waiting for somebody, or watching out for something.

"What's wrong?" she demanded of them.

She had a sudden, intuitive start of wondering—was that what people asked each other twenty-three years ago on the day her father was killed and her mother disappeared? When people saw their neighbors' eyes fill with tears and fear, did they ask that same question with their hearts hammering and their voices shaking as hers was now? *What's wrong? What's the matter? Has something happened?* Rose was a tiny town, some said a dying one, where almost everybody looked out for everybody else. She'd grown up without parents, but cosseted and safe in a town that had sometimes felt to her like a whole community of babysitters.

"Billy Crosby's sentence got commuted," Chase told her, in his blunt way.

She shook her head, not comprehending. "What?"

William F.—Billy—Crosby was in prison for murdering her father.

"He's getting out, Jody," Meryl, the lawyer, reiterated, and then dropped a second bomb. "The governor set him loose this morning." Meryl dropped the third bomb: "He's coming home this afternoon."

Something about the way she looked in response to that news

moved Chase to reach out a hand to grab her right arm to steady her. "Commuted?" Jody said the words as if trying to pronounce something in a foreign language in which she could mimic the syllables without understanding their meaning. Billy Crosby had been in prison for twenty-three years. According to everything she'd ever been told—promised—he wasn't supposed to be getting out anytime soon.

They waited while she took it in.

Jody frowned, still not grasping it. "Are you telling me they let him out of prison?"

Meryl nodded. "Yes. That's what we're telling you."

She gasped, and stared from one to the other. "He's *out*? He's coming back *here*? To *Rose*?"

Still standing guard by the front door, Bobby turned his face toward her, saw her wide-eyed disbelief and horror, and nodded once. But then he said in his deep voice that often sounded on the edge of anger, "It doesn't mean he'll stay." The edges of his lips turned down. "I'll shoot him first."

"I'll hand you the gun," Jody said, trying for shaky bravado, and then she brought her hands to her mouth, whispered, "No!" and burst into tears. "How could this happen?" Her eyes flooded with grief, fright, and accusation as she exclaimed, *"How could you let this happen?"*

2

SOME PEOPLE SAID that the murder of Jody's dad flared from a single nasty, isolated incident that escalated to worse, and then even worse, and then to the unimaginable. Nobody could have predicted it, they said. But other people claimed the trouble was a long time brewing and that Jody's grandfather ought to have known better all along, that he'd been asking for trouble, if the hard truth be told. This was what came from trying to change people who didn't want to change, they said. But Hugh Linder Senior would be Hugh Linder Senior, they also said—a good man, smart, honest, and tough, but maybe a touch too sure of himself where a little humility might have shifted the tragic course of things.

Whichever theory was true—single spark of fury or long-simmering burn of resentment—everybody agreed the final bloody act was set in motion on the fateful day when the rancher came walking around a cattle pen filled with jostling animals and caught Billy Crosby going nuts with rage at a cow.

It was Tuesday, in the early afternoon.

High Rock Ranch was sending cattle through the metal pens by the highway, separating six-month-old calves from their mothers and giving the calves weaning shots to protect them from getting sick during the stressful process of leaving their mothers on this day and then being trucked to feed lots at a later date. The adult cows—pregnant again—were being reinoculated against the bovine disease known as blackleg.

The cow in question was a big rangy old girl, experienced in the routine of cowboys, and so you'd think she would have known better. She'd been a dependable breeder and good mama for years, but she might have gotten a little senile in that long, hard head of hers. It happened to cows as well as to people. On that day, she wouldn't move along, kept turning in the wrong direction, stalling the progress of a bunch of cattle toward a bend in the circular pen. She was bawling for her calf, her eyes rolling wildly, foam spewing from her mouth. The temperature of that September afternoon in 1986 was roasting man and beast as if they were all tied to spits over a Labor Day barbecue pit; both species were overheated, unhappy, angry at each other. The smell of fresh manure and cow bodies filled the dry air with an animal humidity. The noise of the cattle's hooves on the dirt, the bawling of calves for their mothers, the yells of the men trying to control them, created a thunder of its own on a rainless day.

"Move, you *son* of a *bitch*!"

Hugh Senior saw his part-time cowboy poke the cow repeatedly in her side with an electric prod. Billy was one of the rancher's "projects," one of the local boys he had put to work on the ranch over the years, because he believed there was nothing like hard work with animals and machinery to straighten out a path that looked as if it was taking a crooked turn.

Billy had proved to be a tougher "save" than the boys preceding him.

Maybe it was because both of his parents were drunks, and not just one of them, as had been the case with a couple of the other kids who turned out pretty well after Hugh and Annabelle Linder got hold of them. Maybe it was because Billy wasn't the brightest young bull in

the herd, or because he had a temper with a trigger so sensitive a speck
of dust could set it off. Whatever the cause, the result was that Hugh
Linder's regimen of sweat-labor wasn't having much effect, in the opinion of the locals. Hadn't Billy just lost his license again, after his second drunk driving conviction? Didn't his poor little wife look bruised
across her jaw the other day? Wasn't their little boy more serious and
careful than a seven-year-old should be? And wasn't Billy Crosby drinking just as much, acting as belligerent as ever, chasing after women,
and running his dirty mouth off where he shouldn't? The Linders
should have given up on him long ago, people said; anybody else would
have thrown up their hands by now, that was for sure.

Hugh Senior saw that the old cow couldn't possibly respond to
Billy's wishes.

She had gotten herself trapped in the wrong direction. But Billy kept
stabbing at her with the prod. It was clear to the rancher that the cowboy had boiled over and was taking it out on the confused, frightened
animal. Hugh yelled, but couldn't be heard over the other noise. He
picked up his pace, rushing toward Billy, but not in time before the
cowboy climbed the rungs of the metal pen, threw his legs over so he
was seated atop of it, and aimed a vicious kick straight at the head of
the cow. The heel of his cowboy boot hit her left eye. Even as big as the
cow was, the blow staggered her. Her head jerked sideways. Her knees
buckled and she stumbled into the side of another cow, then righted
herself, shaking her head and bellowing louder than ever. A ruckus
broke out in the tight space where she had the other cattle trapped
around her.

Billy pulled back his heel to kick her again.

His lips pulled back over his teeth, his eyes bugged with fury.

Hugh Senior grabbed the young man's shirt and jerked him backward so he tumbled in a twisting fall off the top of the fence, landing
hard at the rancher's feet, sideways, eating dust.

"Go cool off, Billy." Hugh Senior pointed back toward headquarters.

The rancher's voice was loud, gravelly, no-nonsense.

"Why'd you do that, Mr. Linder?" The hired hand grabbed one
shoulder and winced as he struggled to his feet. The twenty-four-year-

old and the fifty-four-year-old stood eye to eye, reminding more than one of the witnesses of a young and old bull challenging each other in a pasture. Nobody could hear what they were saying because of the noise of the cattle, but the body language was clear enough. Even though Billy was six feet tall, the older man had four inches on him, along with a bigger, more muscular frame. The rancher had the light hair and blue eyes of his German forebears; Billy had a dark, sharp-featured resemblance to his own father, whose good looks had long ago dissolved in beer and whiskey. "I didn't do nothin'!" he protested.

"You were abusing one of my animals, Billy."

The rancher's voice rang sharp with disapproval.

"Damned cow's gonna die anyway!"

Contempt joined disapproval in Hugh Senior's response to that despicable defense. "Doesn't mean you get to torture her along the way."

"Ain't fair!" Billy whined. "I seen other men do it."

"If I ever see that, I'll stop them, too. Maybe you ought to just go on home now, Billy."

The words were a suggestion, but the tone was commanding.

"How am I supposed to get home when I don't even have a truck?"

As usual, Billy didn't know when to shut up.

Hugh Senior lost what patience he had on that irritating day and ordered, "Step away from my pens, Billy. Now. Go get yourself something cool to drink. Stick your hot head in it while you're at it. You can wait in the barn for Hugh-Jay to come get you and give you a ride home. And don't be bothering Mrs. Linder up at the house."

"I need a drink, all right," Billy mumbled.

"That's the last thing you need," the rancher snapped back, knowing he meant alcohol.

Wiping dirt from his face, Billy limped away, observed by the disgusted rancher and the other men working the cattle that day. All of Hugh's sons were there, Hugh-Jay, Chase, and Bobby, along with neighbors, a veterinarian, and a couple of other part-time hired hands. A few glances were exchanged among them, but only Chase said anything. "Good riddance," he summed up for every man there.

That was all there was to it, all of them testified later.

It was nothing, and it was everything.

TWO HOURS LATER Hugh-Jay Linder drove Billy Crosby back to Rose, where they both lived with their wives and only children. At the last minute Chase hopped into the backseat of Hugh-Jay's silver Ford pickup truck to ride along. It was three miles from ranch entrance to town limit, all of it along two-lane county blacktop. The pastures of their own High Rock Ranch spread out on either side of the road for the first two miles, followed then by a cemetery on one side and a ranch with a bison herd to the right, before scattered houses began to appear on the outskirts of Rose.

"What the hell's eating your dad?" Billy said to the brothers, right off.

It was four-thirty and hotter than ever, although there was a forecast of rain for tomorrow. It was so hot in the truck that Hugh-Jay drove with his work gloves on the steering wheel to keep from burning his hands. It was too hot for the air-conditioning to kick in before they reached town, so he had the windows rolled down while the AC worked its way up to tepid. He cranked its fan up high, so that between that noise and the sound of the tires, and the hot wind whipping in through the windows, the three of them had to raise their voices to hear one another. From their faces to the back of their necks and on down their clothing, they were filthy from the cattle work. Their boots and their jeans stank of cow shit, a smell they barely noticed after a lifetime of breathing it.

"You are," Chase joked from the backseat. "You're eating him."

They'd all gone through the county schools together. Billy had dropped out of high school on his third stab at a junior year, the same year Belle Linder was a senior, Chase was a sophomore, Bobby was still in middle school, and Hugh-Jay was at Kansas State University.

Keeping his gaze on the two-lane county highway ahead of them, Hugh-Jay said more seriously, "I think you know, Billy."

Billy looked mulish upon hearing that. "I don't know!" He reached under the seat and a beer can magically appeared in his hand when he sat up again.

"Where'd that come from?" Hugh-Jay asked, glancing over.

"Do you have another one?" Chase stuck in.

Billy smirked. "Brought it with me."

Hugh-Jay had given him a ride out to the ranch for the day's work.

Billy popped the top. The smell of beer filled the cab of the truck.

"How can you drink that hot stuff?" Hugh-Jay asked him.

Billy took a drink, then wiped off his mouth with his filthy shirt-sleeve and shrugged. "A beer's a beer, right, Chase?"

In the backseat, too hot to talk anymore, Chase didn't answer.

"Dad said you mistreated an animal," Hugh-Jay continued, refusing to be sidetracked. "You know how he feels about that."

"It was a cow, for Christ's sake, Jay. A fucking cow. She was jamming up the pen. Nobody could get past her, somebody had to get her to move. All I did was give her a couple of pokes and a kick. You never kicked a cow?" He turned around toward the back. "You never did, Chase?"

"Not like you." Chase lolled his head back on the seat and stared at the ceiling.

"I didn't hurt her none! She was just a *cow*."

"And not your wife, you mean," Chase drawled loudly, still staring up.

There was an instant's loaded silence, and then Billy yelled, "What?" This time he turned all the way around to face the brother in the backseat. "What'd you say, Chase?"

Hugh-Jay shot his younger brother a glance in the rearview mirror.

Chase kept staring at the cciling of the truck. "I happen to know the sheriff's been out to see you a couple of times, because some people think you've been hurting your wife. You use a cattle prod on Val, too, Billy?"

"Screw you, Chase Linder. You people are unbelievable! I never hurt Val!"

At the wheel, Hugh-Jay said nothing, but his hands tightened on it.

"I never," Billy muttered, before he chugged at his warm beer.

They covered several hundred yards in silence.

Hugh-Jay finally spoke. "You might want to apologize to Dad."

"For what? I told you, I didn't do nothin'!"

"You might want to work at our ranch again."

Billy threw him an incredulous look. "Your dad's not gonna kick me off for *that*."

"I wouldn't be too sure. That kind of thing's important to him."

"Fuckin' cow."

"You know he doesn't like that kind of language."

Billy muttered the offending word under his breath.

They drove in silence then, until Billy suddenly flung his beer can out his window, aiming at a bison bull as they drove past the herd. The can didn't go five feet, and fell into a culvert.

Hugh-Jay braked the truck so fast that Billy jolted forward, putting out his hands to keep from flying into the dashboard, since he didn't have his seat belt on. In the backseat, Chase nearly slid off the seat. "What the hell?" Billy exclaimed. He and Chase were flung back into their seats again when Hugh-Jay threw the truck into reverse and gunned it.

He made a hard stop again and turned toward his surprised passengers.

"Get out and pick it up, Billy."

"*What?*"

"Pick up the beer can, Billy. What's wrong with you that you'd do that?"

"What is wrong with you people that you care about shit like that?"

"Pick it up or I'll pull you out and leave you on the side of this road."

Billy flung open the door, got out, picked up the can, and threw it so hard into the open bed of the truck in back that when it hit the metal it sounded like gunfire that turned into machine-gun fire as it rattled around. When he got back in, slamming the door behind him, Hugh-Jay asked him, "Was that can empty?"

"You think I'd throw a beer away?"

Billy sulked in the passenger's seat for the remainder of the drive.

Chase eyed the backs of both of their heads and then closed his eyes.

As the speed limit dropped on the approach to Rose, Hugh-Jay slowed to twenty miles an hour. They rolled past grain elevators, a convenience store, a Pizza Hut, a Chinese restaurant, an abandoned train station, and the Leafy Green Truck Stop with its attached café. He turned right onto Main Street, which took them down a four-lane corridor of modest frame and brick homes and then through the three-block downtown with its sprinkling of small enterprises. They passed Rose's three-room public library, the two-room City Hall, the senior citizen center, an art gallery that was open only by appointment, the former bank where Hugh-Jay and Chase's sister Belle were creating a history museum, and Bailey's Bar & Grill, which was a tavern and the only place in town where a person could get served a decent steak, along with a beer or mixed drinks. As they passed other vehicles on the street, Hugh-Jay raised a gloved hand to greet their drivers, who performed the same friendly courtesy to him. His own home would have taken him north onto a block of big houses, but he turned south to get to Billy's poorer neighborhood, where it sometimes seemed as if there were more old cars in the front yards than grass.

When Hugh-Jay parked in front of the small white house where Billy lived with Valentine and their son, he said, "You want cash for today?"

"Yeah." Billy's tone was sullen.

Hugh-Jay pulled out his wallet and counted out enough bills to equal the hourly minimum wage. Ordinarily, and without anybody in the family knowing, he would have added an extra ten, but on this day he didn't do it. He handed the cash to Billy, who took it with an angry, disappointed grab, and said, "You think I'm ever going to see any more of this, Hugh-Jay?"

"I don't know. Whatever you did, maybe you won't do it again."

Billy threw himself out of the truck, slammed the door, and yelled through the open window, "Didn't fuckin' do nothing wrong the first time!" Then he grabbed the rim of the open window, glared into the backseat and said, "Don't think I'm going to forget what you said, Chase."

Chase opened his eyes halfway. "You're not supposed to forget it."

As the brothers drove off, Hugh-Jay said, "Why'd you say that to him?"

"About beating Val? 'Cause it's true."

"You know that for sure?"

"Pretty sure."

"I don't think pretty sure is good enough for an accusation like that."

"Well, that's your problem."

Hugh-Jay glanced back, surprised at the acid in Chase's tone. Instead of pursuing it, however, he said, "Do you think Dad overreacted today?"

"No. I think he ought to have stopped hiring Billy a long time ago."

Hugh-Jay nodded. "You want to ride up here?"

"This is okay. We're not going far, are we?"

Hugh-Jay sighed. "I guess you think you're having supper with Laurie and me?"

Chase, who had a talent for instantly recapturing his own natural good humor any time he lost it, grinned at him in the mirror. "Doesn't Laurie Jo always set an extra place for me, just in case I show up?" Chase and Bobby Linder ate at their brother and sister-in-law's home so often they both kept changes of clothing there, for cleaning up when they came in covered with horse hair and dirt. Suddenly, Chase turned uncharacteristically serious again. "You don't think Billy will take this out on Val or his kid, do you?"

It took Hugh-Jay half a block to think about it.

Then he turned the truck around and drove back.

"Let's make sure," he said.

3

WHEN THEY PULLED UP in front of the small white house again, Billy's wife and young son were in the front yard. In the sparse grass by his mother's bare feet, the boy, Collin, was playing with a toy silver gun, twirling it around his left forefinger, then pointing it, then twirling it some more. His mother was a pale girl, thin, with hair so blond it looked white under the unrelenting sun, but the boy looked like his father—dark, handsome in a sharp-featured way.

The boy was alert to their arrival before his mother was, and looked up.

By unspoken agreement, both of the brothers got out of the truck, slamming their doors behind them. It was only when Hugh-Jay walked up to Valentine and her boy that he realized Chase had hung back and was leaning against the truck, even though it must have felt hot as a branding iron. Maybe he was resting his weight on his belt, Hugh-Jay thought.

"Hey, Valentine," he said politely.

He winked at her son.

The seven-year-old cocked his head to one side as if evaluating the gesture, and then looked down at his toy gun, pausing in his play in the serious way he had, the way that made people worry about him.

"I didn't see you out here before," Hugh-Jay told her.

"I thought you might come in," she said rather mysteriously.

He didn't know why she'd think that, since he never had been in their house before. He looked down at himself. "Not with all this dirt on me."

"Billy wanted us outside." She didn't sound resentful, just resigned, as if this was something to which she was accustomed—her young husband ordering her and their son to get away from him. She looked scrubbed clean and so did the boy. A smell of soap wafted from them, as if she had gone to some trouble to make them both look nice for when their husband and father came home. For all the good it did either of them, Hugh-Jay thought. His own wife, Laurie, didn't do that for him, but then she didn't have to fix herself up to make her husband want her.

"He went into the bedroom to take a nap," Val was saying. "He wants some peace and quiet."

Hugh-Jay frowned but didn't say anything to embarrass her.

He didn't find Valentine Crosby attractive, though he knew some men did. He'd overheard his wife Laurie comment to his sister Belle one time that Val Crosby could be pretty if she put on some makeup and "did something with that stringy hair." Hugh-Jay didn't think any of that would help much; although she had big breasts, he thought she otherwise looked scrawny. She had dark circles around her eyes that didn't flatter her like his wife's eye shadow flattered her brown eyes. He looked for the rumored bruise on Valentine's jaw but didn't see any sign of it. He felt suddenly guilty and grateful that his own beautiful, healthy, loved wife would never look like this defeated-looking girl and that his own daughter would never have the wary look of this somber boy.

Valentine Crosby glanced shyly up at him, a foot taller than she.

She hadn't grown up with all of them the way Billy had; Billy had found her in Scott City, a county away, when he was working a summer job in a cattle feed lot. She'd been a clerk in the office there, sixteen years old, and soon pregnant, and then married to Billy and moving to Rose.

"How old is he now?" Hugh-Jay asked, even though he knew.

"Seven."

She sidestepped a few inches and looked past him, toward his truck where Chase lounged.

Hugh-Jay nodded, unable to think of a single other thing to say about children, and also unable to think of how to ask what he wanted to ask her. He could have kicked Chase for hanging back.

"How's your little girl?" she asked him in her high, light voice.

Every time she spoke now, she glanced over at the truck.

"Jody's fine. Thanks for asking." He gnawed on one side of his lower lip. "Uh, Billy had a kind of rough day, I guess you know."

"What happened?"

"He ticked off my dad—"

"Your dad?" Her pale eyes widened and she looked panicked beyond anything he expected. "But your mom and dad, they're the very last people who'll hire him! Is your dad going to hire Billy anymore?"

He wanted to reassure her but couldn't. "I don't know."

"Oh, God!" She brought both hands to her mouth. "What'll we do?"

"Are things that bad?" he asked, feeling awkward and stiff.

Her eyes filled with tears. "We can't live on what I make three days a week checking at the grocery. And Billy won't take welfare, won't even let me apply for it. He hates charity."

Not enough to decline a free beer, Hugh-Jay thought, or my ten bucks.

He suddenly realized those extra dollars had probably always gone to please Billy, and never to help his wife or son. Hugh-Jay reached for his wallet, took out every bill in it, and handed them to Valentine. "Take this. Don't tell him. I know it's not much, but I'll talk to my dad about hiring him again."

She didn't argue, just took it, and slipped it into a pocket of her shorts.

"Thank you," she whispered. "Your family's always been good to Billy." And then she said a thing that sent shivers down Hugh-Jay's spine on that hot day. He thought at first that it was a non sequitur. "I sold Billy's truck. Just before he got home. I haven't told him yet. What do you think he's going to do?"

"Sold his truck?" he asked dumbly.

Her son stared up at them, frowning, letting the toy gun hang limp.

"It's not really Billy's. He hasn't got any credit. It's in my name."

That didn't mean Billy didn't think it was his, Hugh-Jay thought. He wondered who had the balls or was crazy enough to buy Billy Crosby's truck out from under him.

"Who'd you sell it to?"

She looked surprised at the question. "Your dad."

Hugh-Jay stared at Valentine and felt dumb again. "*My* dad?" he said, as if she must have meant somebody else's father.

"Yeah, he called a little while ago and made an offer." Innocently, she added, "I wouldn't have thought it was worth that much."

"Did he say why he wants it?"

Again she looked surprised at his question. "Because he needs a truck, I guess? He told me you were bringing Billy home. He said to tell you and your brother to pick up the truck and drive it to your house, or out to your ranch." She shaded her eyes to look into his. "I said you don't have to wait on the paperwork, or till it's officially yours. You should go on ahead and take it now. It's out back. The keys are in it. Maybe you can drive it away real quiet so it doesn't wake Billy up?"

Good idea, Hugh-Jay thought wryly. "What are *you* going to do?"

"Me?"

"For a car."

"Collin and I never go anywhere we can't walk." She looked back at her house. "And now *he* won't, either."

"Listen," Hugh-Jay said, and then didn't know where to go from that beginning. When she frowned, he said, "If you need help . . . I mean, if you need anything, call Laurie or me, okay?"

He had a nervous feeling about promising that his wife might help, especially when it came to helping somebody about whom she didn't give two hoots. Which, Hugh-Jay had to admit in that uncomfortable instant, described most people that Laurie had ever known.

But they lived only three blocks from Val and Billy.

Surely, Laurie wouldn't refuse to help if Valentine really needed it.

He heard a car rev up a couple of blocks away. Then he heard the sound of some kid—probably in the high school marching band—practicing on an instrument that sounded hideously like a tuba. It was all bleats and squeaks. Hugh-Jay wondered how the band director would ever get the young "musician" ready to play in time for half-time at Homecoming in November.

We're such a small town, he thought.

Val Crosby glanced away in embarrassment at his implication that she might need rescuing, but then she nodded, with her face bent toward her son. The boy was still concentrating on his toy gun, and in that instant he aimed and "shot" it toward the sound of the tuba practice.

"Bang," the boy said. "Bang, bang, you're dead, but not really."

"Not really?" Hugh-Jay asked him.

Collin looked up at his great height. "On TV. They shoot them, but they're never really dead. It's like a game."

"Real guns aren't a game," Hugh-Jay reminded him.

"I know," the boy said solemnly, and then he aimed his toy at his own head and pulled its trigger.

"Collin!" his mother cried, with a little scream. "Don't ever do that!"

"Not even in play," Hugh-Jay told him, feeling horror-struck by the kid's action and lack of reaction. "Never. Not as a joke. Not playing around. Never on anybody else, and most important of all, not on yourself."

"I'm sorry," the boy said, and looked as if he meant it.

WHEN HE GOT BACK behind the steering wheel, still feeling shaken by what the seven-year-old had done with the gun, Hugh-Jay found Chase in the passenger side of the front seat.

"Did you see that?"

"We all did that kind of thing. On ourselves. On Belle." Chase smiled at the memory of tormenting his sister. "That was fun. Don't you remember?"

"No, we didn't."

"Yeah, it's irresistible. We played around, just like him."

Hugh-Jay shook his head, finding that hard to believe but feeling comforted nonetheless. They were all still alive. Maybe it didn't mean anything. "Dad would have killed us," he said, still skeptical. "Mom would have killed us and then killed us all over again."

"Not if they didn't see it."

"You were a big help just now," Hugh-Jay said then, with mild sarcasm. He told his brother about their father, about the truck, about how Chase was going to have to get out again and drive Billy's truck over to Hugh-Jay's home. "You can park it behind the garage. Make sure it's out of sight. I hope we aren't making things worse for her."

"Again." Chase put a hand on the door handle. "Yeah. Me, too."

"What do you mean, 'again'?"

"That's what I said earlier, that I hoped we weren't making things worse."

His brother shot him a suspicious glance. "You're not screwing around with her, are you?"

"Billy's wife? Are you kidding? Hell, no."

"She kept looking at you."

"Beats looking at you."

Hugh-Jay laughed, and Chase grinned at him.

"Give me some credit, will you?" the younger brother requested.

"For what, respecting another man's marriage?"

Chase grinned again, as he opened the door again. "No, for having better taste in women."

It hit Hugh-Jay wrong, and was one of the few moments in his life when he didn't like his middle brother very much. "Let's go home," he said sourly. "To *my* home. *My* wife. *My* supper. *My* television set."

"Sheesh," Chase joked as he stepped out. "Possessive, are we?"

. . .

THAT EVENING SEEMED to pass peacefully in Rose and on the farms and ranches all around it. Chase parked Billy's truck behind his brother's garage and threw the keys onto their kitchen table, where they remained until he got ordered to set the table. He flirted supper out of his pretty sister-in-law, Laurie, and then pushed his giggling three-year-old niece Jody on the swing in the backyard. Then he walked over to Bailey's Bar & Grill for a few beers before returning to a guest bedroom at his brother's house.

Hugh-Jay called their father to ask about the truck, and Hugh Senior said, "Valentine told your mother in the grocery store last week that Billy was still driving, in spite of his license suspension. She told your mother that sometimes he has their little boy in the car when he's been drinking. Your mother and I discussed it, and we agreed that we could not with good conscience allow that to continue. So we decided to take the truck away from him in the way best suited to help his wife and son. I suppose we could have reported him to the sheriff, who could have set up a trap for him, but how would that help Valentine pay the rent? It wouldn't. But purchasing the truck for more than they can get for it from anybody else will help them, plus it will keep Billy from killing himself or somebody else on the road."

Hugh-Jay couldn't argue with his parents' logic.

He was proud of them for doing it.

Out at High Rock Ranch, Annabelle and Hugh Linder ate a light supper of cold fried chicken with their youngest child, Bobby. Even their daughter Belle was gone, spending the evening at her bank-cum-museum, closing a deal on a stuffed buffalo head. Over Annabelle's cold green bean salad and her radish-potato salad, Hugh lectured Bobby about college, and Bobby lectured his dad about giving tenth chances to "losers like Billy Crosby." Annabelle finally told them to lay off each other or else she wouldn't let them eat the last of her chocolate-vanilla marble cake, which was their favorite.

That being the price of goodness, father and son simmered down.

Inside the little white frame house three blocks away from Hugh-Jay and Laurie and Chase, Billy Crosby woke up late from his nap and went outside looking for the truck he wasn't supposed to drive.

Moments later seven-year-old Collin heard his father yelling and his mother crying. Then he heard his dad slam the front door, and then he went back to reading a book that was two grades above his own level because his teacher recognized a high IQ when she occasionally saw one. His heart was pounding hard, and he knew that if he could get lost in a story, the sad feelings might go away. The book was about a courageous knight on a quest to kill a monster so he could marry a beautiful princess and inherit the kingdom. Collin read until his eyes burned, and then he kept reading to the happy ending.

4

THE NEXT DAY dawned equally hot in that year of drought in Henderson County. A few ranchers' stock tanks had already dried up, and water was being expensively shipped into some herds; crops had turned to brown before they even fully greened, much less reached harvest.

Hugh Senior's wife, Annabelle, watched tempers start to fray early that Wednesday, as Hugh issued commands to their grown children as if Hugh-Jay, Chase, Bobby, and Belle were all still teenagers. He might have tried it on Annabelle, too, if she hadn't shot him a don't-you-dare glance that backed him off.

"Get into town and make those bank deposits," he commanded his third-born, Chase, who had driven in early with Hugh-Jay to get that day's orders. Chase had made the mistake of offering his parents an amiable good morning when he ambled into the kitchen looking for breakfast to complement the eggs and sausage his sister-in-law already served him in town.

His father barked at him, "You were supposed to do that yesterday."

"Dad!" Chase raised his arms in humorous defense. "I was working the pens with you yesterday!"

"You can't accomplish two things in one day?"

If Chase had been with his friends instead of his parents, he might have joked, *Only if one is blond and the other brunette.* Instead he half grinned at his mother, who put a forefinger to her lips to warn him against arguing or getting fresh with his father that morning. "Just do it," her finger said. Chase was smart enough to know good advice when he saw it. Grabbing the deposit envelopes with their checks made out from cattle buyers to High Rock Ranch, he sacrificed a second breakfast for the sake of peace in the family.

Then it was their oldest child's turn when he came into the kitchen.

"You're going to Colorado tonight," his father informed Hugh-Jay.

They had a ranch there, and a third property due north in Nebraska.

"Why?" Hugh-Jay made the mistake of asking, in a perfectly respectful tone of voice. He was, in his mother's opinion, the best natural cowman in the family, not to mention also being the nicest of any of her four children. Hugh-Jay was kind to everybody, good with cattle, even better with horses. His father seemed determined, however, to keep him away from cattle and buried in paperwork and accounting, which was the sort of business for which he had no aptitude at all. Chase and Belle were the ones with the heads for numbers. Hugh-Jay was the diplomat and animal lover, and Bobby . . . well, nobody quite knew what Bobby was good for.

"Dad," Hugh-Jay said calmly, "I want to take that lame horse to the vet."

"He can limp for another couple of days."

Hugh-Jay looked startled at his father's cavalier words. He frowned at his mother, an expression she read as both concern for the horse and confusion at his father's apparent hypocrisy about the welfare of their animals. He opened his mouth, closed it, and then merely asked, "What's going on in Colorado?"

"That's what I want you to find out. Something's funny about the bills. You get out there and see if he's hiding anything from us."

The "he" to whom he referred was their ranch manager.

"Dad." Hugh-Jay's protest was a gentle rebuke. "He's a good man."

"Maybe he is, but it won't hurt to prove it."

Behind Hugh Senior, Annabelle made small sweeping motions with her hands, her way of telling her son to go, get out of here.

"Yes, sir," Hugh-Jay said with a sigh, "but I can't leave until this afternoon."

"Why not?"

He smiled at his father, then at his mother, as he pulled a red feed-store cap onto his wheat-blond hair. He had a plain, pale face that radiated his bighearted nature, and which only burned—or blushed—and never tanned.

"Believe it or not, Dad, I have a life outside this ranch."

He was the only Linder sibling who was married, and with a child.

"We won't any of us have a life if we don't attend *to* this ranch," his father retorted. The elder Hugh Linder was a beefier, more handsome version of his oldest son; he exuded a natural leadership quality that none of his children had yet grown into for themselves.

Instead of arguing, Hugh-Jay winked at his mother and started to leave the kitchen.

"Hugh-Jay?"

He looked back at Annabelle, who asked him, "Are you all right?"

He gave her a friendly, puzzled look. "Sure. Don't I look all right, Mom?"

After an instant's hesitation she nodded, saying nothing more.

His father backed down for a moment, at least about one thing. "Don't worry about that horse, son."

"Why not?"

"I'll get it to the vet myself, if I have to."

Hugh-Jay smiled his gratitude, gave his parents a wave, and

continued on toward the front door, which they heard him thought-fully close, not slam as any of their other children might have done.

Belle almost escaped as she ran out of the house on her way back to her fledgling museum. She'd only come home to shower and change clothes. But she didn't make it out the front door in time to avoid hear-ing her father shout, "Belle! What time did you get in last night?"

Belle backed up, stuck her head in the kitchen and said, "I didn't, Dad. I stayed in town, and I'm twenty-three years old, for heaven's sake, so why are you still asking me questions like that?"

Her expression, more than her words, said he'd insulted her.

"Because you should be thoughtful to your mother."

"What did I do to Mom?"

"She fixed a plate for supper for you, and you never showed up."

"I never asked her to do that, Dad, did I, Mom?"

"You'll be late for work," he said, changing tack.

"What? You don't even think it's real work, Dad."

"Anything worth doing is worth—"

"Mother, tell him to stop."

She sounded pent-up with resentment.

Annabelle smiled at her daughter, who had the blond, big-boned look of her father and her oldest and youngest brothers. If Annabelle could have, she would have waved a magic wand to make Belle, her second child, as pretty and as happy as she was serious and sensitive. Too serious, in her mother's opinion, and too sensitive to slights, but maybe that's what happened to a girl who grew up with younger broth-ers who constantly teased her unless somebody else sat on them. It had never seemed to be in Belle's nature to give as good as she got, except when she was misunderstanding what was said to her. Short of that, she was more likely to run away, slam a door, and simmer until she even-tually exploded out of all proportion to the remembered crimes. Annabelle said lightly, "No, you didn't ask me to set a plate, but you might just as easily have shown up and complained if I hadn't done it."

Belle rolled her eyes.

Her mother observed that but held onto her own temper. In a light, teasing tone, she said, "Tell your dad that if he doesn't like the hours you keep, he can buy you a little house in town, Belle. Then he won't have to know what fathers shouldn't be knowing anyway."

"You know I don't earn enough to pay him rent!"

"Who said anything about rent?" Annabelle joked.

"Don't treat me like I'm irresponsible," Belle shot back.

"What? Belle, I would never call you, of all people, ir—"

Belle interrupted. "Dad, I got that buffalo head I was after, so if you could write me a check and leave it in my room?"

And then she was gone.

"I can't say *any*thing to that girl," Annabelle complained to her husband when Belle was gone.

"I don't know why she rushes to get there," Hugh grumbled back. "That museum is going to get five tourists a year and most of them will be friends of ours from out of town. I think she's only doing it to make me spend money on it." He was bankrolling his daughter's project— which seemed mostly hobby to him—in the hope that it might lead to an actual job for her and her history degree. "Now she wants me to pay for a mangy old buffalo head?"

"Oh, stop it," Annabelle shushed him, but halfheartedly. "She's right. You complain it isn't a real job and then you expect her to act like it is. You offer to finance it and then you complain when she takes you up on the offer." She tugged on her husband's shirtsleeve. She thought Hugh was growing quite distinguished-looking now that he was in his fifties and his thick blond hair was turning silver. She also thought that their children would be shocked—Belle, especially, would be horrified— if they knew how much their mother still loved to be alone in the master bedroom with their father with the door locked. When he turned toward her, she smiled and said, "Why is it that we can't seem to get rid of our kids?"

Chase, Bobby, and Belle still lived—mostly—on the ranch.

He grinned down at her and said, "Well, I'm doing my best here to run them off."

When she laughed, he leaned over and kissed her mouth.

"Have I ever mentioned that you're the prettiest woman in town?"

"Just the town? Not the whole county?"

Annabelle, whom he'd married and brought up from Dallas, was the one from whom their son Chase had inherited both his good looks and his charm. In their family of blond giants, only she and Chase had dark hair and blue eyes and tawny skin; in a family of accomplished and confident people, the two of them carried themselves with the air of people who had always been especially well-loved and admired, and for whom good things came more easily than they did to most people. The fact that Annabelle was also *nice* was a source of some pride throughout the county. People bragged about her, about the whole Linder clan: "Good people, lot of money, but they don't put on airs, 'cept maybe that girl Hugh-Jay married."

Hugh Senior moved in for a longer and deeper kiss with his wife.

She slid her hands around his waist, and he put his arms around her, too.

When she felt the effect of it in his body, she murmured, "No wonder you're so cranky." Annabelle laughed. "You're just horny." He laughed, too, and lifted her hair to kiss the side of her neck. Gently, Annabelle pushed him back a little. "Are you in a mood because of Billy Crosby?"

He didn't get a chance to answer because Bobby, their youngest, wandered in at that moment, looking for breakfast. "Stop that," he commanded his parents, with a look of exaggerated distaste for their show of affection. Then he raised his hands in self-defense and said to his dad, "Don't yell at me like you've been yelling at everybody else, okay? I'm just here for bacon, and I can fix it myself."

"You'd better fix it yourself," his father snapped back at him as he and Annabelle released each other from their embrace. Hugh Senior turned his back, to hide from his son any visible effect of his desire for the boy's mother. At the sink, making a show of washing his hands, he said, "Any child of mine who can't even make it through one year of college had better learn how to fend for himself, because I'm not going to support you all of your lazy life."

"Hugh," Annabelle rebuked him, "don't be mean."

He muttered, "Worthless," as he grabbed a towel to dry his hands.

Then he strode out of the room, brushing roughly against Bobby's shoulder, causing the eighteen-year-old to exclaim, sarcastically, "Excuse me, Dad!"

Annabelle took over the bacon-cooking for her son, to make up to him for his father.

"What's eating him?" Bobby asked her.

"I don't know," she said, although she hoped she did.

She hoped Hugh's foul mood was due to Billy Crosby, or to nothing more serious than too long between times with her in bed. She prayed that it didn't have anything to do with the thing that had *her* worried, the thing she had not confided in him and, with any luck, would never need to say.

A few minutes later she sat down across from her youngest as he forked fried eggs into his mouth.

"Bobby, will you at least *think* about applying to Emporia State?"

When mother and son sat across from each other at the kitchen table at High Rock Ranch, arguing about college, it was seven-fifteen in the morning. They were less than twenty-four hours away from tragedy, and what their family didn't know had already begun to hurt them.

5

After everybody in her family finally left the house, Annabelle made a meat loaf and put it in the oven to bake before the day got too hot for cooking. She planned to let it cool and then serve Hugh Senior's favorite cold meat loaf sandwiches—on homemade wheat bread, with mayo and lettuce—along with leftovers of yesterday's potato and green bean salads. She cleaned up her kitchen, swept the front, rear, and side porches, threw a load of sheets into the machine in the basement, made calls for her church circle, checked by telephone on an elderly friend, answered a couple of calls from cattle buyers, and fed the barn cats. They had temporarily run out of mice, and were looking a little thin as a consequence of their success. She watered her inside plants—she'd given up on her poor flower garden in July. Finally, with yet another chore in mind, she ran upstairs to change into her riding clothes, which amounted to blue jeans, long-sleeve cotton shirt, boots, dark sunglasses, and a floppy straw hat to protect her complexion from the sun.

She wanted to combine responsibility with pleasure.

On her way out to saddle up her chestnut horse—named Dallas for the city of her birth—Annabelle grabbed a banana for her own breakfast.

It was late for a morning ride; the day was already heating up.

But she felt a pressing need to escape from the argumentative air in her home that day. Plus, she had things to think over, including her husband's foul mood. Hugh Senior rarely wavered in his tenderness toward her, but overall Annabelle felt the years were turning him tougher, rather than softening him. The good principles he'd started out with, the ones that made her parents approve of him, had hardened, until now they were deep lines that people crossed at the price of never getting back into his good graces again.

It scared her sometimes, that increasing hardness.

Seeing people encounter it in him was like watching them race headlong into a steel wall and get bounced back violently. From the new distance they rubbed their noses and stared as if seeing him anew. When they attempted to get close again, they encountered a hostile formality in him that kept them at more than arm's length. Permanently. If the ranch manager in Colorado, for instance, was stealing from them—even if only dimes—he would rebound off that steel in Hugh so hard he'd land in another state, where he'd be job hunting.

She hoped it wasn't so.

The irony, to Annabelle, was that her husband's toughness grew from raising three sons whom he loved with every sinew of his being, and from semiraising the boys that Hugh and she had taken under their wings over the last couple of decades. She'd been the lucky one who got to give the boys affection, a sympathetic ear, and lots of marble cake; Hugh was the disciplinarian, caring enough about all of them to say no when it had to be said, and then sticking to it. He'd been as tough on Belle, but it hadn't worked as well on her. Their only daughter had the famous Linder work ethic, but she didn't have the emotional resilience the boys had from being shoved down—figuratively—and expected to get back up again.

When Belle got shoved down, she tended to stay down.

The change in Hugh Senior didn't scare Annabelle for her own sake—she believed her husband would forgive her anything—but for her children. Children—even grown ones—crossed lines. It was inevitable, sometimes even desirable, in her opinion. But it would break her heart if they ever lost their father's respect, and she feared that Bobby was not the only one of them who might be on the path toward that disaster.

Once atop Dallas, she pointed the horse down a rut in the dirt, in the direction she wanted to go, draped the reins over his withers and let him have his head while she peeled and ate her banana.

The grass under his hooves looked worse than dormant, it looked dead.

They hadn't had precipitation since May. Instead of depending on grass to feed the cattle, the ranch was being forced to truck in hay to some of the herds, as if it were already winter.

It was the kind of weather that her husband called expensive.

The morning had a smell of toasted vegetation, even though no sane rancher would have set a match to burn pastures in these conditions. A further fire hazard loomed out west: the threat of lightning in thunderclouds. At this point a storm would be a mixed blessing, welcome for rain, as long as there wasn't too much of it at one time, and unwelcome for the lightning that accompanied it.

They reached a gate and she slid down off Dallas to open it, coax him through, and then refasten the gate and remount him.

She was looking for a particular group of cattle—the pregnant mamas the men had weaned from their most recent calves yesterday. Now that she was in their pasture, she was surprised not to hear any bawling from the mothers or from the calves that had been separated from them. Usually she'd have expected to find all the calves lined up on one side of a fence, crying for their moms, and the cows bunched on the other side, mooing back at their six-month-old babies.

But the pasture was silent this morning.

It was quiet enough to hear a whip-poor-will and to hear Dallas crunch small rocks under his metal shoes, still enough to hear the buzz of a small plane overhead in the distance and catch the honk of a truck horn on the highway.

An especially easy weaning this time, Annabelle thought.

And then, as Dallas led her toward the herd, she saw the reason for the unnatural calm: the supposedly weaned calves were back with their mothers! Some were nursing, some butting and bouncing around each other in play, others pressing so close to their mothers' big red sides that they looked glued to them, as if they wanted to make sure they couldn't be forced apart again.

"Oh, no," she groaned to Dallas. "There must be a fence down."

This was not going to improve her husband's disposition.

It was going to mean another day's worth of hard, hot work, plus the extra physical and emotional strain on the cattle, plus the expense of the hired hands. She thought of Billy Crosby at that moment and said with annoyance, "One fewer hired hand."

Dallas's ears suddenly perked forward, attracting her attention.

When Annabelle looked past them, she spotted what the horse had noticed first: a large mound where it shouldn't be, a big red hump in the grass.

Dallas lifted his feet, one after the other, as if he were nervous.

She had to nudge him hard to get him to move toward the lump.

It was a cow, but it had a "wrong" look to it. Cows spent a lot of their lives lying down, but not stretched out on their sides as this one was, with her legs straight out and her head pressed sideways against the ground.

It lay as no living cow ever would.

She must have simply keeled over and died there on the spot, Annabelle thought at first. Death had to happen to all of God's creatures eventually, and not every one of High Rock Ranch's livestock made it to the slaughterhouse. A few went out the old-fashioned way, as this big old girl appeared, at first, to have done.

A shudder went through the big horse.

Annabelle slid off him again and walked toward the prone cow.

Dallas stepped backward. Annabelle turned to him and said, "Stay there."

Not that she blamed him for wanting to move. The smell was terrible in the heat, because the cow had emptied its bowels and bladder, and there was drying blood . . .

"Blood?" Annabelle felt a touch of dread for the cow's sake.

This was a pasture of pregnant cows that had just been weaned from their latest calves. Had this one miscarried and bled to death?

Why else would there be—

A gush of blood was pooled all around the fallen cow, as if every drop in her had poured out. The ground beneath her was so dry and hard that very little of the blood had soaked in; it remained a viscous, jellylike mass rapidly turning crusty and attracting flies, which also buzzed around the cow's orifices.

"Oh, no," Annabelle murmured when she got close enough to see more.

The blood had not come from the rear of the animal, as it would in a miscarriage, but from the front. It had all poured out of the head, and from a smiling gash across her throat. Coyotes were the only predators, and she knew they didn't normally go after cattle this size. Even the calves were big for coyote prey. Maybe the drought was altering the natural order of things.

Or maybe the cow died first and then the coyote—

But why wasn't any of the carcass torn away or consumed?

There weren't any bulls here; what would scare away a coyote?

None of it was making sense to Annabelle as she struggled to fit what she was seeing with what she knew of life and death on the ranch. Like all the cows in this pasture, this one had been pregnant, which meant an unborn calf was now dead inside of her, so this was a loss to the ranch of two, not just one valuable life, as these things were measured in money.

And then she realized with a shock which cow this was.

It was the cow that had caused all the ruckus yesterday, the old breeder that Billy Crosby had kicked in his rage.

Annabelle had directed Dallas to this pasture expressly to check up on this particular animal, to make sure that Billy hadn't done any terrible damage to her eye, and that they didn't need to call out the vet to treat her. She didn't know all the cattle by sight, not by any means—the ranch was much too big for that—but she knew some of the ones who'd been around a long time, especially the ones she affectionately thought of as "good old girls" and "good mamas." Just like humans, or dogs, or cats, some cattle were "pretty" or "cute" or "handsome," and some were homely ol' critters. This one had been one of those, with a long bony face, a sway back, and knobby knees that only its own offspring could love.

"I'm sorry, old dear," she murmured to it even as she held her breath to keep from breathing in the foul odors of its passing.

Speaking of its offspring, where was its "weaned" calf?

Annabelle looked around, but it was impossible to tell which of all the calves might be motherless at the moment, and they were too spread out for her to count. It had probably been frightened, then spent some time trying to nudge its mother to her feet, or to nurse from her, and then wandered off to graze. This was a hard way to get weaned, Annabelle thought sympathetically, but maybe—for the cow, herself—this was better, more merciful in its way, than going to the slaughterhouse, which was the fate that awaited all the cows past their breeding days.

Annabelle would have liked to place a hand on the cow, to pat its curly rough red hair and feel if its body was cool or if the death had happened recently enough for the carcass still to be warm. But she didn't want to step into the blood, and so she didn't get any closer.

Instead, she pulled herself back onto Dallas without the aid of any bucket or stump and rode home to give her husband the bad news.

UNLIKE HIS WIFE, Hugh Senior didn't hesitate to walk into the blood, or to touch the brutal wound, which was how he came to the conclusion that no coyote had killed her.

"Annabelle," he said, looking up at her, "somebody's cut her throat."

"Oh, Hugh! Oh, no! Are you sure?"

He didn't even bother to answer, and so she knew it must be obvious.

What he did say was, "And we know just who would have done that to this particular cow, don't we?"

Tears came to Annabelle's eyes and she felt pity.

Her pity wasn't only for the poor cow, but also for Billy Crosby, and she thought, Oh, Billy, what have you done?

She thought of the times she'd sat down with the boy and tried to talk to him about high school diplomas and jobs and being a husband and a father. She felt sickened by the blood, and the smell, and sickened for him. Her stomach heaved and she bent over the dirt and grass, though nothing came up. It was then that she noticed the cause of the burnt vegetation smell she had noticed earlier.

"Hugh!" she called, holding her hand over her mouth. She took her hand down and pointed. "He started a fire here."

Hugh stalked over and then walked around, examining the ground and coming to an analysis: "He tried to set a fire to burn her body . . . which means he didn't care if he burned the whole ranch down, and all the animals and us with it." He stood up straight, and was framed in front of the distant, dramatic clouds like a photograph of a rancher in his element. "I wonder why his fire didn't catch."

"Because her blood put it out before it could, that's why."

Annabelle's pity turned to rage with these new facts.

"This is a horrible thing to do, horrible! How dare he, Hugh, how *dare* he?"

"Because that's the kind of person Billy is, Annabelle. I'm sorry I didn't figure that out sooner."

A FEW MINUTES LATER, on their ride home, her anger weakened.

"Hugh, maybe it wasn't Billy." She offered up her one last benefit of the doubt to him. "It could have been anybody. Some crazy person driving by. A trespasser, an illegal hunter."

Her husband threw her a disbelieving look.

"And this stranger just happens to find that pasture and kill that particular cow out of all of our cattle. You can't be serious, Annabelle. You know as well as I do it was Billy. This has Billy's fingerprints all over it, and I mean that literally. I'll bet you that boy's so stupid he's left a trail of evidence."

"What will happen to him? What about his family?"

"His family is better off without a man like him."

She nodded, feeling on the verge of tears for their sakes.

"We'd all be better off without Billy Crosby," Hugh said, and Annabelle recognized his tone. It was the one he used when he came to a hard and irrevocable decision.

"People will say we never should have tried to help him."

"Let them say it," Hugh snapped. "Maybe we stopped worse from happening."

"Maybe we did." Annabelle felt a little comforted by that possibility, because who knew what Billy might have become, even before now, if they hadn't stepped in to try to push him along a better path. Yes, they had failed this time with this one boy. But there had been success stories, like Hugh-Jay's best friend Meryl Tapper, who had found love and inspiration among the Linders. Meryl was going to be a lawyer, and maybe marry their daughter, which could never have happened without their intervention in his troubled life. *He* wasn't out setting fire to pastures, and none of the other boys they'd helped had done anything like this, either.

"*This* could have been worse," she murmured, thinking of the burnt patch.

They were a few hours away from finding out what "worse" could mean.

6

SHORTLY BEFORE NOON, and unaware of what was going on at the
ranch, Hugh-Jay drove his silver truck up his driveway in town and
parked in the gravel behind his own home.

His and Laurie's house could hardly have been more different from
his parents'.

Out on the ranch, his mother and father had an attractive, practical, two-story frame home, unpretentious and perfect for its hard-
working functions. Here in Rose, Hugh-Jay and Laurie lived in an
inherited mansion that was almost 120 years old and rose out of the
ground as if nature had shoved it up from below. Over years spanning
two centuries, the elements had barely softened the edges of the enormous limestone rectangles that formed it, or the hand-laid stone fence
around it. It was a showplace, a nineteenth-century vault, impenetra-
ble unless he and Laurie left the doors unlocked, which they always
did, just like almost everybody else in Rose left their cars, trucks, and

houses unlocked. There just wasn't any such thing as a home invasion, or a murder, or car theft in Rose, although tools had been known to disappear from open garages now and then, which people put down to neighbors forgetting to return them.

Hugh-Jay and Laurie could have built a house out on the ranch, near his folks—or at some distance from them, because the ranch was big enough for that—but Laurie was a town girl. She'd had covetous eyes for the huge house that Hugh-Jay's grandfather had built for his grandmother. It had sat empty for a long while—because Annabelle never wanted to live in it, and there was nobody else in the family to take it—and the family would never consider selling it. With its exterior of foot-thick native limestone, and hand-hewn beams and massive antique walnut furniture within, it had been a fight for them to keep it off the National Register of Historic Places. They wanted to preserve it; they just didn't want other people telling them how to do it. Hugh-Jay's great-grandfather had designed it to warm, cool, protect, and impress, not necessarily in that order.

Hugh-Jay had resisted Laurie's pleadings, at first.

He preferred a simple house on the ranch, like his folks', only smaller.

"Give your bride what she wants," Annabelle advised him before his marriage to Laurie. "That's what your father did for me when I said I *didn't* want to live there, and look how well that's turned out!" His father, overhearing that, laughed. "Yes, all I had to do was build your mother a brand-new house," he'd teased. But he also put his arm around Annabelle and gave her waist a squeeze, which she returned with affection. Hugh-Jay felt he would give anything to have a marriage as good, as *alive*, as his folks' was, so he let himself be moved into a house that felt uncomfortable and pretentious to him. His wife scoffed, "Hugh-Jay, it was built for men your size!" But he felt it was built more for big egos than big bodies; it embarrassed him to live there when most people he knew were scrambling to make a living.

Hugh-Jay stepped out of his truck and squinted west, where clouds were building.

His pair of black Labrador retrievers came trotting up, their tails wagging and their tongues hanging out, to sniff him and to slobber their welcome onto his fingers, his jeans, and his boots.

"Looks like rain toward Colorado," he told them. "We sure need it."

The dogs trotted back to the shade of a tree and flopped down again.

A couple of days earlier he had witnessed an idiot toss a burning cigarette out of a car window. He chased the car down on the empty highway, squeezing it to the side of the road and forcing the driver to stop, scaring the four people inside half to death, so he could give them a piece of his mind about the danger of flipping live butts out of windows.

"You like barbecue?" he'd shouted as he approached their car.

Four hard-looking city faces stared back at him.

He knew he looked imposing. He meant to be.

He hoped the sight of a six-foot-two-inch cowboy rushing at them out of nowhere would scare the hell out of the ignorant fools.

"'Cause if you like your beef barbecued," he said as he came closer, "you're going to get it when that cigarette of yours catches that grass on fire and burns up all my cattle."

Later, thinking about it, he realized he was lucky they hadn't shot him. There could have been guns in that car. They looked like the types who'd carry firearms, and not for hunting deer or pheasant, either. There was no mounted gun rack; the guns these types would carry would be tucked into dark places under seats or in the glove compartment. One of them could have popped him out of sheer self-defense, because he looked and acted like a crazy man. But *they* were also lucky, he thought, that he hadn't jerked open the door closest to him, hauled the driver out of there, marched him back up the highway to where his cigarette lay smoldering and made him stamp it out with his forehead.

Instead, Hugh-Jay had gotten back into his truck, thrown it into reverse, and performed the grinding out—with the leather sole of his boot—himself, while they sped away down the isolated highway as fast as they could escape from him.

He hadn't told his wife Laurie about the incident.

He hadn't told anybody. Well, almost no one. Soon afterward he telephoned the local veterinarian to discuss the lame horse, and was still so full of adrenaline that he'd spilled the story. The vet sounded surprised, not at the stupid behavior of human beings who would throw burning butts onto dry grass, but at Hugh-Jay's high dudgeon about it. It wasn't a reaction anyone expected from him. And now he'd had two such incidents in just the past forty-eight hours, first with those strangers and then with Billy Crosby and his stupid beer can.

Hugh-Jay shook his head at his own volatile behavior.

He placed his gloved hands on the roof of his truck and sucked in a deep breath, trying to locate the calm, reasonable man that everybody thought he was, that *he* thought he was. Even through the gloves, the heat forced him to lift his hands back up. When he did, he saw that the palms of the yellow calf leather had turned gray-white, which told him that dust had traveled from the salt flats and rock monuments west of town. In the thick layer of dust on the metal, he saw his own clear glove prints, from his palms to the ends of his fingers.

"Bad weather for criminals," he thought wryly.

He slapped the dust off his gloves, then turned to look toward the back door of his house. Suddenly, he felt heartburn and tasted bile. He wasn't sure he could eat anything that Laurie fixed for him. While he was at his parents' home, or doing ranch errands, he could distract himself from what he didn't want to think about, but now he couldn't avoid it any longer.

He was headed home for lunch, without calling ahead to let her know he was coming.

This also wasn't behavior she expected from him, which was why he was doing it.

It was his third uncharacteristic act in forty-eight hours, he realized.

Hugh-Jay thought of what his mother had asked him—oddly, out of the blue—that morning: *Are you all right?*

No, was the honest answer to that, he wasn't all right.

He was far from all right. He was worried as hell and sick about it.

And his father's order—also out of the blue—for him to check up on the ranch in Colorado, hadn't made him feel any better. When he heard it, he felt his bowels go loose and he got an awful feeling in his gut. Somehow he managed to cover up his reaction so his dad didn't notice anything, but he hadn't fooled his mother. He never had been able to put anything over on her, not like Chase could by charming her, or like Bobby and Belle could by just refusing to talk about stuff. Hugh-Jay wondered how long his mom would wait to ask him again.

A sudden gust of wind preceding the rain jangled the wind chime on the porch.

Wishing it didn't take courage to walk up to his own back door, Hugh-Jay forced himself to get going. He took off his boots before walking into the kitchen in his stocking feet, so quietly that he had a moment to take it all in before Laurie even knew he was there.

THE BIG OLD-FASHIONED KITCHEN was fragrant with baking pies.

Hugh-Jay saw his wife dressed in her favorite yellow sundress, with her dark pixie hair stuck sweatily to the back of her neck, and he saw her bare arms, shapely bare legs, bare feet. The bones at the backs of her ankles were so slim they looked as if he could break them with a pinch. Her painted toenails—red—made his heart hurt, they were so sexy and perfect. He could have held her feet and played with her toes all day long, if she would let him. Such longings used to make her laugh and tease him; now, they would probably make her run and put on shoes.

He stared at her in silence while she worked at the sink.

She was twenty-two to his twenty-four, and so lovely that when he married her he could hardly believe she was supposed to be his for the rest of their lives. She'd left college to marry him, which sounded like a sacrifice except to anybody who'd seen her grade average. Laurie Linder was far from stupid, but she'd never had any interest in learning about much of anything beyond makeup, clothes, and gossip. Hugh-Jay hadn't cared; he'd loved her from afar for years, awed by her beauty, admiring her sexy walk and exuberant spirit, while he waited until she was old enough for him to ask her out on a date. He knew perfectly well that if he weren't the son of the wealthiest people around Rose, and if he didn't have things like this house to offer her, she'd never have looked at him.

He hadn't cared, not really. He was happy just calling her "my wife."

His parents didn't like her, considered her shallow and self-centered;

he knew they did. They tried to hide it for his sake, but when Hugh Senior or Annabelle Linder disapproved of someone, that fact was hard to miss despite their outward show of warmth. It made him feel protective of Laurie, who might not be "deep," but whom he loved deeply.

"Daddy!" three-year-old Jody squealed, and rushed at him from the hallway.

The child leaped at him with both arms up, trusting him to catch her in midair and sweep her into his arms. In an instant she was cuddled against him with her head tucked onto his left shoulder, and she was chattering away about her day. She had on a blue sundress and was sticky with little girl sweat, which told him she'd been busy that morning, probably hopping up and down the stairs, her current favorite indoor pastime when she wasn't twirling to make her skirts fly out around her. Like her mom, her feet were bare, and like her mom, her toenails were painted red. They also made his heart hurt for love of them and her.

"Hey," he said gently, to both of them, when she paused for breath.

Laurie had whirled at the sound of "Daddy!" dropping her paring knife.

"Daddy's home!" Jody told her, with joy in her lilting voice.

"Hugh-Jay, you scared me! What are you doing here?"

He smiled, hoping it didn't look as forced as it felt.

"I can't have lunch with my wife and daughter?"

"Yes, Daddy!" Jody chirped, and hugged her arms around his neck.

He looked over at Laurie to hear her say so, too.

She turned her back and continued dicing carrots.

Hugh-Jay set his daughter on the floor and gave her behind a gentle swat as she ran off to get something from her bedroom to show him. Then he took a shaky breath and moved purposely toward his wife.

IT SCARED LAURIE that Hugh-Jay had come home without any warning.

She counted on him to be predictable, as he was every time he came in the house. First he'd scrape the soles of his boots on the shit-catcher, a little metal bar attached to two other bars, then he'd pick up his boots, knock them together to dislodge more dirt and cow shit, and then set them neatly side by side beside the back door. Laurie knew that if she looked out there now, she'd see them paired like that. Before he walked into the house, he took off whatever hat he was wearing— today it was a Kansas City Royals baseball cap instead of a cowboy hat—and he knocked it against his jeans to clean it, and then hung it on a hook above the boots, leaving his blond hair plastered down and sweaty where the cap had been. His big square face was reddened, and rivulets of dirty sweat ran down it. That meant that he would come to the sink to wash off.

The routine of his thoughtfulness drove her crazy.

She also depended on it, however, especially lately.

"I missed you," he said, answering her question about why he was there.

"*Missed* me!" she scoffed, still without turning around. "You've been gone, what, five hours?"

She heard the old wood floor creak as he walked toward her.

She tensed as he hovered like a huge tent closing around her, darkening the space, exuding heat from his big body. She expected him to grasp her arms and move her aside so he could rinse his face and arms. Instead, she felt his big arms come around her, felt him bend down to kiss the back of her neck. When he kissed her right ear, she shuddered reflexively. She felt his surprise as he discovered she was naked under her sundress.

"Are you sure you weren't expecting me?" he teased.

"I just got out of the shower," she said sharply. She tried to lean away from him, to reach for a dishcloth. "I didn't have time to put on anything but this."

His hands moved to the straps of her dress.

"What are you doing, Hugh-Jay?"

She heard his breathing quicken, felt him pressing harder into her until the front of the sink bit into her waist. "Hugh-Jay!" He kissed her neck again and started pushing the straps of her dress down over her shoulders until the tops of her breasts were exposed to him. "Don't!"

She bent her head forward, trying to get away from his mouth. She jerked her straps back up. "Stop it!"

He backed off immediately. Then he did what she had originally expected him to do: he gently moved her aside, turned on the water, and washed off his hands, then his face, lower arms, and the back of his neck, until the water finally turned from mud to clear.

He grabbed a nearby towel and rubbed his face and arms dry.

"I can't believe you did that," she accused him.

"Did *what*?" He turned toward her, his broad, plain face looking hurt, his voice plaintive in a way that only annoyed her more. "Try to love my wife?"

"In the middle of the day? In the kitchen? With Jody right here?"

"I wouldn't have done *that* in front of her!"

"You shouldn't have done *any* of it."

"I'm sorry. You're right."

Before they married, she hadn't objected to anywhere or any time, or even to the chance that somebody might see them. He was the one who'd been straitlaced and worried about getting caught. She remembered that; she knew he did, too. Neither of them reminded the other of it.

Hugh-Jay, noticing something shiny under the kitchen table, bent down to pick it up, but his daughter ran back into the room and beat him to it. "Here, Daddy." She placed a silver cigarette lighter into his hands, along with a doll in a new dress that she'd brought down to show him.

"It's Unca Chase's," she said. "He left it. Do you like her dress?"

"It's very pretty. I'll bet Uncle Chase left this at breakfast."

"Nope! Later, when he came back and drank all Mama's coffee, didn't he, Mama? You always say Unca Chase drinks all your coffee."

"I don't say any such thing."

Jody frowned, but didn't argue with her mother.

Hugh-Jay asked, "Chase came back this morning?"

"Yeah, and he swung me!" Jody exclaimed. "On the swing!"

"What did he want?"

"Just coffee," Laurie muttered.

"But Mommy—"

"Jody! Take your doll and go play somewhere else!"

Hugh-Jay saw his daughter's lower lip start to tremble, so he stuck the lighter into his back left pocket and grabbed her onto his lap. Softly, he said, "When did Mommy get your dolly a new dress?"

Laurie whirled around to face them. "What difference does it make? It's just a dress, it doesn't matter when I got it, I can get my daughter a dress for her doll if I want to."

Upset by her mother's anger, Jody started to cry.

It only made Laurie sigh angrily and roll her eyes, leaving the comforting to Hugh-Jay. The oven timer went off, and Laurie put on padded gloves to remove her pies and set them on racks to cool.

"Maybe pie would make us all feel better," Hugh-Jay said, hugging Jody.

"Not yet!" Laurie's tone was still furious. "They're still too hot."

"That's when they're good."

"Yeah," Jody agreed, wiping her eyes with the backs of her hands, hiccuping little sobs. "I'm hungry."

"No, they need to set up more," her mother insisted, which settled it.

LAURIE WOULDN'T EVEN let them have any pie after they ate the tuna fish sandwich and potato chips she put out for them.

"I made the pie for supper tonight," she said.

"I won't be here for supper tonight," Hugh-Jay told her.

"Why not?"

"Where are you going, Daddy?"

Jody had recovered from her tears, helped along by the tuna sandwich.

"Colorado," he said, avoiding his wife's eyes.

"Why?" she asked sharply.

"Dad's sending me."

There was a silence, and then Laurie repeated, "Why?"

Hugh-Jay shrugged, and bent his face toward his empty plate, as if there might be crumbs he'd missed.

"Well, then," Laurie said, her voice hard, "if you're leaving, I guess you won't be getting any, will you?"

"He won't get any pie?" Jody looked anxious. "Are you mad at Daddy?"

"I'm not mad at him."

"Yes, you are," Jody said, starting to cry again.

"No!" Laurie suddenly slammed down a fork and shouted at both of them. "I'm not!"

Her husband and daughter stared at her, but neither of them spoke. Even to a three-year-old, the truth was obvious.

OUT AT THE RANCH HOUSE, Hugh Senior came up with a plan.

"Don't say anything to Bobby about what's happened," he instructed Annabelle. "He'll just go roaring off to find Billy and get himself in trouble. And don't tell Chase, either."

She stared at him, waiting to hear his reasons.

Instead of explaining, he got on the telephone and let her listen.

First he called their eldest child at his home in town. "Son, I want you to bring Billy Crosby back out to the ranch for some work today."

Annabelle's eyebrows rose in surprise.

"Yes," Hugh Senior said into the phone, apparently in reply to his son's reminder of what had happened the day before, "but I have a special job I want him to do. I'm going to need you, too, and if you see your brothers, tell them to show up ready to mend fences." He paused to listen, and then said, "Somebody cut some of our fence lines, son. They let the weaned calves back in with their mothers. But the worst thing is, they killed a pregnant cow. Sliced the poor girl's throat."

Standing a foot away, Annabelle heard their son's exclamation of shock.

And then she heard his father tell a lie.

"No, it wasn't Billy." He listened. "Of course I'm sure of that, or why would I allow him back on the ranch?"

When he hung up, Annabelle said, "You lied to your son."

"Well, I had to. Hugh-Jay can't lie worth beans, and I don't want him giving the game away to Billy on the ride out here."

"What game are you playing?"

"A serious one." He leaned over to kiss her forehead.

"What are you up to, my darling?"

"Getting Billy to clean up his own mess, that's what."

He then made another call, this time to the county sheriff's office in Henderson City. "This is Hugh Linder Senior," he said with easy authority to the deputy who answered. "I am reporting that Billy Crosby killed one of my cows last night . . . Yes, I'm sure. He also cut my fence lines and tried to set fire to one of my pastures. I have arranged for him to be away from his house for a few hours this afternoon. I want you to go there while I've got him safely out of your way. Talk to his wife about where he was last night. Look for evidence while you're there. You should find the knife or some bloody clothes. Look for wire clippers. When you've done all that, then I want you to come out here to the ranch and arrest him."

"Speaking of misbehavior," Annabelle said after he hung up the phone, "what about Colorado?"

"What's wrong out there, you mean? We're getting overbilled on some things. It could be nothing but sloppy clerking. Or it could be that our man is lining his own pockets. Hugh-Jay should have caught it in the bookkeeping. It shouldn't have had to wait for me to find. I'm sending him to clean up *his* own mess. It's the only way either one of them will ever learn; it's the only way anybody learns."

A little later Annabelle said, "He won't appreciate that you lied to him."

Her husband's reply was confident. "It won't do him any harm."

7

LAURIE AND JODY accompanied Hugh-Jay onto the back porch after lunch. He set his suitcase—a battered old leather one that his grandfather had used—on the porch floor beside his feet.

"I'll be driving into rain tonight," he predicted, observing the western sky.

The clouds looked taller, darker, and closer now.

Laurie squinted at his truck, which he'd parked under cottonwood trees at the rear of their driveway. The dogs came running over. When they pressed against her, she shoved them with her knee and said, irritably, "Go on! Get down from here, you hot, smelly things! Hugh-Jay, is there somebody in your truck?"

"Billy Crosby, probably." He took hold of the dogs' collars and tugged the Labs down onto the gravel, away from her. "Didn't you hear me call him on the telephone? I told him to walk on over."

Laurie saw Billy turn his face in their direction as if he knew they were talking about him. He lifted a hand and waved in a halfhearted way. Laurie didn't return the gesture.

"I can't believe your dad would hire him for anything again."

She wasn't trying very hard to keep Billy from hearing her.

"A man gets to have a second chance, doesn't he?"

"But not a fifth and sixth," she retorted sarcastically.

"I didn't know you disliked him so much."

"I don't." It sounded more defiant than convincing. "I don't care about him."

Hugh-Jay bent over to kiss the top of her head, but she moved at that moment, so his affection only grazed her. He stood up straight again. "It's hard for a man to support his family when he's got a suspended driver's license."

"Well, and whose fault is that?"

"Okay. You're right."

She looked up at him. "When will you be back?"

"I don't know. I might come home tomorrow, or I might have to stay a while longer. I won't know till I get there."

"Well, *call* me and let me know what you're going to do."

"All right."

Her expression turned fierce. "Swear."

"I do, I will!" He bent way down to kiss his daughter's tiny nose. "'Bye, baby girl."

She took the opportunity of her father being down at her own level to throw her arms around his neck. "Don't leave, Daddy."

He put his hands on her waist and stood up with her clinging to him. Her breath smelled of tuna fish, and her hair, dark like her mother's, flew into his face, and both sensations made him smile as he hugged her to his chest and picked long strands of her hair out of his mouth. "Got to, baby girl." After a moment he gently unwound her from around him and set her down and pushed her arms back down to her sides, as if she were a tiny bellows. "But I'll bring you back a surprise."

"A *horse?*"

"Not this time." She desperately wanted her own pony, and yet she still adored to ride in front of him while he kept one arm around her and one hand on the reins. "You still need to grow some."

The excitement on her face fell away in disappointment.

"But it'll be a good surprise anyway," he promised her, which earned him a brave little smile accompanied by eyes still moist at the loss of the horse and his impending absence.

"Hugh-Jay, you spoil her."

"I like to spoil my girls."

"No," his wife said in a hard voice. "You don't."

Without looking into her eyes, he grabbed his overnight bag and started down the porch stairs, a big man moving with athletic grace. The dogs labored up and joined him. Laurie expected to see him get into his truck with Billy, but he didn't do that; instead, he set down the suitcase, walked toward one side of their detached garage and disappeared around to the back of it.

"Where'd Daddy go?"

"There's no telling."

In a few moments he appeared again, and this time he did get into his pickup.

"'Bye, Daddy!" Jody hollered in her loudest three-year-old voice. "I love you!"

Her next-to-last sight of him, which would fade from her memory, was of his face framed in his truck window with his left elbow propped on the edge. He had changed into a cowboy hat, and underneath it he was smiling at her out of his plain, pale, wide face, his gaze returning all the love she'd yelled at him.

AT THE RANCH HOUSE, Bobby ambled in past noon, looking for a meal his mother might provide. Instead, he found his parents talking together in the kitchen, where the overhead fan was turning and nothing was cooking. Hungry, hot, and disappointed, he said, "Don't you two ever leave this house?" If Chase had said it, it would have come across as a good-natured joke, but Bobby had little talent for humor, and so it came out sounding aggressive.

His father gave him a sour look. "Sit down. I have something to tell you."

"Yes, sir." It sounded more as if he were glad to sit than to obey his father. Bobby collapsed into a kitchen chair, stuck his long legs out and slouched there, his big hands loosely grasping the top rungs. "You're not sending me to some junior college, Dad."

"I'll send you where you deserve to be sent!"

"Hugh," Annabelle said, in a tone that reminded him he had other problems to discuss with their youngest. Without giving him another chance to argue, she told her son, "Bobby, we have some fences down. Somebody cut them and mixed up the weaned calves back with their mothers."

"You're kidding." Bobby's jaw dropped and he sat up. "Cut them?"

"That's not all," his father said, "they killed a cow, one of the pregnant mamas—slit her throat."

He didn't say which cow.

"Holy shit!" Bobby exclaimed.

"And nearly set fire to the pasture," his mother chimed in, shaking her head at both the event and his choice of words.

Bobby shot to his feet. "Goddamn him!"

"It wasn't Billy," Hugh Senior said, understanding immediately whom Bobby meant. "And watch your mouth in this house."

"Of course it was Billy, Dad! What are you talking about? There's nobody else it could be! He's pissed at you. He was already pissed at you over that stupid thing yesterday, and now he's probably really pissed about his truck. Who else would do something like that?"

"Somebody we don't know, Bobby."

"I'll slit the throat of whoever did this!"

When he left to go wash up, Hugh said to his wife, "And that is why I don't want Bobby knowing ahead of time, before the arrest. If he knew it was Billy who did it, it would be our son who'd end up in jail for murder."

Annabelle stepped into his arms.

"I hate this," she murmured against his chest.

Every time she remembered the poor old cow, so docile, so defense-less, so reliably productive for so many years, she wanted to kill Billy Crosby with her own bare hands.

AS HE BACKED DOWN the driveway with Billy in the passenger seat, Hugh-Jay watched his wife and daughter go back inside. When the sun-light shone through Laurie's dress, it revealed the curve of her hips and her slim legs, and the fact that she wasn't wearing anything else to cover them.

He looked to his right, and caught his passenger staring at her, too.

Billy looked as if he was going to say something admiring, but then he seemed to think better of it, closed his mouth, turned his face, and stared out the windshield. He tipped his cap down to shield his eyes from the white sunshine coming through the glass.

Hugh-Jay, watching him, thought that was a wise move.

He was accustomed to other men admiring his wife, but that didn't mean he liked the fact that Billy now had a mental image of Laurie naked under her thin dress. He wanted to scrape that picture from Billy's mind. He wanted to erase it from *any* other man's mind, but especially from the imagination of a man like Billy. Billy had the kind of bad-boy appeal that baffled Hugh-Jay, because he didn't understand why women ever went for guys who promised nothing but heartache.

He smelled beer again.

"You already drinking today, Billy?"

"That's any of your business, Hugh-Jay?"

"If you're working for my family, yes, it is. Did you?"

Billy let out a martyred sigh. "A beer with dinner, that's all." In the country, they called lunch "dinner," and the later meal was "supper." He shifted in the seat. "What kind of work you gonna put me on today, Hugh-Jay?"

"We've got to mend some fence lines."

"Really. I thought we was all caught up with that for a while."

"We had some vandalism. Somebody cut some wire, mixed up some herds." He refrained from mentioning the dead cattle.

"No shit? Who'd do a thing like that?"

"Dad doesn't know." Hugh-Jay glanced at him. "Sure it wasn't you?"

Billy laughed bitterly. "Yeah, I walked all the way out there. You forgot you took my truck?"

"I'm going to need to get that second pair of keys from you, Billy."

There was a sudden tense silence from the passenger. "Val tell you that?"

"What? That you've got extra keys? No, I just assumed. Who doesn't have extra keys?"

"Me. I don't. Never have. You can ask her."

"Maybe you forgot. Maybe she's got them in her purse."

"She never had any. I never gave her any. I had the only pair. Now you've got them."

Hugh-Jay sensed the unspoken curse words: *goddamn you.*

Billy said, "Does your dad know you hired me today?"

"I told you, this was his idea."

Out of the corner of his eye Hugh-Jay saw Billy relax a little and even smile, close to a smirk.

"Don't make him regret it," he advised.

"Who you think did it?"

"Cut the fences? I told you, Dad doesn't know."

"How you gonna catch somebody like that?"

"Might be hard to do."

"Prob'ly never will catch 'em."

Billy slumped down in the seat, pulled his cap fully over his face, and either napped or pretended to.

Hugh-Jay turned the radio on.

The sweet voice of Dolly Parton singing about a coat of many colors filled the cab with haunting melody.

As Hugh-Jay drove and listened to the music, he thought about how some things are easy to prove: like the amount of mileage that got put on a truck between the last time it was driven and now, and how that mileage matched the distance to the ranch. He'd made a note of Billy's mileage last night after Chase walked off to Bailey's Bar & Grill. It had occurred to Hugh-Jay as he watched his brother stroll down the broken sidewalk that although you took a man's truck, you might not keep him from driving it. In his right jeans pocket he now had a note with two numbers on it: one was the mileage he'd written down last night, and the second number was what he'd written down a few minutes earlier behind his garage where the truck was parked. Now he was going to have to break the news to his father that Billy didn't deserve any more chances, and that the only thing he deserved was jail.

He glanced over at the supposedly sleeping man.

Billy didn't have a clue, Hugh-Jay marveled, that he was now in the worst trouble of his worthless life. He thought he was getting away with it. Billy didn't even sense how deeply offensive it was even to have to sit in the same truck with him. Billy Crosby. Drunk. Wife beater. Fence cutter. Cattle abuser, and now cattle killer.

Or, as Bobby might say in crude summation: Billy Crosby, asshole.

Hugh-Jay's jaw locked, holding in his outrage.

He hadn't lied to Billy. He'd only said, "Dad doesn't know."

That was true; his father didn't know that Billy did the damage.

Hugh-Jay recalled how he'd nearly pulled four strangers out of their car over a tossed cigarette, and how he had threatened to pitch Billy out of the truck for throwing a beer can out the window. That sin was nothing compared to cutting fence lines and killing cattle as an act of cruel revenge. For that, Billy deserved to be thrown out and run over a few times.

And yet, Hugh-Jay was nearly grateful to Billy for distracting him.

Nothing Billy did could hurt as much as what was happening at home.

"Home," Hugh-Jay murmured, moving his lips over the bittersweet word.

Billy stirred a little, as if he'd heard, but then he snored.

Tired? Hugh-Jay thought, glancing at him. You had a busy night, Billy.

The cemetery and the bison herd rolled by.

Hugh-Jay fought to keep his feelings of despair, loneliness, and anger bottled up inside of him so he wouldn't slam his hand against the steering wheel, or beat up on Billy, or worst of all—cry. It was awful when people you helped and people you loved betrayed you and let you down. It made him feel like doing things he never wanted to do, hurtful, violent, shameful things. Hugh-Jay turned into the main gate of the ranch and prayed that the hours of hard work ahead of him would cleanse him and turn him back into the man he wanted to be.

8

IN THE LIVING ROOM of the big stone house, Laurie sat with her back against the frame of a window seat with Jody slumped asleep in her arms. The child had cried after her father left, and then finally gave in to the hot and humid day, to her tears, and to the accumulated exhaustion of a morning spent being a three-year-old who loved to hop up and down stairs, and twirl until she fell down, and run a groove into the carpet around the big walnut dining room table.

Long after Hugh-Jay's truck turned the corner, long after her arms went numb from holding Jody, long after the telephone rang repeatedly and she didn't answer it, Laurie continued sitting in the window seat, staring outside. She was furious and anxious about Hugh-Jay's surprise visit home, and she didn't know what to do about it. She wanted to throw things. She wanted to run out the door and keep running until she was far away from him and Rose. She wanted to scream.

What she didn't want to do was have to sit still to keep Jody from waking up, even though the quiet was a relief.

Why had he come home? It was so unlike him. Was he checking up on her?

Even on such a hot day, she felt chilled and ill at the memory of his voice behind her in the kitchen.

The way he'd grabbed her . . .

She shuddered, which made Jody shift in her arms.

Laurie forced herself to sit perfectly still and barely breathe.

She didn't want to have to deal with a child's wants and needs, but then the truth was, she never did want to play mommy. That's what it felt like to her. Pretend. Not real. Only, it was a joyless game that never ended—like Monopoly, which Chase and Belle loved and played as if the fate of the ranch depended on which one of them got Park Place. She hated that stupid game, because she thought it was stupid to care so much about plastic houses, and because she wasn't accustomed to competing. But at least with Monopoly she could cash in and walk away. With the game of being a mother, she could never win and she could never quit.

She stared down at the sleeping child, feeling resentful and trapped.

Nobody had ever warned her she might feel this way toward her husband or her own flesh and blood. That was a nasty surprise. A child was a whole lot of work and trouble, she was finding out, just like marriage had turned out to be. A baby—like a husband— always had to be considered, even if all the mother wanted to do was take a nap. And God forbid she should want to talk on the telephone or take a leisurely bath or take a few hours off when there wasn't anybody around to babysit.

At least her daughter looked like her, thank God for that much of a blessing.

If she'd had an ugly child, Laurie thought she'd have hated it.

Her child was beautiful, and she lived in the biggest, nicest house in town, and her husband was rich, or would be someday. People thought he already was, just because he was a Linder, but all Hugh-Jay made was a salary like any other ranch employee. He made more than his brothers because he was older and had more experience and responsibility, but still, it was just a salary, as if he was a janitor's kid instead of the oldest son of the wealthiest people in town. In a few years they could share in the ranch profits, but not yet, because his parents didn't believe in giving their children too much, too soon, or too easily. Laurie wanted to shake Annabelle and Hugh Senior for being so selfish! It would be so easy for her father-in-law and mother-in-law to let loose of a few more dollars so that she and Hugh-Jay could have some fun instead of only work.

Fun. It felt like forever since she'd had any.

On days such as this one, when the house and the heat made her feel like an animal who wanted to claw and howl her way to freedom, Laurie thought she would take any escape that anybody offered to her.

And it wasn't as if nobody ever did . . .

She smirked to herself, reveling in that other truth.

Her thoughts made her shiver again, but in a delicious way.

In that overheated moment, she intensely felt her own raw, tingling nakedness under her sundress, longing for hands upon her skin that were not her husband's callused, fumbling, clumsy ones. She felt those other hands moving on her breasts, another mouth pressing against hers, another man's weight on top of her, his eyes admiring her, eating her up, loving her in the ways she wanted to be loved and not in the tame, safe, predictable, infuriating ways she actually was loved. She imagined him commanding her, *refusing* to give her instantly what she demanded, making her wait and beg and do whatever he ordered her to do, holding her arms back, pinning her legs down, tasting her, teasing her, until she exploded with desire for him, and only then would he give it to her—laughing at her, tormenting her as he made her moan and scream and beg again, again, again. Her breath went shallow. She felt consumed by desire for skin she wasn't supposed to touch, obsessed by sex she wasn't supposed to have, wild with longing for things she wasn't supposed to do and would never do with her husband. She didn't believe she had made a mistake marrying Hugh-Jay—Laurie never thought she made mistakes because there were always other people to blame—but sometimes she wondered what it would have been like to marry one of those other boys who stared at her, one of the good-looking, sexy ones who hadn't been respectful and patient like Hugh-Jay, one of the ones who'd been hot instead of lukewarm, who'd been exciting instead of steady, passionate and fun instead of plain and dull. What would her life be like if she went with a man who whispered shocking words to her, and who gave her things that didn't have anything to do with money?

What if she could have had both, the money and the pleasure?

And then she finally saw it, the silver lining that her anger and the sluggish day had hidden from her until this moment: Hugh-Jay was going to be gone that night and maybe longer! She could do what she wanted to do. She could do what she *needed* to do, and had every *right* to do, because didn't she have a right to be happy? And she wouldn't even get in trouble for it, because there would be nobody home to catch her.

In her arms, Jody stirred and opened her eyes.

"Hi, sleepyhead," her mother said, with an encouraging smile that surprised her daughter into smiling back. "How would you like to go out to Grandma and Grandpa's to spend the night?"

9

ANNABELLE FELT NERVOUS as she drove her black Cadillac out to the men working in the pastures that afternoon. She was going to have to see Billy Crosby—after the awful things he'd done—and pretend she didn't know he'd done them. It was vital to keep Billy out here at the ranch while the sheriff did his work in town. Billy wasn't to know what was happening there. He needed to be taken into custody out here in the country, far from his vulnerable wife and innocent son—who should be spared the trauma of watching his father be carted off to jail. Billy needed to be surrounded by strong men who would make sure he didn't do anything crazy or violent. Hugh wanted the arrest made quickly, quietly, with a minimum of trouble. So, with all her heart, did Annabelle. It had slowly sunk in on her and, she thought, on Hugh, just how dangerous a man might be who could do such things, and so she wasn't only anxious, she was also scared of what was going to happen next. She had never seen anybody arrested except on television or in the movies, and never dreamed the first time would be at their own ranch. As she parked on the dirt road that ran through the pasture, she sent up a prayer for everybody's safety.

It was her job now to contribute a touch of normalcy to the scene by doing exactly what all of the cowboys, including Billy, were expecting her to do.

And so she was taking iced tea and cinnamon rolls to them, because she always took treats to them when they worked long afternoons or mornings. When her daughter Belle was younger, she'd gone along, or she'd been up on horseback herself, helping with the cattle work. On some days, Annabelle took coffee and chocolate chip cookies or lemonade and molasses crinkles. Because of the impending weather, she had also stocked her Caddy with rubber rain slickers and plastic hat protectors for any man who'd neglected to bring his own. The clouds had finally moved across the Colorado-Kansas state line, with the main part of the storm now only a county and a half away from them. The first rain had already blown through in thin, intermittent sheets, not enough to stop the work, just enough to cool and mist the cowboys and their horses, all of whom had been working ever since Hugh Senior convened them with his emergency request for assistance.

"What will you tell them?" she'd asked him.

"Same thing I told the boys, that it's vandalism and that's all I know."

Going nonstop, a group of neighbors, hired hands, and Linder men had managed to repair every cut section of fence but one that still awaited mending. A tour of the ranch had revealed other fences cut, other pastures breached, and other herds mixed up with each other. The cowboys were already organizing for getting on horseback to return cattle to their proper pastures, but when they saw Annabelle park on the shoulder of the highway, they tied up their horses again in anticipation of what she'd be bringing to them.

Weather wouldn't stop them from work, unless it turned to lightning, but the smell of Annabelle Linder's homemade rolls could, it was widely claimed, stop a rutting bull in his tracks.

The rain slickers that Annabelle brought, some bright yellow and others black, were heavy. Several of the cowboys jumped forward to assist her in carrying them, along with a big plastic jug of sweet iced tea and plastic cups. They transferred the treats across the grass and the dirt—which was just damp enough to stick to the bottoms of their boots—and set them on the backseat of one of their trucks.

Annabelle followed under an umbrella, carrying the napkins.

She was greeted with "Hi, Mom" from her sons and with courteous, drawled thank-yous from the other men. "Sure am sorry this happened to you folks, Annabelle," one of the neighbors said. "It's a rotten thing," another man commented, which produced a murmur of masculine agreement in bass tones that felt comforting to her, as if they'd put a collective, caring arm around her shoulders. "Hope they catch the sons a bitches," asserted a cowboy, followed by, "begging your pardon, ma'am."

"I agree," she said, and smiled at him.

Red Bosch, the youngest cowboy there, jumped forward with an offer to assist her with the rolls.

"Be happy to carry those rolls for you, Mrs. Linder," young Red said earnestly.

He put out both arms so she might lay the tray on top of them. The rolls, huge and warm, had dripped their powdered sugar icing down their sides into gooey, soft-crusted puddles on the waxed paper she had placed beneath them.

"Don't you let him do it," an older cowboy warned her. "Or there won't be any left for the rest of us."

"Hey," Red joked back. "I'm just a growing boy."

"Exactly," the cowboy said dryly, and everybody laughed, a welcome relief.

"Here, Red," Annabelle said, handing the tray over to him. "You pass them around where everybody can see your hands."

Another laugh went around the group.

The biggest grin came from Red himself. The boy had flunked out of high school and was trying to earn money to buy his own truck. Annabelle often tried to talk him into returning to school, but at sixteen, and from a family where nobody had ever graduated from high school, he had a hard time seeing into the future. "Red" wasn't a nickname; he'd been born with the red hair of his eighteen-year-old father, and so "Red" he had been officially dubbed by his fifteen-year-old mother. He was no pretty boy, people remarked of him, and no Einstein, either, but there was something about Red that made you smile.

Annabelle forced herself to look for Billy Crosby.

Fortunately, he was looking at the sky, so she didn't have to speak to him.

She darted a glance at her husband, who looked at his watch.

Her stomach clenched as she thought of Valentine alone with her boy while the sheriff's deputies searched through their home. She wished there had been a way to warn Val to take the boy to a friend's house before the sheriff arrived.

Poor little guy, she thought, looking down to hide tears in her eyes.

Collin Crosby's childhood was just the kind that produced the sort of boy that she and Hugh Senior tried to help. Boys like his father and Red Bosch. She hoped that one day they wouldn't feel a need to put Collin Crosby to work to keep him out of trouble, or that if they did, they'd have more success with him than they'd had with his father.

Annabelle felt a painful sense of failure with Billy Crosby.

One by one her sons sidled up to her as she stood there.

"Mom," Hugh-Jay said so quietly that nobody else could hear him. "Dad's wrong about Billy. He did it and I've got the proof. I've tried to tell Dad but he won't listen to me. Can you talk to him?"

"What kind of proof?"

He told her about the truck mileage.

Annabelle grabbed one of his hands and squeezed it.

"Let your father handle this," she said.

Hugh-Jay frowned, as if to say there were things that weren't making sense to him, but he didn't ask about them, and Annabelle didn't volunteer to explain anything more.

Next it was Chase who came over and stood in front of her, blocking their conversation from anyone's view.

"I don't know why Dad thinks Billy didn't do it."

Again she said, "Let him handle this, sweetheart."

"But—"

"Trust me, Chase."

He nodded, looking doubtful but willing to believe she knew best. "Okay, Mom."

And finally Bobby came over. "I don't care if he didn't do it. I can't stand to even be in the same pasture with the son of a bitch."

"Is that how your friends talked at K-State?"

He made the same kind of exasperated face at her that she had made several times that day at him, but he walked away without further argument.

Annabelle hoped that whatever was going to happen would happen soon.

Her sons were now bunched together at a distance from the other men, and all three of them looked as if they were just about ready to explode at somebody, and Annabelle knew who that somebody would be with even the slightest provocation. Seeming to sense the tension in the air, Billy Crosby was keeping his own distance from everyone.

Come *on,* she urged the sheriff in her thoughts.

But still he didn't come.

The cowboys gathered around the truck with the refreshments, making appreciative sounds. Annabelle forced herself to walk around to each of them, inquiring about their wives and children, or parents and siblings. She was picking up the remains of the cinnamon rolls just as her husband pushed his arms into a black slicker and called out, "One more fence in this pasture, and then we can move on. Hugh-Jay, Chase, you take care of it."

"Yessir." Hugh-Jay licked his fingers and dropped his empty cup into a plastic trash bag. "Come on, Chase."

"Wait a minute." Chase pulled out a cigarette and then patted his jeans pockets, as if looking for something in them. "I gotta have a smoke first." It was the first break any of them had taken since starting work.

"Quit those nasty things," his father said, looking disgusted.

Chase grinned. "Gotta have *some* vices, Dad."

The other men laughed, as if they suspected Chase of more vices than he was laying claim to.

"Here." Hugh-Jay pulled a rectangle of silver out of his own pocket and tossed it to his middle brother.

Chase caught it with the hand that wasn't holding the cigarette. When he saw what it was, his face brightened and he looked over at his brother. "Hey, it's my lighter! Where'd I drop it?"

"On my kitchen floor."

Chase's grin turned devilish. "Darn, you caught us!"

"You went back there this morning?" Hugh-Jay asked him.

"Yeah."

Their father said, "I thought I sent you to the bank this morning."

"You did, Dad, and I went," Chase said, with an air of humoring both of them. He paused to light the cigarette, cupping his hands over it and the flame to keep the weather from defeating him. When he looked up, after taking a long drag, he blew out the smoke and said, "Then I stopped to bum a cup of coffee off Laurie."

"Hey, Chase," one of the other men joked, "maybe you ought to get yourself your own wife to fix your coffee, instead of messin' around with Hugh-Jay's."

Chase laughed out loud at that, and the neighbors and the hired men grinned.

Hugh-Jay, who didn't laugh, walked off to pick up one end of a brand-new roll of barbed wire. With his cigarette in a corner of his mouth, Chase sauntered over to take up the other side of the spindle on which the wire was rolled. Together they moved toward the broken fence line, while the other men watched them.

The brothers set the roll down on the grass next to the broken fence.

With a gloved finger, Hugh-Jay lifted a strand of wire and pressed the clippers.

Instantly, the high-tensile barbed wire sprang free.

Released from its tight coil, it lunged like a vicious snake toward his brother's legs.

Chase let out a shout and jumped back.

From a safe distance, he gave his brother an astounded look.

"Jesus, Hugh-Jay, watch it! You damn near took my balls off."

Unapologetically, Hugh-Jay said, "Might do the women of Henderson County a favor."

"This family," Chase said, with a shake of his head, "is in one hell of a bad mood today." He took a last drag off his smoke, dropped it to the ground and ground it out with the heel of a boot. Pointing to the dangerous roll of wire, he said, "Let's try this again. A little more carefully this time, all right?"

Annabelle, witnessing the burst of ill-temper between her sons, felt her heart sink.

Cut fences and murdered cows weren't the only problems this family had, she admitted to herself. It was time, she realized, for a visit she didn't want to make to her daughter-in-law. She hoped it wasn't past time to fix something before it got more dangerous than Billy Crosby or barbed wire. And she hoped she wasn't using it just as an excuse to avoid being there when the sheriff came to arrest Billy. Deep in worried thought, she started carrying things back across the muddy grass to her Caddy, with Red Bosch helpfully following her with a full trash bag in one hand and her iced tea container in the other.

She was halfway to town before she recalled that she hadn't even said goodbye to her husband or her sons.

10

Hugh Senior watched his wife drive off, and he wondered what took her away in such a hurry that she didn't even say goodbye. He licked icing off his lips and then said, "All right, everybody. We sure do appreciate your help today. Now let's saddle up and get this over with, so you can get back to your own work."

"You call the sheriff about this, Hugh?" a neighbor inquired.

Hugh Senior nodded. "He's coming."

"Dad," Chase interrupted, looking toward the sky. "So is the rain."

That got the men, and Red, moving toward their horses again.

"Not you, Billy," Hugh Senior called out to his back. "You ride in the truck with me. I've got a special job for you."

Billy Crosby turned around to stare at him.

"What job?" To the ears of the other men who heard it, there was an edge to the question. Some would later remember it as disrespectful, others said it sounded nervous, but every man who was there that day agreed that the statement that followed it was downright cocky.

"I'm better on horseback than them other boys."

"Well, I've got a job just cut out for you."

Hugh Senior's voice sounded hard.

"I'd rather work cattle."

"Oh, you will, Billy."

The neighbors and the other hired cowboys listened to the tense exchange while trying to appear not to. Some of them exchanged covert glances. All of them remembered yesterday and the ugly scene at the cattle pens.

Hugh Senior pointed at his son Bobby and then at Hugh-Jay. "You two get on your horses." Then he pointed at Chase. "You stay here, so if your mother sends the sheriff out here you can tell him where we've gone."

"Where are you going, Dad?"

"To separate the calves from their mothers again."

When Hugh Senior drove into the next pasture with Billy, he pulled up beside the dead cow. "This job's for you, Billy. Use the heavy-duty winch in back and haul her into this truck."

From the driver's seat, Hugh Senior could smell his passenger.

Billy's sweat and breath smelled like beer, a sure sign of being an alcoholic—just like his parents, Hugh thought.

Billy pulled his cap brim over his eyes and obeyed without objection.

That, of itself, was suspicious, the rancher thought.

Billy didn't ask "Why me?" he didn't whine for help, and he didn't complain. He just trudged off to do as he was told, with a strange, nervous grin playing around his lips.

To Hugh Senior all those facts indicted him.

Maybe jail would straighten him out.

The rancher sat in his truck long enough to watch Billy scratch his head over the already rotting carcass. It looked to Hugh Senior as if Billy wanted mightily to kick it in a fury of resentment and frustration but knew he didn't dare while he was being watched. Hugh got out of his truck and called the boy Red Bosch over to help with the dragging and lifting. Cheerful as always, the teenager took his place behind the wheel of the truck and maneuvered it backward to winch up the dead cow. When he saw they might be able to manage it by themselves, Hugh Senior walked off to supervise the other work.

A little later he waved his eldest son over and told him, "We've got enough hands for this. You get going to Colorado."

"Billy rode out here with me," Hugh-Jay reminded him.

"You won't need to give him a ride back today."

"Why not?"

"Because he already has a ride." Hugh Senior pointed to the road where the sheriff's sedan was coming up, followed by two deputies' cars, all of them raising long trails of dust.

AFTER IT WAS DONE, and Billy was carted off and all the cattle were settled in their proper pastures, and everybody else had departed for home, Hugh Senior stood alone in the pasture and looked west and up toward the storm clouds. They were bringing dramatically cooler temperatures, which meant that when the cold front hit the very hot temperatures ahead of it, violent weather was likely.

There could be torrential rain, hail, high wind, tornadoes.

They'd finished up their work just in time to escape being out in that.

"Get a move on," Hugh Senior ordered himself, with another glance at the storm that looked like a dark gray wall moving toward him. He saw telltale vertical streaks of rain in the distance, heard rumbles of thunder, saw flashes of lightning still a few miles away. The rain they'd had earlier was only a preamble. Now the real thing was coming, and it looked as if it meant business.

He worried for the sake of local farmers whose crop fields were so hardened by drought that rain of the sort that was coming would make things worse, not better. What they needed were days of light, steady rain that gave the rock-hard ground a chance to soften and absorb it.

That's what Billy is: rock-hard ground.

What they were going to get instead was runoff, erosion, and flooding.

If he hurried, he could get Hugh-Jay's lame horse to town before the veterinarian closed up for the day and before the rain hit Rose, though he might have to drive back through the storm to the ranch. Their vet made house calls, and night calls, and came on holidays and any other time they needed him, but the Linders didn't like to ask him to make the long trip out to the ranch for just one animal, not if they could take the animal into the veterinary clinic on the outskirts of Rose.

The ranch seemed still and silent, as if it were waiting for the relief of rain.

Hugh Senior felt almost nothing but relief himself.

The culprit was in custody. Billy had gone in handcuffs, protesting, "I ain't done nothin'!" But he had gone, nevertheless, without getting himself into more trouble by resisting arrest. The other men had watched wide-eyed, but without any real surprise. They accepted as reasonable Hugh's explanation of keeping it a secret so Billy wouldn't know it was coming. The sheriff had confided to Hugh Senior that they hadn't found any evidence at Billy's house, "But that doesn't mean there isn't any. Don't you worry, Hugh. We'll get the little bastard to tell us what he's done."

That promise gave Hugh the feeling his world was turning right-side-up again.

The worst was over now.

There had been a satisfying irony in watching Billy Crosby mend the fence lines he'd gone to so much trouble to cut, and even more satisfaction in making him pick up the cow he'd killed. Revenge was a vicious cycle, Hugh Senior mused as he stood in the field with the rain falling a little harder by the minute. The cycle never stopped turning unless somebody made the decision to stop. But then he assured himself that his own words and actions weren't about revenge. He was taking sensible, businesslike precautions by moving quickly to excise a cancer from his ranch.

He got into his truck and headed for the barn to pick up the lame horse. Doing anything less would have made him a hypocrite in his own eyes. He couldn't condemn Billy Crosby for mistreating animals if he didn't care enough about a horse he owned to relieve its pain.

My oldest boy is a better man than I am, he thought, not for the first time.

He felt his heart swell with love for the boy, even if that was a sentiment he might never speak aloud.

"Going on five o'clock," he said to himself.

If he was going to get that horse in to the vet, he'd better get going.

It had been a bad day, but it was already better, or it was if you weren't trying to grow corn.

11

ON HER DRIVE into Rose to try to salvage her son's marriage, Annabelle realized she might need to slide in sideways rather than launch a frontal attack. She needed to dangle a lure in front of her daughter-in-law in the same way she offered apples to her horse to get him to come to her from far out in a pasture. As she drove through the flat landscape, for some reason it made her think of mountains, which gave her an idea, an expensive one that she thought might work with Laurie—especially with luxury-loving Laurie.

Feeling hopeful of her bright idea, she stopped first at Belle's museum in the former bank to use the phone to call ahead. As she stood in front of the nineteenth-century limestone building and glanced up at the corner gargoyles, she realized she might use this opportunity to mend fences with her grumpy daughter while the men mended fences at the ranch. The gargoyles looked no more welcoming than Belle was likely to be, but she loved them, just as she loved her most difficult child—just as she loved *all* of her currently difficult children.

She raised an eyebrow at a stone gargoyle that glared back.

"Oh, come on," she said to it, "look on the bright side."

Since the ugly old thing presided over a failed bank, that seemed unlikely.

She pushed open the elegant front door, with its huge brass knob and murky leaded glass panes.

A brass bell rang over her head, announcing her arrival.

"Who's that?" her daughter's voice called from the back.

"Your mother! Are you in the vault?"

"Yes," came the unwelcoming response.

She walked past the line of filigreed teller cages that lined one wall, wonderful remnants of bank transactions of old, now waiting for Belle to figure out how to use them in her museum. She inhaled, imagining she could smell old money, hear the bustle of commerce, the voices, the clink of coins, the slap of cash on marble.

On her way toward the cavernous bank vault that Belle used as her office, she glanced at black-and-white photos of sod houses, cattle drives, oil wells, stone fence posts, the pictures all lying on tables until Belle could frame and hang them. Despite her own and Hugh's skepticism about the enterprise, she found herself drawn to the photos. When she stopped to look more closely at one, she found herself wanting to look at the next one, leading her to wonder if maybe, just maybe, other people would find them fascinating, too. She looked up at the molded tin ceiling. It really was a wonderful old building.

Tell her so, Annabelle reminded herself.

She hoped she wouldn't have to ooh and ahh over a long-dead, flea-bitten buffalo, but she was willing to do it, willing to murmur, "Oh, what a handsome buffalo," if there was any chance it would please her daughter.

Maybe she and Hugh were too critical; maybe more praise and interest would oil the squeaky hinges of their relationship with their only daughter. If that didn't work, Annabelle knew what would, though she was a little ashamed of herself every time she did it. There was one subject on which she and Belle completely agreed and that was about the young woman who was daughter-in-law to one of them and sister-in-law to the other. Laurie—*bless her heart,* she thought wryly—had a bonding affect on her female in-laws.

She walked into the vault and the sound of typing.

Belle sat at an ancient rolltop desk that she'd scooped up from a farm sale, clattering away on an old typewriter. She wrote articles about local history, geology, and archaeology and shot them off to dozens of different magazines hoping to be published. Now and then she got an acceptance and earned a little money.

"Can you stop for a minute, honey?"

Belle typed a bit more and then halted, making a show out of slowing and then stopping one reluctant key at a time.

She turned in her old leather and wood swivel chair.

"I'm pretty busy, Mom."

"You look good sitting there, Belle. You look like a real writer."

"I am a real writer."

"I know, I didn't mean—those photos out front are fascinating."

"Which ones?"

"The sod houses?"

"They're the weaker ones. I've got better."

"Oh, well . . ." She resorted to her strongest weapon. "I don't want to interrupt you. I just need to use your phone to call Laurie."

"Why?"

Annabelle battled inwardly with her scruples and then brushed them aside in favor of coaxing warmth from her child. "I'm worried about her and Hugh-Jay, Belle. I don't like the way she flirts with Chase."

Belle's eyes got big. "You noticed?"

"Who could miss it?"

"It's ridiculous. I don't know how Hugh-Jay stands it."

"It's got to stop."

They looked at each other in pleasant agreement, but then Belle looked doubtful. "Shouldn't Hugh-Jay be the one to stop it, Mom? And anyway, it's not like she flirts only with Chase."

"Who else?"

"Who *doesn't* she?"

"I've never seen her flirt with Bobby. Oh, I hate even saying that!"

"She's got her ways." A look of disgust crossed Belle's face. "She picks on him and insults him. That's as good as flirting to Bobby 'cause it knocks him down and keeps him interested."

She stared at her daughter, impressed at her perception.

"Has she ever flirted with Meryl?"

"Not when I'm around," Belle said with an indignant and proud lift to her chin. "But Meryl says she tries it at other times."

"Oh, honey."

Her daughter's face was flushed. "Don't worry, Mom. Meryl always makes sure she gets the message that he's not available, not even to *her*."

She felt a rush of compassion for her daughter who had spent her whole life in the shadow of a girl whose pretty face and vivacious manner got her everything she ever wanted. She remembered times when Belle looked as if she'd been crying after parties and other events when she was the wallflower to Laurie's popularity. She recalled Belle's barely hidden unhappiness when her oldest brother started dating, then got engaged, and then married Laurie. *Thank God for Meryl Tapper,* she thought, because he was the best revenge—a boy as nice as Belle's own brother, and one who liked her exactly as she was, which wasn't nearly as prickly when he was around to smooth her edges. When Meryl was with her, Belle was almost pretty, too, and her lovely complexion glowed with the pleasure of his attention. If Laurie ever did anything to threaten that happiness, Annabelle thought she would kill her.

Feeling guilty because Belle looked upset, she changed the subject. "Where *were* you last night, dear daughter?"

"Here." The lift of Belle's chin changed to a stubborn tilt.

"Not out with Meryl?"

"He was working."

"That boy is always working."

"Don't patronize him."

She sighed. "I didn't mean to." She and Hugh both had their fingers crossed for the match between Belle and the boy they loved like a fourth son. They'd helped send Meryl to college and law school and were the first to throw work his way when he hung out his shingle. Hugh liked to joke that maybe they could get a good son-in-law for their money even if he didn't turn out to be a great lawyer. But it was beginning to look as if they had a chance of getting both—a fine lawyer right in the family. "After Belle," Hugh liked to say, "a judge or jury will be a piece of cake for that boy."

Rather than take the chance of falling into other conversational traps, she reached for the phone on the desk and called Laurie. When that was done and she was properly invited over, she gave Belle a long, somber look.

"What, Mom?"

Belle reached over to touch her mother's knee.

"Something bad happened at the ranch last night, honey."

She blinked back tears prompted partly by the wickedness of Billy Crosby, but mostly by the warmth of her daughter's touch and the expression of concern on Belle's face.

AFTER LEAVING THE BANK, she girded herself for her upcoming visit to the other challenging young woman in her family. Alone in her car, she closed her eyes and prayed for her eldest son's marriage. Then, sending waves of love ahead of her toward her granddaughter, she prayed for Jody to always stay as sweet and happy and *easy to get along with* as she was now.

12

"LOOK AT YOU!" Annabelle smiled at the little girl on her lap. "So big!"

Everybody thought it was adorable how Jody—named Laurie Jo after her mother—had been born with naturally dark and pixie hair to match Laurie's. She also had her mother's dark brown eyes and delicate frame. Annabelle, feeling a tad disloyal to her own son, was glad for the child's sake that the gene pool had tilted toward Laurie instead of Hugh-Jay.

A warm, oozing triangle of apple pie sat on the kitchen table in front of her.

Annabelle, who had accepted an offer of vanilla ice cream to go with the pie, also had to admit that Laurie made fine pies. This one had a lattice crust baked to a perfect golden brown. Sugar crystals sparkled on top, exactly as they should. With her free hand, she took up her fork, cut into the triangle, and gave the first fragrant, gooey bite to her granddaughter, who smiled at her around the fork, making Annabelle's heart squeeze with love.

While Jody chewed noisily, Annabelle took a bite for herself.

"Mm, it's wonderful, Laurie."

"It's good, Mommy."

Inside, the filling was just tart enough to make it perfect.

Her gratitude for both the grandchild and the food made it easier for her to smile at her daughter-in-law, who sat across from her at the kitchen table. Laurie, who had an artistic streak, had painted the table sunflower yellow to match her gingham curtains, and pottery that she herself had painted—with big poppy blossoms of orange, yellow, red, and white—and fired in a kiln. They looked like spring bouquets around the circular table. In her yellow sundress, she added the final touch of beauty to the scene. Outside, the day was getting darker and darker by the minute; inside, there was sunshine. Laurie should have gone to an art school, Annabelle thought, instead of trying to make it through a university that expected her to pass freshman biology. When Annabelle had dreamed of having daughters-in-law, this wasn't the one she thought she'd get, especially not from Hugh-Jay. She realized now that she should never have underestimated a young man's—any young man's—vulnerability to a pretty face and figure. And, oh well, she had two more sons and two more chances for the cozy female relationship she rarely had with her own Belle.

In the meantime she had a perfect granddaughter.

Annabelle hugged Jody to her as the child reached for more pie.

"I'll stay here with Jody," she offered, starting casually upon her agenda. "You go do anything you need to do."

Laurie sighed. "I may just take a long leisurely bath."

"It's good to get a break," Annabelle said with careful casualness. "When our kids were little, Hugh and I treasured the times we could get away, even though we missed the children."

"That would be nice. To get away."

This is too easy, Annabelle thought, suppressing a smile.

She observed the unhappy downward curve to Laurie's pretty mouth.

"Are you ready for a little break, honey?"

"Oh, God, yes. A bath will feel great. I may even light candles."

Annabelle smiled. "Actually, I meant a longer break than that, like a couple of days to go somewhere."

"I'm ready for a break of about ten years." Laurie said, and then she sighed. "In Tahiti."

That made Annabelle laugh. Laurie laughed a little, too.

Laurie's parents, who had catered to their beautiful daughter's whims all of her life—had moved to Wichita following the wedding, as if they were turning the care and feeding of their high-maintenance daughter over to the larger, wealthier Linder family. Annabelle had watched them go with bemused understanding. Now, they seemed content to come for suspiciously quick visits to see their grandchild. It was't Laurie's fault, Annabelle reminded herself, that she was spoiled.

"Well, how about taking a weekend off, honey?"

"What?"

"A weekend vacation." This was her big idea. "Just the two of you, you and Hugh-Jay."

Laurie sat up. "A whole weekend! But who would—"

"We will, of course." Annabelle dabbed ice cream off Jody's chin. "We'd love to. I want you and Hugh-Jay to spend a weekend at the Broadmoor—"

"The what?"

"The Broadmoor. It's a hotel in Colorado Springs."

"The one with the spas and the golf, and the—" Laurie began to look excited. "Really? You mean it?"

"Yes, really."

"Oh, my gosh! That's incredible, Annabelle. Yes, yes, yes!"

Annabelle felt a little of her own tension melt away. Smiling, pleased, she stroked the yellow tabletop with one hand, admiring how perfectly Laurie had sanded it down to smoothness before painting it.

When it came to making things look good, including herself, Laurie had the touch.

But then Laurie leaned forward and said, "Hugh-Jay will never go."

Annabelle's hand stopped moving on the tabletop. "Why not?"

"He just won't," Laurie said, in a tone that sounded both dismissive and a little bitter. "He won't leave the ranch for *pleasure*, you know that, Annabelle, not if there's a single cow to herd or a horse to ride. Now, if you sent him to a bull sale, he'd go for a week."

"We'll talk him into it."

"What if I went by myself?"

Annabelle, flummoxed, said, "What? By yourself?"

Laurie nodded, looking suddenly overjoyed, the weariness vanishing from her eyes. In that instant, she looked stunningly beautiful and wildly alive, and Annabelle understood why her son looked so besotted and so sad. This would be a difficult girl for a plain and decent boy to lose, for any man to lose. In Annabelle's lap, Jody stared at her mother as if she were a beautiful princess. "Oh, Mom," said Laurie, "it would be so good for me . . . for both Jay and me, really!"

Annabelle hated when Laurie called her Mom.

"How would it be good for Hugh-Jay?" she asked, with a bite to her tone.

"I'd come back rested and happy to see him!"

"Lucky him."

"Exactly."

Annabelle felt so confused by the sudden turn that she couldn't think of a way to say no that wouldn't come out sounding mean and angry. What she wanted to exclaim was, *You selfish girl! How can you take this generous offer for both of you and turn it into a treat solely for yourself?*

Stalling, furiously thinking, she took another nibble of pie.

She was worried that Laurie had been flirting with Chase that very morning. The business with the barbed wire had shocked her. She hadn't told Belle about *that*. She could hardly believe Hugh-Jay had done it, or that the expression on his face said he didn't regret it. Chase could have been badly hurt. Hugh-Jay was apparently at some kind of breaking point. Even if nothing had happened between Laurie and Chase—yet—it had already reached the point where it set Hugh-Jay off, which meant it had gone too far.

It was Hugh-Jay and Laurie *together* to whom she wanted to give some time alone to rediscover each other, to work on their marriage, to have fun and pleasure without responsibilities for once.

The phone rang, and Annabelle was so tense she jumped.

Listening hard, she heard Laurie's end of the conversation from the phone in the front hallway. "Hello." That sounded normal, but the next words had a funny tone to them, an amused, secretive-sounding tone. "I thought you might be interested . . . Yeah, at Bailey's . . . What?" Annabelle heard her daughter-in-law laugh, a low, seductive kind of laugh. "Oh, you." Then she heard a stilted tone, the kind a person uses when they're trying to get a secret message across to somebody, to let them know they aren't free to say what they want to say. "Listen, my mother-in-law is here." There was a little silence, followed by another low laugh, and then Laurie hung up the phone without saying goodbye.

"That was Belle," Laurie said with a breezy air as she came back into the kitchen. "We're meeting at Bailey's for supper tonight."

Annabelle thought, You refer to me as your mother-in-law? To my daughter?

Laurie leaned forward, looking as if she had mysteriously gained more self-confidence. "May I go for *three* days?"

"Go?" Annabelle said, not understanding at first. Then she blinked at the speed of the escalation from a weekend to three days. "To the Broadmoor?"

"Maybe I'll take a friend if Hugh-Jay won't go."

"A friend?" Annabelle felt queasy. She wondered if she had just made things worse. What she wanted to say at that moment, but could not possibly say out loud, was, *The fact that you're not taking Hugh-Jay does not mean you get to take somebody else, or meet them there.*

Annabelle felt sick at having even worse thoughts.

Who was that on the phone, was that her "friend?"

Of course Laurie meant a girlfriend, of course she did, but if Chase suddenly came up with an excuse to visit the ranch in Colorado on the very weekend that Laurie was gone, she would send him off on errands a thousand miles in the opposite direction. She was also going to suggest to his father that a horse-whipping might be in order.

Laurie wasn't finished asking for things.

"Could you take Jody back to the ranch with you tonight? She'd love to spend the night, wouldn't you, sweetheart?"

The child, made joyful by the warmth in her mother's voice and by the suggestion to go to her favorite place, flung her arms around her grandmother's neck and whispered, "Please." She adored her grandparents and delighted in the ranch, where there were uncles to take her for horsey rides and there was endless space in which to run around and play.

When Annabelle said yes, it was only to that request.

Laurie didn't seem to notice the distinction, and as grandmother and granddaughter were leaving, she prattled about the massages and facials she was going to get and the clothes she was going to need. "I think I've heard of the Broadmoor! It's really famous and really nice."

She appeared to consider it settled, with no requirement to say thank you.

Beaming, the beautiful young mother escorted them rapidly to the front door and closed it as soon as they were standing on the front porch. Annabelle felt as if they'd been put out unceremoniously, like the trash. "Well," she said, looking down at the child whose hand she held, "let's go start supper. While I slice the meat loaf, you can check on the new kitties in the barn."

"New kitties!" Jody jumped up and down with glee.

Annabelle noticed that the child didn't look back for her mother.

AN HOUR LATER, on her way out of Rose with Jody in the backseat, Annabelle jumped when a horn honked behind her. She looked in her rearview mirror and saw it was Hugh-Jay. "Look, Jody, it's your daddy." She pulled over to the nearest curb and parked, and he did the same behind her. Had he already heard about the trip? she wondered, feeling guilty that her good—if interfering—intentions had gone awry, leaving him out.

But when he appeared at her car window, he just smiled and said, "Hi, Mom." Then he reached in a long arm so he could gently squeeze his daughter's left knee. "Hey, pumpkin."

Jody giggled at his touch. "We're going to the ranch, Daddy."

"Well, don't ride any cows, okay?"

"Daddy, you don't ride cows!"

He laughed and withdrew his arm. "That's right. Good thing you reminded me." He smiled at his mother. "I saw the Caddy, and I wanted to say 'bye before I leave for Colorado."

"Is everything . . . taken care of, with Billy . . . at the ranch?"

He answered in similar code to avoid scaring the little girl in the backseat. "All taken care of. Taken away. No trouble at all."

"That's good." She looked into his big, kind, unhandsome face. "Hugh-Jay?"

Teasingly, because of her suddenly serious tone, he said, "Mom?"

"Speaking of Colorado, I may have done a bad thing," she confessed.

"Impossible," he said with a grin.

"Well, wait until I tell you before you judge. I offered a little vacation to Laurie, for the two of you, but it seems to have turned into a spa trip for just her." Wishing to lessen the blow, she gilded Laurie's excuse, to make it sound more tactful. "Laurie felt you might not want to leave the ranch, with so much work to do."

She saw a frown appear between his eyes before he erased it.

"She's probably right. That's fine. It'll be good for her."

"It would be good for you, too."

"Do I look like a spa kind of guy?"

She smiled. "Hugh-Jay?"

Again he teased her, though not quite as lightheartedly. "Yes, Mom?"

"Don't ever let anybody tell you that happiness has to be earned."

His expression turned quizzical and more genuinely amused. She was infamous among her offspring for offering bits of impromptu wisdom to them.

"Okay," he said agreeably. "I won't."

He chuckled, but for some reason, she couldn't work up another answering smile. She felt her eyes start to fill, and blinked it back. "What I mean to say," she said, "is that if happiness had to be earned, then out of all of my children, you would be the happiest." She paused, then plunged in, and said softly so that little ears couldn't overhear, "But you're not, are you?"

"Mom," he said, his voice gentle.

Because he was right there in her window, she placed her left palm against his right cheek, feeling the stubble of the whiskers of her most-grown son. They were so blond they were nearly invisible. She looked at him as if memorizing him. After her first weeks of being a novice at mothering, he had been such an easy child. So simple to manage. Easy to please. As he grew up, a piece of chocolate cake made him happy, any sitcom could make him laugh, Christmas absolutely delighted him. He was never grouchy in the mornings, and now he had his own baby daughter and he thought the sun rose and never set in her.

Annabelle leaned forward and kissed his broad sweaty forehead.

"Mom!" He laughed a protest. "I'm filthy."

"Smelly, too."

"You look dirty, Daddy!"

He grinned into the backseat. "I am, pumpkin. Daddy needs a bath."

Annabelle thought about her daughter-in-law taking a long, leisurely bath and thought about telling him to hurry home. Instead, afraid of interfering again, she just smiled, though her eyes were threatening to fill again. "Well, I never claim that you're my perfect son, just that you're my good one."

He leaned into her palm a little, then straightened his head again.

"Not all that good. But I'm fine, Mom."

"Really?"

"Really. Don't worry about us."

"Your mother loves you," she said, her tone lighter than her feelings.

He squeezed her hand, gently released it, and stood up. He smiled one last time into the backseat, blew his daughter a kiss, and walked back to his truck with a wave. Later, Annabelle would feel those moments were the greatest gift God ever gave her: a last chance to see her firstborn up close, to hold his face in the palm of her hand, to kiss him, to tell him she loved him one last time.

He drove his truck around her car, turned right at the corner, in the direction opposite his home, and was gone.

ABOUT THE SAME TIME Annabelle pulled the Caddy into the barn, with Jody slumped over asleep in her car seat, Hugh Senior led his lame horse back into the vet's stable, where a goat, a llama, and another horse were already in residence. As he led the limping mare into a stall, the goat baaed. The treatment of the horse was overseen by the doctor who had diagnosed an infection requiring some surgical cleaning.

"She's got a fever, Hugh. We'll operate tomorrow."

"How serious?"

"Not very, at least not yet, but if you'd waited a few days—"

"I should learn to trust my son's instincts about animals more than my own. Hugh-Jay knew to bring her in now. I hope he has better instincts about people than I do, too, and not just about horses." His initial confidence about the rightness of his actions in regard to Billy Crosby had ebbed on the drive from the ranch. Uncharacteristically, he was second-guessing his decisions and feeling worried about whether he had done the right things all the way along the line with the young man he'd sent off to jail.

The vet's face took on a knowing expression. "I heard about Billy Crosby."

"Already?"

"Heck, Hugh, he got arrested a couple of hours ago, right? That's a lifetime, in terms of it getting around the local grapevine. I'll be surprised if it isn't already news in five counties."

His patient's owner laughed. "What exactly did you hear, Doc?"

"That he did some bad things. Sliced the throats of a dozen head of cattle, mutilated a couple of them—"

Hugh grimaced. "It was one pregnant cow and no mutilation."

"My my," the vet said wryly, "I'm surprised to hear the news got exaggerated. Who ever heard of that happening around here?"

Hugh Senior stroked one side of the horse's silky neck and smiled.

"I wouldn't worry about your instincts about people," the younger man told the older rancher. "All the boys that you and Annabelle have helped over the years? Not a one of them has turned out like Billy. He's the exception that proves the rule of your generosity in helping these kids."

"I never have understood what that means, 'proves the rule.'"

"Me, either." The vet laughed. "Maybe it's not even true."

"One thing's true. Billy *takes* exception to the rules."

The vet remembered Hugh-Jay Linder's story about the carload of rough-looking strangers who had moronically tossed out a burning cigarette. The idea of a wildfire unnerved him even more than most people, because of all the helplessly caged animals in his care. Whenever there was a story in the news about a burning stable, he broke out in a cold sweat of dread and pity. When it was arson, he could barely contain his rage. He was about to mention the cigarette incident to Hugh Senior as another example of idiots who didn't follow rules, but before he could, he got distracted by the appearance of a swelling on the shank of the horse's injured leg. He walked back into the stall to take another look, and the story faded from his memory.

The rancher traded places with him, walking out of the stall as the doctor walked in. As they passed one another, he clasped the vet's shoulder. "You're a good man, Doc. Thanks for taking care of us." When he walked outside, he was startled to see how much closer the storm had drawn to Rose. The clouds looked like a billowing curtain hung from heaven to earth and extending north and south for miles. Lightning flashed spectacularly throughout them. There was nothing more breathtakingly beautiful in the world, in his opinion, than a thunderstorm approaching Rose from across the wide, flat, empty fields. He wouldn't have traded sights like this for all the nightclubs in New York or trolleys in San Francisco.

The breeze ahead of the gigantic clouds had turned into gusts, and the temperature had dropped already.

Hugh hurried to his truck, holding onto his hat and hoping to get a couple more errands done before he headed back west through the blowing curtain of clouds to Annabelle and home.

13

THE RAIN STILL hadn't started to fall by the time Laurie walked to Bailey's Bar & Grill for supper, letting the wind whip her hair and blow around her bare legs. She'd been so hot all day that the new cool temperature felt good. *She* felt good. She'd had a luxurious long bath, washed her hair, shaved her legs, made a couple of phone calls that left her feeling excited, and then changed into white shorts, sandals, and a rose-colored T-shirt that flattered her flawless complexion. She knew she should take her car, because of the weather, but assumed she could get a ride whenever she wanted one. Her sister-in-law had agreed to meet her there, so Belle could drive her home, if it came to that. If Belle couldn't, then Laurie figured she could bat her eyelashes and several men would hop off their bar stools to help her.

When she walked into Bailey's, heads turned, which pleased her.

A few people called out her name, but she walked on toward the back.

I'm meant for bigger things than this, she thought with scorn.

When they had more money, Hugh-Jay could take her to places she'd always wanted to see, like New York and Paris. Maybe she'd take trips without him, too, like the one she'd talked Annabelle into giving her.

As she walked confidently toward the rear, Laurie smiled to herself. *The Broadmoor Hotel.* That was more like it, where she belonged.

Rose never had fit her right; it felt like a granny dress that nobody with any style would wear. She'd hoped that marrying a Linder could move her up and out in the world, but all it did was plant her deeper. She felt buried here, suffocated, with all her best talents wasted.

On the other hand, she was unique here, and she liked that.

Feeling the pleasure of being admired and the relief of being without her child for a night, she slid onto the long wooden bench in a booth across from Belle. Laurie liked being with Belle, because she looked so pretty and full of personality by comparison. A glass of beer was already sitting in front of her sister-in-law. The scent of grilled burgers, onions, and steaks permeated the big room, and Laurie sniffed appreciatively. "I may get a rib eye tonight," she announced, with the confidence of a woman who never gained an ounce. When a waitress came by, she ordered a bottle of Bud "with a frosty glass and a slice of lime." She'd heard they did that in Mexico—put lime in beer. There was a bowl of peanuts in the shell, and she dipped a hand into it. By evening's end the floor of the grill would be littered with shells and crunchy underfoot.

"Where's Meryl?" she asked Belle.

"At the office. Where's Hugh-Jay?"

"Your dad sent him out to the Colorado place."

"Did you hear what happened last night?"

"At the ranch? Yeah." Laurie took a sip from the beer the waitress brought her, and looked back toward the front door of the grill. "Oh, God, look what the rain dragged in."

Belle looked where she pointed and saw her two younger brothers coming in the door with rain dripping off their slickers and plastic-covered hats. The storm had finally arrived in Rose. A downpour was visible in the brief moment before Bobby closed the front door again. At the same time, the music got drowned out by the sound of rain pounding on the tavern's tin roof.

"I can't go anywhere," Belle groused, "without my family showing up."

"At least you've got family in town," Laurie complained. She was still bitter about her own parents leaving her to fend with marriage and motherhood on her own.

"Got room for a couple of thirsty cowboys?" Chase asked when he and Bobby walked up to the booth.

"Don't you have any other friends?" Belle demanded.

"Yeah," Chase said with a grin, "but they're not as pretty as yours."

Belle rolled her eyes, which made Chase laugh.

Bobby started to slide in beside Laurie, but Chase grabbed his shirt and said, "You're not sitting there."

"Why not?"

"Because she doesn't want to sit by you, do you, Laurie?"

"You're too big for this booth," she told Bobby.

He wasn't fat, but his broad back and big arms and shoulders made him wide. Flushing, he got up without arguing.

Laurie scooted over to give Chase room to sit beside her. He was as tall as his younger brother, but not as bulky; his width was in his shoulders, so his slim hips didn't crowd her, though they somehow ended up touching hers anyway.

They made a striking couple, both dark-haired and good-looking.

Instead of taking the seat beside his sister, Bobby pulled up a chair at the open end of their booth and straddled it backward. "Man," he said, shaking water off his left hand. "Wet out there."

"Don't shake that thing on me," Laurie complained, which made Chase laugh again.

"You," Belle said with a disgusted look, "have a dirty mind."

"Takes one to know one," he told her with a smirk.

"And you're one, all right," an unexpected male voice said, beside him.

"Meryl!" Chase said, looking up at his older brother's best friend.

Meryl had the look of an ex–football player who might one day put on weight, but at the age of twenty-four he was still fit. Unlike Bobby and Chase in their blue jeans, Meryl had on a blue suit and a white shirt accented with a bolo tie—with a sterling silver clasp in the shape of a rearing horse—that Belle had given him for Valentine's Day.

Belle suddenly looked happy. "How'd you get away from work?"

Meryl winked at her. "Got lucky. Power went out."

"Bobby," Chase ordered, "get out of the way and let Meryl sit by his girlfriend." He shook his head in mock befuddlement. "Although what he sees in you, I'll never know—"

"Shut up, Chase," Meryl said.

"No, really," Chase continued to tease. "She can't take a joke, she's oversensitive, and when she talks about all that history stuff, she can bore a stuffed bear to death—"

"Don't talk about your sister like that," Meryl said in a tone that surprised them all into silence. He sounded angry and serious. He looked down on his best friend's brother, his girlfriend's brother, his own potential brother-in-law, and said, "Has it ever occurred to you that Belle is just sensitive like normal people, and she only seems oversensitive to you because you're such an insensitive lout? Has it ever occurred to you that maybe your jokes aren't funny? Have you ever thought that she might be *interesting* to people with brains, people who are actually interested in things like history?"

"Lighten up, Meryl."

"No, you lighten up, Chase. Lighten up on your sister. It's time you gave up that teasing crap. She's put up with it for years, but I'm the one who's sick of it. I ever hear you talk like that about Belle again, I'll stuff a fist down your mouth to shut you up."

For a moment nobody moved.

Laurie looked impressed with Meryl's aggressive defense of Belle.

Belle's eyes shone with tearful gratitude.

Ever irrepressible, Chase grinned. "Did you forget you're a lawyer now? You don't have to get tough. You can just sue me. So if you love her so much, when are you going to marry her?"

Meryl slid into the booth beside Belle and put both of his arms around her, pulling her close to him and then kissing her deeply enough to make his future brothers-in-law hoot at the couple.

When he finally stopped kissing her, he still didn't let her go.

"This isn't how I'm going to ask you," he said, "not here, not in front of them."

"Some people are just born into the wrong families," she told him.

"You're telling me!" Meryl exclaimed, and as the mood lightened, he kissed her again, quick and hard and affectionately, taking all of her lipstick and leaving her looking proudly thrilled.

A little later, when Belle excused herself to go to the ladies' room, Chase leaned across the table and said, "Come on. You're telling me you think my sister is easy to get along with?"

"She is for me, Chase. I don't know what your problem is."

"And you really think the history of this county is fascinating?"

"I'm interested in what she's interested in. You might try that some-time."

Chase leaned back and laughed. "I'm interested in women who are interested in *me*."

Meryl laughed, too. "Well, there's a surprise."

TWO HOURS and several beers later, after they'd all had steaks, the owner of the grill, Bailey Wright, walked up to the head of the booth, behind Bobby. He was a big man in his thirties, beefy, as befit the proprietor of a joint that specialized in hamburgers. Grease from cooking them stained the white chef's apron tied at the back of his neck and around his girth. The jukebox was blaring over the rain and thunder, and his place was festive and cozy with talk and laughter, good smells and flowing drinks. Every now and then the lights blinked on and off, which made the jukebox stop, but each time it happened, Bailey just yelled in his foghorn voice, "No worries! We've got a generator! We'll keep cookin', you keep eatin'."

That always got a laugh, even from the locals who'd heard it many times before.

"I just talked to your dad," Bailey Wright informed the three siblings.

"Here?" Chase started to get up.

Bailey waved him back down. "He's not here. He called on the phone. He gave me a message. He said you three—" He looked from Chase to Belle, then put a hand briefly on Bobby's right shoulder. "—shouldn't even try to get back out to the ranch tonight. You can't get through. He said the highway's washed out in that low place, and you'll get swept away if you try. So he's got a room at the Rose Motel for you boys, and another one for himself—"

"What's he doing in town?" Bobby asked.

"That's what I just told you," Bailey said patiently, if not quite accurately. "He took a horse to Doc Cramer, tried to get home, but got stopped by the water over the highway." He looked at Belle. "You're supposed to stay with Laurie tonight."

"I can stay at the museum," she said in an argumentative tone.

"We could all stay at Laurie's," Chase said.

"No, you can't!" Meryl Tapper and Bailey Wright said at the same time, sharply.

Chase made a show of jumping backward in comic reaction, and Bobby snorted.

"Your father specifically told me to tell you not to do that," Bailey said to him. "He said Laurie's got enough on her hands with a three-year-old, and the last thing she needs is the extra trouble you'd cause her."

"That sounds like Mom talking," Belle said, sounding grumpy about it.

"Jody's at the ranch tonight," Laurie said.

Bailey shrugged. "He must not have known that when he said it."

"Aw," Chase said, "but we could make it a party."

"I wouldn't advise that," Bailey said as he walked away.

"Oh, well, he's got us a room." Chase lifted his latest beer and took a drink, "He'd be pissed if he had to pay for something we didn't use." He twinkled at Laurie. "But, hey, if you want, maybe I can slip out of the motel a little later."

She blushed and threw a handful of peanuts at him.

Meryl, his brother's best friend, eyed him over the top of a beer glass, and said, "You wouldn't want to stay at Laurie's house, Chase. She's not 'interested' in you, are you, Laurie?"

"Not like *that*," she said, and blushed again.

ALL EVENING LONG a progression of people dropped by their booth to say howdy, to ask about what Billy Crosby had done, and to send along regards to Annabelle and Hugh Senior. The four Linders and Meryl didn't notice when the door opened one more time and the din of noise suddenly quieted. They didn't think anything of it when they heard one more voice addressing them.

"Got you a special place back here, huh?"

They looked up and saw Billy Crosby standing behind Bobby's chair.

"Oh my God," Belle whispered to Meryl, who took her hand again.

Billy wore a distinctive straw cowboy hat with its brim tightly rolled on each side and the straw blackened as if it had been burnt. Tied up over the crown of it was a leather chin strap he pulled down when he needed to secure the hat atop his head. He was known for his hat, and perversely proud of being teased that it was ugly.

Chase slid out of the booth and stood up. "What are you doing here?"

"Out of jail, you mean? Why would a man who didn't do nothin' be in jail in the first place, Chase?"

Bobby was standing by then, too. "Answer the question, Billy."

The other man laughed in his face. "No evidence, Bobby. You can't hold a man when there's no evidence. Not even in this county named after your goddamned grandfather, or whoever it was." Billy looked all puffed up with victory and with drink. "There's still some justice in this world!"

"Take it easy, Billy," Chase said in a low voice.

"Ain't nothin' easy, Chase," Billy retorted. Holding a long-necked beer bottle in his right hand, a drink he appeared to have brought in with him, he was swaying on his cowboy boots. "But I guess you wouldn't know that, would you? Everything comes easy for you Linders, don't it?"

Bobby pushed back his chair.

Chase shook his head at his brother, to head him off.

"You got all the money you'll ever need," Billy went on, while the women stared at him, and the men waited tensely to see what might happen next. "Everything you ever want. College, all paid for. Even you, Meryl. They never offered me that—"

"You never got straight A's," Bobby said sarcastically.

"Neither did you," Billy shot back. "But that don't mean you don't get everything all paid for by your mommy and daddy. You just got nothin' to complain about in this life, do you, Chase? Do you, big Bobby? Or you, either," he said, looking straight at Belle. Then he stared at Laurie. "Smart of you to marry a rich rancher, Laurie, instead of some poor-ass county lawyer like Belle's gonna do. Or maybe you're marryin' Belle 'cause you don't *wanna* be a poor country lawyer, is that it, Meryl?"

Meryl let go of Belle's hand and got out of the booth.

"Time for you to take a nap, Billy," he said.

Bobby grabbed the back of Billy's shirt collar.

"Take your fuckin' hands off me, Bobby!"

"Shut up, Billy," Chase snapped.

"What's wrong with you?" Laurie said, looking with disdain at Billy.

"I'll tell you what's wrong," Billy said, staring first at her breasts and then at her face. "What's wrong is how some people treat other people like shit—"

"Nobody has treated you like shit, Billy," Meryl said. "Haven't you had lots of regular work from them? Haven't they paid you what they owed you, and probably extra over that? Haven't they given you the only real chances you ever had? People like Hugh and Annabelle Linder don't come along in every man's life, and you ought to recognize how lucky you are that they came along in yours. Seems like if anybody has treated anybody else like shit, it's you who's treated them—"

"You can't goddamn prove that!"

"I don't hear you saying that you didn't do it, Billy," Meryl observed.

"Why should I? Are you saying any of you'd believe me?"

The bar's owner stepped into the scene again, this time saying, "What's the matter here, Chase? Is he bothering you people?"

"He's drunk," Belle said, stating the obvious.

"I got good reason to be drunk," Billy shot back at her. "Your dad's never going to hire me again, and he'll tell everybody else not to hire me. I got no job. I got a wife and kid and no money. I got no *wheels*." He glared at Chase. "I got nothin', and you people got everything. What am I gonna do 'cept get drunk? What am I supposed to *do*?"

"Go to hell," Laurie suggested in a cold voice.

Billy shocked them all by taking a wild swing in her direction.

Bobby's arms came around him so fast and hard that it knocked his fancy straw hat onto the floor and also knocked the wind out of the drunk man. He struggled for breath and gagged, nearly vomiting.

"You're disgusting!" Laurie looked nauseated herself.

Bailey and Bobby hauled him away from the booth.

"Did he hit you?" Belle asked, breathless with shock.

Chase slid back into the booth beside Laurie and put a hand on her shoulder.

Looking half scared and half excited now that Billy was gone, Laurie shook her head no. Chase didn't move his hand, and she didn't brush it off.

"My God," Meryl said, looking stunned. "I can't believe he'd do that."

"Hit a woman?" Chase turned to stare after the other men while they made their way to the front door. "Why not? He doesn't mind hitting his wife. Why would he mind hitting somebody else's wife?"

Belle muttered something.

"What, Belle?" her brother asked her.

"I said, at least he didn't hit *on* someone else's wife."

Chase took his hand off his sister-in-law's shoulder.

The whole restaurant and bar had gone quiet, all other conversations ceasing as diners and drinkers watched Billy Crosby being thrown out.

"You going to put him out in this weather?" a man at a front table asked.

At that moment lightning flashed, and the electricity in the bar flickered again, causing a murmur of disquiet to go around the restaurant and bar.

"He's not staying in here to bother anybody else tonight," Bailey informed everybody who was listening. "Maybe some nice cool rain on his face will cool him off."

"I don't think you ought to put anything out there tonight," a woman said.

"Not even a drunk," somebody else called out.

"Not even Billy!" a man said, and a few people laughed.

Bailey ordered, "Open the door, Bobby."

They threw him outside into the pouring rain.

The storm, already loud enough to cover conversations, sounded like kettle drums when Bailey opened the door, and when he shut it again, the interior of the grill seemed silent by comparison until a few people broke into applause.

Bailey turned around, his hands on his hips, and looked at some of his customers who weren't clapping. "Don't be mad at me," he advised them. "Billy started it, like he starts any trouble he gets into. I'm just ending it. Everything bad that ever happens to Billy Crosby? You can bet he caused it, and it's about time he suffered some consequences for it."

A LITTLE LATER, after Bobby had returned to the booth and the restaurant settled down, Chase turned to his sister-in-law. "Did you drive over? I didn't see your car outside."

"I walked." Laurie raised her right hand and put it palm up to the ceiling as if to catch some of the raindrops thundering on the tin roof. The din was now so loud that she had to raise her voice so they could hear her even just across their table. "So who's taking me home?"

"We can't," Meryl said, glancing at Belle. "I've got my backseat full of files."

"I'm too drunk," Bobby said. He was too young to drink legally, but that hadn't stopped him from guzzling what his brother provided when Bailey wasn't looking.

"Oh, all right, I will," Chase volunteered, with a feigned sigh of resignation.

On the way out, Laurie noticed they hadn't tossed Billy Crosby's cowboy hat out with him. It still lay where it had fallen on the floor, where it had been trampled in the melee. Serves him right, she thought, remembering the nasty way he had looked at her chest, to say nothing of the swing he had taken at her. Serves him right if it was ruined and he never got it back. She grabbed it from the floor and carried it with her outside to make sure it got soaked in the rain.

IT WAS 10:00 P.M. when they ran through the rain to their vehicles.

Meryl let Belle off at the bank and then left to check on the power situation at his office.

Chase chauffeured his sister-in-law to the big stone house.

When they were inside, dripping all over the kitchen floor, he went upstairs, after saying he would gather up a change of clothing to take over to the motel with him. Laurie stood in the kitchen for a few moments, listening to the thunder and lightning and the powerful downpour that sounded as if it might batter down the walls and wash them all away. She was chilled and shivering and longed to strip off her wet clothes and get warm. Hot shower or bare warm arms—either sounded delicious to her at that moment. Both at the same time would be even better. When she realized she still held Billy's ruined hat, she contemptuously tossed it aside. She followed her brother-in-law up the stairs, trembling from cold and desire, trailing her wet fingers along the banister.

A LITTLE LATER young Red Bosch drove by Bailey's Bar & Grill and thought he saw somebody lying flat on the pavement in the parking lot in the pouring rain. He turned in to take a look, shone the headlights of his pickup truck on the object of his concern and saw it was Billy Crosby lying there. Red put his truck in park, threw open his driver's side door and ran through the rain to see if Billy was dead. He wasn't. He was just dead drunk, from what the teenager could tell. Red managed to prod Billy to his feet, more or less, and guide him to the truck with the heavens nearly drowning both of them before they got there.

He drove Billy home to Valentine and their little boy.

14

ALONE AT THE RANCH with Jody, Annabelle scurried around to get things done before the power went out, as it often did during electrical storms. Her granddaughter trailed her everywhere, chatting up her own storm and "helping" in ways that caused more work, but for which Annabelle had endless patience. It was more patience than she'd ever had with her own children, she knew, but then that was the way of grandkids and grandparents. *Boom!* went the thunder, which didn't scare little Jody at all, but only caused her to clap her hands and yell "Boom!" right back at it. Whenever the lightning flashed and cracked very close, the child flinched, but then giggled, which made Annabelle laugh, too. "Storms are exciting, aren't they?" she said to Jody, who threw her arms up in the air and yelled "Boom!" again.

It pleased Annabelle that this child was so open and fearless.

At the same age, Belle had been a nervous girl, terrified of electrical storms, of horses, of barking dogs, of anything that startled her sensitive nervous system. Annabelle had dreaded storms of all kinds then, and knew that a long night was ahead of her as she tried to calm and comfort Belle.

Eventually Belle got over most of those fears, if not the hypersensitivity.

Annabelle thought the thunderstorm was carrying on as if it might wash the ranch into another state. When it rained like this, she pictured everything sliding east until it landed in one massive mud pile in Kansas City. She could only imagine how it was beating up on the poor little town of Rose.

When Hugh called from the Rose Motel to tell her he couldn't make it home, he told her that the smaller trees in town were bending half over and there was hail the size of ball bearings.

"The highway is already flooded?" she asked in wonder.

"Yes, it is, and I'll bet you've never seen whitecaps in Kansas."

"Whitecaps! You're pulling my leg."

"I'm not. Right there on the highway. It looked like a river."

"Have you talked to the kids—"

Annabelle lost her connection to Hugh just when she was about to ask if he had seen Belle, Bobby, Chase, or Laurie. Surely they'd have enough sense to get in out of the rain without their father telling them to do so. She also wanted to tell him their granddaughter was at the ranch. On the other hand, she was relieved when the phone went out, because it meant she didn't have to tell him why he might have to finance a trip to Colorado Springs for his spoiled-rotten daughter-in-law.

"That was Grandpa," she told Jody.

"I talk to him?"

"The storm knocked out the telephone, sweetheart."

"Pow," said Jody.

Annabelle, wondering if a child that young was smart enough to make a joke like that, laughed and hugged her. When Jody laughed, too, Annabelle realized, with no small wonder, that Jody had heard "knocked out" and put it together with "pow," all the while knowing that's not what it meant.

"You are a smart little girl," she told her.

It gave her an idea: maybe she could "knock out" Laurie's bad idea of going to Colorado by herself—*supposedly* by herself—by getting Belle to go, too. After all, Belle might be jealous and resent the expensive treat for her sister-in-law, and Laurie had already talked about inviting a friend. She and Belle weren't all that close, but they were friends in the way that people who had gone all through school together in low population counties were.

Yes, Belle definitely deserved a short trip to Colorado.

Glad of a solution, Annabelle hurried to get some laundry done.

She occupied Jody with sorting whites from colors.

Annabelle picked up a pair of Bobby's work jeans and started going through the pockets. She found three pockets clean, but he had missed clearing out his back left pocket. She pulled out a wad of stuff: a feed store receipt, an AA battery, a piece of wintergreen gum, which she unwrapped and stuck into her mouth, his (now useless) K-State student ID card, and a small photograph of his sister-in-law and his niece.

Surprised to find such a sentimental thing in his pocket, Annabelle smiled at the discovery.

"Look, Jody."

The little girl hopped up and came over to see.

"Is that baby me?"

"It sure is. That's you and your mommy."

"Where'd you get it?"

"From your uncle Bobby's pants pocket."

"What was it doing in there?"

"He wants to keep you close to him."

"Really?"

"Yes. He's proud of you. You're his only niece."

Annabelle had no idea if any of that was true, but she liked the sound of it, and judging from the way Jody's eyes were shining, so did his niece.

"I love Uncle Bobby."

"Well, he loves you, too."

"Mommy's pretty."

"Yes, she is."

Bobby was better with children than he was with grown-ups, Annabelle thought. Or at least he was better with this one child. He was willing to pick her up and swing her when Laurie asked him to, and not opposed to walking out to the barn with her to visit the cats. She suspected that Laurie only wanted to get Jody out of her hair when she made those requests, but that didn't take anything away from Bobby's willingness to fulfill them. It seemed to make him almost as happy as it made Jody.

Annabelle felt delighted to think that her most difficult son wanted to keep a picture of his niece in his pocket. It was a small thing, and she knew she might be giving it too much weight, but she couldn't help what it made her feel. It gave her hope for Bobby, who could be lazy and sarcastic and sometimes even a little mean. She laid the photo carefully on top of the dryer and told herself to remember to tell Hugh about it. Maybe it would soften him a little bit, and then maybe Bobby would respond to his father's softening . . .

The only thing you should soften by pounding is steak, Annabelle thought. Children were not cuts of beef, and parents shouldn't be meat mallets.

There was a ferocious crash of lightning, and the basement laundry room went dark.

"Grandma, what happened?"

"We've lost power, honey. Here, take my hand. We'll find candles."

"I'm hungry."

"Then we'll find a flashlight, candles, and something good to eat."

Feeling grateful for her gas stove, Annabelle made grilled cheese sandwiches and tomato soup for the two of them, and followed that with a special treat of hot fudge sundaes. "May as well use up the ice cream before it melts." She lit kerosene lanterns, put one on her reading table, and after dinner took her granddaughter onto her lap and read to her, in the flickering light, from *Make Way for Ducklings,* a tattered copy that was now on its third generation of handling and love.

Outside, the storm battered the house.

Inside, they were cozier than any pioneer women could have been.

As she turned a page and Jody snuggled against her, Annabelle thought, I'm the luckiest woman in the world.

AT THE ROSE MOTEL, Hugh Senior peeled down to his skivvies and crawled between the thin white sheets of the lumpy motel bed, for lack of anything else to do. There wasn't any light to read by, except a flashlight, and the television was out, and it was raining too hard to go anywhere, even over to Bailey's Bar & Grill for supper. He would have loved a couple of big fat pork chops with a baked potato and some green beans, but his stomach was just going to have to grumble because it wasn't getting fed anytime soon. Unlike the motel, Bailey's place would have electric generators going, so they'd still be serving, but that didn't do him any good if he couldn't get there. He wasn't hungry enough to pay the price of getting soaked to the skin when he didn't have a change of clothes, and he'd stupidly left his rain slicker in his truck. He thought about forcing his way through the downpour anyway, and driving over to the grill, but decided that he'd had about enough of his own kids for one day. He knew they were at Bailey's because when he'd driven past he saw Bobby's truck and Meryl's. A phone call to Bailey himself had filled in the blanks: his two younger sons, his daughter, and his daughter-in-law; they'd take care of themselves and each other.

Truth to tell, they'd probably had enough of him, too.

He ran his hands over the sheets—so cheap and rough compared to the soft, good-smelling ones that Annabelle used on their bed at home—and wished she was there with him to complain about them.

"At these prices, you'd think they could afford decent sheets," she'd say.

In truth, at the prices the local motels charged, they probably couldn't afford anything but old towels and sheets, but his wife was careful about money, which was one of the things he loved about her—as opposed to some other wives he could think of, including one in his own family.

He liked staying in hotels and motels with Annabelle—well, nice ones, at least—especially now that the kids were grown and got their own rooms. And, frugal or not, Annabelle loved room service. She would never get that at the Rose Motel, but she could have awakened to fresh coffee made in the room by her very own husband.

Hugh Senior crossed his arms behind his head on the pillow and smiled at the ceiling. His kids drove him crazy half the time, the ranches were heavy responsibility and hard work almost all of the time, there were various problems that he'd just as soon he didn't have to deal with, but overall, life was pretty good . . .

Especially now that the Billy Crosby problem was solved.

Any second thoughts he'd had were gone.

We'll be fine, if we don't lose any cattle in this storm, he thought.

He felt a bubble of laughter in his chest, knowing what Annabelle would have said if she'd heard him think that: "You're just an old farmer," she'd say, "always happy to find the cloud in the silver lining," and then she'd put her arms around him and kiss him.

In his imagination, he kissed her back.

He wasn't through thinking, though.

He was convinced—again—that he'd done the right thing about Billy: get him arrested, put him in jail. A lot of things got tolerated or overlooked in small towns because people had to live together, but this wasn't going to be one of them.

Satisfied with his own intentions, Hugh Senior closed his eyes.

Outside, lightning crashed as if the end of the world had come.

Exhausted from the day of stress and hard work, Hugh Senior slept through most of it.

Two doors down from his father, Bobby ran in from the rain.

He'd brought a six-pack with him, provided by a cowboy he'd asked to buy it for him. He proceeded to get started on it by pulling a chair up to the window and drinking while he sat in the dark and watched the deluge. The gutters were lakes by now, water stood deep in the valleys of intersections, and tree branches had come down all over town. There had been a couple of times when he was sure his truck was going to stall, but he'd managed to roll it on through the high water, feeling like a barge captain.

Half a beer down, he smiled with satisfaction, remembering how he had manhandled Billy Crosby at the tavern.

Bastard.

One beer down, he glanced over at the two beds.

He was thinking of fading into one of them, but Chase didn't have a key to the damned room. What the hell was taking Chase so long anyway? All he had to do was drop off Laurie . . .

"What the fuck are you doing?" he muttered to his absent brother.

When he was away from his parents, who forbade such language in their home, he liked to let loose with it. The word "fuck" made him nervous, however, when combined in the same sentence with his brother and Laurie. It wasn't easy being crazy in love with his own sister-in-law and never letting anybody know it. It was painful knowing it was probably never going to come to anything, and always looking for any little sign that she even liked him, and knowing what his fathers and brothers would do to him if they ever so much as guessed what he thought about in bed each night. And when he was driving his truck. And when he was doing practically anything. Like, when he should have been studying.

He'd flunked out of K-State because he couldn't stop thinking about Laurie.

He had this one fantasy he loved, even though he was deeply ashamed of it because it required both of his brothers being dead. It made him feel kind of sick every time he let it play in his brain. He already felt bad enough about betraying Hugh-Jay, even if it was only in his imagination, and this story only made that worse. In his fantasy, they were all back in biblical days and it was the law that when a man died his next oldest brother had to marry his widow, just as things had been back then in real life. That was why in the fantasy Chase had to be gone, too, of the plague or something, or being stabbed by a jealous husband, maybe. Laurie's and Bobby's parents and the whole community insisted on their marriage, so Bobby and Laurie didn't have any choice in the matter. They had to get married to satisfy tradition and religion, so it didn't matter if Laurie didn't want to. In his fantasy, Laurie came around to appreciating that he was honorable and noble, and that he was only doing the right thing because he wanted to help and protect her. And then she'd have a chance to fall in love with him, like he was with her.

It was also hard to be in love with her because of Chase.

When he saw Chase talking and joking around with her, making it look easy, it ate him up with jealousy. It made him want to grab Chase and slam him up against the house and then stomp on him. Talking to women was easy for Chase, like swinging up into a saddle, or smoking a cigarette. Nothing to it, if you had the bullshit for it. It was hard for Bobby to talk to most people, but it seemed like his tongue swelled to twice its size when he was anywhere near Laurie. About all he could get out of his mouth was grunts, which sometimes made her give him a look like he disgusted her. Like this evening, when she'd complained he was too big to sit by her.

That's real attractive, he thought, loathing himself.

Thinking about what really *was* attractive, Bobby reflexively reached for his left rear pocket where he kept a little photo of her.

When all he felt was denim—and he remembered where the picture was—he had a scary moment of thinking, Oh, shit! What if his mother found the picture when she washed his other jeans? He told himself she wouldn't think anything of it, because little Jody was in the photo, too, so it was just an ordinary picture of his sister-in-law and his niece, like any loving uncle might keep.

Next time, though, he would put the photo in a more private place.

He didn't know how he'd explain it if his dad or his brothers saw it, and how ragged and worn it was, which could only be from him handling it so often. Stroking her face. Her hair. Her mouth. And other parts of her. Chase would immediately suspect something, and he would never let go of it.

Where *was* Chase, for God's sake?

This was pissing him off.

Bobby squashed the empty beer can in his right hand.

If Chase didn't show up soon, he thought that he might have to get in the truck and go after him.

BELLE JUMPED when she heard pounding on the side door of the bank.

At first she thought it was noise from the storm, maybe a big branch blown into the door. But when it kept up, she made out a human voice mixed in with the thunder, rain, lightning, wind, and pounding. She weaved her way toward it and jerked the door open. As hard as it was raining, she was surprised that whoever it was hadn't just come on in. Then she saw the screen door and remembered she had latched it to keep it from blowing open.

Meryl Tapper stood outside in the rain, looking in at her with a sheepish expression.

"Meryl! Come in, get in here!"

He had dropped her off and then gone back to his office to check on things there. She hadn't expected him to come back, which made it all the sweeter that he had gone to the effort, especially in the storm. He had his shirt pulled up over his head for cover, leaving his belly and half of his chest and his back exposed. It didn't keep him from looking as if he had been swimming in drainage ditches. His sandy-colored hair was plastered to his face and neck. Water streamed down his raised arms. His blue jeans were so wet they looked as if they'd be heavy to walk in. He looked like the most beautiful drowned rat that Belle had ever seen, and she was so eager to let him in that her fingers fumbled with the latch on the door.

Belle wasn't feeling too steady. She didn't often drink more than one beer, and the three she'd had that evening made her feel dizzy and reckless.

"You're wet as a sponge!"

"It won't kill me."

"It might." She started fumbling with the bolo tie she'd given him, trying to get the silver horse to slide down the twined leather so she could lift it over his head. "You need to get out of those clothes."

He put a hand over her hand to stop her.

"I don't have anything to change into, Belle."

Belle, who was a virgin, swallowed hard and said, "That's okay."

Meryl instantly realized what she was saying. He took her forearms in his wet hands and said, "Then I'm going to ask you now before this goes any further. Will you marry me, Belle Linder?"

Belle laughed a little. "You don't have to marry me to have sex with me, Meryl."

"Yeah, I do."

She stared at him, feeling confused, not sure whether to be disappointed or glad.

"We're going to get married first," Meryl told her, "if you ever remember to say yes."

"What about your wet clothes?" she asked, feeling stupid the second after she said it.

"They're going to get wetter because I'm going on home."

"Did you come here just to ask me to marry you?"

"Yeah." Meryl grinned. "Come hell or high water."

"Are we in love?"

"I'm pretty sure we are, Belle."

"Yes!" she said. "I'll marry you, Meryl Tapper."

He kissed her without holding her, for fear of soaking her, but Belle wasn't having any of that kind of restraint. She pulled him toward her, wrapped her arms around him and got just as wet as he was.

WORKING ON his third beer can, Bobby peered through the heavy rain and recognized a truck that splashed by.

"What's Hugh-Jay doing here?" he asked the storm. He was positive that was his eldest brother's truck, the one that was supposed to be in Colorado by now. Bobby raised up out of the chair so he could follow the truck's rear lights down the dark street. It was hard to see, so he could have been wrong, except there wasn't another silver truck like that in Rose.

He watched Hugh-Jay's truck turn left, toward the big stone house.

15

WHEN ANNABELLE AWOKE the following morning, with Jody warm and sleeping beside her, she knew by the blessed silence that the rain had finally stopped. The storm front had moved on to terrorize eastern Kansas. Batten down your hatches, she thought sympathetically. All night she'd been plagued by awful nightmares that she blamed on the storm. They had awakened her several times, and each time she'd felt an urgent need to do something, without knowing what.

It was a relief to wake up this time, even if she was still tired.

As soon as she looked at her bedside clock, she knew the power was still out, and when she quietly lifted a telephone receiver, she didn't get a dial tone.

Judging by the slant of the sun, she gauged it to be around 5:00 A.M.

She slipped out of bed without waking her granddaughter and took a moment to look back and enjoy the sight of her, all rumpled and flushed with sleep, with her arms flung out. That vision of innocence smoothed the sharp edge of disquiet that followed Annabelle as she put on a robe and went downstairs. She made her first cup of coffee with water boiled on her gas stove, and then carried it out into her yard to check on the damage. She hated instant coffee, but any caffeine port in a storm, she thought as she sipped it and then made a face at it.

The morning had a mildewy smell.

She clasped the mug in both hands, not minding the heat of it.

She observed that her abandoned flower beds had finally been watered, albeit much too late and too heavily to save them. Their poor little root systems were drowned now, after having been parched first. The soil around them—the dirt she worked so hard to improve every single year—would turn to hard-pack clay again. It was the kind of ruined garden soil that cracked when it was wet and when it was dry. If she wanted to make bricks, she could do *that* with the hopeless soil; it was flowers that she wasn't going to get this year.

Annabelle sighed with regret for all that beauty lost.

But she perked up at the sight of intact roofs on the house, barn, and other outbuildings. She felt astonished to see only a few shingles blown off and a slat of wood or two. She saw no fences down around the house, either, and thought bitterly that it took a man with wire clippers to do that, darn him.

"We got off easy," she said to herself, feeling a little guilty.

She was sure that many people had not escaped so easily.

She needed to feed the dogs and horses, but the remainder of the daily chores could wait until her men came home. She tossed the execrable coffee onto the ground and hurried back inside. She was worried about Rose and anxious to get Jody dressed so they could drive into town to see how their little town—and their family—had weathered the storm.

ANNABELLE AND JODY had no problem getting past the low place in the highway. The high water had drained back into the creek by then, leaving only muddy traces of its raging self. She was shocked to see—

by the vegetation clinging to fence rails—how high the water had risen over the road.

Whitecaps! she thought, but stopped herself from saying it aloud, because if she did, she'd need to explain to Jody what they were, and she was too tired to answer any "Why, Grandma's?" Jody was cranky from being pulled out of bed sooner than her body wanted to rise. A big breakfast would help both of them. Annabelle's plan was to round up Hugh, Belle, Chase, Bobby, and Jody's mother and herd them over to the Leafy Green Truck Stop for breakfast. The place didn't look like much, but it served the best pancakes in four counties, even better than she herself could make from scratch. The family rarely went out to eat all together, because why pay money when they could eat just as well— except for pancakes—at her table?

Why do it now? Annabelle yawned. *So I don't have to cook, that's why!*

In spite of her urgent need for better coffee, she took an alternate route to town so she could drive past a local landmark, a set of famous rock monuments that rose high above the ground, looking like a natural, bigger, taller Stonehenge, a startling contrast to the rest of the flat landscape. Testament Rocks, as they were known, attracted about the only tourists her county ever saw—archaeologists, geologists, and paleontologists, for the most part. A great inland sea had once surged through this area, an enormous body of water replete with prehistoric sharks and other seafaring creatures; later, a vast river took its place. Just to look at Testament. Rocks gave Annabelle the sense of being part of something bigger, something almost incomprehensibly old that changed so slowly the alterations were nearly imperceptible unless you watched them for a lifetime. Only erosion, pollution, earthquakes, or dynamite could alter this landscape; cataclysmic change came rarely, but it did come now and then. The head of a high rock formation known as the King had been shattered by lightning a few years before, and she still mourned its disfigurement.

Annabelle didn't drive out to the Rocks, which would have taken too long.

She simply slowed down when she could see them in silhouette in the distance. From that angle, they all looked as she remembered them; the storm had not visibly affected them.

As always, she felt steadied by the sight of them.

"Why are we going so slow, Grandma?"

"So we can see the Rocks, sweetheart."

"I don't want to see rocks."

The early morning light was hitting the Rocks just right to turn them a spectacular white-gold that made them look as if they'd been painted there against the sky, because surely no rocks in nature could shine that brightly. Annabelle thought about insisting that her granddaughter look and appreciate their beauty, then remembered that the child was only three and that her tummy was probably hungry enough to feel as if it had rocks rumbling around inside of it.

"What do you want to see instead?"

"Daddy. And pancakes."

Annabelle decided not to ask for trouble by explaining that Hugh-Jay wouldn't be home for a while yet, and maybe not for a day or two.

"Do you want to see butter, too?"

"Yes!"

"Maple syrup?"

"Yes! And Mommy."

"That we can handle."

As Annabelle sped up again, she had the thought that everyone she knew would be gone long, long before the Testament Rocks fell down. That's what she hoped, because that should be the natural order of things.

Along the rest of the way there were manifold signs of storm damage: trees sundered by lightning, branches and fences down, water standing in ditches, a few telephone poles on the ground. Distracted by the evidence of other people's problems, Annabelle forgot her own disquieting dreams.

WHEN SHE DROVE into Rose, she saw branches down there, too, and streets carpeted with wet leaves. It was clear the power was still out, but otherwise the town seemed to have escaped without major wind damage. How their basements looked this morning was probably a different story, she knew. There could well be dozens of people with their sump pumps turned on, or bailing out water by hand, by the bucketful. She saw one large tree split in two, burned streaks down the inside announcing that the lumberjack had been lightning.

She went to the Rose Motel first and parked in front of the office.

"Where'd you stash them?" she asked the proprietor, whom she'd known for years.

"Your husband's in Seven," he told her with a smile, "and your boys are in Nine. How's the highway from the ranch?"

"Clear. Water was very high, though."

"I heard. We're lucky nobody got washed away."

"We sure *are* lucky. May I have keys to their rooms?"

With a cheery wave and keys in her hand, Annabelle left him to his paperwork. Taking Jody by the hand, she walked past the long row of rooms. She marched past Room 7 to pound on Room 9, and then to unlock it, making as much noise as possible to warn the boys to get decent. Before she did that, however, she gave Jody some instructions. Then she stuck her head in, with her face averted, and they both called out, "Pancakes! In half an hour! At the truck stop! See you there!" Jody didn't get all the words out, but it did achieve Annabelle's goal of giving her the giggles. The room smelled of wet leather and sons. She slammed the door to the muffled sound of "Mom?" in two deep voices, as if she had shocked them awake.

At home they'd have been up much earlier, and already working.

This felt like a vacation day, a special day for sleeping in and eating out.

As quietly as she could, Annabelle slid the key for Room 7 into its lock and turned it, after giving Jody certain other instructions. When the two of them slipped in as quietly as possible, they found it dark. Annabelle saw by the lump of covers that her husband was still in bed. She could barely remember the last time Hugh had slept so late, and although she knew he'd complain about it, she was glad for the extra rest for him.

Grandmother and grandchild ran to the bed and hopped onto the covers.

"Wake up, Grandpa!"

Hugh Senior jerked awake as if somebody had stuck a gun in his spine.

"Wha? Wha?"

Annabelle sprawled on her back and Jody jumped up and down on the bed, both of them laughing so hard that Jody got the hiccups and Annabelle had tears running down her cheeks. When he finally saw who had invaded his room, he started laughing, too, grabbed Jody with both strong hands and lifted her above him. "I should keep you up there all day!" he said with pretend ferociousness. "You woke up the grumpy old goat."

Jody was breathless, so he put her gently down again.

Annabelle got off the bed and said, "I told the boys to meet us at the truck stop in half an hour. And Jody and I are going over to Laurie's now to get her, too."

"What about Belle?"

"Oh, my lord, I forgot about Belle." Pangs of mother-guilt shot through Annabelle. "Where is she?"

"With Laurie. Or else she's at the bank."

"Museum," Annabelle reminded him absently. "You can stop by and pick her up."

"I'm starving!" Jody told them.

"Well, then let's go get your mother!"

16

WHEN JODY SAW Chase and Bobby emerge yawning from their room, she got excited and begged to go with them and her grandfather. And so Annabelle arrived alone at her son and daughter-in-law's home that morning. As she pulled halfway up their drive, she noted that her son would have some yard pickup work to do when he returned from Colorado: the big old pin oak tree in the front yard, the only oak in Rose, had lost some branches. Annabelle smiled, guessing what her optimistic oldest child might say about that: *Well, good. Now I don't have to risk life and limb climbing that tree to prune it with my chain saw.* And then he'd laugh, acknowledging the humor of his absurdly rose-colored glasses.

She saw no lights in the big stone house; their power was still out.

So glad I never had to live here, she thought.

Big old spooky monstrosity full of ghosts and dust. Mostly dust.

At the massive front door, Annabelle turned the old brass doorknob, expecting the house to be unlocked, but it wasn't.

"Locked?" she asked the door, in surprise.

Had Laurie been afraid to stay alone while Hugh-Jay was gone?

She rang the bell and then knocked on the door.

When that raised no reply, she did it again.

"Are you still asleep?" she asked her daughter-in-law, looking up to their bedroom. Why did the idea of Laurie sleeping in annoy her, she chided herself, when just a few moments before she'd been happy for her sons and husband to do the same? It wasn't because they worked hard and deserved it and Laurie didn't; any woman with a three-year-old and a house this size worked hard unless she had a nanny and a house cleaner, and Laurie didn't have either.

Annabelle walked back down the front steps and around to the back.

The kitchen door was also locked, and the windows were all pulled down, probably to keep the rain from spraying in during the storm last night.

She knocked, and then pounded on the back door.

"Laurie Jo!" She felt frustrated. "Answer the door!"

Maybe she had gone out in search of breakfast, too.

Annabelle turned to go, and it was only then that she realized her son's truck was parked in the backyard.

Was Hugh-Jay home already? Or had he driven Laurie's car to Colorado?

This was all very strange, she thought, feeling cranky about it.

And then she realized how she might get into the house.

Hoping that Laurie had forgotten to lock the basement door, Annabelle went around to the side of the house and descended the old cement steps to the basement, where they'd only recently cemented in the dirt walls. She had to stand in dirty water from the backed-up drain at the bottom to test the door, but when she did, it budged. She put a shoulder to it, and it gave with a cracking sound that she hoped didn't mean some kind of expensive repair.

The basement smelled as if it had flooded, as indeed it had by a couple of inches. The water was gone, but mud coated the concrete floor. Annabelle grimaced as she stepped across it, moving carefully so she wouldn't slip and end up lying in the muck. That was some rain they'd had last night!

She saw residue around the clothes washer and dryer.

"Hope they're not shorted-out," she said aloud.

When she climbed the wood steps, treading cautiously on her now slippery soles, she hung onto the banister and prayed the basement door upstairs wasn't locked from the other side.

It wasn't.

Inside the kitchen, Annabelle removed her muddy shoes.

"Laurie? Are you here?"

The appearance of the kitchen startled her.

A chair lay on its back. There was a battered straw cowboy hat on the floor as well. A yellow rain slicker lay crumpled on the floor, too. At the kitchen sink, water was dripping from the spigot. When she went over to turn it off, she saw what looked like blood on the sharp metal rim of the sink.

Suddenly, she felt anxious. Things were not as they should be.

This time she yelled it: "Laurie Jo! Laurie!"

She rushed out of the kitchen and into the front hallway, calling, "Laurie! Hugh-Jay! Is anybody here?" Quickly, Annabelle looked into the dining room and the living room, and then she ran upstairs, her heart hammering and her body trembling when she saw and smelled strange stains on the stairway carpet. It smelled like bleach, and the carpeting had pale blotches in it.

Too frightened to speak now, she raced from room to room on the second floor.

They weren't in the master bedroom. Or its bathroom. Or Jody's room. Or the other bathroom on this floor. Or the guest room across from Jody's room. That left only the small guest room at the far end of the hall. Annabelle raced toward it, pushing its door wide open as she rushed inside.

"Hugh-Jay! Oh, God! Oh, no! My child!"

His body lay on the bloody carpet.

Annabelle screamed his name again and again as her heart broke.

• • •

OUTSIDE, a neighbor who came over to check on the Linders after the storm heard muffled screams through the closed, thick-paned windows and was alarmed. The neighbor, Sam Carpenter, finally located the same unlocked door that Annabelle had and hurried up the basement stairs, slipping on her slimy footprints several times in his rush, while overhead the screams—clearer to his ears now, and more terrible because of it—punctured the air. They terrified him. They were the worst thing Sam had ever heard in his life. They sounded as if a woman was being stabbed repeatedly. He only escaped falling back down the steps by hanging onto the painted railing for dear life. During one slip, he barked his shins through his trousers, but barely felt the pain. At the top, he flung open the door and immediately spotted ominous signs of struggle in the kitchen: the chair, the rain slicker, the ruined straw hat. Without stopping to think about any of it, he followed the har-rowing wails to their source in the small guest bedroom at the end of the hall on the second floor of the old stone house.

When Sam saw there was nothing he could do to help there, he hur-ried in search of his beautiful young neighbor, but Laurie Linder wasn't there.

He returned to the terrible room.

Gasping for breath, he told Annabelle, "I can't find her!"

"Get my family, Sam," Annabelle begged him through her tears.

She told him where they were, and he tried the telephone, but it wasn't working. "I'll get them!" Sam Carpenter yelled back at her. He was so upset he forgot to drive, forgot to tell his wife Louanne that he was going, forgot everything except his mission for Annabelle Linder. His heart pounding, sobs forcing their way up his chest and out his mouth, he ran the half mile to the truck stop, stopping for nobody, hearing no voices that called to him.

He burst in the door of the restaurant shouting, "Hugh Linder! Where's Hugh Linder?"

Waitresses and customers turned to stare.

The smiles that came automatically to some faces faded upon seeing the state he was in.

People pointed: *In there. The Linders are in there.*

"What's the matter, baby?" asked a waitress who was known for calling all of her regulars by endearments rather than their names.

"Oh, God!" he exclaimed as he ran past her. In a flash it came to him who owned that beat-up hat he had seen in the kitchen of the young Linders. Like everybody else in town, Sam knew about the incidents at the ranch the day before, and he'd even already heard about the fight at Bailey's the night before. His mind jumped to a logical conclusion: "Billy Crosby has gone and murdered Hugh-Jay Linder!"

She screamed. Dishes full of eggs and toast slid off her tray.

All around the restaurant people who heard those words stood up, some of them knocking their chairs back. Others demanded frantically to know what Sam Carpenter had said, and then they, too, gasped, cried out "Oh, no!" and stood up, or rocked back in their chairs, or grabbed each other.

After the initial uproar, silence fell over the entire room as they waited.

It was broken only by the beginning of sobs from some of the women.

"That son of a bitch!" someone cried in an anguished voice.

And then they all heard it—a roar of "*No!*" from the other room, where the Linders sat together. When the family came running out into the main room, they were greeted by a restaurant full of people standing, waiting to hear that it wasn't true, that they'd misunderstood, that nobody had actually killed that nice boy. Instead, they saw Chase Linder carrying his scared-looking little niece, and Belle hanging onto her father, who suddenly looked a hundred years old. All eyes followed them as they rushed out the front door.

Bobby Linder still had a napkin tucked in his shirt collar.

Sam, following them, was too exhausted to walk back. He limped slowly into the main room as people gathered around to hear him tell his terrible story.

"Hugh-Jay's dead, shot to death, and his mother's there with his body—"

"Oh, my God!" A woman put her hands to her face in horror. "Annabelle! Poor Annabelle!"

"And I couldn't find Laurie—"

"Did he kill her, too?"

"I don't know. I don't know." Sam sank down onto a restaurant chair beside half-eaten breakfasts now going cold. His shoulders slumped and he wept while one or two people patted his back as they fought to hold back their own emotions.

"How could he do that? How could anybody do such a thing?"

Nobody had an answer at first, because nothing like this had ever happened in Rose before. Then somebody said decisively, "It's Billy. He's just that way. I hope they catch him and kill the son of a bitch."

17

County Sheriff Don Phelps made it to Rose in half an hour from where he was, fifty miles east. He drove with his siren blaring, all the while thinking about the things he didn't know.

He was forty-three years old and had been first a deputy and then sheriff for a total of nine years. Not once in that time, or in any of the years that he knew of preceding it, had there been a murder in Henderson County. Maybe back in the homesteading days some sheepherder had killed a cattleman, or vice versa, but he wasn't much on history and didn't actually know if there'd been any murders back then, either. These days, he handled traffic violations and a bit of larceny and petty thievery, domestic disputes and drunken fights at bars, farm foreclosures and rental evictions. He had never faced a single attempted homicide, much less an actual one. His deputies didn't know squat about handling such cases, and the only things he knew came from one weekend seminar the county had managed to afford to send him to, and the law enforcement journals he read at home. When he got together with cop friends from more populated places, he had to take a lot of ribbing about having nothing to do but put his feet up on his desk. He always shot back with his standard retort: "I don't think that coming from a county where there aren't any murders is anything to be ashamed of."

When he entered the big stone house and climbed the stairs and saw the scene of the crime, he knew the wisest thing he could do was to close the door until the KBI got there.

Since he didn't dare risk gathering evidence, he did the next best thing.

He went after the man he knew to his bones had done it.

It also allowed him to escape from that house where an entire family—a good and decent family, in his judgment—was falling to pieces like a plate thrown against a wall. The sheriff wasn't a homicide detective, and he knew he was no psychologist, so he got the hell out of there carrying feelings inside of him that mixed sorrow, fury, sympathy, and anxiety in nearly equal measure. He thought that if he'd had to look into Hugh Senior's eyes one more time, he'd have started crying himself. And that little girl . . .

He couldn't even stand to think about what this meant to her.

The sheriff figured he had more experience with the worst of Billy Crosby than anybody else in the county, with the possible exception of Billy's wife. In addition to seeing Billy in his jail a few times, Sheriff Phelps had been out to High Rock Ranch the day before. He'd seen the fences Billy cut, viewed the carcass of the cow, heard the story of the animal abuse two days ago. And then, at the house just now, Chase Linder had filled him in on the incident at Bailey's during the storm. The sheriff felt awful about the fact that he hadn't managed to find enough evidence to hold Billy in jail last night. Maybe he'd have cooled off. Maybe this wouldn't have happened. Or maybe it was going to happen no matter what, because once you got a man like Billy rolling down a path toward violence, there was no stopping him.

By the time the sheriff parked at Billy's house, his two full-time and two part-time deputies had caught up to him. One of them had a search warrant in hand, issued by a judge who cried while he signed it.

Sheriff Phelps called them together in the front yard and said, "Do not do what you feel like doing to him. Arrest him like anybody else. Read him his rights. Get him into jail and let the law take care of Billy."

After taking a good look at their faces, he said, "I mean it."

One of them, who had played football with Hugh-Jay Linder, found Billy Crosby asleep in a hammock in his backyard. He dumped the hammock over, spilling its vile contents onto the ground. Billy woke up and yelled, then rolled over and stared up bleary-eyed into the face of the deputy who stood over him.

"Stand up, you fucking scumbag excuse for a human being."

The deputy dragged him onto his feet, snapped handcuffs on him, and shoved him into the barricaded backseat of the sheriff's vehicle.

Billy threw up on the floor of it.

INSIDE THE HOUSE, Valentine was fixing breakfast for her son and for young Red Bosch when the sheriff pounded on the front door. Before she could stop her son, Collin ran and opened it, letting out the scent of bacon and pancakes, letting in the big men in tan uniforms. The boy backed up until his legs hit the couch and knocked his feet out from under him, so that he sat down with his arms flailing. Just as quickly, he shot back up.

Valentine came out of the kitchen, wide-eyed, open-mouthed, wiping her hands on a paper towel while the smell of bacon turned to burning.

"What are you doing here, Red?" Sheriff Phelps asked, first thing, looking nearly as surprised to see the teenager as Red was to see him. Momentarily, it distracted the sheriff from the order he had originally planned to say things.

"I p-picked up Billy last night," Red stammered. "I brought him on home here."

His hair flattened by sleep, his jeans and T-shirt rumpled, and one side of his face still creased from sleeping on the teeth edge of the zipper of the sleeping bag—Red looked confused by the hullabaloo and scared by the sheriff's tone of voice. One of the deputies told people later, with a laugh, that Red had that look teenagers get when they don't know if they're in trouble, the look that says, *Oh, shit, whatever it is, please don't tell my dad.*

"You weren't drinking at Bailey's, were you, Red?"

Red was only sixteen and shouldn't have been drinking at all.

"No, sir," he said with fervor, looking willing to swear to it on a Bible if the sheriff produced one. "I was just drivin' around 'cause I like storms, and I saw somebody lying in the parking lot at Bailey's, and it was Billy. He was drunk as a skunk! I couldn't just leave him there to get run over, so I hauled him into my truck and brought him home to Mrs. Crosby."

"Why are you still here, Red?"

The kid blushed as red as his hair. "Mrs. Crosby, she told me to call my mother and tell her it was too dangerous to drive in the storm and that Mrs. Crosby said I should sleep over."

"Where'd you sleep?"

Red gestured to a sleeping bag. "There, on the floor."

The sheriff turned to Valentine. "What did Billy do when Red brought him home?"

In a high, nervous voice, she said, "He passed out on that couch."

Collin had moved over to stand beside her, and now she tried to get him to leave the room, but he wouldn't budge. He wasn't unpleasant about it, but he didn't move. His mom shook her head and gave up trying.

"Son," the sheriff said to him, in a kind but firm tone, "do you have your own room?"

"Yes, sir."

"Well, you need to go there now and shut the door."

Collin obeyed, and they all heard a door click shut.

They didn't hear it quietly open seconds later.

The sheriff turned back to Red. "Did you see Billy get up and leave?"

The teenager nodded. "I thought he got up to go to the bathroom and then probably went on in to sleep with"—he blushed again— "Mrs. Crosby. He never came back in here."

"What time did Billy leave the room?"

"Had to have been around eleven. Wasn't all that long since he laid down."

"Did he come in to sleep with you?" the sheriff asked Valentine.

"No," she said, her lower lip trembling. She'd asked the sheriff what Billy had done this time, but he hadn't told her yet.

"Did you know he wasn't in the house?"

"Not until I got up this morning and looked out back."

"Do either of you know what Billy did or where he went between the time he got off this couch and the time Mrs. Crosby saw him in the hammock?"

They both said no.

"Where is Billy's truck, Mrs. Crosby?"

She looked relieved to be able to say, "Oh, he doesn't have it anymore! Mr. Linder bought it. It's parked behind Hugh-Jay and Laurie's house."

"No," the sheriff told her, "it isn't there now."

He made that fact sound ominous, which confused and scared her more.

"Mrs. Crosby, does Billy have any guns?"

She looked terrified now. In a whisper, she said, "Yes."

"Show me where they are, please."

All of Billy's three pistols and five shotguns and rifles were where they were supposed to be, in a cheap gun case in their bedroom.

"You're sure he doesn't have any other guns, Valentine?"

The "Mrs. Crosby" had disappeared.

"No!" She was unconsciously tearing apart the paper towel in her hands, and bits of it floated to the carpet. The burning smell was stronger now, but only Collin noticed it. He ran from his room the back way into the kitchen to turn down the heat and remove the pan from the top of the stove. He could hear his mother saying, "I mean, I don't know about any other guns! I'm sorry, I don't think so. Please—"

The sheriff took all that to mean that Billy might have used one of Hugh-Jay's own guns to kill him.

"What's he done?" Valentine's voice rose to a quavering high pleading.

The sheriff took a sort of pity on her and told her. "Billy has gone and killed Hugh-Jay Linder and done something bad with Laurie." The sheriff set his jaw, looking as if he was fighting one urge to cry and another one to detonate in fury. "We can't find her. He may have killed her, too. You have any idea what Billy might have done with Laurie Linder?"

Valentine screamed, *"No!"*

Her little boy came racing out of the kitchen, his face a pale little raisin of scrunched-up fear and worry. He ran up to her side and grabbed her hand. This time, given that he had already heard the worst, nobody made him move away from his mother.

The deputy who'd grabbed Billy came in and reported on it.

"Get him an attorney, Valentine," the sheriff advised her.

"We can't afford—"

"Too damn bad," one of the part-time deputies muttered, before turning and slamming his way out of the house. The sheriff and his other men followed, without offering Valentine any other advice she wouldn't be able to take. "Where is he?" she screamed, running out into the yard after them. She saw him then in the backseat of the sheriff's car and stopped, not attempting to get any closer to her husband. Billy's head was lying back on the seat and his eyes were closed. If he heard her, he didn't look in her direction.

"Are you taking him to jail now?"

The sheriff threw her a look that said she ought to be able to figure that out for herself, and then they all drove away, leaving her standing in the yard with Red and Collin beside her.

ONCE THEY HAD BILLY behind bars in the jail at the county courthouse in Henderson City, the sheriff and his men were free to go looking for Laurie.

What they found instead was Billy Crosby's truck.

It was caught up in a streambed where it had been carried along by last night's flooding. Inside, tied up in a plastic bag that had protected it from the water, was a bloody yellow sundress. Belle Linder was later asked to identify it as belonging to her sister-in-law, which she was able to do. The crime lab at the Kansas Bureau of Investigation connected the blood to Laurie Linder. The conclusion was eventually and regretfully reached that Laurie was dead—even if they never found her body to prove it.

Billy Crosby refused to confess what he'd done with her, so her family never had the solace of her funeral. His final words on the subject that anybody local heard were at his trial: "All right! God Almighty, I killed the fucking cow, but I didn't kill any people!"

18

AFTER THE TRIAL, after his conviction, after Billy Crosby was carted off to Lansing State Prison at the eastern edge of the state, the drought resumed. Northern winds blew away the planted seeds of winter wheat, calves got branded, steers got shipped to feed lots. Bobby Linder went off and joined the Army without telling anybody first, so that his mother suddenly found herself without two of her sons at home. She gained a son-in-law when Meryl Tapper and Belle got married in a small ceremony, followed by a barbecue at the ranch.

By that time it was nearly Thanksgiving.

In a classroom in the elementary school, a teacher called on a quiet pupil.

"Collin? Are you with us today?"

Collin Crosby looked up from his desk, alerted not by the sound of his second-grade teacher saying his name in her gentle way, but by the snickers in the classroom around him.

He nodded at her and whispered "Yes" as she smiled at him.

"That's good. I'm glad you're here with us."

He flushed, because even if the other kids didn't get the hidden meaning, he did, and although he appreciated it, it also embarrassed him. The last thing he wanted was to be singled out or have attention drawn to him, so he realized in that moment that he'd better pay better attention at all times. He was used to doing that, because he'd always had to stay hyperalert when his dad was around; since then, he had started to let his guard down.

He'd been daydreaming when she called him out.

He now realized there were still reasons to keep his guard up.

It was exhausting, having to be like that, but he already knew he could do it.

Collin was learning the ways of his new world, the one where his dad was in prison.

And it wasn't just that his father was in prison, it was what he did to get there.

What people said he did . . .

His teacher, Mrs. Davidson, had been kind from the very first day he'd come back to school, and Collin knew it and he was grateful, as he knew his mother was, too. It could have gone a different way if he had a different teacher. He might have Mrs. Perron, who had a face like a knot in a tree trunk, all twisted up in a constant frown, and who was only nice to girls and hated even the good boys, and who had already stared at him in the hallways as if she'd like to stamp on him like a bug. His mother hadn't had the nerve to go up to the school and talk to the principal about how to make things easier for him when he came back to school, but Mrs. Davidson had made it okay, some of it, anyway. She was young and fun and sweet to him, no matter how any other teacher, or parent, or child acted toward him. She was soft, like her first name, Heather. When no other kid would walk beside him when they formed their double line for the playground or the cafeteria, she took his hand and let him lead the line with her.

"They don't hate you, Collin," his mother had told him. "They're just scared."

He didn't think that was true. He thought some of them probably did hate him, because their parents hated his dad. It all rubbed off on him and his mom. Most of the kids were just quiet around him so far, and awkward, not knowing what to do, as if he was the one who'd had a death in the family. Maybe they'd get used to him, he hoped. Maybe things would eventually go back to the way they were in school before everything happened, back when he had a best friend and got along okay with almost everybody else. Only a few boys and a couple of girls were outright mean, but they were the same ones who'd been snotty before, so that wasn't any different from usual. They just had worse things to say to him now, bigger ammunition, as his dad might have put it. The girls who hadn't paid any attention to him then still didn't, so that wasn't new. The only real and bad difference was that his best friend from "before," Miles Montgomery, was avoiding his eyes, and didn't seem to want to be friends anymore.

Miles lived on a ranch next door to the Linders.

Collin didn't blame Miles for avoiding him, but he really missed him and almost cried the second time that he grinned at Miles to share something funny with him and Miles looked away. The first time it could have been an accident; the second time meant Miles didn't want to be friends. His mom hadn't let him telephone Miles when she kept him home after Mr. Linder died and during the trial. When he wondered why Miles didn't call him, she'd said in her sad voice, "Miles may not act the same the next time you see him."

Collin had hoped so much that she'd be wrong about that, but she wasn't.

He hadn't realized how life wasn't only going to change in a good way with his father gone.

It might change in some unhappy ways, too.

Things weren't all bad right now, though.

Collin was already deeply in love with his nice, pretty teacher, Mrs. Davidson.

And he still *loved* school, in spite of everything. He loved the smell of his school building, thrilled to the look and feel of the books in his hands, loved his sharpened pencils and his wide-lined notebook paper, loved his glue bottle, his sticky stars, and his box of tissues. He didn't even mind so much that he had to keep his enthusiasm a secret now and couldn't share it with Miles. Some of the other boys were acting as if they hated being in school, although Collin didn't believe them, because who wouldn't love to be in school where your friends were and facts were?

And of course he had the gift of Mrs. Davidson as his teacher.

When he'd gone home after the first day back at school, he told his mother, "I want Mrs. Davidson to be my teacher next year, and every year, and in middle school, and high school, and I want her to teach me in college, too."

His mom, who stood alone by the school's front door every afternoon to take his hand and walk him home, had laughed for the first time since his father went to prison. Collin's heart had swelled with pride to make her happy like that. When he laughed, too, he realized it was the first time for him as well.

The boy at the desk to his right leaned over toward him and mimicked what Mrs. Davidson had just said about being glad that Collin was with them. "You dad's not *with* us anymore, is he? They shoulda gave him the death prison."

"Death penalty," Collin corrected him before he thought, and then he flushed again.

"That's right! Ha ha!"

The sentence his dad got was what Collin had heard people call "hard forty plus twenty," which added up to sixty years, which meant his dad would be an old man when he got out.

There were booby traps everywhere now, just like there'd been at home when his dad was drunk. Now there were things he shouldn't say, people to avoid, people who avoided him, places he couldn't go, and friends he couldn't have. Everybody he and his mom encountered was a new test: would they be friendly or not? Some women wouldn't use his mom's checkout counter at the grocery store anymore. "They blame me for what your dad did," she explained to him. "They say I should have known. I should have stopped him." His mom had started to cry again. "And they're right! I should have . . . I don't know what I could have done . . . but I should have."

That was a complication he hadn't expected.

He didn't know people would blame his mother!

That shocked him, and he hated them for making her feel like that. How was any of this her fault? And then Collin had to admit there was a little part of him that blamed her a little bit, too. Why hadn't she fought back? Why had she let it get so bad? How could she let his father hurt her? He hated himself for having those mean thoughts about his mother, and he pushed them aside as soon as they popped up. Being mean to her would make him be like his dad. *I'll never be like him,* Collin told himself over and over.

The new little girl at the desk to his left and catty-corner from him turned around and started to smile at him, but the snotty girl to her left quickly nudged her and shot an unfriendly glance back at him. Collin instantly understood something else: if somebody wanted to be popular, they couldn't do it by being friends with him.

He turned his face to his arithmetic book.

The numbers looked friendly to him, because he liked them and because they wouldn't avoid his eyes. And thus, his sterling academic career began that day in Heather Davidson's classroom, where the only companionship was to be found in his teacher's kindness and in the impersonal facts in the book on his desk. He desperately wanted Mrs. Davidson to be proud of him and to continue to like him, and Collin decided that the way to do that was to listen very hard and always do his homework and make A's on all of his tests. For a moment he had a terrible sinking feeling as he thought, It isn't as if I have anybody to play with now, so I might as well study all the time. He forced those feelings and thoughts down, along with the traitorous ones about his mother. As he looked at $7 + 2 = ?$, he realized—without even looking at the row of seven apples and the row of two apples—that it equaled 9, and he raised his hand to show Mrs. Davidson that he was the first one with the correct answer.

"Forty plus twenty equals sixty," a voice behind him whispered.

Collin doubted very much that particular boy knew that fact about prison sentencing, and he wondered if his mom or dad had told him to say it.

"Yes, Collin?"

"Nine."

19

While Collin Crosby adjusted to his painful new reality in school, Jody was still going out to the front porch of the ranch house every night to watch for her father's silver truck. She lived with her grandparents now, and had the nearly constant company of her daddy's two dogs, which her family had brought along with her and all of her belongings.

She often took her uncle Chase's hand and made him go out to the porch with her and the black Labs.

"He's coming home," she assured him. "Daddy's bringing me a surprise."

After they had stood there together for a while, looking down the long driveway, Chase would walk her back into the house, where her grandmother would give her a bath and put her into her pajamas. Then Chase would read to her, sitting by her bed and holding her hand until she fell asleep, while the scent of dog filled the bedroom with a kind of animal reassurance and comfort. They were the first and only animals ever allowed to live in the ranch house, but even Hugh Senior seemed glad to sometimes find them at his feet in his office.

After a few more weeks, although Jody still went onto the porch after supper to look down the road, she stopped taking her uncle with her and she stopped talking about it. As for Chase, every night after his niece fell asleep, he cleaned up and drove into town, where he drank too much and pursued women as if his life depended on their acquiescence to him. During that fall and the first winter, he worked so hard and loyally for his father that Hugh Senior had to order him to stop at the end of their long days. Once, his father found Chase still driving in fence posts at ten at night, after dark, and when he told him to stop, his big, tough, handsome son bent over the top of a post and sobbed. Hugh Senior patted his middle son on his back and wondered if any of them were ever going to be able to be happy again in this life where even the most simple tasks were now so hard to do.

"WELL, HERE WE ARE, HONEY," Annabelle said at the start of one of those tasks. She slanted the Caddy into a parking spot in front of George's Fresh Foods & Deli on Main Street across from the library and City Hall. At the five-and-dime, the windows were full of cardboard cutouts of Santa Claus and his elves. "Let's go buy a chicken and some potatoes for supper."

It was an unseasonably warm day for December, not requiring coats.

Jody didn't move except to turn her head and stare in a direction that, if she'd had X-ray vision, could have let her see through the two-room City Hall, on through a couple of houses, and directly into her former home. The big stone house with her bedroom on the second floor was two blocks away. Her mouth was open a little, but there was no expression on her face except for a dull resignation that belonged on the face of a defeated adult and not on a three-year-old girl.

Annabelle said, to distract her, "Let's get you out of your car seat."

Resuming a normal life—walking into the bank, shopping at the grocery store, going to the co-op—was challenging. Every time

Annabelle went into Rose, she had to gird herself. People tried to be correct, but nothing they said or did could be right. She knew people were doing their best. She knew she was being unfair. But she was doing her best, too. She couldn't help it if she felt annoyed with them or wanted to run away from their sympathy. She didn't like being the object of pity. She felt grateful to the people who expressed their concern these days with warmth and genuine affection in their eyes but didn't make a big deal of it. She was grateful to the bank teller who simply asked, in a conversational tone, "You want this in twenties, Mrs. Linder?" and to the clothing store clerk who said, "Annabelle, do you know it's three bras for the price of one right now?" Even in such ordinary transactions there were hazards, though. "Three" made her think of three sons, and how she had only one left at home. "Twenties" made her think about how Hugh-Jay was that age when he was murdered.

She couldn't control people's responses to her.

She could barely control her own reactions, so why expect more of other people?

All she could do was breathe, and grit her teeth when need be, and put all her energy into buying a bra without weeping over it the way Chase had sobbed over the fence post. She could only smile and reply, "Twenties will be fine, thanks," and, "Oh, good. I'll add a black one."

She had learned to take Jody with her wherever she went, partly to get the child to do something besides follow her around in the house all day, but also for the selfish reason of manipulating people's reactions. Only the crass would risk talking about Hugh-Jay or Laurie around their orphan. To protect Jody, Annabelle felt no qualms about saying firmly to people, with a reminding glance down at the dark top of her small head, "Let's change the subject, shall we?" She couldn't easily say that for herself, alone, but she could get the words out in defense of her granddaughter—even though she was the person who put Jody in the position to hear such words. But taking Jody along also solved the problem they were having with the child being afraid to stay anywhere without a member of her family near her. Babysitters were still out of the question. The child who hadn't been afraid of much of anything, seemed now to be frightened of everything. Nothing upset her as much as thunderstorms, though, and it didn't take a child psychiatrist to understand that she associated them with the loss of her parents.

Annabelle thought that was desperately sad.

She wanted the child back who clapped her hands at thunder and lightning.

"She's afraid of God," she had told her husband. "She's afraid of God because Laurie made her say that awful prayer every night. You know the one: 'Now I lay me down to sleep, I pray the Lord my soul to keep, if I should die before I wake, I pray the Lord my soul to take.'" Annabelle had thought it was a bad idea to begin with, because good grief, what a thing to put into a child's head that she might die in her sleep! But it turned out to be bad for an unforeseen reason—nobody had warned the child that it was her parents who might die while she slept. Jody didn't trust God anymore. She thought he'd been tricky. He'd distracted her into praying for herself while he sneaked in and stole her parents away.

Tricky ol' God, Annabelle thought bitterly as she helped Jody out of the backseat. *The child has a point, you know,* she said silently, with a sardonic glance to the sky. *You ought to be ashamed of Yourself.* She heard a deep voice in her mind retort: *I never told anybody to say that stupid prayer,* and she laughed a little at her own ridiculous fancies.

"What's funny, Grandma?"

"Nothing, honey." *Absolutely nothing anymore.*

This trip to the store was going to be extra challenging.

It was a Saturday, when the store was usually the most crowded.

Valentine Crosby worked on this day, at this hour.

Until now Annabelle had avoided seeing Val.

WHEN ANNABELLE and Jody walked into George's Fresh Food & Deli, a rolling silence fell over the store, starting with the first people to see them up front. Then the woman closest to them smiled, someone else gave them a little wave, and business went on as usual—except for the feeling Annabelle had that the two of them were being covertly watched by people who were curious or concerned and trying not to show it.

The smell of cooking food nearly gagged Annabelle.

She swallowed hard to keep from throwing up.

This time she was going to attempt to walk up to the meat counter where the bloody fresh cuts were and ask for a whole fryer. The smell and the sight of blood had kept her away from the back of the store before now, but she was determined to change that on this trip.

"George" wasn't a man's first name, but rather the last name of the couple who owned the store. Livia George, the wife, came hurrying up, smiling too brightly. "Hello, Annabelle! Is it okay if Jody has some C-A-N-D-Y?"

Jody grabbed Annabelle's right leg and clung to it.

Annabelle looked down at her and gently asked, "Would you like Mrs. George to give you a piece of candy?"

"No," Jody said, edging partly behind her grandmother. Annabelle wanted to remind her to add *Thank you*, but didn't have the heart to chide her. They could deal with manners later. For now, just getting the child to step six inches away in a public place would be enough.

The store owner bent down closer to Jody. "It's choc-o-late!"

"Another time," Annabelle said, stepping fully in front of her grand-daughter. "Thank you, Livia. That's very kind of you."

When they got a grocery cart, Jody held onto both of them, grand-mother and cart.

With slow progress they managed to pick up fresh fruit and vegeta-bles, cereal, milk, and other staples that Annabelle wouldn't want to cook and nobody would want to eat. Every time she spotted something that her eldest son had loved, or that her youngest son had preferred, her throat closed and she prayed that nobody would pick that moment to ask, "How are you?" *Not good*, that's how. That's how they all were. The Linders were not good at all, including Annabelle's son in Army Basic Training, to judge by Bobby's lack of letters or phone calls home.

Fresh chicken wasn't actually her main goal today.

Even when she successfully took it wrapped from Byron George's hands, she felt no accomplishment yet.

Her main reason for coming waited at one of the front checkout counters.

When she reached the two counters, she saw there were ten people waiting for one of them, and only one customer standing across the moving belt from Val Crosby. Annabelle pushed her cart in behind the single customer, with Jody holding onto her skirt behind her. The customer, a woman she knew only slightly, looked up, saw who was behind her in line, and looked flustered. "I'm sorry," she murmured, although it wasn't clear why. In the same sardonic inner tone with which she tended to address God lately, Annabelle wondered if the woman was offering her condolences or her apologies for failing to snub Valentine Crosby as the other shoppers were doing.

When it was Annabelle's turn, she stood in front of Billy's wife.

"Hello, Valentine."

The girl flinched when she saw who it was. She looked wretched. She had already been thin—scrawny, as Annabelle's sons might have said—but now she looked gaunt, all eyes and bones. She also looked as if she was either going to cry or run away at the sight of the grandmother and child in her checkout line.

Byron George came hurrying up and said, "Annabelle, we can make room for you in the other line if you'd like to use it."

She shook her head. "This will be fine, Byron."

Annabelle straightened her back, took a deep breath and prayed that the frightened-looking young woman standing across from her wouldn't burst into tears, as she looked as if she might. She had something to say to Val. She had practiced it at home, in front of Hugh Senior, and now she desperately tried to remember what came next. At first her mind went blank and she thought she might be the one to cry. But then it came back to her and the words burst out. "My husband and I want you to know that we are always thinking of you and wishing the best for you." She raised the volume a little so she would be sure to be overheard by a number of people, all of whom she was positive were furtively, understandably, watching or eavesdropping. "I hope people are treating you all right, Valentine."

Annabelle knew they weren't. That's why she was here.

The girl's eyes filled and her lips trembled.

Annabelle reached across and took her hand, and as she did, she looked up at the store's owner. "Byron, I'm sure Valentine is an excellent employee and that you will treat her well, as you do everyone who works for you." He looked startled, confused, but then he nodded in a way that looked like a vow rather than just an affirmation. "That's good of you, Byron," Annabelle said.

She turned to look at Valentine Crosby again. "I think we've got everything we came for, if you want to check us out now, Val."

She squeezed the pale, trembling hand and released it.

Val hurried to do her job, taking in an audible breath as she picked up the first item. She could barely ring them on the cash register. She dropped things, which Annabelle picked up and handed back to her. Byron George hovered over them as if he didn't know what to do next.

"I'll call you in a few days, Valentine," Annabelle said in the same clear, loud voice that she intended for as many people as possible to hear, "to see if you need anything. I hope your neighbors and everybody at your church are helping you out while Billy's gone. I hope everyone is being kind and thoughtful to you." She had thought she might say, *That's what my son would have wanted,* but at the last minute she couldn't get the painful words out, and she was also afraid they might wound Valentine terribly. It was better for both of them not to say it.

Annabelle knew how formal and stiff she sounded, and regretted it.

But she couldn't help it. Getting the words out at all was a victory.

She had wept while rehearsing them with Hugh Senior.

He had encouraged her, coached her, cried with her.

They'd heard of meanness in town, of Valentine and her boy being snubbed, or worse, and they had talked about it and decided mutually that they were the only ones who could put a stop to it.

Valentine broke down and began to cry.

Seeing her, Annabelle did, too.

The two women—wife of a convict, mother of a victim—leaned

toward each other over the milk and cereal and embraced. Annabelle whispered in her ear, "You have to eat, Valentine. You're too thin. You have to keep up your strength for the sake of your son."

Valentine whispered back, sobbing, "I'm sorry, I'm sorry, Mrs. Linder, I'm so so sorry," while they held onto each other for dear life.

It was then that Annabelle realized that Jody wasn't clinging to her anymore.

Annabelle broke away and looked around, but didn't see her granddaughter.

Though she knew it was absurd, she panicked. "*Jody!*"

And then she heard it: a little girl's giggle. It was the most beautiful noise she'd heard in weeks, and her eyes welled up with tears again at the precious sound of it. She looked in that direction and spotted Jody standing in a corner of the store beside a card table where a boy was showing her something in a book. Jody pointed to a page and they both giggled.

"Who is that child?"

Valentine turned to see, and she gasped. "Collin!" She abandoned her post and ran toward the children. "Collin, come here!"

The boy and Jody both looked up with surprise on their faces as Valentine grabbed her son's arm, and pulled him off his chair and away from Jody. "I'm so sorry," she said to Annabelle as she came back to her counter with her son in tow. "I'm so sorry, Mrs. Linder. He doesn't know who she—"

Byron George shook a finger in Collin's face.

"Stay away from that girl," he said. "You just stay away from her."

Annabelle was horrified by their good intentions. The boy—a handsome, dark-haired child who reminded her sickeningly of his father—appeared stunned by the grown-ups' actions and words. He looked back to where Jody was still standing. She wasn't smiling or laughing anymore. She looked scared, and ready to cry, too. Annabelle saw the two of them look briefly at each other. Then the boy turned back around quickly and stared at the floor without saying anything.

"Please," Annabelle said, patting the air. "It's all right."

She smiled—or tried to—at the child.

He looked at her with wide, somber eyes.

"Byron," she said, "maybe Livia would like to give Valentine's son that piece of candy that my granddaughter didn't want." Then, as quickly as she could manage it, she completed her transaction with Valentine Crosby, refused Byron George's offer to carry the bag to her car for her, and gathered up Jody to go.

Grabbing Jody's hand, she fled from the grocery store.

OUTSIDE ON THE SIDEWALK, they ran into a friend of hers.

"Why does she stay here?" Phyllis Boren said in her blunt way as she pointed into the grocery store. "Doesn't she know that none of us want her here?"

"This is her home now, Phyllis."

Her friend looked at her with surprise at her tone.

"I don't think she has anyplace else to go," Annabelle added, hoping Phyllis either wouldn't notice her tearstained face or was so used to seeing her that way that she wouldn't remark on it. "From what I understand, her family in Scott City won't have her back. And I doubt she has the money to move even if she wants to."

"We could solve that problem, Annabelle. You and Hugh Senior just say the word, and I guarantee you I'll personally come up with her bus fare. It would be better for her," she added in a virtuous, vigorous tone, "and certainly better for the boy if they started over somewhere."

"How far away would she need to move, do you think?"

Phyllis didn't catch the sharp tone in her friend's voice.

"Far enough that you can't run into her at the grocery store, Annabelle. Far enough that Hugh will never be tempted to take on Billy's demon offspring as one of his rehabilitation projects—"

"Demon offspring? Phyllis, he's just a little boy."

"He's Billy Crosby's little boy, and you know what they say about apples and how far they fall from trees. If none of that convinces you, then let me say this. Val Crosby needs to move far enough away so that her kid and Jody will never cross paths in the same schools."

Annabelle felt startled, having not thought of that probability before.

"That could happen—"

"Sure. He's only four years ahead of her. When she enters kinder-garten, he'll be in fourth grade."

Annabelle glanced down at Jody and saw that she was staring in the window at Collin Crosby, who was back at his corner table, his face determinedly pointed at his book.

"They're just children," she said softly.

"Well, you think about what I said, Annabelle."

"I appreciate your good wishes for us, Phyllis." She straightened her spine, which it seemed she'd had to do a great deal lately. "But I hope you will spare some kind wishes for that poor young woman and her son as well."

Grandmother and granddaughter turned without saying goodbye.

They walked back to the Caddy to stow the groceries that nobody in their family would feel like eating.

COLLIN PEEKED UP from his books and saw the little girl was staring in at him from the fancy black car as it pulled away from the curb. He wanted to raise his hand and wave at her, but he didn't dare cause another fuss. This was where his mom worked. Everything depended on if she kept her job here, because probably nobody else would hire her because of his dad.

Collin felt horrible because of what had just happened in the store.

He hadn't recognized the little girl, hadn't known, didn't mean to—

His sensitive antennae picked up a new conversation going on between the man and woman who were his mother's bosses, Mr. and Mrs. George. They were talking softer than they usually did when they discussed his father around him, but Collin listened hard and heard most of it anyway.

"That poor child," the woman said, and for a moment Collin thought she meant him. But of course she didn't—she was talking about the little girl who'd just been in, the Linder granddaughter, as people called her now. "She used to be so friendly and happy, and now she acts like a chocolate bar would scare her to death."

"She'll feel safer with him in prison," Mr. George said with an air of authority.

"Like we all do," his wife said, and Collin heard a shudder in her voice.

"They should have killed him."

"But then he'd never tell where Laurie is."

"I'd like to get hold of him. He'd tell then."

"He dumped her body somewhere, and we'll never know where," Mrs. George said in the same tone of voice that Collin had heard people talking about scary movies. "Not unless he talks, and why would he? If he admits he killed her, he's in trouble all over again. Lord! Imagine being her child and having to grow up with that question hanging over you all of your life."

"He's a real son of a bitch, that one. Cold. Heartless."

"Well, he'll never do any more harm around here, that's one good thing."

"The only one."

Their voices stopped. Collin heard their footsteps going in different directions, one of them to Produce, the other to Dairy.

He looked over at his mom at work at the checkout counter—where a few more people than usual were lined up now.

It was his dad they were talking about.

It was his dad who was the reason that little girl was so scared and sad.

Collin felt as if he was going to throw up right there in the store.

WHEN HE AND HIS MOM walked home that night after her shift, Collin was the first to notice something different about their home.

"Mom, look!"

Valentine turned her head quickly, expecting the worst.

Instead, she saw, as Collin already had, that somebody had mowed their grass. The yard had been springing up in weeds because their hand mower was broken and they didn't have enough money to get it fixed, much less buy a new one. Collin had felt embarrassed that their overgrown lawn called even more attention to their house and made them look like even worse people than folks already thought they were, and he knew it made his mom feel terrible, too.

"Who would do that?" she said, sounding stunned.

Collin looked around and spotted a neighbor down the street just putting his mower away. The neighbor looked up at the same time and, after a moment of hesitation, waved.

Collin waved back, a big wave, a thank-you wave.

"Mom, I think it was that guy."

When she looked, the neighbor gave her a wave, too, and then hurried on into his garage, pushing his mower in front of him.

"Why'd he mow our grass?" Collin asked his mom.

"Because of Mrs. Linder," she told him, sounding on the verge of tears again, but this time for nicer reasons.

THINGS BEGAN TO CHANGE at Collin's school, too.

At recess the following Monday two boys approached Collin to ask if he wanted to kick a ball around. He'd never really noticed them all that much before, but now they looked like the best people he'd ever seen in his whole life.

He hopped off a step where he'd been sitting while everybody else played at recess and ran after them. He worried it was a trick, at first, that they'd kick the ball around him and laugh at him or kick it at his head, but they didn't. A couple of other boys came over and kicked it out of his reach, and called out insults when they ran away. But his new friends didn't do that—they just kicked it to him as if he were like any other boy.

It felt so good to be included that Collin almost cried the way his mother had when their neighbor mowed their lawn. When he happened to glance at his teacher, Mrs. Davidson, he saw that she was watching their game. Collin saw her dab at her eyes with her fingers as if she'd gotten bits of dust in them.

20

THE NEXT WEEK, storm clouds showed up on the horizon at the ranch and Jody went into a panic over them, just as she had over every storm since her father died and her mother vanished. As the child screamed and sobbed in her arms Annabelle exclaimed in despair to Hugh Senior, "What are we going to do?"

They were on the side porch just outside the kitchen.

The air already smelled like rain. Lightning periodically lit up sections of clouds as if somebody were turning a reading lamp on and off inside them. The three of them, grandparents and Jody, had come outside to look at the new paint job on the porch, without realizing a storm was visible to the west. As soon as Jody saw it, she went to pieces. Annabelle was holding her granddaughter and getting ready to rush back inside. Jody was clutching her and crying as if assassins on huge black horses were galloping toward them with rifles drawn. Hugh Senior was patting her back comfortingly to no effect.

"I'll take care of it," Chase said, striding past them.

"What?" Annabelle asked over Jody's screams, but he was already walking out into the side yard.

Her curiosity piqued, even while her tears flowed, Jody craned around in Annabelle's arms to see her uncle.

Chase stopped mid-yard with his legs apart.

He raised a pistol in his left hand, pointed it at the clouds, and shot them.

On the porch, his mother gasped at the crack of gunfire, and his father started.

Only Jody stared without flinching. Her crying stopped with a hiccup.

Chase turned around and walked back toward them.

"I killed it," he said with dead seriousness, looking into Jody's eyes.

She hiccuped one more time. "Really?"

"Really. Watch, if you want to see it go away."

As if he took the result for granted, Chase walked back into the kitchen.

Within half an hour the storm blew southeast, away from them.

A little while later the sky over the ranch was a perfect cloudless blue.

"How did you know?" his mother asked him later.

"I called the weather service."

"You're a genius."

"You do what you have to do," he said in a somber tone that convinced her that her middle son had changed more than any of them since his brother's murder. He had taken over the duties that Hugh-Jay once performed, and most of Bobby's as well, and he was growing both leaner and harder as he folded himself into the daily routine of ranch work that he had left behind in college. His handsome face was beginning to look sculpted out of golden rock, all cheekbones, long nose, and stern mouth, as if he were becoming one of the Testament Rocks himself. In profile he looked forbiddingly grim, but also compelling, and it was hard for people to look away from him. He was attentive to his mother, respectful to his father, and affectionate but increasingly tough with his niece. He shot off hectoring notes to Bobby to tell him to call home, and he stopped teasing their sister. He grew increasingly bossy with the ranch's employees. His mother missed her flirting, charming, laughing boy, even while she saw that he was becoming an impressive man. She grieved for the cost of it. She wished she could shoot the clouds away from him.

Chase had to "kill" the next storm, too.

Fortunately for his plan, though not for local agriculture, that storm kept to the south/southeast wind pattern and bypassed them. When the one after that showed up and Jody asked him to make it go away, Chase said—knowing it was headed straight at them, "This is a different kind of storm. It's the good kind that we need to give us water and give the animals water and all the crops on all the farms. It's going to be loud and noisy, like Mr. George at the grocery store, but it has a good heart, like him. It's blustery, that's all, big and blustery like Mr. George, but it would never hurt you, any more than he would. It's a good storm. It's our friend. We need it."

"A good storm," Jody repeated doubtfully.

She had seen how Mr. George had spoken to the boy in the grocery store, and so she wasn't sure about how nice he really was.

"That's right," Chase said, seeing her skepticism.

He sent up an order to God: *no tornadoes.*

That storm came and poured, boomed, and flashed, with no damage done.

Jody sat on Chase's lap on a couch against a wall far from the windows and watched it with him. "Do you have your gun?" she asked when a crash of thunder scared her.

"Of course," he said, and lifted the next cushion to show her where he'd tucked it underneath. Jody nodded, reassured, and resumed watching the rain come down.

"What's that?" she said at one point, huddling into his chest.

"Hail," he told her. "You know what hail is. You've heard it before. It's just ice, like we put in iced tea." It was, thank God, only pea-sized, and not the softball-size stones that had taken roofs apart a few years ago. As the storm was easing down, Chase lifted his niece in his arms and strolled casually to a window, and they stood there looking out together, her cheek pressed to his, her arms wrapped around his neck.

"I like rainy days," she said, as if remembering a forgotten fact.

"You've always loved them."

"I do?"

"Yeah. Personally, me, I like blizzards."

She poked him with a finger. "No, you don't! You hate snow."

"You remember that?" The previous Christmas break from school he'd cursed at all the times he had to drive out to break ice in ponds so the cattle could drink. "You were only two."

"I 'member lots of stuff."

I hope you don't, Chase thought.

"Let's go outside and smell the rain, Josephus," he suggested.

"That's not my name!"

"It is now."

"Rain doesn't smell!"

"Oh, yes it does." He didn't try to explain ozone to her, or how raindrops hit rocks, releasing the fragrance of oils that plants had rubbed on them, or how spores in the ground give up their own earthy scent in the rain. He just took her out and let her sniff and sniff until she admitted that, yes, it smelled good outside after a thunderstorm. Then he removed Jody's shoes and socks and set her down so she could run around in the wet, golden grass.

"You do it, too, Uncle Chase. Come on!"

"My feet stink in these old boots."

She giggled and then ran circles around him yelling, "Uncle Chase's feet stink! Uncle Chase's feet stink!"

And that was mostly that, when it came to storms.

There were either good or bad storms now, depending on whether the weather service said they were going away or coming toward. Chase continued to shoot the bad ones away from the house, while Jody agreed to allow the good ones to approach and bring their rain as long as they behaved themselves, and so long as Chase kept a gun nearby in case they acted up. She began to be able to bear them, even enjoy them, without hiding in a bathroom or clinging to a grown-up.

Other fears started to fall away then. The little girl they used to know began to reemerge, the one who chased rabbits and lay down in the hay with dogs, who ran out into the yard by herself, who wanted to be swung "higher!" who giggled when a calf slobbered on her arm, and who didn't cover her ears at the sound of fireworks. On the day she asked her grandfather when she was going to get her pony, they knew that at least in some ways Jody was going to be okay.

21

FOR A LITTLE WHILE after the scene in the grocery store when she was three and he was seven, Jody took peeks at Collin whenever she saw him, and sometimes it turned out that he was peeking at her, too.

When that happened, they gave each other shy, secret smiles.

Then they'd quickly look away as if it had never happened.

But then, "Who is that boy?" she asked her grandma one time after they'd been in the grocery store and had seen him at his homework table again.

Annabelle decided it was best to tell the truth.

"That boy's name is Collin Crosby, sweetheart." She took a deep breath. "It was his daddy who killed your daddy."

Jody looked at her with horror.

Annabelle nodded. "That's why it's best for you to stay away from him."

Jody looked at Collin differently then, as if he'd all of a sudden grown horns.

"I hate him!"

"Oh, honey, that little boy hasn't done anything wrong. You shouldn't hate him. It's not his fault that his daddy is a bad man. You should feel sorry for Collin, and try not to hate him."

"Why?"

"Because it would be awful to have a father like that, wouldn't it?"

Jody nodded slowly. It was awful not to have a father at all.

When she was a little older she wondered if he missed his father like she missed hers.

She wondered if he loved his daddy.

If he did—if he loved that terrible man, even if it was his father—then she would hate Collin Crosby and she would always hate him, no matter what her grandma said about being feeling sorry for him. She tried to stop peeking at him after that when she saw him in the grocery store or other places around Rose, but her eyes kept looking. When he caught her staring—or she discovered he was looking at her—she didn't smile even the teeniest smile at him.

Collin stopped smiling at her, too.

And *still* she couldn't help sneaking glances through the years.

"Do you *like* him?" a middle school friend asked her one time, looking shocked.

"Collin Crosby?" Jody was mortified that she'd been caught staring. "Gosh, no!"

It wasn't that he was cute, although he was.

It was his eyes. His eyes looked serious and kind and somehow gave her the impression that they knew each other better than they did—which wasn't true at all. She didn't understand how he made her feel like that. They were the last people on earth who could be friends. Collin Crosby couldn't possibly know anything about her except for the terrible truth of what his father had done to hers.

When she entered high school and was old enough to entertain the thought, she decided Collin held a creepy fascination for her like a snake, and that it was sick and she should be ashamed of herself and never look at him again.

Soon after that, she turned her head one day and he was looking at her.

Jody whirled around, putting her back to him, but she couldn't seem to make her curiosity about him stop so easily.

As they grew older, they navigated around each other with the help of friends, who whispered, "We can't go that way. Collin Crosby's over there." Or, in Collin's case, "Don't turn around. Jody Linder's by the wall." They averted their eyes when they had to, walked around corners to stay invisible, never joined the same clubs or activities, tactfully slid past each other in school hallways. Jody got tired of always needing to look down rows in auditoriums, gymnasiums, and football bleachers to make sure she wasn't sliding in near him with her bag of popcorn or her soda pop, but that's the kind of vigilance it took to keep from causing trouble.

She didn't know what kind of trouble there might be.

It just felt as if trouble might happen if people saw them together.

He wasn't popular like she was in her grade, but she could see that he had friends of his own, he wasn't one of those loners who might show up and shoot off a gun and kill everybody in school, starting with her.

At least, she hoped he wasn't.

Other people weren't so sure.

Jody had a feeling that Collin Crosby got watched pretty closely by the adults in town, as if they were all afraid he'd end up like his father. She knew what it was like to be watched all the time, because everybody watched out for her to make sure "the Linder girl" was okay. It was nice, even if it sometimes drove her crazy. But that was different from how they watched him.

Well, they could watch him all they wanted, Jody thought, but she wasn't going to look at him at all. And she didn't until the next time.

. . .

ACTUAL FRICTION only happened once, and Jody would have done anything to keep it from happening again. She was in high school by them, and one night she was standing behind the bleachers at a basketball game in Henderson City when she took a step back, colliding with somebody else's back. When she turned to apologize, Collin Crosby was doing the same.

It was only then that she realized she'd spilled pop all down her blouse.

"Nice going, Crosby," one of her male friends said to him, even though Collin was a lot older and bigger. Then Jody's friend reached up and shoved Collin's shoulder. "Back off." His face rigid but otherwise expressionless, Collin took a step backward. When he started to say again to Jody, "I'm sorry," her friend got between them. "Shut up, Crosby. Just shut the fuck up! Your goddamned father already did enough to her. Stay the hell away from her."

Without a word, Collin turned and walked away.

Jody felt breathless from the episode that hadn't lasted more than a few seconds.

Her boy friends didn't usually curse that way around the girls.

There'd been real anger there, and protectiveness.

For a moment it unveiled something hidden and violent that scared her and that she had never known existed in the people around her.

Jody was quickly enfolded in her circle of friends again and they moved en masse back to the basketball bleachers. Nothing was said about the incident. Nobody seemed to think their friend had done or said anything wrong, but nobody seemed to want to talk about it, either. Talking about it would have meant referring to her parents. Jody's heart kept beating hard. She was just glad it wasn't worse and that Collin decided not to shove back. Did that make him smart, or did it make him a coward? She didn't know. She felt she should have said something, but she hadn't. What did that make her? She felt bad, as if she had done something wrong. Or failed to do something right. And she felt bad for him. Her attention was badly distracted from the game and she kept scanning the bleachers, pretending to look at the players as they moved up and down the court, but really looking to see if a tall, broad-shouldered, dark-haired boy had come in and found his seat again.

She didn't see him again that night or for a long while afterward.

When she finally did, it was their first real contact since they were children, and this time the two of them were the only ones who knew it happened.

SHE WAS SIXTEEN, fresh from getting her driver's license and being able to drive solo, and one day her urge to drive and drive and drive alone took her out to Testament Rocks. She went as if pulled there by some strange magnet that compelled her to go, even though she knew that girls weren't supposed to go out there alone. It was too isolated, too far away from help, too likely to attract the kind of man who would take advantage of its isolation and of her.

Her new used truck, a birthday gift, just kept speeding in that direction, over the asphalt, then over the dirt. She was still getting the hang of this driving-on-highways thing, even though she'd been driving tractors and trucks around the ranch since she was thirteen. Now, with a truck of her own, she loved going fast a little too much. The truck was old and she didn't care as much as some people would—teenage boys, for instance—about dings in its chassis. So she sped down the long road toward the huge rock formations as if in training for an off-road race.

Once there, she wasn't sure why she had come.

And then she saw she wasn't alone.

A male figure came out from around one of the tallest formations, wearing climbing gear.

Jody thought, I'm not the only crazy person who does things alone that you shouldn't do alone.

She looked at how he was all wrapped up in ropes and belts and carrying equipment and decided that whoever he was, he was too encumbered to be a hazard to her.

Then she recognized him.

She thought about turning her truck back on and leaving.

Instead, she got out, grabbed an old backpack from behind her seat—because she liked to collect things at the Rocks—and stood there, looking at him. It was the only time she had allowed herself to do that, to stare openly at Collin Crosby.

Something—what the heck was wrong with her? she didn't know— pulled her toward him. With a boldness she barely recognized in herself, she walked straight up to him and stood in front of him with her hands on her hips, while he looked a little flabbergasted.

"Isn't it kind of stupid to climb alone?" she said.

"Like coming out to the Rocks by yourself?" he retorted.

"Like that, yeah."

"I can be stupid sometimes," he admitted, with a slight smile. "So far it hasn't killed me."

"I climb that one," Jody bragged, pointing at a rock called the Sphinx.

That was stretching reality a little. What she did was clamber up a few yards to a good place to sit so she could gaze out over the landscape. When he turned to look in that direction, she stared at his profile.

He was disturbingly good-looking and he acted like he didn't know it.

"The Sphinx?" he said, squinting at it.

"Yeah, but not with all that fancy gear. Where did you get all that stuff?"

He turned back toward her, making her take a quick breath. "Last summer I worked in a sports equipment store."

"Where?"

"Denver."

"Really?" She was kind of wowed. But then he was twenty, and probably going into his junior year in college. "Are you in college somewhere?"

"You don't know?"

"I don't keep up with your every move."

He smiled that slight smile again. Her heart did things in response that she wished it wouldn't do and for which she had no good excuse.

"Darn," he said. "And all this time, I thought you did." He paused, suddenly looking less sure of himself. "I keep up with you."

Jody stepped back. "Huh?"

"Well, not like I'm a stalker or anything. It's just that I hear things. People talk about you around Rose. They're proud of you."

"Me? Why? They are?"

"Yeah, because you're pretty and you're smart and—"

"Wait. Stop." Jody stepped back, too, and turned her back on him. She felt more flustered than she'd ever felt in her life except for the time when her friend had cursed Collin and pushed him back away from her. When she turned around, she said, "I don't want to hear about that."

He looked surprised. "You don't want to hear praise?"

She laughed, kind of. "Do you have any idea how spoiled I am?"

He took in a breath, said, "Right," and then gave her a look she couldn't decipher. "Are you meeting somebody here?"

She thought about lying and saying yes. "No."

"Have you got time to wait for me to get out of this stuff?"

She thought about saying no. "Yes."

While he shed himself of everything draped over him, she fidgeted, not looking—as if he were stripping off his clothes. She felt as if she wanted to run away, back to her truck, and reverse her trip out here. But she hung on, pacing a little, feeling stupid and not understanding what was going on inside her own body when she looked at him, thought about him, talked to him . . . did anything in regard to him.

"Okay," he said, and she turned around to face him again.

Now he was just an ordinary good-looking guy in shorts and T-shirt, except he seemed very sophisticated—two years in college already!—and it made her feel very young.

"I think I need to go home," Jody said as her face grew hot.

A look of disappointment crossed his face.

"In a few minutes," she said quickly.

They talked for a while about nothing—his school, her school, how his mother was, how her grandparents were, and then out of the blue, he said, "I've never told you I'm sorry."

She was honestly puzzled. "For what?"

All she could think of was the time they'd bumped into each other and she'd dumped soda down her front. She was on the verge of saying *It was my fault* when he said, "For what happened to your parents."

Her breath caught in her throat.

It was too much: what he'd just said and who he was. It was too much to hear from him and she couldn't take it in. It frightened her and upset her and confused her. It brought up feelings of anger and grief and all of the powerful emotions she was always trying to submerge.

Suddenly she wanted to hit him, push him, hurt him.

"What *happened* to them? Like, it just . . . *happened?* Like nobody *did* it?"

Grief-stricken, helplessly furious, and suddenly without the words to express any of it, Jody turned and ran away from him, back to her truck, back to Rose, back to the ranch.

For many nights afterward she tossed and turned, unable to sleep as she kept hearing his voice calling after her, sounding as sorry as he'd said he was and as upset as she was, *"Jody!"*

22

June 9, 2009

IT WAS A beautiful June day in a season bursting dangerously with hope when she saw Collin Crosby again. By that time she was twenty-six years old and he was thirty. They were twenty-three years away from her father's death, her mother's disappearance, and his father's incarceration. On this particular day, Jody wasn't worried about anything worse than how to ease away from her lover and whether or not she'd prove to be a good high school teacher. And then her uncles walked into her parents' house and reinforced her belief in bad following good as inevitably as the moon chased the sun.

Billy. Crosby. Released from prison. Coming home.

Following that announcement, the sun still shone through Jody's new curtains, but now it cast malevolent shadows. A breeze still blew through the screens, but now it carried no sweet, imaginary scents of lilac and honeysuckle. In the front hallway of Hugh-Jay and Laurie's house, in the space of a few words, their daughter's world turned brittle as a winter field. She shivered like a slender weed taken by surprise and caught defenseless by an early, killing blizzard.

"How could this happen?" she screamed at them. "His sentence got commuted? What does that *mean*?"

"It means he gets out with time served," Meryl told her.

"He got *pardoned*?"

"No, not pardoned, Jody. Commuted."

"What's the difference?" She felt lost in a terrifying thicket of jargon.

"He would have to prove actual innocence to get a pardon."

She stared at him, aghast. "They let him out, but they still think he's guilty?"

They're not saying that. They're saying it was a smelly trial."

"The smell is all over them," Chase said. "He *is* guilty."

"Smelly?" She was deeply sarcastic now. "Is that the official legal term, Uncle Meryl? What was *smelly* about it?"

"The county attorney has cooperated with Billy's lawyers to say he messed up the case. He says his conscience got to bothering him as the years went by." At the doorway, Bobby made a sound of incredulous disbelief, but Meryl kept talking. "He says he withheld evidence from the defense attorneys. Billy's new attorneys got the original defense attorney to say *he* messed up, that he didn't provide an adequate defense or file timely motions. They even got a juror to claim she wouldn't have voted for conviction if she'd known all this at the time."

"Withheld what evidence? What about the honest evidence that he's guilty?"

"Governor doesn't think it's so honest."

"Governor's a liar," Chase said.

"Somebody is," Meryl agreed.

She looked from one familiar face to the other, feeling as if protective walls were washing away, leaving her shaking and frightened on the edge of an abyss. "Don't you have any clout up there? Can't you *stop* this?" Billy Crosby was the monster of her life, the boogeyman of her childhood. Ever since he had stolen her parents away from her, she'd had nightmares where he was chasing her and she was running, out of breath, tripping and stumbling and feeling as if she would die of fright even before he caught her. The nightmares tapered off as she grew up, but lately they'd reappeared, and now she knew why: they were warnings, predictions of this shocking day.

Shock turned to tears again. She started to sob.

Meryl stepped forward to put an arm around her while she pulled a tissue out of her pocket and fought for control of her emotions. "Governor knows this county will never vote for him, or for anything he wants," he reminded her. "And nobody outside of this county gives a damn about"—his voice turned bitter—"our little murders."

She flinched at his use of the plural "murders."

"Somebody else has clout, though," Chase said.

Jody looked up through her tears. "Who? Who would care enough about Billy Crosby—or hate us enough—to do this to us?"

"Just one person."

She waited, hiccupping, crying.

"His son."

"*Collin?*"

"Kitchen," Chase suddenly ordered, and led them there.

AT THE TABLE her mother had painted yellow, in the room where Laurie had cooked meals for her and her daddy, Jody sat with her shoulders hunched and her hands clasped between her thighs, waiting for somebody, any one of them, to start making sense.

"It's weird," she said, sniffling, taking stuttering breaths. "Don't you think this is a weird coincidence? I move back to town for the first time—and he gets out of jail and moves back, too?" Her shoulders lifted in a shudder and more tears escaped before she trapped them with the tissue. "I don't understand any of this. When did all this happen? *How* could it happen? Why did they let him go? You're going to have to explain this to me."

To her right, Chase leaned against a kitchen counter only inches from the spot that had tested positive for Laurie's blood type. It always felt strange to Jody when she cleaned the sink there—just as cleaning other parts of the house took a little courage. She had found a way to do it, though, by thinking of her mother with love and by murmuring a prayer for her, thereby turning the bad moment into something better. Now she watched Chase cross his arms over his white shirt. He still hadn't removed his sunglasses and his jaw still looked clenched, as if a dentist had told him to bite down. In the past when she had seen her uncle Chase look like this she'd gone out of her way to avoid him— even walking clear around the house and coming in another door if necessary. He looked in the kind of mood that started with him blaming somebody for something, then turned into a loud argument, and finally ended with doors slamming.

Sounding angry, barely opening his mouth to speak, he said, "Bobby, make us some coffee."

Jody started to get up to do it.

He waved her back into her chair. "He makes better coffee than you do."

It was true. It had been her mom who was the good cook. Jody had always heard that great coffee and piecrust were two of Laurie Linder's specialties. Chase, particularly, had loved her coffee, people said, and everybody had loved the pies she baked, with their flaky, sugary crusts. At that moment, Jody would have given anything for a bite of her mother's piecrust and a cup of that coffee to relax Chase.

Sitting across the table from Jody, Meryl said, "Give me a minute, sweetheart." He glanced at Chase, then at Bobby, and then gazed out a kitchen window toward the backyard. For a moment, Jody thought anxiously of Red and hoped he wasn't hiding there in plain sight.

"I need to get my thoughts together," Meryl said. "I wasn't ever expecting to have this conversation."

Jody bit her tongue on the questions that sprang to it, and gave him his chance to get organized. She was almost relieved to wait, to delay the words she didn't want to hear. She stared down at the top of the table and thought about how it must have looked bright and cheerful when her mom painted it. Now it was dingy. The old paint was bare in some places, bubbled in others—she brought her hands above the table and rubbed some of the rough places with her fingers—but she wasn't ready to redo it. She had the superstitious feeling that if she did, her mother would never come back in any way, not as a living woman or a corpse. Everybody assumed her mother was dead, but there was a part of Jody's brain—or her heart—that still held out hope. A bloody yellow sundress had been found in a truck, that was all. It didn't have to mean she was dead, did it? The fact that not a single sign of her, any- where at any time, had shown up in the last twenty-three years was taken as proof that Laurie Linder was truly gone, but her daughter lived in a fugue state, haunted by the slimmest of possibilities that her mother was alive.

Jody suddenly wanted her grandmother Annabelle in the worst way.

It made her heart hurt to think of what this was going to be like for her grandparents, having their son's murderer so near, where they might run into him at any time. She knew they would worry for her sake, and that made it essential for her to get a good grip on herself.

She would *not* cause them more pain. Clasping her hands atop the table, Jody sat up straight in her chair. She looked at her uncles and felt such sympathy for them that it nearly undid her and started her tears again. This was going to be *hard* for everybody.

Meryl looked straight at her. "Tell me what you know about why Billy was convicted, Jody."

She wasn't expecting the question, but she focused and obeyed.

"Physical and circumstantial evidence," she recited, having been taught it all when she demanded to hear it years ago.

"What physical evidence?"

"Hair in the guest room and a bathroom drain. Fiber from his socks, on the carpets." She swallowed. "His hat in this kitchen."

She kept her eyes on Meryl, forbidding herself from looking over to where Billy Crosby's cowboy hat once had lain, stopping herself from wondering if the chair that had been turned over was the very one in which she sat now.

"What was the circumstantial evidence?"

"The cow. The arguments. The fences. The fight he got into with you guys at Bailey's. The way he looked at Mom. How he tried to hit her." Fury surged in to suffocate her sadness. She took a ragged breath and beat on the table with her fists. "I hate him! How can they let him go? How can they!"

"Calm down," Chase ordered.

She threw him an infuriated look.

Meryl snapped his fingers to get her attention back. "What did all of that circumstantial evidence establish that was so damning to him at the trial?"

"A pattern," Jody recited, answering by rote. "It formed a convincing pattern of events leading up to the crime."

"Yes." He sighed. "Well, here's the bad news about the physical evidence. Hair and fiber comparisons are considered faulty science in some quarters now, and our governor's office is one of them."

A sickening, sinking feeling rushed through her.

"I didn't know that," she said in a near whisper, and then angrily, "Why didn't I know that?"

"Most people don't."

"But you did, right? A lawyer would know. Why didn't you say anything?"

"Because I think the science is *fine*. And because even without the physical evidence, there is still enough circumstantial evidence to support his conviction."

"So what *happened*?"

Meryl glanced over at Chase, who still leaned silently against the counter, while Bobby banged around looking for Jody's coffee and filters. Driven nearly mad by the clatter and tension, Jody yelled at him, "They're in the left-hand drawer, Uncle Bobby!"

"I don't have a left hand," he growled.

It was a bitter reminder of one more thing Billy Crosby had done to them.

"This is where withholding evidence comes into play," Meryl said, calling her attention back. "The county attorney withheld evidence from Crosby's defense attorney—"

"What evidence?"

"He had witnesses who said Billy lost his hat at Bailey's and that it was your mom who picked it up."

"What?"

"Hold on. There's more. The county attorney also did not reveal that Doc Cramer—remember him, used to be our vet?—told a deputy that your dad had told him about some men he'd confronted in a car passing by the ranch the day before his murder."

"What men?"

"Strangers. One of them threw a lit cigarette out of their car, and your dad got so mad he forced them to the side of the highway and then gave them holy hell for doing it. Your dad told Doc Cramer they looked like tough customers."

"So what?"

"So they could have been suspects, Jody."

"Oh, bull, Uncle Meryl!"

"Bull*shit*," Bobby muttered at the sink.

"No doubt," Meryl agreed, "but prosecutors are required by law to share exculpatory evidence with the defense, and they didn't do it."

"Why not?"

Meryl sighed. "So it couldn't be used to try to establish reasonable doubt."

Jody stared at him, and after a moment, she said, "Okay, I get it. I get all that. But none of that proves Billy didn't do it."

Meryl smiled slightly in approval of her quick analysis.

"Goddamn right he did it," Bobby muttered, his back still turned.

"Why now?"

"What?" Chase interrupted.

She turned to look at him. "Why is all this coming out now? Why is this *happening now*?"

"Because that boy of his got out of law school, that's why."

"Collin." She felt her face flush at the memory of him.

Over the years since that day at the Rocks, she had thought of him more often than she wanted to. Each time, she'd had to fight the impulse to keep thinking about him. Now she felt a molten flash of resentment and fury and humiliation as she recollected those moments and the "sorry" he had claimed to feel for her. She tasted gall as she thought, So this is his idea of sorry.

"This is really Collin Crosby's doing?" she asked them.

"He went through law school with the governor's son," Meryl told her. "And apparently the young son of a bitch has been active in political campaigns since he was old enough to figure out how to get what he wants."

"Paving his way," Chase said.

"Working up to this," Meryl agreed.

Jody thought about the boy she remembered—how quiet and self-contained he seemed, how carefully he moved through the streets of Rose and the halls of its schools, how hard he studied and what good grades he got, the scholarships he earned, the fact that he could have gone to college and law school in other places, but stayed in Kansas to do it. She thought about the day she'd seen him at Testament Rocks, about his climbing gear, his athleticism, his obvious ambition to surmount obstacles in literal and figurative ways. If any boy was going to grow up to be the man who accomplished what Collin had achieved on this day, it was that boy. Now, too late to stop him, it was clear what he was after all the time.

"Didn't we—us, our family—get any say in this at all?"

The uncles exchanged glances again. "We got a hearing with the governor," Meryl told her. "There's not much statutory guidance on these things, so I'm not sure he had to do it, but it didn't make any difference anyway."

"Don't give him credit," Chase growled. "He did it so he could say he heard us."

"When? When was this hearing?"

"Last night in Topeka."

"What? Last night? Who went? Did you all go?"

Meryl nodded, looking wary.

"Why didn't I know? Why didn't you tell me? You did all this behind my back?" She was furious. All of her life they'd protected her from hearing the worst; all of her life she'd had to fight for any bit of truth and information, until finally she thought they'd loosened up and started treating her as an adult. Obviously, that still wasn't the case. "The governor needs to see me. I want to talk to him. I want to tell him what that man did to my life. Maybe I'd make him feel some sympathy. Why didn't you give me a chance?"

"Mom and Dad didn't want you to be there," Chase said, his voice harsh. "They wanted to protect you. Dad was sure it was all for show, and he was right. The governor already had his mind made up, and there was nothing we could do to change it. They wanted to spare you."

"They shouldn't have. You shouldn't have!"

He shrugged. "Maybe not, but it's done now."

She glared at him with all the force of how infuriated, helpless, and frightened she felt.

"Don't blame us." He looked disgusted at the idea of it. "Put the blame where it belongs, on that kid of Billy's. Like father, like son." Finally, his own bottled-up rage burst out of him. "Liars, both of them!" He let his anger flow toward his brother. "Isn't that damned coffee ready yet?"

Bobby answered by swinging his right arm into the coffeepot.

The force of the blow sent the pot full of water and coffee grounds flying into the metal sink, where it shattered. Chase and Meryl both jumped and Jody gasped with shock.

Bent over the sink like a man who might throw up into it, Bobby propped himself up with his one arm. "He's moving back," he said, as if the words hurt and sickened him to say. "That murdering bastard who killed my brother and took Laurie is coming back here to live as if he never did anything to anybody. We can't let this happen."

"Too late," Chase said bitterly.

Jody got up from her chair, ran to Bobby, put her arms around his thick waist and hugged up against his back. It felt good to know they were all as upset as she was. It was a mark of just how bad things really were. She had rarely seen any of them lose control; Bobby's outburst was a welcome revelation. "It's not our fault, Uncle Bobby," she consoled him. This time she didn't cry. Anger at Collin Crosby had dried her tears.

It felt good to have someone to blame.

23

"PACK A SUITCASE, JOSEPHUS," Chase told her before the uncles left her house. He had an unlit cigarette in one hand, as if he could barely stand to wait to get outside again so he could smoke it. "You're coming to the ranch with us."

"I'm not moving back there, Uncle Chase."

"Yeah, you are. Mom and Dad want you to."

They were all standing in the front foyer again, Jody and her uncles.

She had stopped crying. Her anger at what Collin Crosby was doing to her family by getting his father out of prison had rejuvenated her, giving her back some spirit and spite.

"But I don't want to. I just moved in here!"

It wasn't only that she'd only recently moved in, it was also that she'd done so much work to the huge house to turn it into her home—sanding and polishing its original wood floors, taking down ancient draperies and putting cheerful new curtains back up in their place. She

had painted and wallpapered with the help of her aunt and her grandmother. They had all given hours to dusting, washing, shopping, tossing out and replacing things. It had been, Jody hoped, a restorative time
for all of them as they began to transform a mansion of bad memories
into a happy and beautiful house again. With every swab of a wet
sponge, Jody had felt as if she were exorcising *him*. She was *not* going
to let Billy Crosby force her out of her own home a second time.

"Do you want them to worry about you?" Chase demanded, the
set of his face looking grim around his sunglasses. "Do you want them
to lie awake nights thinking about how he's only a few blocks away
from you?"

"God, Uncle Chase, that's so not fair."

He shrugged. "Well?"

She gave in to her own concern for her grandparents' feelings.

"All right. All right! But I'll drive myself out there."

"When?"

"When I've packed!"

"Six o'clock," he told her in a tone that brooked no further argument. "Supper. Suitcase."

Chase grabbed his cowboy hat off its peg and stalked out of the
house, letting the screen door slam behind him. Within moments the
smell of cigarette smoke wafted back inside.

Jody turned toward her other two uncles.

"Don't you just want to kill him sometimes?"

"Frequently," Meryl said with a brief grin as he grabbed his own
hat, then gave her a passing hug. "Don't you worry. He'll screw up.
He'll end up back in a cell where he belongs."

"Uncle Chase?" she managed to joke.

Meryl laughed. "I'll see you tonight at the ranch."

"I may still have questions."

"Anything you want to know, honey. Just ask."

He hurried out to his truck as if he had things to do and not enough
time to do them.

When the other two were gone, Bobby surprised Jody by asking,
"How are you?"

"Shocked," she said, after taking a moment to consider it.

"Are you scared?"

That startled her. It was so unlike him to acknowledge that anybody might ever have a reason to be scared of anything. She lifted her chin. "Not in the least." Then she admitted, "Okay, yes. It makes my heart pound just to think of ever seeing him around town."

"Good," he said, surprising her even more. "You *should* be scared of him."

"Uncle Bobby! Why?"

"Because we have no idea what he'll do."

"He just got out of prison! He won't want to get into trouble, will he?"

"You heard Meryl. He's Billy Crosby. Don't expect him to have gotten any smarter. And remember that he hates us, he hates your grandparents, he hates Chase, and Meryl, and me, and probably even Belle. And I'm guessing he hates you, too."

"Me? But why?"

Bobby shrugged, looking like his brother Chase when he did it, because they both had the same dismissive lift of their big shoulders. "Billy Crosby has never needed a good reason for what he does." He stepped closer to her. "But listen to me, Jody. If there's anybody who should be scared, it's him. Billy Crosby should be looking over his shoulder every second of the time he's here in Rose, because we will be watching him." Bobby put his hat on his head. "That's why you need to go out to the ranch until he's gone. We don't want to have to keep an eye on you, too."

"What do you mean gone?"

"He won't stay."

"How do you know?"

"It won't be comfortable for him here."

On his way out the door he said, "I'm sorry about your coffeepot."

"It's okay, Uncle Bobby." She smiled shakily at him. "You can buy me a nicer one."

"And teach you how to make a decent cup of coffee," he said gruffly, and was gone.

. . .

AFTER THEY LEFT, Jody didn't know what to do with herself.

At first she wandered from room to room downstairs, looking at all the labor she'd put into them and regretting the need to leave them even for a day, much less for however long it took to put Billy Crosby safely away again. "Shocked" didn't even begin to describe how she felt. Things that she had assumed were settled suddenly weren't, and none of the reasons made sense at their deepest level. So what if none of that physical evidence held up? So what, even if the county attorney had withheld evidence from the defense attorney? So what if the local defense attorney hadn't tried very hard? If Crosby did it, and everybody knew he did—because of his low character and because of all the events leading up to that night—then he was still as guilty as ever and nothing about his sentencing should ever change.

Collin Crosby.

Furious at him all over again, Jody trudged upstairs to pack.

When she reached the second-floor landing, she stood for a moment looking up and down the long hallway with all of its rooms and doors. As if her cowboy boots were moving of their own volition, she turned left and started walking toward the small guest room at the far end. She kept its door open at all times so the sun could shine in during the day and so she could see lights coming from the room at night.

People wondered how she could live there, especially by herself.

This was my home. I want it back.

"But it's so big," people objected.

"I like big," she replied.

She was used to it: big land and sky, big animals and cowboys, big plans for being a really good teacher and meeting a nice man and raising a family right here in this house with plenty of room for them. But first she had to tame it—both this house and her fears of it.

Jody stepped into the doorway of the little guest room.

She looked at the carpet without flinching.

Her father had lain there, shot through the abdomen, blood gushing from him. She'd seen photographs. She'd read the trial transcripts. She had insisted on hearing it all, seeing it all, and learning it all, even when it meant dragging facts out of her family that believed she'd be happier not knowing, even when it meant going behind their backs to ask other people, or going on the Internet, which wasn't much help for a crime back then. It was the only way she could walk through life without always suspecting that people were keeping dark secrets from her. She didn't like feeling as if people were staring at her and knew things about her life that she didn't know, so she had set out to learn all of it, or as much as she could. She knew that her dad couldn't have survived for long after he was shot, but nobody knew if he'd been conscious or how much pain he'd felt. She prayed that he hadn't known what happened to him.

There was still so much that nobody knew, but at least she wasn't the only one in ignorance. Why was her dad in the house that night? He was supposed to be in Colorado. There were unanswered questions about him, not to mention the huge gap of knowledge about her mom. Jody suspected that she had scrambled to get all the details she could about her father's death to compensate for all she didn't know about her mother's fate.

It hadn't helped much.

What she didn't know about her mother ate at her, always.

She realized there were other important things she hadn't known, like for instance that Billy Crosby might someday return to Rose, or that it could happen this soon.

A noise outside made Judy startle and whirl around to look down the hallway.

There was nothing there, but she was good and spooked.

She felt as if she had to get out of the house where *his* vile, contaminating presence seemed more real to her now than it ever had before. She forced herself to walk down the hall, down the stairs, to the front door, and then she ran for her truck.

SHE WAS ABOUT TO turn the key in the ignition when a man's voice made her jump as if somebody had stuck a gun in her ribs.

"Hey." Red Bosch grinned at how startled she was.

Jody leaned back against the seat and inhaled deep sucking breaths, trying to get her heart going in a normal rhythm again. "My God, Red, don't sneak up on me like that. You nearly gave me a coronary."

"Sorry." He laughed again. "Where are you going?"

She tapped her fingertips on her steering wheel, resisting the question.

In the glare of midday, her lover's face showed all thirteen of the years he had on her, but she didn't mind that. It was merely evidence of hard work in the great outdoors, which she loved, too. Red just missed being good-looking, but he was appealing in a sexy, cowboy way. He wasn't educated past twelfth grade and he talked with a country drawl that would have been laughed out of the movies for being excessive. But there was a sweetness about him—always had been, people said—that seemed to stem from his own easy acceptance of himself and of everybody else. He could gab with anybody and he laughed easily. Red had never had any trouble attracting women, except for the fact that there weren't many available ones in his own county.

Jody looked at him standing beside her truck and felt glad to see him.

He was a relief from the angry intensity of her uncles.

She'd known Red all of her life. He looked like comfort to her.

They probably would never have bridged the divide of employer/ employee, however—the age thing wasn't a big deal to either of them— except for one night when she'd stopped by his house to give him a message from her grandfather. Red had handed her a cold beer and then another one, and before either of them quite knew what happened, they were staring at each other, naked in his bed, and Red was drawling, "Oh, shit, Jody, what have I done?"

"We both did it," she said. "Let's do it again."

He had laughed, and that was the start of something good for a while.

It just hadn't developed beyond that easy fun for Jody, and she was pretty sure it never would. Now she knew she had to do something about it because it looked as if it had passed that point for Red. It wouldn't be right for her to encourage him.

"Don't know where I'm going," she lied.

"What do you mean you don't know?"

Red had been asking her things like that lately, demanding to know where she was and what she'd be doing. It was beginning to sound like possessiveness or jealousy, and she hated it.

When she shrugged, he said, "You want company?"

"Don't you have to work?"

"Not if they can't find me."

"Are you forgetting they're related to me?"

"I never forget that, babe, but they don't seem to want to get anything done today."

"How do you know that?"

"I tried calling a few times."

"Red? Did you hear what just went on in my kitchen?"

"What?"

"They came to tell me that Billy Crosby has been let out of prison and he's coming back here to live."

"Yeah."

Red looked down at his boots, leaving Jody to stare at the fabric button on top of his cap. "What do you mean . . . 'yeah'?"

He met her eyes again, but with a squint, as if he found it difficult to face her all of a sudden. "I mean yeah, I know."

"You know? How do you know?"

"Everybody knows by now. And . . ." He got a look in his eyes that she had never seen there before, as if he was wary of her, or had a guilty conscience. Jody tensed, waiting for something she had a feeling she wasn't going to like. "I guess I may as well tell you. You're bound to hear it eventually." Red cleared his throat and looked away from her again. "The thing is, Jody, I kind of kept in touch with Billy."

She recoiled as if he had thrown a live snake into her lap.

"You what?" Her words were quiet, but the syllables were drawn out slowly, imparting the impression that she had a warning rattle. "In prison?"

"Yeah, in prison. There's a reason—"

He hadn't heeded the warning, and she struck.

"A *reason*? You *slept* with me, Red. In my parents' house. In their bed. We *screwed*. You work for my family. You take their money. You eat at their table. And all this time you kept in touch with the man who murdered my father and did God knows what to my mother?"

He got a confused look on his face as if he didn't know what to say, and then Red picked the wrong thing. "You shouldn't talk that way about what we do together, Jody. It means more to me than—"

"You son of a bitch!"

She threw her truck into reverse, laid her right arm up on top of the bench seat, glared behind her down the long driveway, and gunned it, spraying gravel at him so he had to raise his arms to protect his face.

Jody was so angry at Red Bosch that she drove down the Main Street of Rose faster than she should have, but not so fast that she missed spotting all three of her uncles' trucks at Bailey's Bar & Grill. "That's what you were all in such a hurry to do?" she said out loud inside her truck, feeling willing to be angry at anybody right at that moment.

At the edge of town her tires screamed around a corner and sped west toward the one place where she always felt closer to her mom than anywhere else in the world.

24

IN A CERTAIN LIGHT, the Testament Rocks turned white as bleached seashells. At those times, when Jody walked into that landscape, she felt like a black dot on a white slate, as visible as a prairie dog to a hawk, as uncomfortable as if she were naked in public. It was her least favorite light at the Rocks, because it washed out all other color, all subtlety of tone, and it was blinding. Sunglasses were not enough to make it possible to look at the rocks under such light, and so she donned a cap for its additional shade.

But being there, even like that, beat not being there on some days.

She stuck her hands down in her back jeans pockets and squinted up to the tops of the Rocks where golden eagles nested and red-tailed hawks flew by. She wouldn't have gone so far as to claim she experienced instant peace of mind just from looking at them, but it was true that her heart rate slowed down and so did her breathing.

There was wind on this day, blowing bits of white dust around her.

Dust of chalk, she thought, dust of limestone, dust of bones.

She saw no other humans. No fossil hunters. No rock climbers. No tourists with cameras, no strangers taking potshots at beer cans or teenagers making out in their cars.

She had the place to herself, the way she liked it best.

After squinting at the Rocks for a few moments, she walked back to her truck, took a swig from a water bottle, and then pulled on her work gloves. They were soft and tough and they grasped her fingers like old friends that knew her well. If my uncles knew I was coming out here, they'd have made me bring along a snake hook and a pistol, she thought. But fortunately they didn't know, and she had never seen a single snake out here anyway.

"I'll leave you alone," she said to any lurking reptiles. "And you return the favor, okay?"

Still, they were the reason she kept on her cowboy boots with their high-tops and thick leather instead of switching to shoes more suited to clambering around rocks. That was the thing about the Testament Rocks, she thought as she contemplated them—they were eighty-foot piles of contradictions, accessible yet distant, wild yet serene, safe if you were smart and lucky, but dangerous if you weren't. They'd injured a lot of stupid or clumsy climbers, killed a couple of them, and snakebites weren't unheard of, either. But they were also the backdrop for many of the county's marriage proposals and not a few conceptions of its babies. There was a legend that if a girl closed her eyes at the Rocks and made a wish for love, the first boy she saw when she opened her eyes would be her husband.

Some girls should have kept their eyes closed, Jody thought.

A hawk screamed overhead as if to underscore the sentiment.

There had been boyfriends in Jody's life, but nobody had ever proposed to her at the Rocks or anywhere else. She figured there was something about her that looked normal but that on closer inspection wasn't—the part that made her wake up screaming, kicking against the bedcovers and hitting at the air to fight off her demons. Or rather demon, singular—the one named Billy Crosby. She tended to delay the moment when she had to tell a new man after a few dates, "Oh, did I mention my dad was murdered and there's a man in prison for it, and my mom's been missing ever since I was three years old?" At first, some men were sympathetic and fascinated, and they seemed to think they'd comfort and cure her. But the wise ones—in her judgment—knew there might always be places in her they couldn't reach. They were smart enough to foresee distant and difficult times when she wasn't with them in body, mind, or soul, and that they wouldn't want to be with her at those times, either.

"You come with a lot of stuff," a man had once told her.

She had long felt as if nobody but her family could understand her "stuff," although Red probably came as close as anybody. He just held her when she had bad dreams, because he knew their source. He had them, too, as did most people who were around when Billy did his worst.

Remembering that, Jody felt even more betrayed by him.

Red *knew,* and he *still* kept contact with the man of her nightmares.

It was equally true that her "stuff" had so far kept any guy from marrying her for her family's money. Or maybe it was just a case of how intimidating her grandfather and uncles were to any male passing through her life. Grandpa Hugh was intimidating simply by being who he was. Her uncles intimidated by forming a wall of height, muscle, and distrust around her when a date showed up.

Sometimes she didn't mind that; sometimes she was grateful.

Jody started to shut the truck door again, but before she could stop herself she did something she didn't want to, following an old compulsion that she had not been able to break. She dug into the tight space behind the seats until she got her gloved fingers on familiar canvas, lifted out an old green backpack and hoisted it over her shoulders.

"Idiot," she said to herself, with only lizards as witnesses to hear it.

With the pack on her back, she hiked across the white ground to the gently slanted rear rise of the formation known as the Sphinx. She began ascending, not easy in boots, but getting traction with her gloved hands. After a bit she stopped, pausing on the golden haunches where she liked to sit and stare.

Once there, Jody checked for scorpions, brushed off the top layer of eons of dust, and plunked her butt down on the rock. As the formations eroded, "new" fossils appeared—sharks' teeth, brachiopods, and other souvenirs of ages past. But those were not the kind that she had addictively collected for years and hid in backpacks like the worn green one she set down beside her now.

Ever since she was a child, she had searched for a different kind of remnant. She was looking for human detritus, things her mom might have left behind, and she'd been looking for them since she was old enough to know that the Kansas Bureau of Investigation had searched the most exhaustively for Laurie here. It had never made much logical sense to Jody that they'd look here for so long, but then maybe it took them a while to understand how impossible it would be to dig a grave and hide it in this hard flatness where every anomaly showed up like a fox on snow. Conversely she knew, as perhaps they didn't for a time, how quickly things got covered up or uncovered, how an engagement ring could get dropped and sparkle in the sun on Tuesday, be buried in windblown dust by Wednesday, and then be found by a stranger thirty years later when it popped up to the surface again. A search for clues here could take centuries, not days or hours. Eventually the KBI had abandoned their search, but Jody didn't. She had a lifetime to wait for any bit of evidence that suggested her mom had been here at the Rocks that night or at any time. Maybe one day an SOS or Help Me would appear. Maybe she'd look down and read LL Was Here. She thought of this place as a gigantic Etch-A-Sketch: with even the slightest twist of the weather dial, everything shifted in subtle ways. The KBI and the sheriff might have given it their best effort, but the entire surface of this landscape could have altered every moment while they looked, then change again the moment they quit looking, and they wouldn't even have detected the differences. They could have missed something that wind or rain revealed at a later time.

Like an amateur archaeologist, in her secret backpacks Jody stowed bits and pieces of human lives, always hoping for the "big find" that might startle with its revelation and answer the questions that haunted her. If scientists could find a single tooth that revealed the presence here of prehistoric sharks, could she not find a telltale sign from mere years ago?

As a child, she had shown her first finds to her grandparents, to Chase and to Uncle Meryl and Aunt Belle.

"What's this?" her grandpa asked her, holding up the artifact she'd found, a hair clasp or key, something lost to memory now. The family had driven out to the Rocks with some out-of-town relatives that morning, a sightseeing trip they always took with visitors.

"It might be something Mommy dropped," she answered.

She recalled even now the look he passed to her grandmother over her head when she said that. She was six, old enough by then to know her mother was missing and that people had looked for her and that a lot of the looking had taken place at the Rocks. They got cemented in her mind when she was little as a place her mommy might have gone.

She was old enough to sense that she'd said something wrong.

She remembered Grandma Annabelle coming over to her.

"Is that why you picked it up, sweetheart?"

"What?"

"This?" Her grandmother held out the object for her to see.

"It might be Mommy's."

That was all Jody remembered of the incident. She didn't know what was said next. She just remembered getting the feeling they didn't like it that she'd picked up the thing because of her mother. It may have been the first hint she'd revealed that she didn't totally believe that her mother was as dead as her father. She was only a child, though, so she didn't give up trying to snag their interest in her discoveries. The next time she found something, she showed it to Chase.

"Not a good idea," he said, or words to that effect.

That criticism struck her to the core. It also pissed off her six-year-old self.

"It is, too," she insisted.

"The reason it's not a good idea," he instructed her, "is that hundreds of people leave stuff out there every year. All you're going to bring back is dirt and germs and other people's trash. You don't want to do that."

But oh yes, she wanted to.

With Uncle Bobby still in the Army, he never saw her fossils.

Uncle Meryl was sympathetic, but did not encourage her macabre hobby.

Aunt Belle took action, lifting her treasures out of her small hands and walking them to the trash bin near the barn. Belle dumped them there, over the rim above her niece's head, and deep, where not even a child standing on a bucket could reach them.

"No," Belle said to Jody, as if she were a puppy to train. "No!"

Yes! the child thought, and from then on kept her secret from all of them.

They started monitoring her visits to the Rocks.

She had to wait until she could go with other families, or her Girl Scout troop, and after that she had to wait until she was old enough to drive out to the Rocks on her own or with girlfriends or boys.

"What are you doing?" her friends would ask.

"Picking up the litter," she'd claim. It earned her an undeserved reputation for being an ecological good citizen. Or, she thought more likely—just a nut. Every now and then she had to stop her well-meaning friends from "helping" her. Sometimes she resorted to offering to get rid of their collections of trash for them, just so she could go through it in her room late at night down on the carpet in the space between her bed and the wall.

Jody couldn't stop looking, because she couldn't be sure.

There had been a Kansas playwright, William Inge, whom she hoped to introduce to her honors classes if she ever got to teach any. He'd written *Picnic, Bus Stop, Splendor in the Grass,* and a play called *Come Back, Little Sheba,* in which a lonely wife kept going to her back door in the vain hope that her lost dog had returned. Sometimes Jody felt as if she had to keep opening doors in case her mother might be standing there.

Partway up the Sphinx, she examined the ground, not the horizon.

That was why she missed seeing dust rising on the road from an approaching vehicle.

25

It was a beat-up old truck speeding toward the Rocks.

Soon its driver was parked and walking toward her, daylight visible through his bowed legs.

"Aren't you even goin' to ask me what my reason was?"

Red Bosch stood with his hands at his skinny hips, looking up to where Jody sat on the haunches of the Sphinx. She resisted her desire to pick up rocks and hurl them at him.

She could barely make herself look at him.

"You followed me." She made it an accusation.

"You could give me the benefit of the doubt, you know."

Jody did pick up a rock then, but only rolled it around in her hands, looking down at it instead of at Red, feeling sick at the thought of what she had done with him without knowing what he'd been doing behind her back, behind the backs of everybody in her family.

"He was too drunk, Jody."

She looked off into the distance, not at him.

"When I picked Billy up in Bailey's parking lot, he was almost unconscious drunk. There was no way he could sober up enough to get from his house to your house, not drivin' and not on foot. No way. Not within the time frame when your dad got killed, that's for sure."

"You were sixteen!" Her tone mocked his interpretation of events.

"Well, I knew what drunk was. I wasn't a sheltered kid, Jody."

She flushed. *Not like you,* he meant.

"Jody, they didn't give him a breath test."

Finally, she glanced at him, but then quickly away again.

"Did you hear me? I'm tellin' you they didn't check his blood alcohol level. Now why do you suppose that was?"

She didn't say anything but was thinking furiously, back to all the transcripts and records she had read over the years. She couldn't remember ever seeing the results of a breath test, or any testimony about one. It never occurred to her to realize one was missing.

"I'll tell you why that was," Red persisted. "It's because it would have screwed with their assumption that he did it. A blood alcohol test would have proved he couldn't have functioned anywhere near well enough to do what they said he did. Hell, Jody, he was still stumbling when they picked him up the next morning. He could barely put two words together. There is no way on God's green earth that he got off that couch, crossed three blocks in thunderin' rain, got into your parents' house, climbed the stairs—"

"Stop."

"—And then drove his truck somewhere with your—"

"Stop!"

Her right foot jerked reflexively as if she were trying to brake. It dislodged pebbles. They rolled to the ground, coming to rest near Red's boots, raising a faint clatter and tiny puffs of white dust. Red stepped forward onto one of the pebbles and ground it to powder.

"I'm sorry this makes you feel bad," he said.

"It doesn't make me feel bad," she lied. "It makes me furious."

He smiled slightly, ruefully. "I get that. But this is why I kept in contact with him. You can understand that, right? I never believed he did it. I thought Billy got a raw deal. I was young and maybe idealistic, I guess. Or maybe I'm just a dummy, but I know what I know. I'm not saying Billy wouldn't have done it, but just that he couldn't. Not that night anyway. And nobody listened to me about how drunk he was because, like you said, I was sixteen and what did I know? Especially since they all had their minds made up already. He did it, that was that, and nothing different was ever going to be considered." The look he gave her was pleading. "But he didn't do it, Jody. I'm not sayin' I like the guy. And please understand, when I say I kept contact with him, I mean like three Christmas cards and one five-minute visit over twenty-three years—"

"You went to see him in prison?"

Warily, Red drawled, "Yeah, I did. And I wasn't impressed and I never went back. It's not like he changed in prison into a saint, 'cause believe me, he didn't. I'm just sayin' it wasn't right what they did, even if they thought they were doin' it for the right reasons."

"'They' being my family?"

"They being everybody but me, I guess."

"You and Collin, apparently."

He blinked, then nodded. "Yeah."

"What do you mean he didn't change into a saint in prison?"

Red glanced behind him, back toward the dirt road leading into the Rocks. "Jody, you need to leave here now."

"Leave? Why?"

He looked back up at her. "Like I said, I went to visit him that one time. He told me if he ever got out of jail the second thing he wanted was a pork tenderloin from Bailey's. The next thing he wanted was to get laid. But the first thing Billy wants is to see this place."

"Why?"

"Because it means, like . . ." Red struggled to find what he wanted to express, and finally said, ". . . home."

Jody didn't want to understand that, but she did. Because there was nothing like them anywhere else, the Rocks meant home to most people who lived near them. When people from Rose got a glimpse of them after being away, they knew they were back. She didn't want to share that feeling with a murderer—an alcoholic, wife-beating, animal-abusing, lying, ex-convict murderer.

She dropped her face into her hands.

What if he wasn't all of those things?

"Jody?" Red stepped forward, concern on his face.

When she looked up, she was leaking tears again. "Oh, Red. Every-body I know—except you, I guess—believes he killed my parents."

"Yes, they do. I know."

"But you're telling me they're wrong. I'm wrong. We're all wrong."

"That's what I'm sayin'. I suppose you don't have to believe me."

She stared at him, knowing he was a man who'd always rather tell the truth than not. Of the two of them, she was the one who felt most comfortable with the lies they told so they could keep playing together. If he'd had his way, and even though he'd scampered like a scared weasel out of her bedroom that very day, Red might have taken his chance with the truth. She knew that was because he thought that much of her and of her family.

"Why'd you run out of my bedroom today, Red?"

"Why'd I what?" He laughed a little at her unexpected question.

"Did you run off just because of your job?"

"I left 'cause if they're goin' to find out about us, it's not goin' to be like that."

Out of consideration for her. That's what he meant.

Maybe she wasn't the more mature of the two of them after all, she thought.

She dropped her face into her hands again. "Oh, dammit, Red."

"What's the matter, babe?"

This time the wry laughter was hers. "What's wrong? Red, I don't want to have to be fair. I don't want to start believing what nobody else that I love believes." She didn't see the flinch that passed across his face at those words. "I don't want you to be right."

She sighed, every fiber in her resisting his story.

"Listen to me, Jody. One thing you have to believe right now is that you've got to get out of here."

"Why? What's he going to do to me if he shows up and I'm here?"

"That's the thing, babe. I don't know. I just know he was angry when he went into prison and he was angry that time I saw him and he's had more years since then to build up an even hotter head of steam."

Old anger burst out of her again. "As if he has any right to it!"

"Jody. That's what I'm saying. He has a right to it."

She felt emotionally exhausted, scared of what he'd told her, and confused by it.

"I've hated that man for twenty-three years, Red."

"Babe, it doesn't matter if you hate him. It only matters if he hates you."

That sent a shiver down her spine.

"He's for sure coming back today?"

"They let him go this morning."

There was increasing urgency in Red's tone.

"I suppose his son is driving him back."

"So I hear."

Red looked back toward the road. Nervously, he shuffled his boots in the white dust. It was about a five-hour drive from Lansing, where the prison was.

"Come on, Jody. I'm not leaving unless you do."

She thought about staying, on the chance of getting a look at Billy Crosby, but the only defensive weapon she had with her was her backpack. "I find it really hard to believe he'd make a special trip just to look at the scenery," she said, with an edge of sarcasm.

"Maybe not. I'm just tellin' you what he told me."

"Criminals like to return to the scenes of their crimes, though."

"Babe." He shook his head at her. "Come on."

"Go on ahead," she said, working up to her feet. "I'll follow you into town."

Appearing satisfied with that, Red turned to go, but she stopped him.

"I'm not saying I believe you."

"You believe me they didn't give him a drunk test, don't you?"

"Yes. I mean, I guess. I'll find out for sure from Uncle Meryl."

"Do that. Do you believe me when I say he couldn't have done it?"

"I don't *know* what I believe right now, Red! But I do believe that you believe that."

He let out a breath of relief at that admission from her.

She made it better by adding, "I'm sorry I didn't let you explain."

Red made a gesture that brushed away hurt feelings. "Not a problem." And then suddenly he was scrambling up the rocks to where she sat, using his bare hands and the toes of his boots to get to her.

"Wha—" she started to say, when he planted a kiss on her lips.

Then he plunged down the slope again, making her hold her breath for fear he'd break his neck. Once on the ground, he kept moving. When Red was halfway to his truck, he turned back to yell, "You're coming, right?"

"I promise!" she yelled back at him.

Jody stared at the back of his truck until it was well on the way out.

It was strange to think of Red, when he was only sixteen, being so intimately involved with what happened that night and the next day. He'd been right there in the house with Billy, and he'd been there when the sheriff showed up in the morning. It must have been a lot for a kid like him to take in, Jody thought. Maybe he had devised his theory about Billy's drinking because it was too frightening to think he'd been in the house with a murderer. Or maybe Red couldn't bear to wonder if he might have stopped Billy and prevented it all from happening. What if he hadn't picked Billy up? What if he hadn't taken him home? Could that have changed anything? And then on top of everything, he'd gone to work full-time for the family of the murdered man and missing woman.

Breath test or no, there were all sorts of reasons he could be wrong. *But what if he was right . . .*

Almost everything in her resisted the idea. And yet . . .

Come what may, I have to know what happened to my mom.

Jody stood up on the haunches of the Sphinx, shaded her eyes and looked in every direction as far as the huge rock formation would allow. Only the scenery at her back remained blocked from her view.

Why do I keep coming here for searching and solace?

With a catch in her breath, she thought, Because it is huge and solid and it changes so slowly. Unlike her own life, with its devastating, breathtaking alterations, this landscape shifted minutely over centuries, its dust sloughing off of these rocks no more dramatically than cells shed by her own skin. That made it comforting, even while it was also painful because she mysteriously felt so close to her mother here.

She sat down again, feeling a little stunned by her epiphany.

After a bit, she slid on her butt back down to the ground.

Again, she paused to look into the distance, and had another stunning thought: What if this commutation of Crosby's sentence is opportunity rather than disaster? What if it shifts all the evidence, bringing a new truth to the surface like wind moving the dirt around here at the Rocks?

After a few moments she trotted back to her truck, feeling as if something within her had both opened and focused, like a long-slumbering dinosaur waking up to turn its eyes toward dinner.

THE NEWLY ALERT FEELING lasted until she reached the edge of town.

There, Jody saw a rough, hand-lettered sign:

go back where you belong in jail!

A frisson of instinctive, unstoppable, vindictive pleasure shot through her, bullying her epiphanies out of the way and letting all the pain and fury of the past twenty-three years pour in again. The bulk of the evidence still pointed in one direction. She'd heard Red, himself, suggest that Billy Crosby was more dangerous now than when he'd gone to prison.

She sped past the sign, nodding her heartfelt agreement with it.

26

Before running inside to stuff a suitcase she didn't want to pack, Jody grabbed the green backpack she had thrown onto the seat beside her in her rush from Testament Rocks. It wasn't any heavier, because Red Bosch had distracted her from searching.

She unzipped it. A mildew smell wafted up to her nose.

Inside, she saw a woman's scarf—navy blue and yellow with a pattern of keys and locks. There was also half of a rat-tail comb—the business half—and a single clasp earring with a reddish stone in its center.

Once inside her house, she decided to throw away the broken old comb, because who could ever possibly remember if such a thing had belonged to her mother? She chose to keep the scarf and earring, though, and ran into the kitchen, where she washed off the jewelry until the fake stone glowed. She took one of her own earrings out of the hole in her ear and tried on the found earring, crying "Ow!" when her fingers slipped and allowed the clamp to pinch her lobe.

"How do women ever wear these things?"

After carefully taking it off again, she dropped it into her shirt pocket, put her own back on again, and proceeded to wash the scarf with dishwashing liquid. She rinsed it out, wrung it as dry as possible, shook it and slapped at it to get some wrinkles out, and then walked it out onto the back porch, where she laid it on top of a railing, weighted down a corner with a flowerpot, and left it to dry in the sun and the breeze. Then she raced upstairs and headed back down to the smallest guest room at the far end of the second floor. She moved fast this time, to keep the shivers at bay.

Inside the room, she opened the closet door.

There, piled in a heap, was the rest of her collection of backpacks.

It was a collection of a couple dozen packs in which she'd gathered objects from the rocks over many years. Some were crammed full, others held only a few things.

She knew it was strange, maybe even crazy.

She could only guess how it would look to anybody who happened upon it, which was why she had never shown her stash to anybody. It was why she stored them in this room—because nobody in her family ever wanted to enter here. They could barely tolerate the idea that she did. Prior to moving in, Jody had stored her treasures in various places like hollow tree trunks or old wells, often having to shift them elsewhere. But now she had what she figured was a permanent hidey-hole for backpacks and Christmas presents.

As she closed the door on them, she remembered what a poet had written about "the quivery earth," a phrase she had never forgotten. The ground in Rose had gone all quivery on her this day—dirt and rock turning without warning to gelatin that wobbled under her boots. If she lived in San Francisco on top of a fault line, she couldn't have felt any more shaky. Foundations were cracking and giving way—her trust in Billy Crosby's prison sentence, and now her belief in how much he deserved it . . .

Red had to be mistaken, that's all there was to it.

Jody shook off her doubts. There was too much evidence.

Billy had to have done it. No one else was ever suspected, and the idea of those strangers driving back to take that kind of revenge was nonsense. How would they even have known where her father lived, and why would they have done such a thing in such a storm?

"They wouldn't," she told herself decisively, and went to pack.

As she tossed underwear into a suitcase, the resentment she felt about having to go back to the ranch eased a little, and she found herself feeling glad to be going. If there was anywhere in the world that put firm ground beneath her boots, it was High Rock Ranch, where her grandparents ruled. She wanted to be with them, where her life felt solid, familiar, and reassuring.

Before she left the second floor, Jody went to the guest room a third time.

Standing in the doorway, she stared at the room where her father had died.

"We'll get him back in prison, Dad. Don't you worry."

How that could happen she did not know, although finding out what he did to her mother could do it.

At the last minute she remembered to grab the scarf from the porch.

As she lifted the flowerpot off it, she felt chilled again and looked up to see if clouds had been blocked by the sun. But no, they hadn't. The chill was another inner one. She stared all around the backyard. *There.* Her father's truck was parked there the morning Annabelle found him. *There.* Crosby's truck was supposed to be parked behind the garage, but it wasn't. Instead, it was lodged in a streambed with a bloody yellow dress inside. *There.* That path around the house led to the basement door where Annabelle and a neighbor—Samuel Carpenter, who still lived next door—had to enter because Laurie had the other doors locked, and nobody knew why she did that, either. Was it the storm that scared her? Had Billy tried to get in the house earlier?

Feeling spooked again, Jody went back inside.

She had to rummage around several kitchen drawers before she located them, but she finally found the old house keys. She put them in the same pocket that held the earring and then went around the perimeter, pressing old button locks that had not been used except when the big house stood empty. *This is silly,* she told herself, but she locked up anyway.

27

IN HER TRUCK, Jody used her cell phone to call the ranch.

Sometimes she wondered how her life might be different if her mother or father had owned cell phones. What if they could have called for help even though their land lines were dead? Now and then, when her phone rang and there was nobody there and she didn't recognize the number, she wondered if it was her mom calling. It was crazy to think that, she knew, but the flash of hope came to her anyway.

When the soft, steady voice of her grandmother answered, "High Rock Ranch. This is Annabelle Linder speaking," it had a greater calming effect on Jody than mere landscape ever could. They always answered phone calls like that at the ranch, because all of their business was conducted there alongside their personal lives. In her mind's eye Jody saw the familiar figure of her father's mother. If today was like most days in the spring and summer, Annabelle would be wearing a pair of her favored Capri pants, with a soft cotton shirt worn loose over them—to hide the tummy that only she could see—and sandals. She only put on cowboy boots these days when she donned blue jeans for riding her horse. Her hair, a beautiful silver—which it had turned after her son's murder—was always cut very short so she didn't have to think about it.

"Hi, Grandma." She dropped her voice to a gentle tone. "Are you and Grandpa okay?"

"We will be as soon as we see you coming up the road."

Her grandmother wasn't given to laying guilt trips on people—that was the job of her sons—so Jody took her statement at face value as a simple statement of truth. She also took it as an example and held back her urge to lay a guilt trip on her grandparents for not taking her with them to see the governor. It was done. This was awful for them; she would not make it worse.

"I'm just leaving. Do you need me to pick up anything for you?"

"Child, I do. I have enough milk to mash the potatoes, but not enough for gravy."

"Oh, no, not that!" Jody teased. "Uncle Bobby can't live without gravy."

"I think his veins run with it." Even under these circumstances, there was humor in her grandmother's reply. "That can't be good, can it?"

Jody thought that if a person didn't know her grandmother well, they'd never suspect from her voice on the telephone that anything was troubling her. It was only in person, where you could see her expressive face, that a stranger might get a glimpse of pain or trouble.

Jody said, "One day science will discover that your gravy cures cancer."

"In that case, I'd better take out a patent on it." There was a smile in the warm voice. "Pick up two half gallons, please?"

Her granddaughter knew without asking to get two-percent milk. "I'll do it."

"How are *you*, dearest?"

Jody's throat closed on tears for a moment and she waited until she could talk. "Let's see." She cleared her throat. "I'm stunned. Confused. Sad. Pissed off. That about covers it, I think."

"Yes," Annabelle said gently. "That would about cover it."

"I'll be out as soon as I can get there, Grandma."

"If you run into your uncles, tell them to be on time for supper unless they want cold fried chicken."

The words "fried chicken" made Jody's stomach rumble with hunger.

"I'm pretty sure I can smell it from here."

"Well, then, I'd better check to make sure it's not burning."

"Chase and Bobby aren't there yet?" They'd been in such a hurry to get *her* out to the ranch. "Where are they?"

But her grandmother had already murmured a soft goodbye and hung up.

JODY FELT ON high alert during her short trip to Main Street where George's Grocery was still located. As she spotted people she knew and waved to the ones who noticed her, she wondered if she was only imagining that they, too, looked wary. Was everybody as nervous about seeing Billy Crosby as she was? Many of them had known him a long time ago, and they probably wondered what in the world they would say to him or he would say to them.

A couple of them had served on his jury.

She wouldn't have wanted to be in their shoes today, either.

Jody walked into a grocery store that was far different from the bustling enterprise it had seemed in her childhood, when it was called George's Fresh Food & Deli. With a falling population in the county, Byron George had been forced to cut back in every way, including closing a quarter of his floor space. There wasn't any deli now; if you wanted a ham sandwich, you bought the bread and made your own at home. Everything about his store seemed smaller to Jody, and she knew that wasn't just because she was bigger. The ironic exceptions were the products that kept arriving in ever larger containers containing ever less inside.

At least a half gallon of milk was still a half gallon of milk.

She walked into a store kept dim to save on the lighting bill.

Just inside, Jody halted, because she heard raised, heated voices.

She looked to her right and saw Byron surrounded by three of his customers who had him backed against a soft drink refrigerator. Taller than all of them, he looked red-faced and frustrated above his butcher's apron.

Even from the rear, Jody recognized her grandmother's friend Phyllis Boren and also one of the men, her own next-door neighbor, Samuel Carpenter. It might have seemed a coincidence, since she had just been thinking about him only minutes earlier, but it was hardly ever a coincidence to run into somebody she knew in Rose. There just weren't that many people, and they basically all had the same errands to run. The other man wasn't anybody she knew, which likely made him somebody from one of the neighboring towns that had lost its own grocery store and whose citizens were forced to use a lot of gas to pick up bread and milk. All three of them were in their seventies, at least, but that wasn't weakening their voices or tamping down their anger.

"You can't possibly believe what you're saying, Byron!"

As Phyllis Boren yelled at Byron George, Jody decided the wisest thing to do was slip down the bread aisle to avoid them. Everybody knew Phyllis was argumentative, and Byron wasn't any shrinking violet himself. Sam Carpenter was a tenderhearted sweetie who'd brought Jody housewarming flowers and tomato plants, and she had a soft spot for him because of how much he always cared about what happened to the Linders. He was as thoughtful a neighbor as anyone could wish for, but even Sam Carpenter looked as if he'd like to kill somebody.

Then she heard Byron say, "I *do* believe he didn't do it, Mrs. Boren."

"That's just sex talking," Phyllis shot back, shocking Jody into standing still as her grandmother's very proper friend said with a nasty tone, "You and that wife of his."

"That's insulting," Byron retorted, looking ready to strangle one of his oldest and best customers. "Don't you talk to me like that and don't you be talking about Valentine like that!"

Jody flinched at the name. She looked around for its owner.

A lot had changed for Valentine Crosby, too, in the years since she'd been left at home with a child and a part-time job. She had hung onto one of the few steady jobs in Rose and done it the old-fashioned way. Byron had once told her Aunt Belle, "It's real hard to fire somebody who works as hard as three people and never misses a day of work." His wife, Livia, had passed away of a brain aneurysm five years ago, and he'd moved Valentine up to manager. The talk around town the last year or so was that he'd have married her if she didn't insist on staying married to Billy.

Jody didn't see Valentine in the store.

At her grandmother's insistence, she had never been anything but polite to Mrs. Crosby, who had without exception returned the courtesy. But now her feelings toward the woman who was welcoming Billy Crosby home were not so friendly.

The other man—the one Jody didn't know—stuck his own opinion into the fray: "If you'd of married her by now, he'd never have come back here."

"Oh, now you want us to get married?" Byron's words were sarcastic. It made Jody remember how offended a lot of people were when it became obvious that he and his manager were keeping company outside the store.

At the ranch, nobody had felt that way, or if they did, hadn't said so. "They're probably the two loneliest people in Rose," Annabelle had remarked at the time, "and this may be a good thing for both of them."

But now the gossip worm had turned, Jody observed, as Byron said, "Well, Val believes she needs to stay with him to show she believes he didn't do it, which she does and which he didn't!"

Jody's neighbor, Samuel, said with a deep sarcasm that shocked her, because it was so bitterly different from his usual manner, "Oh, well, yes, let's make sure he looks good, the murdering bastard."

"I swear to you he didn't do it," Byron insisted to them.

"No!" Samuel got up in his face, his own kind features twisted with anger. "He's telling *Val* he didn't do it, and she's telling *you* that, and you're an old fool to believe it. Don't you tell me he didn't do it, Byron George. You didn't see what I saw that day. You didn't hear Annabelle Linder scream over the body of her dead son. You didn't have to go fetch her poor family. Don't you stand there and try to tell me Billy Crosby's innocent!"

Jody brought her hands to her face and stood frozen.

Oh, God, she thought, silently pleading with them to stop.

"I never said he's innocent!" Byron shouted. "I'm saying he's not guilty!"

"Oh good grief," Phyllis Boren said in disgust. "Are we talking about the same Billy Crosby? The one who used to get drunk and hit his wife? That's the Billy I knew, and I'm betting he's exactly the same person he always was, and now you're glad he's coming back here. If you loved Valentine like you supposedly do, you ought to be horrified that he's coming back to live with her!"

"I didn't say I'll be happy to see him! I said he's not guilty!"

"And who told you that?" Phyllis challenged him. "His wife and his son? Of course they think he didn't do it. But where's your evidence, Byron?"

"It'll all come out someday, Phyllis."

She made a disgusted noise.

"Not guilty?" Samuel launched in again. "On which planet? That man murdered that wonderful young man and his wife and it couldn't be any plainer unless he confessed—"

"Which he's never going to do," Phyllis interjected.

"Because," the third man said, "that would mean taking mercy on their family and especially on their daughter, who's never going to know for sure—"

He stopped when Phyllis, who had just spotted Jody, tugged on his shirtsleeve. "What?" he asked her, sounding annoyed at being cut off in mid-tirade. "Who's that?"

Phyllis's whisper could have been heard in the back of the store. *"That's Jody Linder!"*

Far from stopping out of consideration for Jody, he now pointed at her: "*That* young woman. What do you think all this is going to do to her, Byron George? You want to look her in the eye and tell her how you believe Billy Crosby didn't do it? Go on, I dare you. Walk up to her and tell her how—"

Jody didn't wait for more. She hurried toward the back.

She was used to being recognized or pointed out by people she didn't know, because of her family's infamous history, but she'd never gotten over finding it an appalling experience. She might not have minded being recognized for some worthy accomplishment of her own, but she minded very much being "famous" because her father had been murdered and her mother might have been. When she was thirteen, a couple of tourists asked for her autograph, which shocked her so badly she had thrown their pen back at them before running away. Behind her, she'd heard one of them call her a rude little brat.

When she was out of sight, she clutched the side of a table holding apples and bananas and waited to see if the four people would keep yelling at each other. Her heart was pounding even harder than when her uncles broke the news to her and she felt like crying again.

All she wanted at that moment was to be invisible.

The yelling stopped, but then she felt an arm come around her shoulders. She looked up into the lined face of Phyllis Boren, who laid the side of her head against Jody's and whispered, "I'm so sorry."

Jody nodded, and didn't know what to say to her.

Phyllis took hold of her left hand and squeezed it. "Please give your grandparents my best wishes."

"I will." Then she made herself ask what she didn't want to ask. "Phyllis? Are there many people who think Billy didn't kill my dad?"

Her grandmother's friend—who could be counted on to tell the truth as reliably as she could be counted on to be tactless—said, "There are a few. Always have been. They're the ones who think he was railroaded and that he wouldn't be in prison if your family hadn't forced it."

"People blame my *family*?"

"Not many, just a stubborn few. Probably jealous of you. And then there are people like Bailey who don't think Billy did it, but they don't mind if he got sent to jail anyway."

Jody frowned at the idea of the tavern owner's betrayal. "*Bailey* thinks he didn't do it?"

Phyllis sniffed. "Nobody ever accused Bailey of being a genius."

She finally moved away, leaving Jody alone. Blindly, Jody picked up an apple as if she was considering buying it. Then, feeling hideously self-conscious, she made her way to the dairy section and got the two half gallons of milk for her grandmother. Their handles felt cool and damp in her hands as she walked back to the front again with every intention of purchasing them. But when she saw Byron George at one of the checkout counters, she felt swept by outrage at his defense of Crosby. It was different for Red Bosch to feel as he did—he'd been there that night, he'd actually seen Billy, and even if Red's perceptions were wrong, at least they were drawn from firsthand experience. Not so Byron. All he was doing was taking the word of people who could be expected to defend their husband and father. In all the years that her family had bought groceries here, they'd never suspected the worm in all the apples they'd bought from Byron.

Jody took the milk to the checkout counter.

"Hi, Byron," she said to the red-faced man who stood behind one of them. She put the sloshy containers down on the conveyer belt. It was hard to keep antagonism out of her voice, so she grabbed the first superficial topic she could think of, even if it must have sounded like a non sequitur to Byron. "My grandma's making gravy tonight."

He looked apologetic as he said, "I hear your grandmother makes the best gravy in five counties."

"And my mom made the best piecrust."

She looked him in the eyes.

Byron's face flushed even redder. "I can't claim I ever had any of it. But that's certainly what I always heard."

Jody didn't say out loud her contemptuous thought as she took her change from him. *You believe things you don't know anything about, don't you, Byron? You believe what anybody tells you?*

"Where's Valentine today?" she asked him.

He looked both sad and embarrassed as he said, "She stayed home." He busied himself with packing the milk into plastic bags. "To get ready."

Jody swallowed. "Is he in town yet?"

"I don't know, Jody. I'm keeping my distance."

"Probably a good idea for all of us," she replied, and realized she sounded like a self-righteous version of her grandmother.

"I hope you weren't offended by—"

"Not at all," she lied, with a bright smile.

But then she heard her grandmother's voice in her head.

If you don't get down off that high horse, you're going to have a very long way to fall, young lady.

Jody's false smile wavered. A smaller, truer one took its place. Byron couldn't help it, she realized. He was in love, and sometimes love wasn't only blind, it was also stupid. Maybe that wasn't a kind thought, but it was the best she could do at the moment.

"'Bye, Byron," she said quietly.

"'Bye, Jody. Thanks for coming in."

When she got back into her truck, she pointed it in the opposite direction of the ranch.

28

WHEN SHE WALKED into Bailey's Bar & Grill, the scent of beer and fried food was overwhelming, as it always was. Sometimes she thought she'd go to her grave with the scent of Bailey's cheeseburgers still clinging to her hair and clothes. After every meal she'd ever eaten there, she went home and scrubbed, even if she had loved every fatty bite. Before Bailey outlawed smoking—because he wanted to quit—it had been even harder to wash out the stink.

The place was even dimmer than the grocery had been.

A few early diners had their suppers in front of them, and a couple of them raised their hands to her in greeting. Bailey had installed a pool table years ago, and now it was bracketed by men with pool cues in one hand and bottles of beer in the other.

Bailey himself, standing in front of a neon sign behind his bar, looked up and gave her a nod. He was wearing one of his Denver Broncos T-shirts, she saw. On game days between the Broncos and the

Kansas City Chiefs, Bailey's tavern could get rowdy. As usual, he had his beloved country-western music playing too loud, because as Bailey got older and deafer, he kept turning the music up, until enough of his customers complained about it. People wondered what the magic number was to get him to turn it down—three customers? ten?—and joked about running an organized test on that someday.

Jody went over and hoisted herself up onto one of the chrome and red vinyl bar stools.

"Rascal Flatts?" she asked, not recognizing the song.

"Yeah. My boys. Want a beer while you wait?"

"I'm waiting for something?"

"Aren't you? Friends? Your family?"

"No, I came to see you, Bailey."

He quirked a bushy eyebrow.

Over the years, Bailey had become a man of fewer and fewer words. He poured your drinks, cooked your steaks, took your credit card, and tossed you out on your ear if you broke his house rules, which consisted of: don't upset me, my waitresses, or my other customers. Most people knew he was sick of running his tavern; he wanted to move to Florida, but for years now his business had dropped off so drastically that he was lucky to pay his bills on time, with nothing left to save for retirement.

Jody reached for a handful of peanuts, shelled one of them and ate it.

She raised her voice to be sure he heard her.

"I hear you don't think Billy Crosby killed my dad."

She could be very direct herself, as encouraged by her family. As Chase liked to say, "Life is short. If you have something to say, either spit it out or forget about it." It had been hard for her to ask Phyllis Boren in the grocery store about opinions that conflicted with her family's, and hard to face a man who held such opinions, and her heart was still pounding too fast, but the questions she had to ask were coming easier now.

Bailey didn't look fazed by her blunt question. He gave her a long look and then confirmed it. "No. I don't think Billy did it."

"Why not?"

He put down the shot glass he'd been wiping dry. "Too drunk."

"That's what Red Bosch says, too."

"Red's right."

"Then how come he got convicted and sent to prison, Bailey?"

He shrugged.

"No, really." She dumped the rest of the peanuts back into their bowl and brushed her hands together to get the shell dust off. "If he didn't do it, how could he end up in prison for it?"

This time Bailey gave her a look that made her feel as if she was the stupid one in Rose. It was a look that said, *What? You think that never happens in this country?*

"I've read the trial transcripts, Bailey. You didn't testify."

"I told the cops what I saw. They never called me back."

Jody started to say something, but Bailey wasn't finished.

"Didn't matter to me," he said, "Billy needed to go to jail and stay there. He was bound to do something similar someday."

"Bailey," Jody said to him, "the system's not supposed to work like that."

He shrugged again. "It wasn't supposed to let him out this soon, either."

"He might say twenty-three years isn't soon."

"And I say it's not long enough."

Jody, feeling a little shell-shocked by all the opinions she was hearing for the first time from people she thought she knew, said, "May I have that beer now, please?"

"Are you going to eat something with it?"

"No, I'm due out at the ranch for supper."

"Soon?"

"Yeah, why?"

"You can't have a beer."

She gave him a look that said, *Why not?*

"Because you're too little to absorb the alcohol that quick, and your grandpa would kill me if I let you drive out of here tipsy."

"Oh, for God's sake, Bailey."

She whirled around on the bar stool, hopped down and stalked out, even though she knew he was right.

JUST OUTSIDE the tavern's front door her cell phone rang.

When she saw who was calling, she punched Talk and said, "I'm on my way, Uncle Chase."

"What's taking so long?"

"I had to pick up some milk for Grandma."

"Did you go clear to Topeka to get it?"

People were coming up the walk toward her, so she stepped to one side and turned her back. "No, I didn't go to Topeka," she said with exaggerated patience. "It just took a little longer than usual, that's all."

She felt her left arm being squeezed and turned in that direction to see who had done it. It was the mother of a girl she'd gone to school with. The woman smiled sympathetically at her and then went on inside with her husband. Jody turned back toward the shrubbery.

"What? I didn't hear what you just said, Uncle Chase."

"I said, why did it take longer than usual?"

Jody heard a man say loudly, "If I want a goddamn pork tenderloin for supper, that's what I'm going to have." She was turning to look to see who was saying that so unpleasantly when the same raspy voice said, "I've waited twenty-three goddamn years for one of Bailey's pork tenderloin sandwiches. You can goddamn wait one more night to cook your damned spaghetti."

In one chaotic moment Jody heard her uncle call her name over the phone, dropped the cell phone onto the cement walkway, and realized she was looking straight at Billy Crosby, who was coming up toward Bailey's with Valentine and a tall good-looking man who could only be their son Collin.

"Dad," the younger man said, "we're here, aren't we?"

Jody bent to pick up her phone and saw that she had cracked its case. She opened it with fumbling fingers and said, "Uncle Chase, I've got to go. Don't worry about me. I'll be there in twenty minutes." She clicked the phone shut before finding out if it was even still working.

She didn't know what to do next.

They were coming closer.

He looked about five foot ten and muscular, as if there'd been a weight room at the prison and he had used it often. His hairline was receding at his temples but his hair was still dark with no visible gray. It was a shock to see he looked no older than her uncles. She realized that in the last few years she'd started picturing Billy Crosby as an old man, worn-down and neutered by prison. This man coming toward her was nothing like that; he looked full of hunger, anger, and testosterone. She'd heard he was considered good-looking by some women, and she supposed the same kind of woman would think that now, too, but all she saw was a top-heavy man with big shoulders and biceps and a pinched, aggressive expression on his face. He had on sneakers, blue jeans, and a black T-shirt, and it all looked new.

Collin looked up and saw her standing there.

He put a restraining hand on his father's arm, but Billy shook it off.

Collin was taller than his dad, Jody saw, a bigger man altogether, and he didn't look overjoyed to have his father home from prison. Jody barely noticed Valentine.

She had eyes only for the father and the son.

"What the hell is she looking at?" Billy said, nodding toward Jody as they came closer still. "People think I'm some kind of fucking tourist attraction? Like them rocks you wouldn't take me out to see!" He put on a falsetto, like a crazily enthusiastic girl, and waved his hands in the air: "Fly your freak flag, Billy!" Then he raised an eyebrow and smirked in Jody's direction. "I see the girls have gotten better lookin' since I was here. You know that girl, Collin? She's lookin' at you."

"Shut up, Dad. For God's sake, shut up."

Such a powerful surge of reaction went through Jody that she thought if she'd had a gun she would have used it. Every bit of information she'd heard that day that purported to exonerate this man fled from her brain and her heart. All she could remember at this moment was how he had haunted her nightmares, how she had grown up hating him, how one violent night had devastated her family, and how terribly much she missed and longed for her parents. Her next impulse was to turn and run. *No,* she thought, and stood her ground until the trio were only a few feet away from her. She stepped to her right then so that she was in the center of the sidewalk, blocking their path into the tavern. Any warnings she'd heard that day, any fear she'd previously felt, vanished as if they had never happened. He wasn't getting by her without acknowledging her. *He wasn't.*

"You the bouncer?" he joked, right in front of her.

"Jody," Collin said, and then, "I'm sorry."

"No, I'm not the bouncer," she said, looking straight into eyes that hurt her to see. "I'm Hugh-Jay and Laurie's daughter. I'm Jody Linder." She raised her eyes to look at Collin. "Why did you do this? Why?" she asked him.

"You're a Linder?" his father said, stepping even closer.

"Dad, you touch her and I'll kill you myself."

"I'm not gonna touch her."

"I'm not 'a' Linder," she said to him. "I'm 'the' Linder. I'm the kid you left without any parents."

"I didn't do nothin' to either of your parents."

She wanted to beat on him and scream at him, *What did you do with my mother?* Instead, she stared as he looked threateningly at her.

"You tell your wicked old grandfather that I don't forgive. Him and those sons of his put me in prison for things I never did, just 'cause they could. You tell them Billy Crosby ain't never going to forgive or forget."

Jody looked from him to his son as coolly as she had it in her to do.

"I'm never going to forgive or forget, either," she said, staring straight at Billy Crosby's son.

Praying she wouldn't trip, praying her legs still worked and would carry her, Jody slowly turned and walked at a steady pace to her truck. From inside of it, she watched the three of them go into the tavern. For a moment Collin hung back, looking at her, and then he followed his parents inside. She thought bitterly that Bailey would probably be happy to serve them pork tenderloin sandwiches for dinner. Since business was so bad, even murderers were welcome if they brought cash.

Her hands shook on the steering wheel all the way to the ranch, and her foot trembled on the gas pedal as if she had palsy. It got so bad that she stalled out the truck a couple of times and had to roll to the shoulder to start it up again. As she finally neared the ranch's front gate, she drove past the two-bedroom house where Red Bosch lived free, one of the perks of working full-time for her grandfather, and also one of the disadvantages. To hide her visits, they resorted to putting her truck in the garage and closing the door on it. Jody saw that the garage door was open to let his dog in, as it always was if she wasn't there. She thought about stopping to tell him about Crosby—and how right Red had been about the Rocks and the pork tenderloin at Bailey's—but she decided not to delay seeing her family.

Inside the gate, just after she turned in, she opened her truck door, leaned over and threw up in the grass.

29

THE HENDERSON COUNTY sheriff's SUV was parked in front of the house when Jody drove up. She took a quick swig of water from the bottle in her truck—water that was tepid now—swished it around her mouth and spat it out. Then she popped in a couple of breath mints, and hurried to the kitchen door with the milk in both hands. Once inside the kitchen, she put one half gallon into the refrigerator, then went up to her grandmother—who stood at the stove turning over pieces of chicken with a long fork—kissed her on the cheek and set down the other half gallon on a countertop near her. She still wanted to say, Why didn't you let me go with you to see the governor? Instead, she held back again.

Forcing herself to sound normal, she said, "Am I in time for the gravy?"

"Just right." Her grandmother gave her a tired smile. "Go listen to what the sheriff is saying and come back and tell me."

"Would you rather that I stir and you go?"

Annabelle shook her head. "No. I might say something I'll regret."

"You? To the sheriff? Why?"

"Just go on."

Obediently, Jody followed the sound of a male voice coming from the direction of the living room. She passed through the dining room, where plates, napkins, and silverware were stacked, waiting to be placed around the big oak table with its man-sized upholstered chairs. Surprised to find that it wasn't set yet—with her grandmother so far along toward finishing supper—Jody surmised that the sheriff's visit was unexpected and interrupted the routine.

When she walked into the living room, she saw Sheriff Don Phelps standing beside the oak coffee table in front of the couch that her grandmother had recently redone in yellow silk to match the elegant floral print of her armchairs. It was a beautiful, feminine room, a contrast to the more traditional western appearance of the family room, her grandfather's office, and the study that the men used more often, and where the decor ran more toward brown leather and dark wood.

Everyone was standing, like the sheriff, leading her to think he had only just arrived. She slid in beside her aunt Belle, who stood in front of the wall just inside the room. Jody crossed her hands behind her, swallowed the bit of mint left in her mouth, and leaned back until her palms touched the wall. She felt shaky and upset from her encounter with Billy Crosby, and it was hard to concentrate on what was going on in front of her. Her mind kept jumping back to him—what he'd said, what she'd said to him, how vicious he had sounded, how crude and intimidating and aggressive he was. Clearly, he was not a convict whom prison had softened into remorse, or rehabilitated. She was proud of herself for standing up to him, though she doubted she had disturbed him in the least. He'd laughed at her, made fun of her, threatened her family and showed no feeling at all for what he'd done to her. And his son! Collin Crosby was almost worse—purposely throwing his psycho father back into the path of innocent people, like tossing a hand grenade down the main street of Rose.

An involuntary shudder went through her.

"Where have you been?" her aunt whispered.

Jody turned her shudder into a shrug. "Where's Meryl?"

"Coming. Shh."

"—talked to Billy," the sheriff was saying.

Hearing that name, Jody stood up straight and paid more attention.

Phelps was in his sixties now, paunchy, and gray-haired under the brown felt cowboy hat he had taken off and was revolving in his beefy hands. His name and fame had been made locally by his quick arrest and conviction of Billy Crosby. Since then, only rarely had another man—and never a woman—campaigned against him for the office of sheriff of Henderson County. Jody knew him only because he liked to stop teenage drivers and check for drugs or alcohol, and she had been in a few cars that he pulled over when she was younger.

"Your parents will thank me," he was famous for saying.

Now she listened as he informed his small audience, "I stopped by their house just before I came out here. I warned him that if anything bad happens to any member of this family, anything at all, I'm coming after him. I told him if Hugh-Jay's girl gets so much as a flat tire, I'm going to check the nail to see if it's his. If Mrs. Linder stubs her toe, I'm going to assume Billy tripped her. And the same holds true for the judge who tried him, the members of that jury, the county attorney, his own lawyer, and every one of my deputies who worked the case at that time. I told him he is under suspicion for every bad thing that happens in my county from now until he leaves again, and he'd just better live and conduct himself in a manner that befits that."

He sounded forceful and looked proud of himself.

Jody expected to see the men in her family nodding their appreciation.

Instead, they were staring at him with less than friendly expressions on their faces.

"You should have run an honest investigation, Don," Chase said, launching an attack with no preamble.

Jody gasped imperceptibly and touched her aunt's arm.

Belle glanced at her, but Jody noticed that neither Belle, nor her grandfather, nor her uncle Bobby appeared surprised or offended by Chase's bald accusation. Instead, they just kept steadily staring at Phelps, whose face had taken on a reddish hue.

They've discussed this, she thought, whatever it is.

Jody also had the thought that the sheriff didn't know what he was walking into when he'd shown up at their front door. She'd seen it before in her lifetime, when her family came to a unified decision and joined forces. Most of the time it was for ordinary reasons—whether to tear down an old barn and build a new one, or alter the composition of their cattle feed with the goal of boosting calf weights. Often it was directed toward civic beneficence—funding a senior trip, electing a judge. But sometimes it was directed at a common enemy—a breeder who lied to them, a buyer who shorted them. In those cases, Jody didn't envy anyone who stood in the path of her family's will and decision. She just didn't know, this time, what that decision was, or why they'd come to it. Maybe that's why they'd been after her to arrive sooner, she realized—so she could be part of it. Out in the kitchen, her grandmother obviously was involved, to judge by what she'd said to her.

"Well, now, that's one hell of a thing to say, Chase." The sheriff had gone rigid, and now spoke in a tone as cold as the looks he was getting from the people around him. "You're going to have to explain to me just what the hell you mean by that."

"It's not hard to figure out, is it?" Chase said with a wry hard tone. "You chose not to investigate things you should have investigated and question people you should have questioned. You withheld evidence that should have gone to the defense."

Jody was shocked. She had never, *never* heard Phelps criticized in this house before now. If anything, he'd been put on a pedestal. Linders contributed to his reelection campaigns, as much as the law allowed. They sported his motto, "Reelect the Law," on their truck bumpers, and her grandfather still had one of those stickers on his Cadillac.

"Evidence that should have gone to the defense?" Phelps repeated, with barely contained anger under his drawl. "Why would you want it to, Chase?" It seemed to be an admission that he'd done it, but that he wasn't backing down from considering it the right thing to do.

For the first time, Jody's grandfather spoke up, in a somewhat milder tone than his son, a tone that suggested he was speaking more in sorrow than in anger. "So we wouldn't end up like this, Don, with a guilty man getting out of prison."

The sheriff looked around the room at all of them before returning his attention to the patriarch. "Is that what you think, Hugh? You're going to stand there and accuse me of being dishonest like your son just did?"

"What else would you call it?" Chase challenged him.

Hugh Senior said, in the same regretful tone, "There wasn't any need to withhold that evidence, Don, and if I'd known you had it, I would have told you to show it. You had a strong enough case without hiding anything. You could have withstood the silly business about the hat. You could have easily dismissed any suspicions about those strangers that Hugh-Jay supposedly saw that day."

"I don't appreciate this," Phelps said, looking cornered and as ready to attack as they were. "We did the best we could, and we did it as honest as we could. We were young and green. Call it incompetence if you want to, but don't you call it dishonest. Don't you do that. You think we had any experience investigating a major crime? We had zero. We didn't know what the hell we were doing, and we still managed to hand the county attorney a damned good case."

"Doesn't look so good now," Belle said in a harsh voice.

"Seems to me I remember getting a lot of pressure from this family to arrest Billy Crosby!" the sheriff shot back at her. "It didn't used to be 'you' when you talked about it, it used to be 'we.' My department and the prosecutor's office and this family, we were in it together, remember? Helping each other put the son of a bitch away. I don't recall you folks wanting to help the defense back then," he said with deep sarcasm.

"What they 'wanted,'" Meryl Tapper said as he strode into the room and took a stance in the middle of it, "was a clean case that couldn't be commuted as this one just was. That's what they 'wanted,' Don. Now, because we didn't get that, they have to live with the killer of their son and daughter-in-law ten miles down the road. Now their granddaughter has to move out of her parents' home so she isn't living three blocks from Billy Crosby."

Meryl still wore the reddish polyester trousers, the plaid jacket, and the bolo tie that made Jody roll her eyes whenever she saw them, but any pretense of country bumpkin lawyer was gone.

"You shouldn't talk to me like this." The sheriff put his cowboy hat back on, shoving it down on his head, and then looked straight at Hugh Senior. "This isn't right. I never thought I'd hear this kind of thing from this family, and especially from you, Hugh. I thought as highly of your son as anybody else did in this county. I was just as upset as everybody else was. My wife cried about it. I worked my butt off to bring his killer to justice and make it stick."

He started to walk out, brushing against Meryl, who didn't budge.

Then he turned and said, "When I told Billy that if anything happened to any of you he'd be in trouble, you want to know what he said to me?" The sheriff paused and looked each of them in the face. "He said he didn't give a damn. He said that if somebody killed another Linder, that was one crime he'd be happy to go to jail for this time, whether he did it or not."

He let that sink in and then he shifted his weight and jutted his chin as if daring them to swing at it.

"But hey, if you're all fired up to help the defense, I think I can be of some assistance, folks."

Jody sensed a tightening of the tension among her family.

"You know that hair evidence that got thrown out?" the sheriff asked with a sly and aggressive look in his eyes. "Well, Billy's boy came to me wanting some of those strands for DNA tests, 'cause we can do that stuff now where we couldn't back then. I told him there wasn't any left, that it was all destroyed in the earlier testing. But you know what? I think I might be able to come up with a few little hairs that got stuck back in an evidence box. You just never know what we might manage to find back there—since you're all so eager to help him out."

With that last volley, the sheriff slammed out the front door.

Within moments they heard his SUV spin gravel as he drove away.

"Why does he think a DNA test will help Billy?" Belle asked in a complaining tone. "It's only going to prove once and for all that he did it. That doesn't make any sense."

"He's just trying to shake us up," Chase said, with a contemptuous downturn of his mouth, "because we pissed him off. We should have run somebody against him years ago."

"Hell, I should have run against him years ago," Bobby chimed in. "I couldn't have been any worse at the job than he is."

"Well, start thinking who we can put up for the job," their father commanded, leaving Jody more astonished than ever. All her life she'd heard there was no finer lawman than Don Phelps, and now he was the enemy? Her grandfather was a self-pronounced lover of justice, and it was certainly true that she hadn't been old enough to know what was going on at the time, but something about this whole situation with the sheriff didn't sit right with her.

Maybe it would all come clear. It had to, she hoped.

"This outcome was unnecessary," her grandfather was saying. "Billy would have been convicted without the shenanigans. There's no excuse for it. Don can say what he wants to about how they didn't know what they were doing, but inexperience or incompetence is no excuse for a lack of basic principles. It's dishonest to circumvent the law like that, and look where it's got us now."

When he saw Jody, his intimidating formality melted and he smiled at her. "Hello, Granddaughter."

After a moment's hesitation, she ran over to get enveloped in a hug and then stayed close to him.

"Dad," Belle said, sounding worried. "I think we just alienated our best protection."

Meryl snorted. "The sheriff's department is no protection for any-body, honey. Too few of them and they're too far away to do us any good. We're our own best protection. Always have been, always will be. That's why we have guns." He looked at his father-in-law. "I prom-ise you this, sir. I'm an older, wiser lawyer now. Billy will screw up, we'll get him again, and next time it will stick."

His mother-in-law appeared in the doorway.

"Who's setting the table for me?"

It made Jody feel anxious to think about what Billy's "next time" might be, but none of the rest of them seemed to be worrying about that as she followed them in to supper.

30

As Jody Trailed her aunt around the table, laying dinner plates down between the silverware that Belle distributed, she said cautiously, "That was kind of rough in there."

Belle retorted, "This whole situation is rough, don't you think?"

"I know, but—"

"What in the world have you got on your head?"

Jody reached up a hand and touched the "found" scarf, which she had forgotten she was wearing, having tied it on after she left her own home. "Just a scarf."

"You must have found it in a trash bin."

"It's clean, Aunt Belle."

Her aunt shook her head at her niece's fashion sense.

This was how Jody played what she thought of as her obsessive little game without anybody knowing what she was up to. She was waiting for the time when somebody in her family might blurt out, "Your mother had a scarf just like that!"

"Did my mom wear scarves?" she asked.

Her grandmother entered the room just then, followed by Bobby carrying a huge bowl of mashed potatoes and Meryl balancing fried chicken on platters in both hands. Hugh Senior was pulling out his chair at one end of the table, and Chase was in the kitchen fetching the gravy, green beans, and biscuits. The butter, jam, and a bowl of Waldorf salad were already on the table. Belle and Jody were setting the table with the "good stuff," as Hugh Senior liked to call it. Apart from Thanksgiving and Christmas and other events of note, Annabelle only went formal at her dining table when she thought it might increase the likelihood of keeping her family on their best behavior. "There's nothing like white linen napkins to keep a man in check," she liked to advise her granddaughter.

Belle asked her mother, "Did Laurie wear scarves, Mom?"

"Not that I recall, no."

"What about earrings?" Jody asked them. "Her ears were pierced, right? Did she ever wear those clip-on things?"

"Oh, God no," Belle said, and laughed. "She wouldn't have been caught dead—"

She bit her lip.

"Nice," Chase said sarcastically, hearing her as he came in.

"Oh, Aunt Belle, don't listen to him. You didn't say anything wrong."

"Everybody's hypersensitive right now," Meryl said, with a glance at his wife.

"We'll all feel better after we eat," Annabelle remarked. She looked around her table, checking things. "Which I believe we're finally ready to do. We'll begin with a prayer tonight, Hugh."

THE TABLE SEEMED both fuller and emptier than usual to Jody that night—fuller with the additions of Chase and Bobby from out of town, but emptier because they'd arrived without any of their kids. Neither was married at the moment, so the table seemed short of wives, too. When Jody was young, she'd loved sitting at the "children's table"—two card tables jammed together with a spill-proof plastic cover thrown over them—with her cousins.

At Annabelle's command, any further talk about the day's events was delayed until dessert and coffee. "I won't have that man ruining my family's digestion on top of everything else," she announced, and so most of supper was a quiet affair, since there wasn't anything else on their minds. There were long spaces where Jody heard nothing except the scrape of forks on plates and requests to pass the biscuits or some other favorite food. When anyone started to bring up Billy Crosby, Hugh Senior tapped his water glass with his knife to remind them of Annabelle's decree.

Finally, the supper plates were cleared away and taken to the kitchen and Belle's apple crisp à la mode was passed around on dessert plates. Jody, surprised she could be so hungry, ate it all right down to the melted vanilla ice cream that she scooped up with her spoon.

"There's something I have to say," Meryl announced. He looked over at his father-in-law. "Chase and Bobby and I spent some time in town today, sir, testing the temperature, if you know what I mean, and I would say that it's hot, very hot. People are upset, they're scared, and there's some big talk going around about forcing Billy out of town. Some of it is just silly—egging his house, that kind of thing—but some of it is downright ugly. Setting fire to their house—"

"No!" Annabelle exclaimed, one hand flying to her mouth.

"Yes, ma'am. That's what we heard one old boy say."

"We can't control what other people choose to do," Hugh Senior observed.

"No, we can't, sir, and I'm not suggesting that we try. We can control what we do, however."

"What does that mean?" Bobby asked, sounding irritated.

"It means that, speaking as your attorney, I want all of you to keep track of everywhere you go and everything you do and who's there with you, for at least the next few days, until this maybe begins to die down."

"Alibis?" Belle asked her husband with disbelief.

"Yes, alibis. Chase and Bobby, it might be better for you to go on back to your places sooner rather than later. If somebody shoots Billy Crosby between the eyes or runs him off the road, I want every member of this family to have a cast-iron alibi for that period of time, and I'd particularly like the two of you to be a couple of hundred miles away. I don't care if all that happens is that somebody eggs his car, I want every member of this family to be able to prove you weren't holding the empty carton."

In the moment of fraught stillness that followed, Jody blurted, "I talked to him today."

They looked at her with puzzled expressions.

"Talked to who, sweetheart?" her grandmother inquired.

Her heart pounding, she said, "Billy Crosby. I met him."

Amid the outcries of consternation, it was Chase who exclaimed, "What the *hell* have you done?"

"I didn't do anything," she defended herself. "I'd just been at Bailey's and when I was leaving you called on my cell phone, Uncle Chase. I was just standing there talking to you—"

"You hung up on me."

"No, I dropped my phone because I heard him. And then I saw him."

When she finished telling them about it, she looked across the table at Meryl. "You said I could ask you anything," she reminded him.

"Shoot," he told her.

"Why didn't they test Billy Crosby's blood alcohol level?"

Tensely, she waited for his answer.

He smiled wryly. "Because we only had one breath alcohol tester in the entire county and it was broken. Remember that, Chase?" His smile widened. "Some drunk kicked it to death, as I recall."

"I remember," Chase said, nodding.

Jody's grandfather caught her eye and interrupted, impatient to say something. "I don't want you anywhere near him, ever again." She wanted to protest that she hadn't meant to be around him at all, but kept quiet rather than be argumentative, because it wasn't even the point. The point was his concern for her. She felt like crying out of sheer gratitude at being surrounded by strength and love that made her feel so much safer than she had after meeting Billy Crosby. When she felt Belle's hand come over hers, she had to blink back tears.

Hugh Senior looked around the table at his family.

"As for the rest of us, we'll do what Meryl wants us to do." He gave them a small, grim smile. "It's clear to me from the looks on your faces that you'd all like to kill Billy Crosby, so we'd better all get alibis." His gaze rested on his wife's beautiful face. "Even you, my dear."

"How dare that man speak to her?" Annabelle looked frightened and worried as she stared across the long table at her husband. "How dare he say a single word to our Jody?"

"That's the kind of man he is, Mom," Belle reminded them all.

31

AFTER THE DISHES were put away, Chase joined his niece as she sat alone on the front porch swing listening to music on her iPod and looking up at constellations that couldn't be seen in any city, but only in places as isolated and dark as the ranch was at night. When he sat down beside her, the swing jolted, rattling the chains that held it to the porch ceiling and breaking the rhythm until he got it going again with a push of one boot heel on the wooden floor.

"How long are you and Uncle Bobby going to be here?"

"Until we don't have to be."

"What does that mean?"

He didn't answer, but lit a cigarette instead.

Jody removed the iPod buds from her ears.

"Why didn't you bring the boys with you?"

He had three teenage sons whom she loved a lot.

"Because I don't want them around any of this."

"Can you ship me away, too?"

"I'd be happy to."

"I wouldn't go."

"There's a surprise."

They swung silently for a while. He blew his smoke away from her when Jody waved a hand at it. Sometimes she liked her uncle Chase's company more than anybody's—when he was quiet and thoughtful and not bossing her around. She felt safe with him, although she didn't quite remember why, and she trusted him to make things right. She wished he was a happier man, for his sake. Two wives hadn't made it so; he seemed to come the closest to it when he was working cattle with his sons. She wished she had known him—or could remember him—when he was young and lighthearted and funny.

"What was my dad like?"

"I've told you a million times."

"I like to hear it."

He shifted in the swing, making it temporarily slide jarringly from side to side. Jody held onto the armrest on her side until the swing went in the right direction again.

"You like to hear it," Chase said in his smoke-roughened voice. "And I like to tell it. Hugh-Jay was a big guy, bigger than any of us." She heard a smile in his voice when he said, "But not nearly as good-looking."

"You say that every time."

"Can't be said too often." He chuckled, a low masculine rumble of amusement that she loved to hear. "But what he lacked in handsome, he more than made up for in decent."

"Was he the nicest person you ever knew?"

"I think he was."

"Nicer than you?"

He laughed. "Well, yeah, but how hard is that?"

Jody giggled. They swung in companionable silence while coyotes called to each other from hill to hill. A single bulb over the barn doors shed the only light at any distance from the house. Jody took solace in the beauty of the evening and pride in her father's good character.

"What about my mother?"

"Hmm."

"You always do that, you go 'hmm' when I ask about her."

"Prettiest girl in the county."

"Was she as nice as my dad?"

Usually Chase answered that by smiling and saying something like, "Nobody could be, but she made a damn nice blueberry pie." This time he did something different. He stopped the swing with his boot so they were sitting still. Jody's heart started to beat fast as she got a feeling she was going to hear something he'd never told her before.

"You mother was spoiled and stuck-up and a little mean."

"What?" She felt shocked, even though she'd long heard allusions to her mother "wanting what she wanted when she wanted it." But nobody had ever gone this far. "Are you kidding me?"

"I wish I were. But here's the thing. She was young. If that bastard had given her a chance to live a normal life span, Laurie might have gotten humbled a few times and she might have grown up to be a nicer person. I always thought there must be more to her than what people saw in her because—after all—your father married her. That was the highest recommendation she could get, so I have to put some stock in that, since I put so much stock in him. Most people thought he married her for her looks and she married him for his money—"

"Uncle Chase!"

"But the older I get, the more inclined I am to think he saw something good in her heart." He laughed, a rueful sound. "Or maybe it's just that the older I get, the dumber I get."

"Why are you telling me this?" She felt desperately unhappy to hear it.

"Because it seems as if all kinds of truths are coming out, and you may as well get them all laid out for you."

She had to fight back tears. "You're the mean one."

She heard him sigh. "Don't you want to know who she really was?"

Jody didn't answer. Maybe later she would want to know; at this moment it made her sad. In a kind of revenge, she suddenly said, "What if he really didn't do it?"

"What if who didn't do what?"

"Billy Crosby. What if he didn't kill my dad?"

"Where the hell are you getting this?"

It pleased her to have made him angry, too.

"Do you know that Byron George thinks he didn't do it?"

"Well, then I guess he doesn't want this family as his customers anymore."

"Bailey doesn't think so, either."

Chase halted the swing again. She saw him turn to stare at her.

"He told me so today," she said. "He says Billy was too drunk."

Jody was about to tell Chase about Red Bosch's opinion, but thought better of doing that; Red should get to tell the family himself, and not have her tattle on him.

"Is this where that question about the drunk test came from at supper tonight?" Chase asked, and then he snapped at her, "Try to remember you're the victim here, all right?"

"You didn't bring me up to feel like a victim."

"No, we didn't, but maybe you need to feel that now and then, so you can know the deep wrong this very bad man did and how he doesn't deserve anybody's sympathy, least of all yours."

"I'm not sympathetic to him, Uncle Chase."

"Good. Don't ever be. And stop this ridiculous talk."

They sat in a much less comfortable silence then, until Jody got up from the swing. Faking nonchalance, she stretched up her arms, spreading her fingers until their tips seemed to touch the stars.

"Are you coming in?" she asked, her tone chilly.

"No, I'll stay out here awhile."

"Uncle Chase?"

"Yeah?"

"What if he doesn't leave Rose?"

"He's not going to stay here."

"How do you know that?"

"Some things are inevitable."

"But—"

"Go to bed."

Something in his tone made Jody walk to the screen door and go inside without questioning him any more.

THE RANCH TELEPHONE rang just as Jody was going into the shower. She delayed long enough to hear Bobby call out to his parents from his old bedroom, "Who called so late?" It was only a little after ten, but it had been an exhausting day and they were all worn down.

Her grandfather opened the door to the master bedroom. Standing in the doorway in his pajamas and a robe, he said, "There's been trouble in town. Some teenagers outside of the Crosby house were throwing rocks and yelling things."

"Was that the sheriff who just called?" Bobby asked, appearing in the hallway, still fully dressed in his boots, jeans, and shirt.

His father nodded. "You have to give the man credit for calling to let us know, even after the things we said to him."

"Oh, come on, Dad. He's just doing his job, which he should have done in the beginning. What did he do about the kids?"

"Warned them off. Put deputies at either end of the block."

"That should calm things down."

Bobby returned to his room and shut the door.

Hugh Senior spotted his granddaughter, who had her head stuck out of the bathroom, listening. "Thank you for coming out here, Jody. Your grandmother and I feel better knowing you're here with us."

She decided to say it, rather than let it fester.

"I wish you had let me go with you to the hearing."

"It wouldn't have changed anything, honey."

"But at least I would have known I tried."

"It doesn't feel better to have tried," he said surprising her. "It may even feel worse. I can't stop thinking of other things we should have said . . ." He shook his head slowly, with a look of heavy regret on his face. "Be glad you weren't there. Be glad you don't have to feel you failed."

"Oh, Grandpa. You didn't fail. You never had a chance."

Feeling sorry she'd said anything at all, she murmured good night and slipped into the bathroom. As she stood under the hot water, her mind took an unexpected turn away from her own family's woes. Against her will, because she didn't want to feel any sympathy for the Crosbys, she wondered what it would feel like to have people hurling rocks at you, and cops who didn't do any more than shoo away your attackers and tell them to be good boys? She wondered if she'd be teaching any of those hooligans in the fall. If they were in her classes, they'd probably assume she approved of their actions, maybe even considered them heroes, and they'd be wrong.

BEFORE JODY could crawl into her bed in her own old bedroom, her grandmother came in to see her. Annabelle's hair, looking spiky from her own bath, made her appear younger than her years. She had on a pretty mauve bathrobe with a matching nightgown underneath, and brought a familiar creamy scent of soap and lotion into the room with her, which took Jody back to the days when her grandmother got into bed with her and they read together until one or the other of them fell asleep. Annabelle was always gone in the morning, but there had definitely been times when she had been the one to kiss the cheek of a sleeping grandmother instead of the other way around. It must have been hard, she often thought, to have to raise a young child when you had believed those days were over for you.

"May I come in?"

"Of course!" Jody patted the bed beside her. "Come sit with me."

After Annabelle did that, she said, "Dearest, I want to ask something of you that may be hard for you." She paused and then said a most unexpected thing: "Please try not to hate Billy Crosby's son."

"What?"

"Everyone seems to be so angry at Collin, but really, none of these years have been easy for him, either. All I can think of is that little boy, so diligently doing his homework in the grocery store while his mother worked. He probably loves his father and missed him as much as you love and miss your father."

Jody remembered what she'd seen and heard outside of Bailey's.

"I don't know, Grandma," she said with some skepticism.

Annabelle, not catching the doubt in her voice, continued, "It's only natural he'd want to get his father out of prison. I think we can only admire the grit it took for Collin to put himself through college and then law school in order to help his father."

Her grandmother was a great admirer of grit.

"You're too good, Grandma."

"No, I just know that children want to believe in their parents."

"In that case, I need to ask you something."

"All right."

"Just a little while ago, Uncle Chase called my mother spoiled, stuck-up, and mean. Is that true? Was she?"

"Oh, honey." Annabelle took one of her hands to hold. "I'm sorry Chase said that to you. She was young, that's all."

"It's true then, isn't it? You haven't said it wasn't true."

Her grandmother sighed. "Laurie may have been a tiny bit selfish, but she took good care of you, and your father loved her very much."

"Did I?"

"Did you love her? Of course, you did! You adored both of your parents."

This time it was Jody who let out a big sigh. "Okay. I'm glad."

Annabelle put an arm around her, hugged her, and kissed her hair. "Do you think you can sleep tonight?"

"I think so, can you?"

"I won't get a good night's sleep until that man is out of Rose again." Annabelle got up from the bed, but then turned around to look down at Jody. "You know, I hardly ever listen to the radio when I'm driving, but today for some reason I turned it on. There was a song I'd never heard before, and I believe the idea of it was that a young mother was singing to her child. I've forgotten the words, but they had something to do with keeping her baby safe. When I heard that, I had to pull over to the shoulder because I couldn't see for crying. I must have cried for half an hour before I could drive again."

"Oh, Grandma . . ."

"I didn't keep your father safe." Her voice caught, but she kept going. "So far, you have been safe with us. I want to keep it that way forever."

Annabelle slipped out of the bedroom before Jody could get to her feet and catch her for a hug. She watched her walk down the hallway toward the master bedroom and close the door, then she shut her own door and leaned her back against it. Tears started to roll down her cheeks until she had to run to get her pillow and put it over her face to cover the sound of her sobs. She wasn't even sure who she was crying for this time—her grandmother, her lost parents, herself, or for everybody whose lives had changed so much on that violent night twenty-three years ago.

32

JODY COULDN'T SLEEP because she couldn't stop feeling miserable and because she was afraid of what she might dream. Finally, around eleven-thirty, she threw off her covers and got up and dressed again, feeling as if she had to get out of there. She didn't want to worry her grandparents—or piss off her uncles—but she longed for her own home, her own bedroom, and her own bed. Knowing there were sheriff's deputies stationed at either end of Billy Crosby's street made her feel she might safely get what she wanted. The desire to leave was so strong it surprised her. She hadn't realized how completely she had already transferred her allegiance to her parents' house in Rose and how powerfully it could pull her toward it. She was a little worried about whether she'd get spooked inside of it again, but also determined not to let that get to her.

She wrote a note and taped it to her bedroom door.

Please don't worry about me. I couldn't sleep. I've gone for a drive.

It wasn't as irresponsible as it might have seemed to an outsider. In the Linder family, "going for a drive" at any time of day or night—in a car, a truck, on a horse, or even on a tractor—was a time-honored tradition that signaled, *I'm losing my mind. See you later.* It wasn't remarkable for any of them to wander in the middle of the night, rendered sleepless by ghosts and painful memories. Her grandmother had been known to ride her horse around the yard at three in the morning with the horse practically walking in his sleep. Her grandfather took his truck out to scare the coyotes with his headlights now and then. When her uncles visited, they often drove to Bailey's tavern late and got home later.

She had her cell phone, which still worked.

They could reach her at any time.

As she hurried through the kitchen, Jody grabbed a couple of leftover biscuits and a bottle of cold water from the refrigerator. She sneaked out of the ranch house, where the only interior sounds were a ticking grandfather clock and a snoring uncle. Outside, it was so quiet she could hear the whir of the occasional truck tires on the closest highway.

Three of the ranch dogs trotted up silently to sniff her.

She cracked open a biscuit and divvied it up for them, letting them grab the pieces from her open palm and then lick her clean. And then, with a sigh, she divvied up the other biscuit for them, too.

Worried about the noise she'd make by starting her truck, she got it rolling downhill without the engine on and didn't start it up until she was many yards away from the house.

She switched on the CD player as she drove toward stars on the horizon.

Johnny Cash—her father's favorite singer—crooned into the cab of her truck. She rolled down the front windows so he could serenade the cows as well. It was a Johnny that might have shocked her dad, Jody thought—not a country-western song, but a cover of the Nine Inch Nails' song, "Pain." With all the emotion, honesty, and life experience that Johnny poured into it, it was enough to break your heart. When it finished, Cash's voice rocked out of the truck speaker again, this time singing a cover of Depeche Mode's "Your Own Personal Jesus."

Jody figured her dad would like the singer if not the songs.

"Hey, Dad," she murmured, feeling love for him, "times change."

She let the cool night air roll in while the music rolled out.

She passed Red Bosch's house, with its garage door left half open for his dog. For a moment she wanted nothing more than to crawl into bed with him, but as Red's home passed in her side mirror, so did the moment of desire.

She wasn't afraid of being out on the road by herself at night.

Wide-open spaces didn't scare her. She felt as if she needed them in order to keep breathing; the way other people needed oceans or mountains, she needed the plains. And anyway, she was fairly sure there was nothing to fear on this night. Billy Crosby was inside his house with law enforcement outside to make sure he stayed there. As for herself, she had a big powerful vehicle with plenty of gas, and a cell phone with its battery fully charged, and there were people she knew living down almost every road and around every corner, even if the corner was a mile and a half away. This was her territory, which she knew like the soft comfortable feel of her saddle.

The night smelled to Jody like fresh-plowed dirt and new things growing.

WHEN SHE DROVE into Rose, it was close to midnight.

Most of the streetlights were out, because the town couldn't afford to turn them on all night anymore. "We're safe," was the sad local joke, "if anybody ever wants to bomb us from an airplane." No bomber pilot could spot them in the vast Kansas darkness below. In truth, Rose had already been bombed by the economy. "You want a growth industry?" one wag had said about struggling rural towns like Rose. "Sell the lumber people use to board up their store windows." Surprisingly, at least to Jody's family, her aunt Belle's museum was a rare bright spot and success story in the county's economy, a fact that Chase claimed "only goes to show how hard up this place really is."

But Rose still had a high school, and Jody had a job teaching in it come fall.

She was thinking about that as she drove slowly down the street that crossed at the north end of the Crosbys' block. As she neared it, she saw a deputy's sedan blocking the entrance, and when she drove up parallel to his car, she spotted a second one blocking the other end of the street, just as the sheriff had told her grandfather they would be.

Through her rolled-down window, she called to the deputy next to her.

"Hi, Ray." He was an old friend of her uncle Meryl's.

"Jody? What are you doing out so late?"

"I just wanted to see you maintain the peace."

She smiled to make sure he knew she was being nice about it. She didn't know what, if anything, his boss had told his deputies about the tense standoff at the ranch that evening.

"We cleared everybody out hours ago."

"I'm glad."

He gave her a curious look. "I wouldn't think you'd care."

"I care about what happens three blocks away from my house. And I don't want anybody to get hurt or arrested because of Crosby."

"We're not going to arrest anybody, don't you worry."

Jody nodded her head in the direction of the Crosby place.

"What about the rear of their house?" she asked.

"What about it?"

"The alley in back? Might be kind of vulnerable?"

Ray glanced in that direction. "If he's nervous, he can stay up and watch." Sounding resentful, he added, "Like I am."

"This citizen appreciates it."

He softened a little and smiled up at her. "Does the citizen happen to have fresh coffee with her?"

"No, but I'll bet she could bring some back with her."

"Nah, I'm just kidding. You go on home, Jody. It's going to be a peaceful night in Rose, just right for sleeping."

She gave him a grateful wave and drove on home, but didn't go inside.

Instead, she left her truck parked behind her house and started walking to Bailey's Bar & Grill. Since supper, she'd felt a growing need to talk to somebody who wasn't in her family *about* her family.

. . .

FOR THE SECOND TIME that day Jody walked into the dark tavern.

As before, country-western music was playing loud enough to require earplugs, and the pool table was the most popular spot in the joint. Bailey had closed the kitchen, so there were only the pool players and a few drinkers left in the place.

Jody hopped onto a bar stool again.

When Bailey came over, she said, "I ate a big supper, Bailey. I left my truck at my house. I walked over here. I'm going to walk home. Now may I have that beer, please?"

"Corona with a lime and a glass? Your mom always drank from a glass."

Bailey had told her that before, so she only nodded. "Yeah."

"But she was satisfied with domestic beer."

"Well, I'm un-American."

The big man smiled slightly, and Jody saw how weary and bored he looked as he leaned over to pull her beer out of a refrigerator under the bar. Maybe what she had to ask him would wake him up.

"Bailey, I would never confuse you with a priest."

He plucked a glass off a shelf and located a slice of lime in the refrigerator, too. "Good to know."

"And as far as I know you're not a lawyer or a shrink."

"Where's this going?" he asked, setting what she wanted in front of her.

"Where it's going is . . ."

He watched her pick up the glass, tilt it and pour beer down its side. When it was upright again she ran the lime slice around the rim and then dropped it into the beer and took one swallow. Finally she said, "I got to thinking about you tonight." She took another swallow, because it tasted so good and because she hoped it could relax her. The glass was cool in her palm, the beer was sweet and bitter in her mouth. "And what I thought is that I've been coming here all of my life and I've never heard you pass on gossip about anybody."

Bailey looked at her with an impassive expression, but she thought she saw a hint of pride in his eyes.

"Which leads me to believe," she said, after wiping her upper lip with a bar napkin, "that I can ask you something and it won't go beyond us."

He frowned a little.

"Don Phelps was out to the ranch this evening," she told him. "My family pretty much accused him of making all this happen by running a dishonest investigation." When Bailey didn't say anything, she pushed a little. "So I wonder what you think about that?"

Bailey shrugged. "I think he ran a dishonest investigation."

"Shit," she said, involuntarily, and took another drink. "You do?"

"Well, yeah, didn't the governor say so?"

"I guess, but—"

"You guess? No, he did say so. And as much as I respect your grandfather and the rest of your family, I think they have some nerve blaming Don Phelps for all of that."

It was a lot of words for Bailey, and he looked like he had more to say.

Jody worked up her courage and asked, "Why, Bailey?"

He sighed and propped himself on his bar with his hands spaced wide on it. "Listen, your granddad is the biggest property owner in this county, right? Everybody thinks he shits gold. Nobody's respected any more than him and Annabelle. They have the most money, so they wield the most power and influence, right? You know that's true. And one night their oldest boy—who just happens to be a kid that folks think is the nicest young fellow around—gets murdered and those nice, rich, powerful people point to Billy Crosby. They *believe* he did it. They are *sure* he did it. They're not lying. They really do believe it, and they expect him to get arrested and tried and convicted and be sent away for a long, long time."

Bailey took a breath and backed off from the bar a little, then leaned in again toward Jody, close enough that she could see the gray hairs amid his whiskers and the broken capillaries in his nose. He leaned one meaty forearm on the counter and turned his back to the couple of customers farther down the bar who looked as if they needed refills. "And let's say you're the sheriff of this county where the Linders are royalty. And you're an average guy, no Colombo, just a young guy who got elected sheriff because you always wanted to turn on a siren and drive a car real fast and, anyway, it's a job. And you don't know eff-all about investigating a homicide. If you're that man—I'm not saying if you're you, but if you're *that* man—what are you going to do?"

"Find and arrest Billy Crosby," she answered with reluctance.

"Are you going to waste time lookin' for anybody else?"

"Probably not."

"No probably about it. Are you going to give the time of day to anybody that suggests that somebody else might have done it?"

She hesitated too long, and Bailey said, "Trust me, you're not."

Jody asked, "Are you saying my grandfather—or somebody in my family—told the sheriff to ignore that other evidence?"

"No, I'm not saying that, Jody. I don't know if they did or not, although knowing your grandpa, I'd guess not. But they wouldn't have to, I do know that much. Don Phelps may not be a genius, but he's no dummy, either. There was an *atmosphere,* there was a rush to judgment— if you want to call it that—and he knew enough to lead the rush. But let me tell you something. In my opinion, it's a damned good thing Don did that, because if he hadn't taken Billy to jail first thing that morning and kept him there, we would have had other violence in this town. There were people who would have dragged Billy out and either beat him to death or hung him. So I'm not blaming Don for what he did, and I don't think your family ought to be blaming him, either, because they're the ones who set him up for it."

"Set him up?" She was shocked by his words. "Bailey, are you saying you think they did it on purpose?"

"No, they most likely did it out of honest grief and sorrow and a belief that they were right, but the result was just the same."

"You mean the wrong man went to prison?"

But Bailey only shrugged again. "Oh, I think Billy Crosby was an absolutely right man to put in prison."

Jody took a sip of her tart beer, looking down to hide her emotions.

When she finally looked up again, she said, "There's a flaw in your logic, Bailey."

"Which is?"

"If Billy didn't kill my dad, then somebody else did who's more dangerous than he is."

Bailey said, "It was those strangers your dad stopped that day."

"And so we'll never catch them and we'll never know?"

For the first time, he let some sympathy into his eyes. "Probably not, Jody. It might be best for you to accept that fact." He grabbed his lone waitress as she tried to squeeze past behind him to get to some bottles. "Sylvia can tell you what I mean."

The waitress, older than Bailey, said, "Tell her what, baby?"

"Tell her about that day over at the truck stop when you were there."

"Oh, honey," she said, looking at Jody, "are you sure you want to hear this?"

"Yeah, she does," Bailey insisted, before Jody could say anything.

Sylvia—white-haired and still shapely at over seventy in her T-shirt and blue jeans—leaned against Bailey but looked at Jody. "I used to waitress at the truck stop, did you know that, honey?"

Jody shook her head. Sylvia was fixed only to Bailey's in her mind.

"Well, I did work there, so I was there that Saturday when that poor Sam Carpenter came running in, just so out of breath you'd have thought he would die right there. He came in yelling, 'Where's Hugh Linder, where's Hugh Linder!' and then he said that Billy Crosby had killed your daddy."

"And how did everybody react to that?" Bailey prodded her.

"Well, shock!" Sylvia said, her hands flying up into the air as if she'd just been shot. "Pure shock and grief was what it was, people weepin' and yellin'. We just wanted to go get that little bastard and string him up right then."

"See, that's what I was saying," Bailey interrupted, releasing Sylvia back to her job. "It was a good thing Don Phelps did what he did that day. If he's responsible for sending the wrong man to prison, then we're all responsible for it, because there wasn't anybody—including me—who really stood up and suggested we might be convicting the wrong guy. Oh, I told them how drunk Billy was, but that's all I did. We all just went along, most people because they believed he did it and a few because maybe they knew better but they didn't want to cross your folks, and a few of us because we didn't mind so much if Billy got sent away. That probably saved some-other-body's life, like his own wife or his kid, or who the hell knows who Billy might have ended up killing someday."

Bailey went off to sell a few drinks, and Jody took the time to gulp down half of her beer, only to realize she didn't want any more of it. She was already disoriented enough from everything that had happened and everything she'd heard since noon. When Bailey came back, she said, "But why would my family be so hard on the sheriff?"

This time there was no mistaking the depth of sympathy in his eyes.

"Ah, Jody. Think about it. Think about your grandfather and what kind of man he is. How's he ever going to live with himself if he admits he sent the wrong man to prison?" Bailey took up a wet rag and began wiping down the counter around her glass. "When you don't want to face what you did wrong, it's easier to find you a scapegoat."

Jody sat quietly for a moment, working hard to keep her emotions under control, and then she said, "Thank you for being honest with me, Bailey."

He shrugged. "There's nothin' much else to be most of the time."

His last remarks to her before she left the tavern were a warning: "Watch out for Billy. Maybe he did it, maybe he didn't, but if he didn't, that don't make him any less dangerous. He went into prison a bad kid and he came out a worse man. I had him in here today, and you don't want to meet him in a dark alley, Jody. I don't want to, either, leastwise not without a gun or a baseball bat. He is one pent-up angry dude with a grudge as big as your granddaddy's ranch, for which I can't really say that I blame him. If I was him I might want to kill somebody, too. If I didn't know he was locked up on his block with deputies at either end of it, I'd walk you home myself."

"I'll be all right, Bailey," she said, and paid for her beer.

• • •

IT WAS GOING on 1:00 A.M. when Jody stepped outside onto the front walk where earlier that day she'd confronted the man she had always been convinced was the killer of her father and probably of her mother. She took a deep, shaky breath, feeling suffocated by the air inside and by what she'd heard there. Had her family sent an innocent man to prison? It was almost impossible to connect the word innocent with the name Billy Crosby, so she settled for what Red Bosch had said: *not guilty*. Had the Linders taken Valentine's husband away, and Collin's father, and locked up a human being for twenty-three years inside a maximum security prison—because they had connected the dots of various pieces of circumstantial evidence and used them to draw the wrong picture?

The possibility was so disturbing she felt sick to her stomach.

Above her, the sky was a clear dark blue with a sliver of moon.

There was the Big Dipper and Orion. There was the Milky Way, which was impossible to see anywhere near a city. The June air was cool, but not so chilly she wanted a sweater. Her head felt tight and she realized she had never removed the tattered old scarf. Had she showered in it? She almost laughed. Was she that preoccupied? Hadn't she even washed her hair? She untied it and looked at it briefly. *Whose scarf were you?* Not her mother's, at any rate. Jody dropped it into Bailey's trash can outside the tavern and then combed and lifted her hair with her fingers, liberating it to the breeze.

I'm never going to know what happened to her.

It stabbed her heart. *I must learn to live with it.*

Her boots on the cracked sidewalk were the only sounds she heard except for trucks passing infrequently on the nearby highway, and music coming out of somebody's windows, and an owl hooting every few minutes. Jody stuck her hands down in her jeans pockets and hunched her shoulders as if against a cold wind from the north.

At the end of the last block downtown she looked to her right and saw the other deputy's car at the southern end of the Crosbys' block. Unable to bear the thought of going home yet, and still desperate for fresh air, she struck out diagonally in that direction. She aimed for the center of the block she was on and then slipped between houses to get closer to the guarded block. When she was across the street from the Crosby home, she sat down beside a parked car in a driveway where neither of the deputies could see her. When her butt landed on crumbled concrete, she raised up enough to sweep it out from under her and make a less bumpy spot to sit cross-legged. She wasn't sure why she'd come, except she was following a need to look without flinching at the home of the family to whom it was possible that her own family had done great harm.

The Crosby house was completely dark, without even a porch light.

The whole block, the whole town, was equally dark, dimmed by its budget and the night. Rose wasn't a town that stayed up late. Very few houses, and none on either side of this block, showed any interior lights, though a few had porch lights on. It was so dark that Jody thought she could probably have sat out in the middle of the street and the deputies still wouldn't have been able to see her.

She surmised that the Crosbys' lights were all off because they didn't want to call attention to themselves, not after the trouble they'd already had that night. What was it like in there? she wondered. Were they sleeping? What was it like for Valentine having her husband home after more than two decades? Did Billy sleep soundly in the silence or did he toss and turn? And what about Collin—

With a jolt she realized she wasn't the only person sitting on pavement in the middle of the block. Her heart stuttered with anxiety and her breath caught as she recognized that what she had thought was a shadow was actually a man seated on the curb with his knees apart and his hands dangling between them.

She had a feeling he had heard her and been watching her.

Collin Crosby stood, using his hands to push himself to a standing position, and immediately moved toward her. She saw that he was wearing an unlikely wardrobe—long basketball shorts and an oversized sleeveless T-shirt, along with sneakers—huge ones—and socks pushed down around his ankles. He looked as if he'd just finished a pickup basketball game in the city park, but she doubted that, considering he didn't have any friends in Rose right now.

Jody stayed where she was, hoping he'd turn around and go back.

He kept coming, and then he started talking in a low voice before he reached her, a voice so calm she could hardly believe it. "There's nothing to see here," Collin Crosby said, sounding like the most reasonable man in the universe and not at all like one whose house had been stoned that night.

She saw the moment when he recognized who sat there in the dark.

"Oh." He stopped about five feet from her. "I didn't realize it was you." Collin cleared his throat. "Why are you here, Jody?"

She thought for a moment about how to answer. "I'm trying to figure things out."

"What things?"

"Did your father kill my father." She made it a statement, not a question. "Or not."

His eyebrows lifted. "I wasn't aware you had any doubt. You didn't seem to this afternoon."

"I didn't. But the governor says I should. Red Bosch says I should. He says your dad was too drunk to do it. Bailey says the same thing. But it's hard for me to take in information like that, because I've grown up hating your dad and being really scared of him."

"Me, too."

"What?" Jody stood up in surprise, brushing off her jeans. "What did you say, Collin?"

He turned his head and looked toward where Ray's car was parked at the other end of the block. Looking back at Jody, he said, "Billy scares me, too, and he always has. When he used to come home drunk, I'd make myself stay up all night to keep an eye on him."

"Why?"

"In case he started beating on my mom."

"Oh, God, Collin. And beating on you, too?"

He shrugged, sloughing off whatever was the truth of that.

"Then why'd you do this for him, Collin? *Why?*"

"You mean beyond the fact that we're not supposed to convict people unless they're guilty of the crime for which they're charged?"

"*Is* there more to it than that?"

"Yeah, there is." His face—his handsome face, she thought—looked grim, and he gave her a probing look as if to try to figure out how she might take what he said next. "I've known from the beginning that he didn't do it, Jody. The night your dad died? It was one of those times I just told you about, when I stayed awake all night to watch Billy."

Her heart was pounding so hard she almost couldn't hear him.

She noted how Collin called his father by his first name, as if he didn't want to call him "Dad."

"That night, he passed out on the couch and I watched him from the hallway. When he got up to use the bathroom, I followed him. It was exactly the sort of thing I'd done a lot of times before. He went out to the backyard and climbed into our hammock. I thought he was going to dump himself onto the ground, and if he had I wouldn't have helped him up. I would have let him lie there. But he didn't. He fell into it and started snoring. I sat on our back stoop and watched him until the sun came up. He never left, Jody. He didn't go anywhere. He didn't go to your house and hurt your parents. I've always known that, because I watched him all night."

Chills were running through her nonstop.

"You were, what, seven? Maybe you fell asleep and you didn't know it?"

"But I didn't. I never did. I felt responsible for my mother's life. I couldn't fall asleep."

She felt so confused and overwhelmed that she couldn't speak.

Her voice came out sounding choked. "Why didn't you say anything—"

"I did. Nobody believed me except Mom and Red. Mom and I went to the sheriff to tell him and he lectured her for using her son to lie for her husband. That was awful." He shook his shoulders in a voluntary shudder and looked away, down toward the other end of the street and the other deputy's car. "After that, she didn't want me telling anybody." Collin looked back at Jody again. "People wonder why she stuck with my dad, don't they?"

She nodded. "Are you aware that they think she hooked up with Byron at the grocery store?"

He snorted. "That's all in Byron's mind. To her, he's just her boss."

"Why *does* your mom stay with your dad, Collin?"

"Because she knows he didn't kill anybody and she used to love him and she feels guilty about him and she always hoped he might change." Collin shook his head. "He'll never change. She's seeing that now. They've already been fighting. My mom refused to let him in her bedroom tonight and he was so angry about it that I know he would have hit her if I hadn't been there."

Jody couldn't keep her hands from flying to her mouth.

"Here's an irony for you," Collin said, sounding bitter. Jody wanted to go to him and take his hands and squeeze them to comfort him, but she brought her hands down from her mouth and kept them at her sides instead, and stood there listening. "He's sleeping in the hammock again, just like he used to do. Only this time he doesn't even have the excuse of being drunk. We couldn't stop him from having a few beers at Bailey's, but I wouldn't buy him any more to take home. Now he's just a stone-cold sober son of a bitch. *You* saw how he is. I'm getting him away from her as soon as she'll let me, which I have a feeling may be first thing in the morning."

Jody swallowed. "So you felt you had to get him out of prison because . . ."

"Because otherwise I'd have to go through my life *knowing* my own father had been wrongly convicted and I hadn't done anything about it. And because my mother knew it, too."

"You remind me of my grandfather."

He looked askance at that. "Why?"

"Men of principle, both of you. It can cause a lot of grief."

Collin looked taken aback at that, but then he said, "Yeah. I'm afraid I've caused you some of that today."

"Oh, hell, what's a little more?" she said with false lightness, and then felt ashamed for the self-pitying sound of it. She lowered her head so she didn't have to look him in the eye. Although she heard his feet moving over the distance separating them, she was still surprised when she felt the heat of his body right in front of her. They stood on an incline with her slightly above him, which still didn't bring her face level with his. Somehow gravity pulled her close to him and she found herself pressed against him. Collin's arms came around her, and hers went around him, and he rested his chin on top of her head as she breathed in the scent of his skin. They stood like that for several minutes, neither of them saying anything, but their arms getting tighter around each other, holding on as if this were the only chance they'd ever have to embrace. There was a moment when Jody thought she felt him kiss her hair. She shivered and pressed even closer into his body, feeling more deeply comforted by his touch than she had ever felt before and wanting with all of her heart to give back to him the same profound feeling.

It felt so wonderful and so impossible that she wanted to weep.

Finally, she pulled away and Collin released her.

Jody looked into his eyes once more and then turned and walked away from him. One hesitant step. Two steps. She didn't hear him do the same so she guessed he was watching her go. Unable to bear leaving him, she turned around to see if he was there, which was why she could see the shocked and frightened look on his face—which mirrored hers—when they both heard a sound that could only have been a gunshot coming from the direction of his parents' house. There was no other sound, no scream that followed it, no other boom of gunfire, just the one shot that cracked the night silence as if it had broken a sound barrier.

Jody started to run with him toward his home until he turned to say, "No, please! Stay here. Get out of sight. Don't make me worry about you." And then he said, "I've always loved you, Jody." Shocked as much by those words as by the gunshot, she stopped where she was, then ducked back into the shadows beside the car in the driveway and watched Collin Crosby run home, his long legs covering the sidewalks, the street, and his yard faster than either of the screeching cars of the deputies could get there. Her heart screamed *No!* when Collin pulled open the front door and disappeared inside. She prayed frantically for his safety. She watched Ray and the other deputy park at strange angles in the street, saw neighboring lights come on, watched the two sheriff's men advance cautiously toward the house with guns drawn.

And then she saw Collin come back outside.

Jody stood up where she was.

He walked past the deputies as if they weren't there while they called to him, "Is anybody hurt? What's going on inside?" Instead, he came straight to Jody and faced her.

Her voice shaking, she asked, "Is your father—"

"It's not Billy," Collin said, his face distorted with all of the emotions running through him. "It's Mom."

Too shocked to speak, Jody stared at him.

"He shot her. Point-blank in the face. Killed her. He took her car and he's gone."

She stammered. "But I didn't see a car—"

"Hers was parked in back."

There were potholed alleys that ran the length of some blocks, emptying into other streets.

He put his face in his hands and began to weep. "This is my fault, this is all my fault, Jody. I should have left him there. I never should have tried to get him out."

Jody reached out to grasp his shaking shoulders, with hands that were also shaking, but he broke away without another glance and returned to where the deputies still waited with their guns out, ignorant of the fact that it wasn't Billy Crosby who'd been killed by some local vigilante, it was Valentine Crosby—who had waited for her husband all those years only to have him kill her soon after their reunion. Staggered by the shock of it, Jody watched a few more moments and then, sensing that her presence was useless, she turned and went slowly toward her own home. She wanted to run, to escape, to get as far away from Rose as she could go, though only if she could grab Collin and take him with her. Instead, frightened, sad, confused again, and bone weary, she climbed back into her truck to drive out to the ranch to tell them before they heard it from anybody else.

33

IT WASN'T EVEN two o'clock in the morning yet.

Jody drove fast, taking advantage of the fact that every law enforcement officer in the county had more important things to do now than to chase speeders like her. Her high beams showed her fence lines, sleeping cattle, sweet young growths of soybeans and sunflowers that she flew past as she navigated the curves in the road with a skill that came from familiarity—which was a good thing, since as she approached the gate, she couldn't even remember how she got there. The whole drive was a blank in her mind.

All she could think of was Collin's face as he told her about his mother, Collin's arms as he held her, Collin's grief, and Collin's confession of love for her. She tried to recall how his mother had looked yesterday in front of Bailey's, but she couldn't remember anything about Valentine. She'd been aware only of Billy and his son. She felt grieved and guilty about that, realizing she had totally ignored a woman who—at that moment—had only a few hours to live. If she could have gone back in time, she would have run at Valentine and pulled her away, yelling, "Get away from him, get away from him now!"

As Jody neared the ranch gate, she drove past Red Bosch's place again. This time she saw that his garage door was all the way down and she felt a tweak of surprise. Since it wasn't her truck hiding in his garage, it must mean that some other woman's was.

That didn't take long, she thought as she drove on by.

It appeared that Red had read the signs correctly and already moved on. Jody felt no jealousy; she felt relieved that their ending was so easy and relatively painless. He'd be sad about Valentine, though. She hoped that he and his new friend got to sleep in a little on this morning, to delay the moment when he found out.

JODY HALF EXPECTED to find her grandparents and her uncles awake and already talking about the shooting, but instead she found her grandfather in the kitchen alone, with only a light on the stove to illuminate him. He was noisily puttering around in the near-dark, trying to fix coffee and only managing to make a mess of grounds on the counter and water in the sink.

Her first instinct was to blurt the news, but she didn't.

"Here," she said, flipping on an overhead light and hurrying toward him. "I'll do that."

He blinked in the sudden light and then smiled down at her. "Your coffee isn't any better than mine is."

"Why does everybody say that?"

"Because it's true?"

"Yes, well at least I'm tidier."

He laughed and turned and walked over to the kitchen table.

He doesn't know yet, she thought, observing him from behind.

"What are you doing up so early, Grandpa?"

"Couldn't sleep. What are you doing dressed and sneaking in the back door?"

"Didn't you see my note? I wasn't sneaking."

She turned and tried to smile at him.

It hurt Jody's heart—a lot more than seeing Red's closed garage door—to note how slowly Hugh Senior moved this morning. He was a big man, but his skeleton was never designed for years of the hard physical abuse he'd given it on horseback and in cattle pens.

If he didn't know about the shooting yet, it wouldn't do any harm to let a few more minutes slide by before she told him and ruined his morning. Besides, that would give her own heart a little more time to stop pounding and her eyes to stop prickling with tears, so she could tell it all to him calmly, as he would want her to do.

"You feeling okay, Grandpa?"

He sank down into a chair, laid an arm on the table as if needing the support of a hard surface. "I'm fine. Just the usual aches and pains. They get better as the sun comes up. I'm like an old dog. I need the sun to warm me up and get me going. You're smart to be a teacher instead of a rancher like the rest of us."

"I'll always be a cowgirl, Grandpa."

"It's in your blood. Just don't let it break your bones."

She held up the leg she'd fractured years ago when a horse bucked her. "Too late."

He chuckled and then sighed and settled farther back into the chair, causing it to creak.

"Nobody else is up yet?" she asked, still stalling.

"Up and gone."

She turned to look at him over her shoulder again. "Chase and Bobby?"

"They both took off early for home."

"In the middle of the night?"

"Not more than an hour ago. I came down for coffee with them."

"I guess they couldn't sleep, either," she said, but he didn't reply. "What about Grandma?"

"She got up to see them off, then went back to bed."

"Did I wake everybody up? Was it because I left?"

"Did you leave?"

She glanced back at him and saw his blue eyes had a twinkle in them.

Jody washed wet grounds off her fingers and then turned to face him.

"Grandpa, you don't know, do you?"

He frowned a little. "Know what?"

"Something happened in Rose less than an hour ago." She swallowed hard, forced herself to tamp down her emotions. "Somebody got killed. Shot."

Hugh Senior's jaw dropped and he leaned forward. "Who?"

"Valentine."

"Oh, no." He looked grieved to hear it. "Oh, that's terrible. I'm so sorry to hear it. Did they arrest him, Jody?"

"Arrest him?"

"That . . ." Her grandfather wanted to say bastard or son of a bitch, she could tell, but he wouldn't in front of her. ". . . murderer."

"They haven't caught him yet. Billy took her car and escaped."

"Well, I guess this ends any of that stupid talk about how he didn't kill your father."

"Does it?"

"Of course!" He slapped the kitchen table so hard that it shook, and then he quoted what his daughter had said the night before at the dinner table. "That's the kind of man he is."

Jody didn't join him for coffee.

She poured a cup for him and then dragged herself upstairs and fell asleep on top of her covers, so tired that not even confessions of love could keep her awake any longer.

34

JODY WOKE UP at two-thirty in the afternoon, stared at the passage of time on her clock with dismay, and hurried down the hall to shower. Once dressed, she clomped downstairs, intending to apologize for sleeping so late. One look at her grandmother's face told her that Annabelle was worried about more serious matters than a lazy grand-daughter.

Jody hurried over to give her a kiss on the cheek.

"Why'd you let me sleep so late?"

"I thought you needed it."

"You know about Valentine?"

"Of course. That poor child."

"Which one? Her or her son?"

"Both of them."

"Have they caught him yet, Grandma?"

"Not yet. And people are scared to death. They're locking their doors and loading their guns and just generally acting as if he's going to break into houses and start shooting people. Personally, I think he's a long way from here." Annabelle looked her up and down. "You look nice and fresh. Now go back up and change into some old clothes, honey. Red hasn't shown up yet today and we're trying to catch up on his chores. I can't imagine where that man has got to. Did you hear him say he was going anywhere today?"

It must be love, Jody thought, remembering his closed garage.

"Maybe Uncle Chase or Uncle Bobby sent him off on some errand and just forgot to tell you before they left."

"That's what I told Hugh. Go change clothes."

"What are we doing?"

Her grandmother smiled at her. "Your favorite job."

Jody groaned as she turned to go upstairs again.

"NOBODY EVER GOT close to her," Annabelle remarked as she and Jody worked in the barn together in the mid-afternoon, after turning the horses out into their pasture.

Both of them had on long-sleeve shirts, rubber gloves, and jeans tucked down inside rubber boots so they could muck out the horse stalls, a daily chore that Red usually performed. As a teenager, Jody had learned a lesson about stubbornness when she insisted on wearing her leather boots to clean the stalls, and horse urine ate through the stitching on the soles.

Continuing her thoughts about Valentine Crosby's quiet personality, Annabelle added, "I never heard of anybody being a close friend to her except maybe Byron at the grocery store."

"Her son felt close to her," Jody said, a little sharply.

"Oh, honey." Annabelle was contrite. "I'm sure he did."

They were removing twenty-four hours—and more, thanks to Red's absence—of manure and laying in fresh straw bedding. They'd hauled the feed and water tubs out into the corridor, giving themselves room to work. Shooting Jody a curious look before returning her attention to her pitchfork, Annabelle plunged the five prongs into the horse's bed and then lifted the manure and soiled straw into the metal wheelbarrow Red used for the job.

"Grandma, he told me he always hated his father."

Annabelle put down her pitchfork again. "Collin said that?"

Jody nodded. "He said he used to watch his father all night when he was drunk, to make sure he didn't hurt Valentine. He claims he was watching Billy all that night—the night everything happened—and so he knows his father didn't do it. I said, maybe he fell asleep and just didn't know it, but he swears he never did that, ever. Red says Billy was too drunk to go all that way in the storm and do all those things. Bailey says the same thing."

"Good grief." Annabelle sounded a little stunned. "When did you hear all this?"

"Yesterday," Jody said, omitting the part about how some of these discussions had gone on around midnight and later.

"When did Collin tell you that? Was it when you ran into them at Bailey's yesterday?"

"No. Later. Between then and when his mom was shot."

She realized her grandmother was staring at her.

"I sneaked over there to get a look at their house, Grandma. Last night, after I left here. I never intended to talk to Collin, but he was sitting outside on the curb and he saw me and came over to talk to me."

"He was just a little boy."

"Red and Bailey weren't."

Nervously, she waited to hear what her grandmother would say to that, but when Annabelle spoke again, she changed the subject completely: "Your mother would never have done this job."

Jody didn't say anything at first, partly to adjust to the abrupt change of topic, but then she said, "That doesn't make me better than her."

"I think it does."

Jody propped her shovel against a wall. "Uncle Chase thinks that if she'd had a chance to grow up more, she'd have been a better person."

"He may be right." Annabelle seemed about to add to that, but then closed her mouth.

"What?"

Her grandmother glanced up. "What do you mean, 'what'?"

"You started to say something else. What was it?"

"Oh." Annabelle stopped working again, too. "I started to say that if it had been your uncle Bobby who said that, I'd have put it down to the crush he had on her—"

"Uncle Bobby had a crush on my mom?"

"He did. I found a photo of her in one of his jeans pockets shortly before she—disappeared—but it took me a while to put the clues together. I suspect grief over her was one of the reasons he took off for the Army. I think he had a huge crush on her. I don't believe your uncle Chase did, so I'm more inclined to take his opinion on this matter."

"I would have thought it would be the other way around."

"Why's that?"

"Because Uncle Chase is so handsome and women fall for him."

"Well, maybe that's why, since he had lots of other girls."

"Poor Uncle Bobby."

"Well, he shouldn't have had a crush on his own sister-in-law!" Annabelle eased off a little on her indignant tone. "Not that he could help it. Your mom was just as pretty as you've always heard she was."

"What? You did it again, Grandma. You started to say something and you stopped yourself. What is it?"

"Nothing. Really, it was nothing."

"Please, Grandma. Please tell me whatever you were going to say."

Annabelle started to push her hair off her face, but remembered she wore now-filthy gloves. She brought her hands back down to her sides. "I was just going to say—" She hesitated, and Jody could see that her grandmother really didn't want to say whatever it was she was forcing her to say. "I was going to say that your mother was as pretty as she was dishonest."

"*What?*"

"I know that's a mean way to put it, and I'm sorry, but the truth is, she stole from us, honey. Little bits of cash from one of the ranch accounts. We found the evidence after she was gone. I'm pretty sure your father knew about it and he was worried about it. And about her.

And I was worried about them, without knowing that was the cause of it. I hate the fact that she gave him any trouble or grief at all. I don't think I've ever quite forgiven her for that. So I don't know if your uncle Chase is right or not. Maybe she would have changed, maybe she would have grown up to be a nicer person. I want to think it's true. I want *you* to think it's both possible and true."

They finished their dirty job in an uncomfortable silence.

At one point Annabelle said in a voice full of regret and a bit of accusation, "You wanted me to tell you."

"I'm glad you did. Well, maybe not glad. You know."

"You want the truth."

Jody nodded, and then pretended it was straw dust that was making her take off one glove and raise her fingers to her eyes to wipe the tears away. Her grandmother, sniffing as if she, too, was affected by the dust, didn't try to comfort her, but left her alone to absorb this new information that her beautiful mother—her spoiled and snobbish mother—had also been a petty thief.

Nothing more was said between them about Collin Crosby.

Jody spent the rest of the afternoon working near her grandmother, but thinking about him. Where was he now? What was he doing? *How* was he doing? Was there anything she could do to help him—

She shook her head, feeling heartsick for him, and lonely.

It was impossible. The violently intertwined lives of their families stood between them. Her own family, alone, was an obstacle bigger than the Testament Rocks, as hard and unyielding as stone when it came to the subject of Billy Crosby.

I should stop thinking about Collin and stay away from him, because that is the best and only way I can help him.

FOUR HOURS LATER Jody found out she wasn't the only one who would determine when and how she could help Collin Crosby. When the ranch phone rang after supper and she went to answer it, she saw his name in the caller ID window. Quickly, she picked up the portable receiver, said, "Hold on," and hurried out to the porch and then kept walking into the front yard, away from ears that might overhear her.

"Collin," she said. "How—"

He didn't give her a chance to ask anything.

"Jody, I need to tell you something that nobody else wants to hear." There was no "Hello," no "How are you?" and no news. He just launched right in as if he didn't have much time, or thought that maybe she wouldn't. She clung to the receiver, but she was really clinging to the sound of his voice, not knowing if and when she'd hear it again. "If you can't talk, just listen. I don't think Billy killed Mom. It took me about half an hour to get over the first shock and then I realized—where'd he get the gun? There was no gun in the house. He sure didn't come out of prison with one. There wasn't one in my car, there isn't one in my mom's car, and I swear to you there wasn't one in the house."

"Could he have hidden one away, years ago?"

"He could have, yes, but it's not a big place and I've been over every inch of it doing things for Mom. Painting, fixing the roof, replacing insulation, taking down old cabinets and putting up new ones. I've looked in every nook and cranny of the basement and the attic, I swear, and there was no gun. Jody, the only way Billy could have gotten hold of a gun is if somebody came into the backyard and dropped one on his chest while he was in the hammock."

"And that didn't happen."

"Right. That's fantasy."

"I don't know what to say. Why would anybody want to kill your—Oh."

It hit her, of course, that somebody would do exactly that if they wanted to frame Billy.

"Oh, God, Collin. I don't know what to say."

"It's enough that you didn't say bullshit."

"I wouldn't. I won't. Where are you?"

"In the motel in Henderson, waiting to find out what happens next."

"Do you know where your father is?"

"No. If I did, I'd tell them."

"Even though you think he didn't do it?"

"I'm afraid of what he *will* do if he's as desperate and angry right now as I suspect he is. He doesn't have any money. He doesn't have anything except Mom's car, and he can't even refill the gas tank when it runs out, which it probably already has. He's not a smart guy, Jody. He's just a physically tough man who runs headlong into trouble, and he'll probably keep doing that until it kills him. I don't want it to kill anybody else first."

"What can I do?"

He said nothing for a moment. "I probably shouldn't even have called you. I must sound like I'm possessed and I suppose I have been, in a way, for years."

"That's okay," she said gently. "We're both a little crazy."

"I called you because I just . . . needed to." There was another pause, and then Collin said, "I meant what I said to you last night, Jody." And then he said, "I've got another call coming in. I'd better take it in case it's about Billy." A quick goodbye and he was gone. Jody punched a button to see his phone number again and memorized it. Maybe she would never call him, but it made her feel better to think she could reach him.

Jody turned to find her grandfather striding toward her across the grass.

She held the phone against her chest, hoping he wouldn't ask about the call.

But all he said was, "Would you run down to Red's house for me, Jody? I've called a dozen times, I swear, and all I get is voice mail on his cell and his phone at the house. I'm getting pretty fed up that he hasn't let us know where he is and what he's up to. I called Chase and Bobby, and neither of them sent him out of town, so I don't know what's going on."

"Sure, Grandpa."

"I've got half a mind to go with you and give him what-for."

"No, no, you stay here. I'll do it."

If anything could have struck Jody as funny right then, after her call from Collin, this situation would have. Yesterday she'd been trying to keep her family from walking in on her and Red; tonight she was trying to keep them from walking in on Red and some other woman. As she faced the embarrassing prospect of knocking on his door, she thought: Red? Whoever she is, buddy, she'd better be worth this.

35

IT WAS ONLY a couple of hundred yards to Red's place, down an incline that put him out of sight of the ranch house and gave both Red and the Linders some privacy from each other. When Jody was small, now and then her grandmother had sent her down to the mailbox at the front gate near the hired hand's house just to let her run off some energy. Now she walked, not ran, in that direction, mentally working through a list of single women she knew in the county to try to predict who it was going to be. Thinking about Red's new romance was easier than thinking about Collin's phone call and all the things it might mean to her, to him, to her family, to a whole lot of people.

It was a beautiful evening on the ranch, fragrant and fresh.

The time was past twilight, with full night closing in.

She'd brought a flashlight with her to show her the way home, but she didn't turn it on yet.

Red's house came into view and she halted at the sight of it.

His truck was there and the garage door was still down.

She would just walk up, ring the bell like a proper visitor, and if his woman friend opened the door, she would ask with an innocent air, "Hi. Is Red home? May I speak to him, please?"

At the front door, she rang the doorbell and then knocked.

Nobody answered, though she could hear the television blaring from the bedroom. She rang again and knocked harder, giving them time to get dressed, if that was the problem. After waiting several more minutes with no results, Jody walked around the bushes at the side of Red's house and went over to the garage. Red's dog was pacing in front of the closed garage door.

She didn't try to pet the stray that Red called Mangy Beast.

She looked like a blue heeler with a touch of husky in her, a gray and tan dog that he'd found by the side of the highway near the front gate. Red considered it a major miracle of his life that an actual hunting dog had materialized there, needing a home. She had acted liked a whipped cur for a long time before her curved, bushy tail began to wag when Red went out to feed her.

Mangy Beast wasn't mean, but she wasn't friendly, either.

The sturdy, muscular creature with the strange light eyes stood in front of the garage door, staring at her.

"Are you hungry, girl?"

It wasn't like Red to neglect to feed animals, whether cattle or dogs, and it appeared to Jody that he had committed several of those sins today—neglecting horses, cattle, and his own pet.

On the far side of the garage—where any woman watching from the house couldn't see her—Jody found an old bucket and put it under the window frame. She stepped up and looked inside a dirty window.

Red's visitor drove a red Ford Taurus that looked familiar to Jody.

Where had she seen that car before and who was driving it?

She stepped down and walked to the back door this time.

Beyond the illumination cast by the lights inside the house, Red's yard was totally dark, so she turned on her flashlight and trod carefully, watching where she placed her feet so she wouldn't stumble over a garden hose or anything else in her way. As she neared the back stoop, she realized Mangy Beast was with her, keeping silent pace with her. The dog's hackles were raised on the back of her neck, as if she didn't approve of Red's visitor inside, and she was growling low and deep in her throat.

Jody noticed the screen door was closed but the door behind it was ajar.

She pulled at the screen, expecting it to be locked, but it wasn't.

Never before had she found it unsecured. In a town where hardly anybody locked anything, Red locked up out of respect for the fact that he lived in a house owned by his employers.

Getting more annoyed by the second at his obliviousness to responsibility, Jody knocked loudly and then pulled open the door and shouted, "Red! Are you home?"

When he didn't answer, she stepped inside the kitchen.

The dog came with her. Jody closed the door.

She looked down at the bristly mottled coat at her side and said, "Go find him, girl."

Beast went straight through the kitchen and on into the living room, where she paused to look and sniff around. The television was so loud Jody worried it would hurt the dog's ears, but it didn't stop Beast from aggressively hurrying toward the noise. Jody followed as the dog ran into the little hallway where the bedrooms were and then into the room where Red slept.

She heard Beast bark and then the dog started to howl.

Jody ran after her into Red's room and screamed when she saw what the dog had found: Red Bosch lay on his stomach on his bed, alone, his back a bloody mess, ripped apart by the bullet that killed him. In the same instant that Jody realized he was dead, she also remembered where she had seen the old Ford Taurus before and who owned it.

It was Valentine Crosby's car, which Billy had stolen last night.

She looked up then at the big gun case that stood against a wall of Red's bedroom and saw that the glass front was shattered. If Billy Crosby hadn't had a gun when his wife was killed, he did now.

• • •

JODY DIDN'T STOP to think or weep, but simply followed a knee-jerk, basic instinct for self–preservation, because it was all she had left of her emotional and physical reserves at that moment. Her first instinct wasn't to call the sheriff or to call her grandparents up at the ranch house. Instead, her fingers punched into the face of her cell phone the number she had only recently memorized. As she walked like a zombie out of the awful, noisy bedroom, through the living room, and toward Red's front door, she heard the number at the other end ring once before he answered with her name.

"Collin, I'm at Red Bosch's house. He's been shot dead."

Before he could say anything else, as she opened the front door, she said, "I think your father has a gun now, or more than one, and since your mother's car is in Red's garage and Red's truck is still parked here, that probably means your dad is somewhere around here, too."

She heard Collin say her name again just as she stepped outside, closing the front door behind her.

Out of the darkness, a strong hand grasped her arm, the one that held the phone.

Jody screamed as the cell phone fell from her hand and the hand that held her whirled her around so that she was looking into Billy Crosby's face. She screamed again when she saw that his other hand held a pistol. "Shut up," he told her. He pulled at her so she had to go with him or fall down. Struggling to keep up, trying to avoid the gun he held on her, Jody half walked and was half dragged back to Red's truck and shoved into the passenger front seat before Billy pushed himself in behind the wheel. He had been drinking—she could smell it—but she didn't know if Billy was drunk.

She heard Red's dog crashing against the back door and barking furiously.

Gasping with the pain of being violently shoved into the passenger's seat, grief burst out of her.

"Red! You killed *Red!* He *believed* in you. He went to *see* you—"

"Once. He came one time. Where was he all the rest of those years?"

"But *Red.*" Her cry, her protest, was anguished. "He was a good man, *a good man!*"

"He wouldn't let me have his guns."

"So you killed him?"

"I needed those guns!"

Horrified by the brutal banality of it, she fell back against the truck seat, breathless with shock, fear, and sorrow. It struck her with terrifying force again that even if this man had not harmed her parents, that did not make *him* a good man. A person could be not-guilty without being innocent, Collin had said. Now, with Red's murder, his father was neither.

"*Red,*" she whispered, in dull shock.

"Shut up."

"You've really done it now, haven't you?"

He turned to look at her in the dark cab of the truck. "Why not? After a while you get tired of being accused and punished for what you didn't do, so why not do it? You know? Why the fuck not just do it. When I was young I was just a dumb fuck punk. You know what I mean? I did stuff like drunk driving, cut a few fence lines, big deal. You get ninety days for that shit. But what do I get? Forty years! I was a punk serving a murderer's sentence. Is that fair? I been serving some other guy's sentence! Some guy who was smarter and meaner than me. That was *his* jail cell I was in, that was *his* slop I ate, that was *his* *life* they gave me and they took away my own. And where is he? Living my life? Married, maybe? Has kids? Has a job? If I could kill *him*, that's what I'd do."

He had Red's truck keys. They shone in the dashboard lights when he switched on the ignition. As he stepped on the gas and started up the long gravel drive with the headlights off, he said, "They took everything away from me. Let's see how they like it when I take everything away from them."

36

It was all she could do to keep breathing and not do anything to make him pull the trigger. She couldn't tell how sober he was or how much control he had—or didn't have—over his mind and muscle. But judging by how overconfidently and fast he drove and how he had to zigzag repeatedly to keep from going over into the shallow drainage ditches that ran alongside the driveway, she thought he must be drunk. Red kept a supply of beer and whiskey in his house, and she had no doubt now that Billy had been heavily into it.

He began to talk nonstop, turning his head frequently to stare at her.

"I was a young guy and they took that away from me. They took all those *years* away from me. I had a wife and a kid and they took me away from Val and Collin. I had a job, and your granddad was going to fire me and take all the money I earned away and leave me with nothing."

He shouted some words, uttered others with ominous quiet.

"They made me look guilty of stuff I never did. I never killed your father! I never did nothin' to your mother! Your dad was okay, but she was a bitch. Why would I want anything to do with her? I never did any of that stuff. And now they've killed Valentine and made it look like I did it. Why did they do all this to me?" He glared at her across the darkened front seat, taking his eyes off the road so the truck veered too far left, and then Billy corrected it too sharply, sending Jody rocking against the door frame, moving her away from the gun barrel for an instant and then slamming her back against it so that she cried out from the sharp pain of metal against bone.

"Why, why'd they do that? They ruined my life. They took my whole life away. Now I got nothin' left. So what if I'm out? My wife's dead. My boy hates me. I can't go home. They want to put me back in prison. They'll do it, too, if I let 'em. I'm not goin' back. I'm not. They'll have to kill me first, and I don't give a shit if they do. Life is shit. *My* life is shit. So I'm gonna make their life shit, too. They took everything away from me? Well, their time has finally come, and now I'm takin' everything away from your bastard grandfather."

She hated herself for believing him. She didn't want to feel even a sliver of sympathy, didn't want to understand his fury, didn't want to have to think, *In his place, how would I feel? What would I do?* And she kept thinking, *He's Collin's father. His* father. Collin might not like or respect this man any more than she did, but he had devoted his life to giving Billy another chance. Part of her wanted to attack Billy, disable him, hurt him, kill him if she had to. Another part of her wanted to tell him she was sorry. *My God.* She didn't want to be sorry, not for him. "Remember who's the victim here," Uncle Chase had told her, but there wasn't just one victim, and what she had reminded him was even truer: She wasn't brought up to be a victim and she didn't feel like one, inside.

"They thought you did it," she said.

"Don't matter what they thought. Matters what they did. And anyway, somebody knew it wasn't me, didn't he?"

He slowed as they neared the house, not only slowing the truck but also his slurred speech. Finally, in near silence, they rolled to a stop about twenty yards from the front door and he threw the truck into park. Grabbing Jody's left arm, Billy pulled her after him, over the bench seat, banging her against the steering wheel, dragging her out into the grass violently so that her body hit the steering wheel, the side of the truck, the door, the ground. She gritted her teeth to keep from crying out and lay stunned at his feet until he dragged her to a standing position again.

This time he stood behind her with the gun between her shoulders.

He shoved her forward in the darkness, closer to the house.

Jody saw lights on inside, both upstairs and downstairs.

Where are the dogs? This time of night they sometimes liked to wander, hunt, roam the pastures looking for coyotes, nudging calves closer to their mothers if they found any awake and standing. In her mind she begged them, *Come home!* Here was a predator worse than any coyote, closer to a rabid wolf, and he was closing in on their home and hers.

"Stop," he ordered her.

She heard Billy digging in one of his pockets and then he shoved something in front of her face with his free hand and she smelled tobacco.

"Get me out a cigarette."

Jody reached for the pack of Camels and dug out a cigarette with her shaking fingers. She held it over her shoulder and he took it.

"Now light it," he said, and handed her a matchbook.

She lit his smoke for him and breathed what he blew out.

For several silent minutes they stood like that while he smoked. Jody had the sense that Billy didn't have a plan. He was making it up as he went along, just as he had grabbed her when the opportunity presented itself. The fact that he didn't know what he was doing didn't make her feel any better, it only made him seem more unpredictable and dangerous.

Billy flicked the still burning cigarette onto the grass.

It was dry, and not more than a few seconds passed before it caught a few blades of the tinder-dry growth on fire.

Jody instinctively moved to stamp it out.

He grasped her shoulder and pushed the gun in deeper.

"Hold the fuck still." And then he said with pleasure in his voice, like a boy discovering a new toy, "Well, look at that. Caught the damn grass on fire, didn't it? Don't that make a pretty light?"

He pushed the matchbook into her hands again.

"Start moving. And light another one."

She walked, and tossed the next lit match onto a different spot in the dry grass when he told her to. He nudged her with the gun again and she repeated the arson. They moved slowly closer to the house, each time starting little fires while the older fires built behind them. Jody prayed the blazes wouldn't join and get out of control, while at the same time she prayed that they *would* get large enough to attract her grandparents' attention from inside the house. In her mind she saw Annabelle looking out the window, her forehead creasing as she noticed an orange glow that wasn't supposed to be there. She imagined her grandmother calling out in a worried tone, "Hugh? Hugh!" If they saw it, they could call for help. They could escape out the back.

Please don't come out the front to check on it.

But of course that would be the natural thing for them to do.

They would walk out their front door and put themselves directly in Billy's line of fire.

If that happened, Jody resolved, she'd throw herself at him, even if it meant he shot her. She just had to hope it didn't kill her right away. She would do whatever it took to keep him from harming the two people to whom she owed everything.

She didn't let herself think about what life would be like for her grandparents if they lost her, too. They were smart, she told herself, they would do *something* to save themselves.

Finally, she spoke to him again.

"I know you didn't kill my father."

"Hell no, I didn't."

It wasn't the surprised and gratified response she hoped for, but she tried again. "And I know you didn't do anything to my mom and I know you didn't kill your wife." She wasn't even sure she believed these things, but she said them anyway, borrowing Collin's conviction that his father wasn't guilty. She didn't mention Red. If Billy had not been guilty of any murders before, he was guilty of one now. Her immediate goal was to keep him from becoming guilty of any more of them.

"Collin got you out of prison once and he'll do it again."

"Too late now."

Her heart sank. Billy knew he'd cast his own lot by killing Red. Just as he'd told her, he had nothing to lose.

Hearing a crackle and feeling heat, she turned her head just enough to check on the fires behind her without angering Billy. What she saw terrified her. It was her worst fear about them coming true. The separate fires were combining, devouring the dry tinder of grass as they rushed toward each other and then merged and got bigger, hotter, higher.

Soon it would be on their heels.

Had he thought of that? Did he know they might be caught by the fire before the house was?

She was just about to turn back and shout at him when she saw something else terrifying that was marching toward them through an opening in the waist-high flames. *Grandpa!* Tall, broad-shouldered, grim-faced with hatred and determination, his white hair shining in the light of the fire, he appeared to her like a vision, an Old Testament figure, but one who bore a shotgun in his big hands.

How had he got there? How could he be here?

Quickly, heart pounding, she turned around and kept walking next to Billy.

She listened hard, wanting desperately to help her grandfather, waiting for the right moment to do it.

When she heard what she thought was his step on gravel, she stumbled to distract Billy. It slowed them down and so he jabbed at her again with Red's pistol. The push gave her a reason to stumble again, which gave her an excuse to drop to the ground as fast as she could, getting herself out of two lines of gunfire, Billy's and her grandfather's. Crumpled onto the grass that might soon be burning, she gulped for air and prayed for deliverance.

"What the—" Billy got out before her grandfather's shotgun barrel slammed into his gun hand, sending the pistol flying and shoving Billy aside. He screamed with pain and stumbled, and then fell to one knee.

On the ground, Jody lunged for the pistol just as he did, too.

She had her right hand near it when she heard her grandfather say, "Lay still, Billy, or I'll shoot your head off."

In that moment, she wondered if Billy really would rather die than go back to prison. *We'll find out now. Collin, I'm sorry.* Billy's left hand was only inches away from the gun that she was reaching for, too. Jody shot her hand forward the small distance, but Billy didn't move to compete for it. She got her answer as she wrapped her hand around Red's gun and watched Billy pull his own hand back and lie still. With Red's firearm in hand and her finger on its trigger, Jody got to her feet, and joined her grandfather in holding Billy Crosby at bay.

"I've got this," he told her as he pressed the shotgun barrel into the side of the other man's face. "You'll find your grandmother near the barn. We've been waiting there for you. Tell her it's over. The two of you can put the fires out while I wait here with Billy for the sheriff. And this time there won't be any problem with the evidence."

"How did you know?" she asked him before she ran to do it.

Her grandfather never took his eyes off the man on the ground. "We got a call from Billy's son."

37

Two nights later Jody walked up to where Collin stood beside his car in front of the Testament Rocks. His father was in jail, charged with so many crimes that once he was convicted of any of them, the question of his guilt or innocence in the death of Jody's father would no longer matter. One way or another, Billy Crosby was going to spend the rest of his life behind bars.

"Let's walk," she said. "Okay with you?"

He nodded, and took her hand to hold.

"Is the ranch okay?" he asked her.

"Yes. Grandma and I hauled a couple of big tarps out of the barn and laid them on top of the fires and pretty much stamped it all out. That, plus a garden hose, took care of it. There are some burnt spots, but that just means new grass will grow there."

Collin stopped and pulled her around so he could look at her.

"What about you? How bad did he hurt you?"

Under her jeans and long-sleeve shirt she was black and blue; her ribs and other spots on her body still hurt so much she had to move carefully. "I'll be fine. Thanks. A lot more fine than I'd have been if you hadn't called my grandparents."

"You scared me to death when I heard you scream. And then I heard his voice. I'm so sorry, Jody."

"Not your fault." She saw how sad he looked. "This is impossible, isn't it?"

"Yes," he answered in a low voice that held all of the regret she felt inside of her. "Your family—"

"Still believes your father killed my parents. And they blame you for Red's death, because you set your father free to do it." At the mention of Red's name, Jody's throat closed and she had to look down to hide the tears in her eyes.

"I doubt that's ever going to change," Collin said.

Tears or no, Jody looked up at him. When he saw her eyes, he gently took her in his arms for a moment. When he felt her wince—in spite of the fact that she tried desperately hard not to—he released her. But she'd been raised by her family to be bold, and so now she was. "Then we may never have another chance to be together, Collin. I can't abandon my family." She looked into his eyes. "But I can't bear the thought of never loving you."

They walked together back to his car.

Like teenagers, like the couple they might have been if life had allowed it, they made love in the backseat, at first carefully because of her wounds and then with more abandon as her body loosened from its stiffness and she refused to let pain stop her. They laughed and cried and said goodbye to each other. Afterward, hours afterward, Jody drove home to her own house and Collin drove back to his home in Topeka.

Jody went to sleep in the smallest bedroom, the guest room at the end of the second-floor hallway, where nobody else in her family would go. She lay down on the bed in the room where her father had been murdered. It couldn't be said that she cried herself to sleep. Instead, she thought the whole night through about how her life was now defined by the word "never." *I'm never going to be with Collin again. We're never going to know who killed my father. I'm never going to know what happened to my mother.*

38

September 3, 1986

LAURIE STEPPED ONTO the second-floor landing and lifted her fingers from the banister. She looked back and saw that she had dripped rainwater all the way up. Ooops, she thought, feeling tipsy and reckless, and then: It'll dry. She felt excited from the run into the house through the heavy rain and by the feeling now of being trapped inside with her handsome brother-in-law.

Chase stepped out of a guest bedroom carrying dry clothes in his hands. He had wrapped them in towels to try to keep the moisture off them from his own wet body and clothing.

"You going to be okay here tonight by yourself?" he asked her.

"I'll be fine," she said, a little dreamily. "Just fine, Chase."

He tilted his head and smiled at her. "I think Laurie's drunk. Is Laurie drunk?"

"She might be." She giggled. "Are you?"

"Nah. That business with Billy sobered me up, darn it."

"He's a jerk."

"Yeah. Seriously, what if your power goes out?"

"Seriously, it's night. I'll be asleep. And I have candles."

He waggled his eyebrows at her flirtatiously. "I could keep you company."

"You could go on and get out of here before your dad comes and gets you."

They both laughed. She loved flirting with Chase and leading him on, and anybody could see that he loved flirting right back at her and being led, but that's as far as it would ever go, she had figured out, because for all his wild ways, there were certain things Chase would never do. Fooling around—really fooling around—with a wife of one of his brothers was high on that list of taboos for him. Sometimes Laurie thought that Chase, unlikely as it seemed, was the most like her father-in-law of all the Linder siblings, and that his playboy appearance was a cover for a rigid set of principles: you did your work, you respected your elders, and you didn't mess around where you could cause a mess. Hugh-Jay was more forgiving than that. And it wasn't Chase who had flunked out of K-State, after all, it was Bobby. Everybody in Rose had expected Chase to be the Linder brother who lived up to his name and pursued Laurie, but he never did, and she had figured out it was because he sensed early on that Hugh-Jay wanted her.

"Sleep tight," he said, and took the stairs two at a time.

"'Night, Chase," Laurie sang out, and laughed, because he was hurrying as if he were afraid of her. For a moment she considered calling him back and making it difficult for him to leave, but she was just sober enough to recognize that for the bad idea it was—he wouldn't weaken, and she'd be mortified.

Also, as much as they annoyed her, she liked being a Linder.

She liked being given a trip to that fancy hotel in Colorado, for instance.

Even before she heard the back door slam behind Chase, she was undoing her wet clothing, unzipping her shorts, pulling her T-shirt over her head, unhooking her bra, and letting it all fall to the floor as she danced in circles toward the bath in the master bedroom.

She stepped into the shower and let the water cascade over her. It was dangerous, people said, to bathe during an electrical storm, but Laurie wasn't concerned about that. Her life seemed to have come equipped with its own lightning rod that deflected bad luck away from her.

When she got out, she didn't dry off.

She'd dripped up the stairs, she would drip down the stairs.

It felt wonderful to have the whole house to herself.

At the top of the stairs she suddenly realized she was standing in a completely dark house. She flicked a light switch and nothing happened. While she had been in the shower—where she'd opened the shades to get the illumination of the lightning and lit a candle instead of turning on the lights—the power had gone out.

She felt an urge to walk naked through the dark house where nobody could see her from inside or outside. She took a step toward the stairs and then another few steps and found it lovely and pleasurable to be moving without clothing, feeling the touch of her thighs against each other, her own bare arms brushing against her body.

She looked down at herself, and approved of what she saw.

How many boys and men had wished they could look at and touch what she was seeing and touching? From the time she was a child she'd been aware of the attention of men and that it was edged with something that gave her little thrills in deep places. She crooked her right arm, raised it toward her mouth and licked it, tasting honey. So this was what men tasted on her skin, she thought with amused pride, something sweet and sexy, making her a perfect pastry.

She laughed at that as she started down the steps.

The drinking she'd done made her thoughts scattered, and now they focused briefly on her other—pathetic—brother-in-law. Bobby only made her laugh. Did he think she didn't catch him looking at her with moon eyes?

She wondered if Hugh-Jay noticed his brothers' attentions to her.

She hoped he did, because jealousy might make him more eager to please her, and anyway, she was so mad at him that she didn't care what he thought when she flirted with other men.

How *could* he? How could her own husband accuse her of stealing?

It *wasn't* stealing; it was balancing the scales. Making things more fair.

She was taking money from the accounts of the Colorado ranch, but just a little.

"I have a right," she said out loud in the dark house as she stepped onto its first floor. The Linders were stingy, in her view; if they weren't so stingy, she wouldn't have to pad her own bank account with such pitiful little amounts of . . . *change,* really, just a few dollars here and there to buy herself something nice, or to make Jody look pretty so people would admire her daughter. Besides, she was doing the work that Hugh-Jay was supposed to be doing but had no aptitude for, and so therefore what she was taking was only a *salary,* the one they were too cheap to give her.

"They owe me."

TWO MILES AWAY, on the front porch of an abandoned farmhouse where he had sat and watched the rain for hours, Hugh-Jay finally made up his mind about what he was going to have to do.

He'd gone to the farmhouse after seeing his mother and daughter in Rose. Upon leaving them, he had mentally kicked himself for turning right—in front of his mother's car—instead of turning left so she would believe he was heading for the highway to Colorado. It didn't matter, he tried to convince himself. She would assume that he had errands to run before he left town; she would never suspect that he wasn't going at all.

So he had made his right turn and kept driving out of Rose.

Five or so miles east he signaled and turned into a road leading to a farm that had failed a few months before and hadn't been sold yet. Hugh-Jay was depressed to see that prairie dog towns had already popped up in several places. Eventually they'd join into one huge underground mammal city with upright furry sentinels spaced outside atop their holes. He might have found them cute if he didn't know the destruction they wreaked on farm and ranch land. His sympathy was for the farmer who had gone bust and whose belongings had been auctioned as his family looked on.

Agriculture was hard, Hugh-Jay thought as he parked beside the empty farmhouse.

But not as hard as marriage was turning out to be.

He got out of his truck and slowly walked up to the front porch.

The wooden slats creaked under his boots.

He put a hand on a post and felt the rough surface of peeling paint, inhaled the smell of dirt rising from the humidity beneath the broken steps.

People he knew had lived here. There'd been small children playing on this porch and in the yard, filling the air with their laughter and the crying that accompanied skinned knees, bumped heads, and hurt feelings. He'd have sworn he could still hear one of them yell, "Mom!" It made his own heart hurt to think that if he didn't find a way to fix the rift in his marriage, it might be his house that would be haunted by the sounds of a family that didn't live there anymore.

Hugh-Jay had sat down on the porch swing and pushed off with one boot.

He had a bad decision to make and felt paralyzed by it.

His dad wanted him to check out the honesty of the Colorado ranch manager, but Hugh-Jay knew that it didn't need checking. There was nothing wrong with the man's honesty, or ethics, or morals, or whatever else you wanted to call it when a person either did or didn't take money that didn't belong to him.

The ranch manager didn't even know there was anything amiss.

When the manager sent his bills, everything was in order.

It was only when it left Hugh-Jay's own house that holes appeared in it.

Because he hated office work, he had asked Laurie to help him, and she gradually took over responsibility for the accounting that he was supposed to do. They'd both been surprised—and pleased—to discover she had an aptitude for it, and even though she complained about doing it, Hugh-Jay thought she took pride in being better at it than he was.

He'd been proud of her, too, and relieved to let go of a job he knew he'd botch. He'd looked forward to telling his father that he and Laurie were a team now. He hadn't anticipated that she'd find a way to siphon a few dollars here and there for herself.

That came as an awful shock.

Hugh-Jay had felt sick to his stomach ever since he realized the truth.

He'd raised the subject, ever so delicately—he thought—two days ago, and Laurie had gone through the roof, accusing him of "calling me a thief!" He knew their fight was part of the reason he'd gone off so furiously on those strangers who threw the cigarette out of their car on the highway, and also why he'd overreacted to his brother's return visit that morning to Laurie. He couldn't bring himself to yell at her, so he took it out on other people.

She was still furious at him, and letting him know it.

It was why he had surprised her at lunch. He'd wanted to make peace with her, show her he still loved her, but he didn't want her building up a head of angry steam before he got there.

It hadn't worked so well, he thought, with wry, grim recall.

He'd be lucky, at this rate, if she didn't kick him out of their bedroom.

Hugh-Jay knew he could go out to the Colorado ranch and lay the blame there, but there was no way he could blame an innocent man. That left him two choices, because his father wasn't going to be satisfied—or let it go—until the problem was solved and the thief revealed. There was just enough money missing, and the disguising of it was just suspicious enough that Hugh-Jay knew he couldn't pass it off as his own bad arithmetic. That left him the choice of telling the truth, which meant that Hugh Senior would never forgive his daughter-in-law or think of her the same way again. His mother would never forgive her, either, and they didn't like her very much to begin with. And if he took that way out, Laurie would never forgive *him*. The whole thing could just spiral forever.

He had one other choice: he could take the blame himself.

If he did that, his father would never trust *him* again.

Hugh Senior drew lines in the dirt, and honesty was one of them.

As the day pulled to a close around him and rain started to fall, and prairie dogs popped out of their holes to check the weather one last time, he stopped the movement of the porch swing, bent over and put his head in his hands.

He felt anguished. Lose his wife's affection, or lose his father's respect?

"It's such a little bit of money!" Laurie had cried out to him. "Who cares? Why are you making such a big deal of it?"

And it was, just a little bit, really, compared to all that the ranch owned, earned, spent.

But in his father's eyes, stealing a dime was as bad as stealing a dollar.

It was a big deal to Hugh Senior, a mark of character or lack of it, maybe not as bad as cutting fences, but still, a sign of . . . badness. He might forgive a starving woman for doing it, but he would never forgive a woman who had all the food she could eat, and pretty clothes, and the house she'd always wanted.

Hugh-Jay remained there as the rain got heavier and night settled in.

Near midnight, when the roads were flooding, he gave in to what he had to do and then worked up the courage to do it. If he had to choose between the respect of his parents or the love of his wife, he would choose his wife so that he could keep their little family together.

He prayed that his parents would find it in their hearts to forgive him.

Hugh-Jay ran through the pouring rain to his truck.

He was going to tell Laurie that he would take the blame, if she would promise never to do anything like that again. And then he would face his father and tell the necessary lie, and the old man was never going to forgive him, but he could spend the rest of his life, if need be, trying to regain his father's trust again. His decision killed him, because he respected his father above all other men, but his love for his baby daughter wouldn't let him brand her mother a thief.

Hugh-Jay drove back into town, barely aware of the pummeling rain.

. . .

SHORTLY AFTER Hugh-Jay drove past the Rose Motel and turned the corner toward home, Chase opened the motel door that his brother Bobby had left propped open with a pen to keep it from locking. When he walked into the dark room, he saw Bobby seated by the window, drinking beer, and staring out at the rain.

"What took you so long?" Bobby asked him in a surly tone.

"What are you talking about? It didn't take long. Long enough to grab some dry clothes, is all. Here, I brought some for you. I can't believe you're sitting there sopping wet like that."

Chase tossed dry jeans and a shirt at his brother, who parried them with his left hand so they fell to the floor.

Chase started getting out of his own wet clothing.

"I saw Hugh-Jay drive by a few minutes ago," Bobby told him.

"Couldn't have. He's in Colorado by now."

"No, he's not. It was his truck, plain as thunder."

As if on cue, thunder actually rolled at that moment, so loud they had to wait before they could hear each other speak.

"You sure?"

"Hell, yes, I'm sure. I think I'd know that truck!"

"Did you tell Dad?"

"Why would I? If Hugh-Jay didn't get on the road, it's not like Dad can do anything about it now."

"I guess not. And it's not like he doesn't have a home to sleep in."

Bobby took a long drink from the lip of a beer bottle. "Laurie okay?"

"Fine, why wouldn't she be? A little drunk. How drunk are you?"

"Shut up."

Chase was glad to do that and went right to bed to prove it, leaving his younger brother still at the window, morosely looking at the rain until he fell asleep in the chair. A crack of lightning woke them both up a few minutes later, along with waking up their father two doors down.

• • •

ON THE STAIRCASE, Laurie let the tips of her fingers slide along the wall so that her arms were spread out as if she were about to take off and fly. When she reached the first floor, she wandered into the dining room, touching things, letting her hands slide up and down the curved tops of the walnut chairs, clicking her fingernails over the spines of the books on the living room bookshelves. She lay down on her back on one of the sofas and stared out the window at the rain coming down, spreading her legs as if for a man, imagining making love in this storm, in this room, on this couch, in the darkness lit by lightning.

She got up and went to a window, naked and invisible to the world.

Finally, she walked lightly through the foyer, past the mirrored, walnut tallboy against the wall, stopping for a long admiring look at herself, turning to the right and the left and then all the way around to see herself from every angle, trying to view her body as men saw her, voluptuous and lush, a special woman to stroke and please and pamper and adore. She sighed with the contentment of the moment. Then she walked on and pushed through the swinging door into the kitchen and went to the sink to get a drink of water, running her fingers under the water first, then drinking slowly, breathing between every sip. The thunder was crashing all around, blocking out every other sound, and intermittent lightning illuminated patches of the world outside her windows.

She felt safe inside the great vault of a house, and protected by the storm.

And yet, what she wanted to do in that instant was leave. Not forever. Just for this moment, this wild moment when she felt the thunder in her bones. She wanted to run outside, naked, into the rain and lightning and let it pour on her and flash around her and scare her, and she wanted to keep running until she was out of Rose, out of her marriage, out of her life, away from her child, just for a little while.

"Or, maybe I'd never come back," she dared herself, putting the glass down.

She thought she heard noises on the kitchen porch, muffled by the storm.

At the sink, she tensed, listening, but didn't run to put on clothes.

Then she heard the kitchen door open behind her, heard the rushing sound of the noise of the storm coming in, heard it cut off when the door closed.

She gripped the edge of the sink and closed her eyes.

The storm was so loud she couldn't hear the stocking-clad footsteps coming toward her, so the first she knew of his presence at her back was when his hands came around and cupped her breasts.

She gasped and leaned back into him.

"I thought you'd be with Belle," she murmured as Meryl's hands moved down, and she gasped again. "Why aren't you with Belle?"

"Because I can't be until we're married," her husband's best friend said as he turned her to face him. "Because it practically killed me not to screw her tonight when she begged for it. Because you called me, you little troublemaker, and told me he'd be gone tonight. Because it could be a long time before we get a chance like this again."

"What?" she mocked him. "Not because you love me?"

"No," he said, leaning down to kiss her. "Because I want you, and you want me."

She always had wanted him in this way and this way only, in those years when Meryl Tapper was still slim, and athletic, good-looking and sexy. They'd been Homecoming King and Queen together when he was a junior and she was only a freshman, but she'd never had her eye on Meryl for anything but fun, and he'd never had his eyes on her for anything but that, either. They had their hooks set for bigger prizes—the Linders, Belle and Hugh-Jay, and even managed to convince themselves, sometimes, they loved them.

"Did you park in back?"

"I left my truck at my office and walked over."

He was in his socks, which were wet clear through.

"Walked?" she laughed. "You really wanted this."

"So much I barely *could* walk," he said, making them both laugh at his dirty joke.

She gave him a teasing look. "What are you waiting for?"

Without taking off his own clothes, just unzipping his jeans, Meryl lifted her and took her once with her back against the sink, the metal rim cutting into her until her skin broke and she bled and complained to him. Then he led her upstairs—moving so fast they knocked over a chair, and laughed about that, too. On the second floor, she stepped ahead of him, pulling him to the small guest room at the end of the hall, where they always went, because they didn't want to leave any clues in the master bedroom for Hugh-Jay to find, not that he'd ever in a million years suspect what they did now and then, they assured themselves whenever they did it.

"Do you feel guilty?" she asked him as he pushed into her again.

Hugh-Jay never talked during sex; he treated it like a sacred ritual, making love to her in reverent silence as if she were a virgin every time. It irritated and bored her so much that she did everything she could to get it over with quickly. Sex was supposed to be *fun*, it wasn't supposed to be church.

"No, I don't feel guilty, do you?" he asked. "It's not as if we don't care about them."

"I know. Want to meet me out of town somewhere?"

"What?" Right in the middle of things, he laughed, which she loved. She loved the fact that they didn't take it seriously. Her back felt raw and bruised and it stung where he had rammed her into the edge of the sink, but the pain pleased her, as if it were a badge of sexual merit, like hickeys and whisker burns used to be when they were kids in high school. The evidence of their mating had changed, but the cause remained the same, and she also loved that and wanted to show it off by wearing hip-hugger jeans or a bikini.

"Where?" he asked.

"The Broadmain Hotel. In Colorado."

Meryl laughed again. "You mean the Broadmoor?"

"Yes! Annabelle is giving me five days there."

She'd inched it up from three days.

"On your own? Without Hugh-Jay?"

"Uh-huh. You could come, too. They'd never know."

"Why would she do that?"

Laurie grinned. "Because she loves me best."

"Everybody does," he said, and pushed in deep enough to make her squeal.

Even now, when Meryl was an attorney with the potential for making okay money, she still felt she'd made the right and practical choice in marrying Hugh-Jay. Maybe she could have had it all by marrying Meryl, but the "all" that Meryl could offer wasn't anywhere near as much as being a Linder could do for her—and for her children's future, she thought with righteous virtue. And marrying her wasn't anywhere near as helpful to Meryl as marrying the Linders' only daughter might be. He would be their attorney, the ranches' main attorney, recommended to all their friends; his future was made, as was hers . . .

Provided Hugh-Jay overlooked that little money thing . . .

"Think about it," she murmured, meaning the trip.

"Are you kidding? That's probably all I'll be thinking about now."

She laughed, and made excited noises to encourage him, which made him groan and work harder. He imprisoned her wrists above her head, slamming them hard against the backboard of the bed, which startled and thrilled her. She played as if she were trying to get away by twisting and turning beneath him, and that turned him on more. He told her she was the most beautiful, sexy woman in the world and no other woman would ever be as good in bed as she was, and he would always want her, and that she would always know this was what he was thinking of whenever he looked at her, wherever they were, in church, at their in-laws' house, across a supper table, even when he was standing at the altar of his own wedding, and when she heard that, she let him do whatever he wanted to do to her.

It was just for fun, no harm intended, no feelings to be hurt.

39

IN SPITE OF THE STORM—or because he was so worried and anxious he was oblivious to it—Hugh-Jay made a quick stop at Bailey's for a shot of courage and a hamburger before going home. There, he heard from several people about the argument—and near physical fight—between Billy Crosby and his brothers. He heard about the swing Billy took at Laurie, and how he got tossed out into the driving rain by his youngest brother and Bailey. He heard that his father and brothers were staying at the motel, that Belle had gone to spend the night at her bank/museum, and that his brother Chase had seen to it that Laurie got a ride home.

He stayed for a second beer, just to hear about the whole thing.

By the time he left, whatever small bit of tolerance Hugh-Jay had left for Billy Crosby was gone, just as all sympathy for Billy had disappeared from the hearts of the rest of his family and from nearly every other person in Rose.

He felt so angry about Billy's swinging at Laurie he could have killed him.

He ran through the rain again, climbed into his truck one more time, and drove home past the motel where the other men in his family were. When they wanted to know in the morning why he was home, he'd tell them he started to Colorado late and the storm had prevented him from going all the way. He hoped he could lie about it. According to his mom, he was terrible at lying.

He parked behind his house and hurried from his truck to the back porch with his head down against the rain, seeing nothing but the ground ahead of him, which was how he noticed boot prints in the mud. Some man had come this way, running at a loping trot, from the look of the spacing and depth of the prints. Hugh-Jay stepped into them, squashing them to flatness and mixing them with his own prints. They were filled with rainwater almost a second after he lifted each boot, and eventually they disappeared as the rain flattened the mud and everything ran and eroded. At the porch, Hugh-Jay took off his own wet, muddy boots and then his socks, which would only get soaked on the floor of the porch if he left them on. He looked for the boots the other person had worn but didn't see them. Maybe whoever it was had knocked, Laurie didn't answer, and he left again. Hugh-Jay looked back for prints going in the other direction, but it was too dark to see.

He stepped into his house barefoot and dripping.

A lightning flash showed him a picture that jolted his adrenaline.

Beside the table where'd he sat for lunch, a chair was overturned.

A familiar straw hat with a tightly rolled and blackened brim lay on the floor, as if it had fallen off its owner's head and then been crushed, as if somebody had stepped on it during a struggle.

Billy's hat.

The moment Hugh-Jay saw it, he panicked and thought, *Laurie!*

Billy was drunk, he was angry, he was crazy, and he'd already tried to attack her at Bailey's.

He raised his face to the ceiling, heart pounding, listening.

He pulled off his rain slicker, let it fall, and kept moving.

He wanted to shout his wife's name but didn't dare. What if Billy had a gun?

Desperate to find and rescue his wife, terrified of what kind of revenge a drunken Billy Crosby might be taking on her even at this moment, but also realizing the urgent need to move silently, Hugh-Jay took long strides to his office on the first floor and went immediately to his gun case, where the key was in the lock.

He pulled out a long-barreled pistol, his favorite of his small arms.

It was powerful, sharp of aim, straight of shot, and after the thirty seconds it took him to arm it, loaded.

The gun held in front of him, he hurried down the first-floor hallway, finally grasping that the noise of the storm covered every sound he made, though that meant it also covered every sound that might be coming from upstairs.

What if Billy hadn't taken her to the second floor?

He raced through the other rooms on the first floor, cursing himself for the delay when he didn't find anyone. He reached the upper landing and quickly checked the rooms there. Master bedroom and bath, second bath, large guest room, Jody's room, leaving only one to go. With a speed born of fear and fury, he covered the remaining few feet of carpet, burst into the room, and saw the two figures on the bed, the man on top of the woman. His heart clenched with the pain of heartache, betrayal, and outrage as he yelled, "Billy! Get off of her!"

Hugh-Jay's voice—harsh, furious, frightened, and sounding nothing like normal—was unrecognizable to the couple in bed. Laurie, seeing a dark and threatening figure in the doorway, screamed. Meryl, rolling off of her, saw the same shadow, but also saw the shape of the gun, and he lunged at the man's waist. As they fell together to the floor, Hugh-Jay pointed the gun down at the man he still thought was Billy Crosby, but the man moved at the last moment, shoving the gun backward. The bullet fired into Hugh-Jay's own abdomen, knocking him back onto the carpet.

Deafened and shocked by the noise and light of the shot, Meryl saw and heard darkness for several moments. It was only when Laurie began screaming Hugh-Jay's name that he realized whose blood he had all over him.

"Oh, my God," he said. "Oh, my God. Oh, no. Oh, God, please no."

Meryl Tapper helplessly watched his friend and his future bleed to death on the carpet.

40

MERYL STOOD in the shower in the spare bathroom on the second floor with his clothes on, holding a naked Laurie by her upper arms as she screamed and wept. Hugh-Jay's blood washed from his face, his hair, his neck and arms, his clothes. Her arms where he held her washed pink from the blood on his hands and from the spots on her body where it had splattered onto her. A bit of it had reached her lips, which terrified her when she realized it by tasting it. He thought she might claw her own tongue out in her frantic attempts to get the blood off of it.

Afterward, he wrapped her in a towel and held her.

"What will we do?" Laurie cried, shaking and sobbing. "What will we do?"

Meryl went over multiple scenarios in his head, just as if he were still in law school reviewing evidence from case histories and trials. There were no working phones. They couldn't call the sheriff, or call for help for Hugh-Jay, even if it weren't too late for that. He was dead, not instantly, but quickly from the gushing blood they were helpless to stem.

They could drive to Henderson City to report it, they could . . .

We could what? Meryl asked himself as his own teeth chattered with cold fear.

He made himself keep thinking: If they told the story truly, then Laurie was an adulterer and he was as good as one, and they would forever be held responsible for Hugh-Jay's death even if nobody thought they'd meant to kill him. But how many people would believe that? Who would believe it was an accident?

Not many, Meryl thought, wanting to throw up.

And the Linders . . . oh, God, he thought, the Linders.

"I can't have been here," he finally said to her. "I was never here tonight."

"What about me?" she screamed at him.

"You have to leave."

"Leave? But—"

"This house. Rose. So people think somebody took you."

"What?" She looked at him as if he were insane.

"Laurie, we have to get you out of here. It has to look as if somebody broke in here and raped and kidnapped you and killed Hugh-Jay when he tried to protect you."

"I can't do that!" She looked stunned, confused. "Where would I go?"

"We'll figure that out. I'll take you somewhere tonight, and then we'll figure out the rest of it."

"Come with me!"

"What?"

"Meryl, come with me. We'll go away together! It will be all right."

"No, it won't, it will never be all right if we do that. I have to stay here. I have to go back to my office and get up in the morning and act as if I was there all night after I left Belle. You have to be gone, where nobody can find you, and then when they do, you have to pretend you were taken."

"I can't do that!"

"Yes, you can. You *have* to. Get dressed. Don't bring anything. Not your purse. Nothing."

"I don't want to, Meryl!"

"Would you rather be charged with his murder?"

"What? But we didn't—"

"Can you prove that? They'll want us to prove that, and we can't."

"Maybe he killed himself, we could say he—"

"Because he found us in bed? No, I don't think we want that, either."

"Meryl, I can't do what you say I should do. I can't—"

"Go put on some clothes. Whatever you need later, I'll get it for you."

When she wouldn't budge, he ran into her bedroom and took the first thing he saw: her yellow sundress. He came back and put it over her head, pulling it down over her body. Then he picked her up and carried her outside before he remembered he didn't have his truck. "Shut up," he told her, so the neighbors wouldn't hear her during moments when the storm died down. Fearful of being witnessed now, she acquiesced to his plan, even telling him to use Billy Crosby's truck, which was behind the garage.

They rolled it silently down to the street.

With the storm still boiling all around them, Meryl drove her out to Testament Rocks over dirt and gravel roads that made the going slippery and treacherous and threatened to dump them into ditches. They drove through low places where the water came halfway up the tires, and once the truck got stuck and he had to rock it from drive to park and back again several times in order to rock it into moving again.

"Why *here*?" Laurie screamed at him when he stopped the truck. The windshield wipers revealed glimpses of the huge rock formations that loomed over the dark, desolate landscape.

"Because nobody else in the world will be here during this storm."

"What if you get stuck on your way back into town, or on your way back to pick me up?"

"I won't get stuck. You saw how I got out of that already."

"You can't leave me here alone like this!"

"I have to go back and take care of things at your house before the storm stops," he yelled back at her. He knew he couldn't think straight about how to cover their tracks if he also had to cope with her hysteria. "You can get under that shelf of rock over there. You'll be okay. Wait for me—"

"Like I have a choice!"

"I'll come back for you when I finish cleaning everything up and we'll figure this out."

When she wouldn't budge from the truck, Meryl came around to her side, flung open her door and forced her out. She was sobbing and screaming about rain and Hugh-Jay and Jody, and she beat on Meryl as he picked her up again and carried her to where he wanted her to be.

"Laurie, our lives depend on this. I swear I'll come back for you!"

She clung and he forced her to let go and pushed her away. She tried to run after him but he was faster. He left Laurie standing in the middle of nowhere with only the furious storm and the huge rocks for company.

When he drove away, leaving her in rain, thunder, lightning, and isolation, she was so terrified and furious that she half climbed, half ran up one of the huge rock formations to watch his headlights abandon her.

She was forty feet up when her shoes slipped and she fell, landing not only on chalky ground but on rock as hard as centuries could build it.

41

BLEEDING AND BROKEN, Laurie lay on the chalky, rocky earth in a daze of shock and pain. Her consciousness faded in and out as her five senses surged in to startle her awake and then disappear again: smell of her own urine soaking her sundress; tastes of dirt, of beer and catsup; sounds of the wind that whipped her dark hair stingingly into her open eyes and moaned and sang around the rocks; sight of enormous clouds rushing east; painful stab of rocks beneath her shattered back.

It all blinked on and off as she woke up, faded out, woke up.

At first she felt terrified of lying helpless on her back, because she feared drowning with her face to the sky. Thunder rumbled the ground beneath her, making her shudder involuntarily, making her broken bones rattle agonizingly inside of her like seeds in a gourd. Flashes of lightning illuminated the landscape in nightmarish relief, turning rocks to gargoyles looming over her.

But then the first storm passed, and she found herself staring up into a sky so clear and deep blue-black that it hurt her heart to see it. In a moment that changed her, Laurie felt grateful to have been flung onto her back, her poor ruined back, so that she might see this astonishing beauty.

She had not known the world could be so lovely.

She'd always thought of the landscape of Rose, Kansas, as boring, had never understood when other people raved about its supposed glories, its famous soaring rock monuments and its sunsets, its flat horizons and dramatic cloud banks. Now she understood: it was wonderful! It looked transformed and magical in the shifting, changing light of the moon, stars, and clouds. Light rolled over the Rocks like waves, changing their colors from soft orange to gold to white to silver to black and back to gold again.

It appeared strange, enchanted, like the landscape of a fairy tale with a tragic ending. She had thought herself a princess, too special, too beautiful for her own hometown. Hugh-Jay had played her wealthy prince, and the big house in Rose had been their castle where they were going to live happily ever after inside its thick stone walls that were supposed to keep the three of them safe.

The Rocks above her looked now as if they had been washed in delicate pastels she would have stolen for a dress.

She had literally never noticed such beauty in the world before.

If her arms could have moved, she would have reached up to touch the amber moon and the winking stars that appeared from under the clouds as they scudded west to east. A memory from high school surprised her, because she couldn't remember ever having paid much attention: *From Missouri to the Colorado border, Kansas climbs nearly half a mile in altitude.* Which teacher had said that? She couldn't recall, and wouldn't previously have cared, except that now the memory felt like someone kind had come to keep her company in her loneliness.

Thank you, she sent to the unremembered teacher.

Thank you, she repeated, to taste its novelty in her mouth.

But then that memory of the slant of Kansas gave her a sudden dizzying feeling of lying on a bed with her head lower than her feet.

Oh, God!

The world tilted back into flatness again, and she stopped worrying about dying by choking on her own seasick vomit.

She stared up, and felt entranced by the sky again, and soothed by the cool wind between storms. She felt embraced by the vast landscape that had previously felt so barren and dead to her. *It wasn't lifeless at all!* The eighty-foot rock formations that rose beside, and above, and all around her looked like living creatures now, protectively watching over her with their sharp, cold faces.

Why did you let me fall? she asked them, sadly, but without blame.

Everybody in her county was proud of them, these Testament Rocks.

Geologists and archaeologists traveled from all over the world to study the soil or dig for fossils here, and yet she had declared these formations—these amazing, huge, natural sculptures—stupid and boring. There was a sphinx! There was a castle! Over there were towers and pyramids and eagles made of rock! At other moments those same rock formations stood out starkly on the plain like giants who had paused in a long walk; she now thought they looked wise and fascinating, like living beings who knew the secrets of the ages.

And yet the Rocks had let her feet skid, let her hands grasp air, let her plunge screaming through darkness and rain, falling through sickening yards of space, falling like a bird with oiled wings that wouldn't fly, like an angel in a spinning dive to earth.

I'm no angel, Laurie admitted to the Rocks above her.

She had a feeling they already knew that about her.

Tears leaked from the corners of her eyes.

Once they would have been tears of self-pity; now they were for Jody.

She felt a pang of love so painful it made her cry out with pity and sorrow for her child. For a few moments, for her three-year-old daughter's sake, she fought what was coming. She tried to move, to rise, to run, but it was torture, and impossible.

Her heart and thoughts continued the fight for a little while longer.

When that made no difference, she tried pleading.

Please, she feverishly begged whatever might be listening, *take care of her and protect her.*

She wished her daughter could know that her mom had fought hard to live.

Headlights like two distant tiny moons would soon be coming if Meryl had told her the truth, but Laurie didn't believe their puny light would reach her in time to save her.

42

MERYL DROVE BACK into Rose and ran back into Hugh-Jay's and Laurie's home, going in again through the back door. Hugh-Jay's boots were in their accustomed spot by the back door, and Meryl left them there. The first things he saw inside were Hugh-Jay's yellow slicker, a straw hat, and the overturned chair on the floor.

He left them where they were.

It dawned on him the hat was Billy Crosby's.

He walked over to the sink where he had first had sex with Laurie that night and examined it for anything linking the scene to him. He saw the bit of her blood on the metal lip of the sink, and decided it was smart to leave that alone, too. Whatever he had done, let the sheriff decide that Billy had done.

It wasn't as if Billy *wouldn't* have done it, if he could have.

Meryl knew his own fingerprints were all over the house.

Did that matter? It would seem odd if they weren't, he decided, although the guest room and bathroom upstairs might be a problem, albeit not one he couldn't solve with a dust rag and a can of dusting aerosol for the bedroom and cleanser and a sponge for the bathroom.

He looked at his watch and then outside at the storm.

It looked as if it would keep pouring and thundering for hours.

There was plenty of time to do all that needed doing.

His only real worry was exactly what Laurie feared, which was flooding that might keep him from getting back to her. He had to get back to her. She was an emotional unguided missile aimed directly at both of them if he didn't stick with her and control her.

There was time, but he couldn't afford to waste it.

He washed the bathroom first, watching out for hairs in the shower, getting rid of as much blood as he could, although he wasn't particularly worried about that as it was only Hugh-Jay's blood and not theirs. If someone else—Billy, for instance—had committed these acts, that person could have been expected to use the shower to wash off, too.

They had left bloody footprints on the upstairs carpets.

Meryl ran to the basement for bleach, made a solution of it with water, grabbed a scrub brush and went back upstairs. He flooded the bloody floors and carpet with the solution and rubbed at the footprints until they ran together and their outlines were indistinguishable by size or footfall.

Now the upstairs smelled hideously of acrid bleach.

He preferred that to the worse smells that it covered up.

He had told Laurie he would bring her what she needed.

But he wouldn't do it now, and it wouldn't include anything she owned.

It would have to be all new. She would have to have a new identity.

He felt overwhelmed by how much would be required to save both of them from here on out. She didn't think she could do it, and Meryl wasn't at all sure she could, either.

He would deal with that later; right now he had to prepare the bedroom.

He stripped the sheets, for fear of hair fibers. Hair from his head anywhere in the house was one thing, but pubic hair in a bed with semen stains on it was something else entirely. He wiped down all the surfaces, rather than try to remember which of them he had touched.

Meryl left the gun where it lay loose in Hugh-Jay's right hand. He had, essentially, shot himself, which took care of the problem of fingerprints. If people didn't jump to the conclusion that Billy Crosby had murdered him, then maybe they'd think Hugh-Jay had killed himself. But when Meryl stepped back and viewed the obvious signs of violence and struggle in the room, and those downstairs in the kitchen, he doubted that scenario would convince anyone.

All the while he stepped around his best friend's body.

Best friend, he thought several times.

Had they been best friends? Brothers was more like it. Brothers raised at first by two different families and then merged into a single one, the better one. Everybody knew Meryl loved Hugh-Jay, and they would expect him to be incredibly upset by his friend's death. There'd be no faking there: he *was* incredibly upset by this. Whoever had killed Hugh-Jay was going to be hated. Meryl had to make sure that wouldn't be him. He worried a little over the fact that he didn't feel very sad, that he only felt worried about what this night might mean to his own life. And then he put that behind him, because if all went well, he would have the rest of his life to make it up to the Linders—and to Hugh-Jay's daughter—the best way he could, with attention and hard work and taking care of them and their business.

"I'm sorry, buddy," he said when he was finished. "We didn't mean to."

After throwing the thin quilt aside, he gathered up the sheets and pillowcases and walked them downstairs, knowing that his footprints in wet socks would dry and disappear before morning. He stuffed the linens into a black plastic trash bag and put them in Billy's truck, still unsure of what he was going to do with them. He'd worry about that later, because he had to get back out to Laurie before the roads were too flooded to allow him through.

Meryl stood in the darkness and the rain taking a long last look at the house that looked like a huge gravestone to him now. Had he taken care of everything? Had he thought of everything? Feeling unsure, he went back inside and rechecked every room to look for things he'd missed, nearly fainting when he spotted his own bolo tie down on the carpet between the far side of the bed and the wall. He had removed it when he got undressed to get into bed with Laurie and put it on the end table, where it had fallen off.

Feeling shaken, Meryl stuffed it down inside his suit coat pocket.

Then he hurried down the stairs and went around the first floor using a knuckle to push the button locks closed on the outside doors, hoping to make it just that much harder, and delay that much longer, anybody's entrance into the house.

SHE WAS DEAD when he found her, and it wasn't hard to discern why.

A large shred of her dress had caught on a rock sticking out of the formation she had apparently tried to climb. Meryl realized she must have gotten a long way up for a fall to have killed her, or else she just happened to hit at a fatal angle. He also realized this was going to make his life much, much easier. All he needed to do now was get rid of her body, Billy's truck, and the damned bed linens in time to walk back to Rose and climb into his own bed to await the moment when someone called to tell him the terrible news.

Her body, shed of its clothing, went into an abandoned feedlot waste pit in the next county. Billy's truck—with her yellow sundress tied into a plastic bag Meryl found in the truck—got sent into the flood-waters over the highway. In desperation, out of ideas and running out of time before sunrise, Meryl picked up the plastic bag with the bed linens and carried them back to Rose with him. He felt ridiculous doing it. He could get rid of a body and a two-ton vehicle, but he couldn't figure out how to do the same with some sheets? He'd been afraid to throw them into the feedlot waste pit, for fear they wouldn't sink fast enough, and he didn't want to leave them in the truck to be found there. As he walked home, daring the lightning to get him, Meryl nearly started laughing hysterically at this last dilemma. It seemed so stupid compared to everything else he'd had to take care of this night.

When he woke up to the phone ringing in the morning, he knew what to do about the bedclothes that were his remaining problem. He was afraid to wash them for fear Belle or someone else would see him doing it; he was also afraid to take them to the dump, or put them out with the trash. He knew he was being paranoid about something that probably should be easy, but it felt as if all of his fears had centered now on the damned sheets and pillowcases. So after emptying out a cardboard file box, Meryl folded the sheets, put them inside it, and closed the lid on top of them. He found threaded mailing tape in his desk and wrapped the box in it so tightly and completely all around that even scissors would have a hard time finding a place to cut. Then he put it aside to give to Belle to store unknowingly in her basement for him, "because it's full of a client's personal records and your bank is more fireproof than my office." Later, much later when nobody would be paying any attention related to Hugh-Jay or Laurie, he could go back and get the box and finally destroy it. And if he didn't, maybe the wet fabric would mildew so completely in the box that it would eventually disintegrate and be no threat to him. It wasn't as if they were much of a threat anyway—hair fiber analysis was an inexact science; a good defense lawyer would cast doubt on it.

Having thought his way out of his last problem, Meryl hurried off to help his future wife and her family in their sad time of great need. He absolved himself with the sentence that became the source of his confidence and his reassurance: *It wasn't a crime, it was a tragedy.*

43

IN BETWEEN the first and second semesters at Henderson County Consolidated High School, Jody decided to clean out her collection of backpacks. Her idea was that if she destroyed her collection, then maybe that would end her nearly lifelong obsession with it.

It took her two days of going through each pack individually, examining each item and deciding if there was anything worth keeping or giving away. In the end she dumped almost all of it into black plastic trash bags, which she took to the county dump. The packs themselves ate up additional trash bags. She thought about trying to clean them up so they could be donated—to the school where she taught, for instance—but there wasn't one of them that any self-respecting kid would have wanted to use. They were beaten up, torn up, filthy, out of fashion. But there were a few interesting objects inside of them, a dozen or so, that she wanted to show her aunt Belle, in case Belle might see any value in them for her museum.

. . .

HUGH SENIOR had been forced to eat crow about the Rose Historical Museum.

"I thought it was just a little hobby for her," he admitted freely to people, more freely than his daughter liked, given that he also said, "I thought I was throwing money away, just to let Belle pretend she had a job."

But he'd been wrong, as he was happy to say now.

Jody thought it was remarkable that during years when Rose was failing in almost every other way, her aunt's museum-in-a-bank thrived. Belle had turned out to be a great curator with a superb eye for historical artifacts and a talent for displaying them. Plus, she was a public relations fool, as her brother Chase liked to say with admiration in his voice. Belle didn't like that praise, either, given that he followed it with, "Who would have guessed?"

As for Belle's writing, what Annabelle used to call "Belle's little articles" turned out to be good enough to attract assignments from major publications. She became what Meryl called "the go-to girl" for historians and archaeologists, geologists and paleontologists, writers, photographers, and artists, even for the occasional television documentary about ancient seas and rivers, not to mention the busloads of schoolchildren who journeyed to Rose to run around the famous Rocks and giggle their way through her museum. The scientists who arrived in Rose contributed to the local economy: they ate at Bailey's and the truck stop, and they bought bottled water and suntan lotion at George's. Some of them got invited out to High Rock Ranch for supper and horseback riding for them and stimulating conversation for the Linders. Jody's grandfather was especially proud of the Nobel Prize–winning scientist from China who had loved Annabelle's homemade barbecue sauce.

Jody was proud of her aunt's "little hobby."

BELLE'S CHARM still didn't extend very generously toward the family, and sometimes especially not toward Jody. Sometimes Jody worried that she was the reason Belle and Meryl never had children, because they'd had to spend too much time helping take care of her.

"You got these where, and how?" Belle challenged her niece.

"Out at the Rocks. It's just stuff I happened to see and pick up."

"Just happened to," she said, casting a skeptical eye from the objects to Jody. Her aunt had always been a large woman, patterned on Hugh Senior's family rather than on Annabelle's; over the years her good cooking had broadened her as well, so that she cut a formidable figure. "Like you did when you were a little girl?"

"Maybe."

"I didn't know you kept doing that."

"Well, I did. No harm done."

"Hmm," Belle said, sounding skeptical.

"Mostly junk," she declared after a few silent moments of close examination of the first batch that Jody spilled out onto the glass countertop.

"Which ones *aren't* junk?"

"This one." Belle held up a bit of old wood that had a groove in it like old school desks did. "And this one"—a locket without a chain, but with an old-fashioned photo of a girl in it—"and this one"—a metal hinge that might also have come from a desk. "There used to be a one-room schoolhouse near the Rocks. It was ripped apart by a tornado in 1882. Killed the teacher and all six children. I suspect these could be remnants of it."

"I found them together."

They had worked themselves up to the surface, as things did at the Rocks.

"You did? I'm glad to hear it. That makes it even more likely."

The locket tugged at Jody's heartstrings, given that it might have been worn by the schoolteacher or one of the children.

"Will you display them, Aunt Belle?"

But her aunt didn't answer. She was staring at the second batch of items that Jody was rolling out onto the glass. When Belle finally spoke, her voice sounded choked and she didn't look at Jody.

"Where did you find this?" she demanded.

Belle held a tarnished little sculpture in the palm of her hand.

"At the Rocks, like everything else. Remember one time I asked you if Mom wore a charm bracelet? I thought maybe that's what this was, a charm."

"It's not a charm," Belle said, her voice harsh. She turned it over, showing a circular clasp on the back of it. "It's designed to hold the ropes of a bolo tie."

The "charm" was a silver rearing horse.

Jody took it from her, noticing with alarm that her aunt's hand was trembling, and looked more closely at the back of it. "Is this an inscription? *M.T.* M.T.? Meryl Tapper? Aunt Belle, did this belong to Uncle Meryl?"

"Yes," Belle whispered, and then she finally looked into her niece's eyes. Her own were filled with tears and she looked frightened. "Jody, I gave it to him for Valentine's Day that year."

"That year?"

"The year your parents . . ." She couldn't finish her sentence. "The last time I saw him wear it was the night they died. He told me the next day he'd lost it. I never saw him wear it again. Jody, if he lost it at the Rocks that night . . ."

Belle suddenly ran from around the counter.

Jody, her heart pounding with dread and her mind trying to refuse what it was hearing, ran after her aunt. She followed her down the basement stairs into the storage area where Belle kept box upon box of things she had been given, had bought, had found, herself. Like a woman gone mad with terror, Belle pulled at the boxes, destroying her neat piles, reaching back farther and farther until the reached a row at the farthest remove from the front line of boxes. She knocked boxes aside, heedless of what emptied out of them until she reached one on the bottom. It looked different from the others—not like ordinary storage containers but like a cardboard box that a law firm might use to store old transcripts. Jody had seen old ones just like it in her uncle Meryl's law office.

"Get me scissors!" Belle ordered her, pointing to where they hung.

Jody got them and gave them to her aunt, who ripped into the old, threaded wrapping tape that had been wound around the box as if its contents were valuable enough to be stored in Fort Knox.

When the tape was undone, Belle lifted the lid off.

Jody saw only what looked like rotten fabric inside, but Belle saw something that made her burst into tears and rock back and forth on her knees and moan. Scared, anxious, Jody knelt beside her and put a gentle hand on her aunt's shoulder, only to have it shaken off.

"Aunt Belle, what is that in the box?"

"Sheets," her aunt sobbed. "The bloody sheets from the bed in the room where your daddy died. Meryl gave me this box to store the next morning. He said it had confidential records of one of his clients and it would be safer stored here than in his office." And then she said two things that shocked her niece. "Damn her! Damn her, damn her! I saw her flirt with him, but I thought, well, she flirts with every man. I should have known, I should have known." She lifted the loathsome sheets— and what looked like pillowcases—out of the box and said the second thing that shocked her niece. "Why didn't he just destroy these? Why, oh why, did he leave them here?"

Jody stood up and backed away in horror.

"Uncle Meryl killed my dad?" She began to shriek, over and over, until Belle had to come and take hold of her to stop her. But she couldn't stop Jody from screaming, "What did he do to my mother, *what did he do to my mother?*"

MERYL MIGHT NOT have confessed, even when confronted with the irrefutable DNA evidence of the remaining hair strands that the sheriff turned over to the state crime lab, since any old semen stains on the sheets were long past using. He still might have pleaded not guilty and gone to trial. There wasn't any other evidence to connect him to the murders, and the fact that he'd had sex with Laurie Linder didn't prove he'd killed her husband. Based on past and recent events, his defense still could have built another case against Billy Crosby to provide the jury with reasonable doubt.

But Jody and her grandfather visited Meryl.

Hugh Senior sat across from him and stared without speaking.

Jody begged her uncle to tell her where her mother was.

She thought it was her grandfather's stare that broke him, rather than her pleading, and even then he didn't say it directly to them. He told the sheriff, claiming that he felt squeamish about telling his niece that he'd put her mother's body in a feedlot waste lagoon.

Jody doubted that he confessed out of pity, but shame worked fine, too.

After that it was easier for him to admit to killing Valentine as well.

"None of it was murder, it was just one terrible accident after another," he maintained to the sheriff and to everyone else who'd listen to him, as if he had never intended to kill anybody. This, despite the fact that he confessed to killing Valentine in order to put all the investigative energy into a new murder trial instead of the old one, because he felt threatened by the sheriff's taunts about using the hair for DNA analysis. "The other deaths," Meryl protested, in full lawyerly self-righteous dudgeon, "Hugh-Jay and Laurie, they were tragic accidents, too. It was all a terrible tragedy, not a crime. Hugh-Jay was my best friend, he was like a brother to me, and I loved—I love—the Linders, I owe everything to them."

Two weeks after his arrest, Meryl Tapper had a massive heart attack.

The weight he had gained over the years—perhaps unconsciously to disguise the fact that he had ever been a man whom a beautiful woman might desire—helped kill him. The Linder family was grateful for the easy ending; after Billy's rampage at the ranch, they had no appetite—not even Bobby or Chase—for more revenge.

44

"GRANDMA," JODY SAID, after she finished telling about her day, three months later. "I need to ask you something." They were in her kitchen in the big stone house in Rose, and not at the ranch, because her uncles and their children were in town and some of them were staying with her. Even in Jody's house, it was Annabelle who was doing the cooking on this night, which was a wonderful luxury for a young schoolteacher coming home from a full day of teaching.

On this early winter evening, Jody felt exhausted and exhilarated, all at the same time. One of her shyest students had shown courage in raising her hand and answering a question that afternoon.

Jody felt inspired to speak up, too.

"Do you remember what you advised me about Collin Crosby?"

Annabelle was peeling potatoes, but she stopped and looked over at Jody.

Jody could tell that she didn't remember.

"You told me to be kind to him."

"Oh." Her grandmother went back to peeling, but slower than before. The burden of guilt she and Hugh felt for wrongly accusing Billy, and for Red's death, and for harboring their son's killer in the family was almost unbearable sometimes. It had aged and humbled them, given them new nightmares, turned them softer and sadder, made them more forgiving of other people, if not of themselves yet. Sometimes Hugh Senior had forgetful moments when he still thought Billy had done it all and hated him for all of it, and then later he'd remember with a shock that was brand new again.

Jody sensed she couldn't do anything for them except love them.

Gently, she asked, "How do you feel about him now?"

Annabelle laid down the peeler and stared out the window above her sink.

"I feel . . . I feel so guilty about him, honey."

"Anything else?"

"Grateful. He saved your life by calling us when a lesser man might have let us reap the whirlwind that we sowed."

"Maybe we should invite him to supper some evening."

"What?" Annabelle turned so fast that she brushed a potato off the counter. It bounced once, then rolled toward Jody's feet. She picked it up, sniffed at the raw freshness of it, and then put it down on the table where she sat. Before Christmas, she'd painted the table and chairs bright blue.

"Jody, we can't do that. It would be so awkward for everybody. Worse than awkward, it would be awful. He wouldn't come anyway, and I don't blame him. I'm sure he doesn't want anything to do with us."

Jody swallowed, and then plunged into the deep end.

"He wants something to do with me, Grandma."

Annabelle looked for a moment as if her knees would give out, and Jody started to get up to go to her, but then her grandmother gripped the sink and straightened into her usual good posture. "No, that's not a good idea. Sweetheart, it just can't be a good idea. There's so much, too much—"

Chase was visiting, and he picked that moment to walk into the kitchen.

"What's not a good idea?"

"Collin Crosby," her grandmother said in a stunned voice.

"And me," Jody finished for her.

Chase got very still for a moment, still enough to remind Jody of how Aunt Belle had been when she saw the silver horse. Her heart pounded as she waited to see what harsh judgment he would make on this dramatic announcement of hers.

"Have you been seeing him?"

"Yes."

"When?"

"Every chance we get, Uncle Chase."

"Where?"

"Any place we can find."

"Those weekend trips you take to see friends . . .?"

"Right. Those."

He stared at her without speaking for a long moment. "When did this start?"

"When we were children, I think. We've always felt drawn to each other." Jody looked at her uncle and then at her grandmother. They didn't know how she and Collin talked and talked and talked, examining their strangely intertwined lives from both of their points of view, seeking and finding understanding in each other that they'd never found in anybody else. She took a deep breath. "He's the happiness that follows all the sadness. I never used to think that was possible for me—or for anybody, not really—and I know it's still no fairy tale. I know bad things will come into our lives, as they do in everybody else's life, but—" She was near tears, wanting so much to convince them. "In the tough times, it's his hand I want to hold. I have to tell you one of the reasons he worked so hard to get his father out of prison. Yes, it was for the principle of justice. Yes, it was because he knew Billy didn't do it. Yes, it was for his mother. But he also did it because he believed it was the only way to force a new investigation. And the real reason

Collin wanted a new investigation was because he thought that otherwise I'd never know what happened to my mother."

When she saw them frowning as if they didn't quite understand what she was saying, Jody took another deep breath as if she were on a horse and lining up to jump a final fence.

"He did it for me," she said, making it absolutely clear.

Chase looked over at his mother, who stared back at him.

"Well," he began, while Jody crossed her fingers. "I don't see why he shouldn't come to supper, provided he can stand to be in the same room with the rest of us."

She could hardly believe what she was hearing.

"He's probably the only man in Kansas who's crazy for the exact same reasons you are. It's either a match made in heaven or in hell, but it sounds like a match to me," Chase said. Annabelle stared a little open-mouthed at him. "Chicken," he said next, suggesting the menu for their first supper together. "If the boy doesn't like your fried chicken, Mom, then he's not fit for this family. And if he does like it, then next time maybe I'll grill some steaks if I'm in town."

Chase walked out of the room, taking Jody's gratitude with him.

But then he walked back in and said quietly, "If he doesn't want me around, I will stay away."

Jody thought it was the most thoughtful thing he'd ever said to her.

"We'll all get used to each other," she suggested.

"I expect he hates us."

"He's not like that, Uncle Chase."

He squinted at her, as if gauging her capacity to decide such things.

"I'll be the judge of that," he said as he left the room again, but then he came back again, this time to say something else to his mother. "We need a new lawyer in the family, you know."

It was nearly a joke. A grim and unfunny one, but almost a joke anyway.

Annabelle was looking as if she might cry, too, and she said to Jody, "I suppose you'll end up moving to Topeka."

"I'm just suggesting supper, Grandma, we're not getting married!"

"Yet," she said as she picked up her paring knife again.

"And I have a whole school year to get through, remember?"

"There are schools in Topeka," Chase said, unhelpfully.

"Which is not that far away," Jody said quickly.

She got up and went to her grandmother, wrapping her in a hug. The two women stood together like that until Chase left the room and the water for the potatoes began to boil.

About the Author

NANCY PICKARD is a four-time Edgar Award nominee, most recently for her Ballantine debut, *The Virgin of Small Plains*. Hailed by mainstream critics, the novel was also honored by the State Library of Kansas to be the "Kansas Reads" book for 2009. Pickard is the winner of the Anthony Award, Macavity Award, Agatha Award, Barry Award, and Shamus Award. Pickard has been a national board member of the Mystery Writers of America and president of Sisters in Crime. She lives in Merriam, Kansas.

About the Type

This book was set in Sabon, a typeface designed by the well-known German typographer Jan Tschichold (1902–74). Sabon's design is based upon the original letter forms of Claude Garamond and was created specifically to be used for three sources: foundry type for hand composition, Linotype, and Monotype. Tschichold named his typeface for the famous Frankfurt typefounder Jacques Sabon, who died in 1580.